THE
SECOND
MARRIAGE

BOOKS BY JESS RYDER

Lie to Me
The Good Sister
The Ex-Wife
The Dream House
The Girl You Gave Away
The Night Away

THE SECOND MARRIAGE

JESS RYDER

Bookouture

Published by Bookouture in 2021

An imprint of Storyfire Ltd.
Carmelite House
50 Victoria Embankment
London EC4Y 0DZ

www.bookouture.com

ISBN: 978-1-80019-850-0
eBook ISBN: 978-1-80019-849-4

For my family

PART ONE

CHAPTER ONE

'Lily, will you marry me?'

He was down on one knee, holding out a tiny black box, the lid hinged open. A beautiful diamond ring was wedged into a white satin cushion. I let out a gasp and put my hand to my chest. Edward looked up at me, smiling. The corners of his mouth and eyes were etched with fine laughter lines. His grey hair shone in the candlelight like polished steel.

'Well?'

The other diners had put down their forks and were watching us openly, nodding and smiling like we were part of the evening's entertainment.

I hadn't seen the proposal coming, even though he'd told me to dress up for the evening and brought me to one of the most expensive restaurants in Soho. Not even the bottle of vintage champagne had given the game away. I wasn't used to love moving so fast. My previous boyfriend had taken seven years to decide I wasn't the one for him, but Edward had made up his mind after as many months.

'Please say something,' he said. 'This is getting embarrassing.'

'Yes, yes, of course I'll marry you.'

His eyes lit up and his shoulders dropped. The whole restaurant burst into applause.

'I didn't realise we had an audience,' he said, blushing.

'They're just happy for us.' The ring was a large solitaire, simple and elegant, exactly what I would have chosen myself. 'It's stunning,' I said. 'Must have cost a fortune.'

'Never you mind about that. Put it on.'

'What, now?'

'Of course now.' He slipped it onto my finger and it came to rest perfectly. I splayed out my hand and let the diamond catch the candlelight.

'I can't believe it. I never dreamt I'd have a ring like this. My mum is going to go crazy when she sees it. And as for my friends…'

'I can't wait for you to be my wife,' he grinned. 'Let's get married as soon as we can.' He sat back down, then leant across the table and kissed me full on the mouth.

'Hey, steady.'

'Oh.' He pulled back, looking hurt. 'I'm sorry. Am I embarrassing you? It's because I look old enough to be your father, isn't it?'

'You *are* old enough to be my father,' I teased.

'Barely. There's only fifteen years between us. It's the grey hair.' He smoothed it back self-consciously. 'Makes me look ancient.'

'No, it makes you look sexy and distinguished. Anyway, you know I couldn't care less about that. It's just that everyone's staring.'

He glanced around. 'Yes, you're right. Sorry. I wasn't thinking.'

'Shh, no need to apologise. It's fine.' I lifted my glass. 'I love you, Mr Morgan.'

Our eyes locked as we chinked. 'I fell in love with you at first sight,' he said. 'From when you came for the interview. I was trying so hard to be professional. There were all these questions I was supposed to ask you, but they went straight out of my head.'

I laughed. 'I have to say, it *was* the easiest interview of my life.'

'I was so frightened you'd turn me down.'

'No way. I needed the job.'

'No, tonight, I mean. You've made a forty-five-year-old man very happy, Lily, I can't tell you.' He picked up his napkin and wiped his forehead. 'Sorry, I'm feeling a bit overwhelmed.'

'It's okay, Edward, everything's going to be fine.'

He excused himself and went to the bathroom. I sat there turning my hand this way and that to admire the diamond, remembering how it had all started. To think that I'd nearly not bothered to turn up for the interview…

The uphill walk from the Tube station had taken longer than I'd expected; I'd got lost in the maze of twisting side roads, hitting dead ends and having to retrace my steps. Even when I found what had to be the correct house, there was no number or name outside to confirm it either way. I felt irritated. This was taking privacy too far, I thought as I pushed the buzzer on the security gate.

A warm male voice answered and asked for my name. 'Lily Baxendale,' I said. 'I'm here about the teaching job.' There was a buzzing sound and then the gate swung open. I walked across the expansive paved driveway and up the steps to where my potential employer stood at the open door.

'Lily! Great to meet you. Sorry about all the security.' He beckoned me inside. 'Sadly, we have to be careful these days.'

He was older than I'd expected for someone with an eight-year-old son; casually dressed for the occasion in jeans, a white linen shirt and leather flip-flops on his bare feet. I remember thinking he was very attractive for a man of his age. I guessed he was in his mid forties, although I wasn't sure. Maybe a few years younger? My stomach flipped over, but I put it down to the butterflies that had been plaguing me since breakfast.

He showed me into the living room and sat me down on a large, squashy sofa. I waited, assuming that his wife would join us, but then it became clear that there would be just the two of us. After I'd refused tea and coffee, he took the chair opposite and we talked. I had all my answers prepared – why I'd quit my career as a primary school teacher, what my approach to home-schooling would be, how I'd balance academic studies with field trips, group activities and physical education – but he didn't ask me any of the normal questions. Instead, he wanted to know what books I'd read and films I'd seen, what countries I'd visited, what food I enjoyed, whether I liked to cook.

'I've brought my certificates,' I said, reaching into my bag.

He waved them aside. 'I'm sure the recruiters did all the necessary checks. I'm more interested in your personality, to be honest. I'm a financial adviser and I work mainly from home, so we'll be seeing a lot of each other.'

'Yes, I understand.'

'The last tutor was very experienced but too strict. Like Mary Poppins but without the magic.' I laughed appropriately. 'We didn't see eye to eye about the best way to handle Noah.'

'Oh... Yes, well... I can see how important it is that everyone gets on,' I agreed.

'Just one thing I should make clear. I only have one rule in this house. And that's that nobody ever talks to Noah about his mother.'

'Oh,' I said, rather taken aback. 'Can I ask why?'

He paused to swallow, as if it hurt to get the words out. 'She died when he was only three years old. He has no real memories of her, and that really upsets him. Any mention of her, or even talking about mothers in general, can trigger a serious panic attack. That's why he can't go to school – he'd be bullied without a doubt. So please avoid the subject at all times. Is that okay?'

'Yes, of course,' I replied, privately thinking it was a strange way to deal with a child's grief, or anyone's grief for that matter. But my curiosity was piqued. I immediately wanted to know more about this mysterious woman who couldn't be mentioned. Had she been the same age as Edward, or a young trophy wife? And how had she died?

'Noah is a special child,' he continued, 'and he needs sensitive handling. We live very quietly here. He spends a lot of time in his bedroom playing video games, and he loves drawing.'

'Does he do any sport?'

'He used to have swimming lessons, but it, er… didn't work out. There's a basketball hoop and a trampoline in the garden. He likes playing on those. But team sports aren't really his thing. He's a solitary child, prefers his own company.'

It sounded like he didn't have much choice. 'How do you feel about trips out?' I ventured. 'Educational visits, I mean. To museums, art galleries…'

'That's fine as a treat, but not every week.'

'No, of course not. I didn't mean—'

'He likes his own home – he feels safe here. Once you get to know him, you'll understand.'

We seemed to be talking as if I'd already got the job. 'Is Noah around?' I asked.

'Yes. Would you like to meet him?'

I nodded. 'Please. If that's okay.'

Edward went into the hallway and called up the stairs. Left briefly alone, I glanced around the room, expecting to see family photos, but there wasn't a single image of the dead wife. Instead, there were several pictures of two young women whom I later discovered were Edward's grown-up daughters, Tara and Georgia.

A minute later, a boy appeared. He was a miniature version of his father, with bright blue eyes and a shock of jet-black hair that patently hadn't seen a brush in a while.

'This is Lily,' Edward said. 'She's going to be your new teacher.' He quickly turned to me. 'At least, I hope she is.'

'Hi, Noah.' I smiled at him and he almost smiled back.

'Will I have to do maths?' he asked.

'Yes. Some. But we'll do other stuff. Reading, writing, making up stories… some science, a bit of history. And art, of course. I hear you like drawing.'

'Yes, but I'm not very good at it.'

'I bet you are, but it doesn't matter as long as you enjoy it. I'd really love to see your pictures sometime.'

'Really? Okay.' He seemed genuinely pleased and surprised that I was interested. My heart went out to him. I felt an immediate bond with this small, gentle soul, and wanted to prise him out of his shell. But it didn't occur to me for one second that one day I would be his stepmother.

Edward returned to the table and the restaurant suddenly came back into focus. 'Glad you like your ring,' he said, sitting back down.

'I love it.'

'Would you like to see the dessert menu?'

'No thanks. I think we should go home now, don't you?'

'Good idea.' He called for the bill.

'I've been wondering about Noah. How do you think he'll take the news?'

Edward considered for a few moments. 'I'm not sure. I think if we play it down, don't make a big thing of it, he should be okay. He thinks the world of you, so hopefully…' His face clouded over. 'It's Tara and Georgia I'm more worried about.'

'Really? I thought we got along.'

'You do, they like you. It's just that… me having a girlfriend is one thing, but marrying again? That's a big change for them.' He picked up his napkin and folded it nervously. 'Tara's so volatile, you never know how she's going to react. Georgia's more easy-going, but she usually follows big sis.'

'They're both grown up. They should understand,' I said firmly. 'Clare died five years ago – why shouldn't you move on with your life?'

'Yes, you're right,' he said, taking my hands. 'I'm sure they'll be happy for us, once they've got over the shock. We'll invite them over to Sunday lunch, tell them at the same time. You know how competitive they are.'

'Whatever you think best.'

Edward settled the bill and we took a taxi back to his house. The champagne and excellent food, not to mention the beautiful rock on my finger, were making me feel hot and fuzzy around the edges. We kissed and cuddled on the back seat like a couple of teenagers. I couldn't wait to get back to the house and show Edward how much I loved him, but Georgia was babysitting and would be staying the night in her old bedroom. Edward always felt inhibited when the girls were around. The real celebration of our engagement would have to wait.

'It's just occurred to me,' I said as we pulled up outside the front gates. 'Georgia will spot the ring straight away.'

He grimaced. 'Shit, you're right. Sorry, darling, would you mind taking it off? Just for now.'

'No worries.'

He fished the box out of his pocket. I gave my hand one last admiring look, then removed the ring and put it back on its cushion. The lid closed with a snap. It was a shame to be parted from it so soon, but I understood. At least, I thought I did.

CHAPTER TWO

The following day, once I'd finished teaching, I told Edward I was going back to my place for the night.

'Do you *have* to?' he said. 'I thought we could spend the evening looking at the calendar. We need to pick a date for the wedding. Make some plans...'

'I really want to do that, but there's no rush, is there? I need to pick up some clean clothes, do a few chores, that kind of stuff.' I also wanted to tell Marsha that I was getting married and moving out of her flat for good.

Edward shrugged resignedly. 'Okay, you can stay at Marsha's one night, but no longer.'

I gave him an arch look. 'I assume that's a joke.'

'Of course it is. I can't bear sleeping alone any more, that's all.' He kissed me goodbye as if we weren't going to see each other again for months.

Soon after I left the house, I took my engagement ring out of its box and put it back on. It felt strange and heavy on my finger, and as I walked down the hill towards the Tube station, I wondered if I would ever get used to wearing it. I didn't normally bother with jewellery – a pair of discreet stud earrings or a simple silver chain around my neck was about as far as it went. My mother would be thrilled when she saw the diamond, of that I had no doubt, but I was less confident of Marsha's reaction. She was a defiant singleton and hated anything that smacked of male possessiveness.

Not that I saw my engagement ring in that way. For me, it was simply a sign of Edward's love and generosity.

Marsha's flat was a period conversion on the first and second floors of an Edwardian terrace. As soon as I got in, I set about preparing dinner. It had been weeks since we'd sat down to eat together, and as I chopped some onions and peppers for a pasta sauce, I reflected that I hadn't been a very good flatmate of late. Now I was about to desert her altogether. Marsha and I had been close since childhood. She had taken me in a year ago after I split up with my boyfriend Alex, pouring the wine, listening to me as I ranted and raved into the night. She was the only one who supported my decision to take a break from my stressful teaching job.

We decided to take a year out and go travelling together. Her career as a museum curator had stalled, and she was up for a change. All I needed was a temporary job so that I could save some money. Home-schooling an eight-year-old boy in upmarket, leafy Hampstead seemed like the perfect fit. I never had any intention of falling in love so quickly, even less of getting married. Now I was wrecking my plans with Marsha. I was sure she would forgive me, but I still felt anxious about breaking the news.

I heard the key turn in the front door lock and the sound of her footsteps coming up the stairs. I strained the spaghetti and started to serve up.

'Hello, stranger,' she said, smiling. 'What are you doing here?'

'I was worried you weren't eating properly,' I joked.

'Oh yes, I starve when I'm on my own. But seriously, thanks.' She went to wash her hands, and when she came back, two steaming bowls of pasta arrabbiata were sitting on the table. As I passed her the Parmesan cheese, my diamond glinted and she gasped.

'OMG, is that what I think it is?' she exclaimed.

'Yup.'

'When did this happen?'

'Last night.' I told her the story of Edward's romantic proposal, and her eyes widened in amazement.

'Obviously you said yes…' She gave me one of her penetrating stares. 'But are you sure this is what you want? I mean, I was expecting you to move in with Edward – you virtually have already anyway – but *marriage*? That's a different league of commitment.'

'Yes, I know it's a bit sudden, but actually, I feel surer about Edward than I ever felt about Alex. When I'm with him, it's like I've come home, like I don't belong anywhere else. He feels the same. We love each other. What's the point of waiting?'

'You've only been together a few months, Lily, you don't really know him. You come from completely different worlds, different generations. You're only thirty and he's a middle-aged widower with three kids. From what you've told me before, he was deeply in love with his wife. The whole family's still grieving. That's a hell of a lot of baggage to dump on you.'

I looked up from my bowl of pasta. 'I have baggage too – we all do. I like the fact that Edward's a grown-up with proper real-life experiences. I'm sick of relationships with boys who are afraid to be honest.'

'Like Alex.'

'Yes. Like Alex.'

'I understand, but… dead wives…' she muttered. 'Such a tough act to follow.'

I frowned at her. 'Come on, Marsha. I thought you'd be happy for me. I was going to ask you to be my bridesmaid.'

She put down her fork. 'Of course I'm happy for you, and I'd love to be your bridesmaid. I just worry, that's all. Alex hurt you really badly. If you're marrying Edward to get back at him…'

'I'm most definitely not. I'm completely over Alex.'

'Okay, that's good.' We started eating again and I sensed the atmosphere easing. 'So, when's the big event? Do I have enough time to lose some weight?'

I laughed. 'We haven't decided yet, but Edward doesn't want to wait too long. He's sensitive about his age. It'll only be a small, quiet wedding. Close friends and family. He doesn't want to hire a venue or anything. It'll be a registry office ceremony, then back to the house for a party.'

'Oh. That's a shame.'

'He thinks it wouldn't be appropriate. In the circumstances.'

Marsha frowned. 'You mean because his first wife died?' I nodded. 'But that was five years ago.'

'I know. It's Tara and Georgia he's worried about. Well, mainly Tara – she's the spiky one. And Noah, I guess, although I don't think he'll take much notice.'

'Hmm… see what I mean about baggage?'

I sighed. 'Yes, Marsha, you're right – as ever. But have faith. We're both going into this with our eyes open. It's not the wedding that's important, it's being married, spending the rest of our lives together. It's going to be fine.'

As I'd guessed, my mother was far easier to win over. 'Oh, I'm so thrilled! How wonderful! You lucky girl!' she exclaimed when I rang to tell her the news. She'd never been a great fan of Alex (too laid-back, not enough ambition), and had been instantly charmed by Edward on the one occasion they'd met. Her enthusiasm waned a little when I told her the wedding was going to be low-key, but then redoubled when I sent her a picture of the ring.

Now we just had Edward's children to deal with. I'd only met his daughters a handful of times. As Noah's tutor, they'd taken virtually no notice of me, but when I became Edward's girlfriend, their interest had suddenly increased. To be fair, they'd seemed okay with the idea, even though I was closer in age to them than I was to their father. Of the two, I preferred the younger sister, Georgia – she was more open and friendly. Twenty years old, she was following in her father's footsteps and was in her second year of a business studies course at university. Tara, two years older, was what my mother would call 'a cold fish'. She was about to graduate with a degree in fashion marketing from the famous Central Saint Martins and was extremely ambitious. The girls shared a flat in north-west London, the considerable rent paid by their father. Although very different in looks and personalities, they were inseparable.

Edward was busy in the kitchen, lovingly slaving over roast lamb. He was a good cook, but used to doing everything himself. I'd already learnt not to try to help, and was upstairs sorting out the last of the clothes that I'd brought from Marsha's. There wasn't room for everything. I still had several boxes of books and cooking equipment sitting in the garage.

When Edward and I had started our relationship, I'd hardly ever thought about his first wife, but now that I was about to replace her, the woman was constantly on my mind. I kept wondering about her personality, how she and Edward had worked as a couple, whether they'd really been as deliriously happy as he made out. I even worried about their sex life and whether she had been better in bed than me. I knew it was unhealthy, but I couldn't seem to stop myself.

With no photos of her in the house and online searches producing no credible results, I had to create her from my imagination. Naturally I gave her all the qualities I felt I lacked. She was voluptuously beautiful, with long hair that fell in waves down her back. I gifted her a flawless skin, with not a wrinkle in sight.

Edward never wanted to talk about her; it seemed to hurt him too much. When I asked questions, I received the briefest of replies. She'd been an events manager, specialising in outdoor concerts – classical music with fireworks, ageing pop stars performing their greatest hits, that kind of thing. She'd had a severe nut allergy and had died after eating some bread containing sesame seeds. That was about it. Despite spending hours scouring all the usual social media platforms, I couldn't find any more information about her. It was as if all evidence of her existence had been deliberately erased.

There were noises below. The girls had arrived, by the sound of it. I checked my face for make-up smudges and reapplied my lipstick, then went down to greet them.

'Hi, Lily,' said Georgia, looking up. 'Loving the dress.'

'You should have told us it was a special occasion,' added Tara. They glanced at each other suspiciously.

Edward put an arm round each of them. 'Seeing you two is always special,' he said neatly, then turned to me. 'Lily? Would you mind calling Noah?' He led his daughters into the sitting room and sat them down on the sofa. I shouted up for Noah, then followed, perching on the edge of an armchair.

'Lunch smells good,' said Georgia. 'Who's the cook?'

'Me, of course.' Edward pointed to his apron. 'Roast lamb with all the trimmings. Your favourite…' He hovered nervously. 'Anyone for an aperitif? G and T?' We all shook our heads. 'Where is that boy?' He went to the foot of the stairs and called Noah again.

Tara twisted her mouth. 'What's going on, Dad? I feel like we've been summoned.'

'Is it bad news?' Georgia asked.

'No, quite the opposite.' Finally Noah slunk into the room. He barely acknowledged his sisters, and stood by the door as if in preparation for a quick escape.

'Well?' demanded Tara.

Edward came and stood by me, resting his hand on my shoulder. 'I've asked Lily to marry me, and I'm thrilled to say that she's said yes.'

There was a stunned silence. The girls exchanged a glance, but nobody said anything. Noah didn't display any emotion at all. I realised – too late – that Edward should have told them on his own.

'I know we haven't known each other long, but we both feel very sure about our relationship,' he continued bravely. 'It'll be a small wedding, nothing showy or fancy, but we very much hope you'll join us.'

'Can I go now?' asked Noah, seemingly unbothered.

'Um… yes, I guess so, unless you've got any more questions?'

He shook his black mop of hair, then scooted off. Another ticklish pause followed.

'So when's the big day?' drawled Tara, without enthusiasm.

Edward smiled. 'We've booked the registry office for the end of next month.'

'Next month?' echoed Georgia, somewhat alarmed. 'That's a bit quick.'

Tara immediately looked me up and down. 'Are you pregnant?'

'No,' I replied quickly, silently adding, *not that it's any of your business.*

'Thank goodness,' she muttered under her breath.

'Shh…' hissed Georgia.

'One late accident's enough, isn't it?'

I cut in. 'I would love to have a child with your father, but it's not possible. I had an ectopic pregnancy when I was a teenager and had to have emergency surgery.'

Georgia gasped. 'Oh, gosh, I'm sorry, how awful for you.' She shot a reproving look at her sister.

'How was I supposed to know?' Tara protested.

'It's okay. I came to terms with it a long time ago,' I replied smoothly. It was almost true. 'Look, I want you both to know that I've no intention of barging into your family and trying to take your mother's place. You're grown women, it would be absurd for me to act like your stepmum. But Noah's still little, he needs a mummy.'

Edward squeezed my arm. 'And a wonderful job you'll make of it too, darling.' He turned to his daughters. 'See? It's all fine. Nothing will change. Life will go on as before in its normal quiet way, only I won't be so lonely any more.' He looked from one daughter to the other, and I sensed a secret unspoken dialogue going on between them. 'I think I deserve that, don't you? After everything I've been through?'

'Sure. It's your life, Dad,' said Tara. 'You don't have to ask our permission.'

'I know, but I'd like your blessing. We both would, wouldn't we, Lily?' I nodded, but I was starting to think I no longer cared about their approval, particularly not Tara's.

'Well, I think it's brilliant news,' said Georgia. 'I was just a bit surprised, that's all. But hey, congratulations all round.'

Tara forced a smile. 'Can I have that G and T now? A strong one.'

CHAPTER THREE

'Lily, relax, please! You're screwing up your face.' Adina, the hair and make-up artist, raised her brush and tutted.

'Sorry…'

'Too late to change your mind now!' She cheerfully painted on an eyebrow.

'It's not that,' I assured her. 'Just feeling a bit nervous.'

'Oh, you'll be fine. This is the happiest day of your life.'

I smiled at her, but inside my stomach was churning. I couldn't tell whether it was anxiety or excitement. A bit of both, I supposed. The big day had come around so quickly, I'd barely had time to catch my breath. In less than four hours' time, I would become Mrs Morgan. The *second* Mrs Morgan. I immediately sensed Clare's spectre gliding into the room, summoned by my thoughts. She would be with me all day now, the uninvited guest, lurking in the shadows.

In fact, it was the real guests I needed to worry about. We'd invited sixty people to the wedding, but nobody on Edward's side, apart from his children, had responded to their invitations either way. His parents were still alive, and he had two brothers, both of whom were married with kids. There were also a few aged aunts and uncles. Perhaps they were intending to roll up at the registry office, dressed up to the nines, bags of confetti at the ready, but it seemed unlikely. When I'd asked him to chase them up, he'd refused, saying he didn't want to pester.

'What about your parents?' I asked. We'd never met, and I was starting to wonder if we ever would.

'Unfortunately, they're going to be on one of their cruises,' he replied. 'Bad timing, I'm afraid. It's my fault, I didn't give them enough notice.'

He was trying to spare my feelings, but I had a good idea what was really going on. His family had adored Clare. They thought I was too young, a gold-digger. Edward insisted it wasn't so, but I didn't believe him, especially as not one of his close friends was attending either, just a few neighbours he hardly knew. It was all making me feel extremely uncomfortable.

'Ta-dah!' cried Adina, bursting into my thoughts. 'Transformation complete!' She stood back to admire her work. 'You look stunning. Absolutely stunning.' I thanked her as she cleaned up, stacking boxes of cosmetics onto a little wheeled trolley. 'Have a wonderful day.' She trundled towards the door. 'Send me a photo and I'll put it on my website.'

I examined my face in the mirror and saw a stranger. Her chestnut-coloured hair was swept into a dramatic chignon. Bronze cheekbones shimmered under the lights, and enormous grey eyes gazed out questioningly from beneath false lashes. It was still early, not even breakfast time, but I looked as if I was ready to hit the town. Everything felt so unreal. My skin already itched underneath the layers of creamy foundation. Part of me just wanted to scrub it all off. We should have got married privately, I decided – dragged a couple of witnesses off the street, then gone for a pizza.

There was a knock on the door. Before I could answer, it slowly opened. Noah entered hesitantly, still wearing his pyjamas, his black hair sticking out at angles.

'Hello, sweetie, come in.' I waved him forward and he sidled around the door like a curl of steam. 'Well? How do I look?'

He peered at me. 'Not bad,' he said finally. 'Quite pretty, actually.'

'Aww, thank you!' From him, that was praise indeed.

He shuffled towards the wardrobe and lingered there, twisting his fingers. 'Lily...' he began.

'What's up, chipmunk? Something wrong?'

'There are people in the kitchen.'

'Yes, we told you there would be, remember? They're getting the food ready for the party.'

He shifted from one foot to the other. 'But I'm hungry *now*.'

I laughed. 'You don't have to wait. Go ahead and have breakfast, they won't mind.' He stared down at the carpet. I silently reprimanded myself. Noah often felt uncomfortable with strangers, especially when they were in his space.

'Actually, I'm hungry too,' I said. 'Shall we go together?'

We went downstairs and into the large living room. The sofas had been pushed back against the wall and all the surfaces had been cleared. Somebody was standing on a ladder, fixing balloons. In the kitchen, three caterers were dancing expertly around each other, chopping and slicing, ducking and stretching, leaning across to fill pastry cases or sprinkle garnishes.

'They'll be gone soon,' I whispered as we munched away at our cereal. 'And the party won't go on for long. If you feel uncomfortable at any point, or even just bored, you can go up to your room, okay? Nobody will mind.' I watched Noah chase the last soggy grains around the bowl. 'Come on. We need to get our special clothes on.' I gestured at him to follow me upstairs.

'Where's Daddy?'

'I don't know. I think he might have gone to get his hair cut. He'll be back soon to help you get ready.' We reached the landing and I hovered at the door of my bedroom, hoping he'd take the hint. 'Right... See you in a bit.'

He didn't move. His mouth opened, then quickly shut again. 'What is it, Noah? Is there something you want to tell me?'

'Um…'

'Go on.'

'I was just wondering why Daddy's marrying you when…' He drifted off.

'When what?'

'Nothing. It's okay, doesn't matter.'

My heart lurched with love and I knelt down. He let me hug him for a few seconds. 'I know things have been hard for everyone these past few years, but I'm going to do everything I can to make Daddy happy. To make us *all* happy.'

'I do solemnly declare that I know not of any lawful impediment why I, Edward Anthony Morgan, may not be joined in matrimony to Lily Christina Baxendale.'

He pushed the ring onto my trembling finger and we stood, hands clasped, gazing into each other's eyes while the registrar pronounced us husband and wife. The audience broke out in applause as we performed the customary kiss.

We sat to sign the register while a cellist played my favourite Adele song and our guests broke out in lively conversation. I glanced up, briefly taking in my people, who had turned out in force, some of them travelling a long way. Marsha looked amazing – it was lovely to see her wearing a dress for once, instead of the usual combat trousers and boots. The pale blue satin really showed off her dark brown skin.

Mum had gone for the whole 'mother of the bride' look. Despite being disappointed by the scale of the wedding, she hadn't stinted on the hat. She stared at me from beneath the wide brim, jaw tense, lips set in a line. I gave her an encouraging smile and she returned it, but I knew she wasn't happy. There was an embarrassing imbalance in the room, weighted heavily on the bride's side, and she was taking it as an insult to her daughter. She was right, too – there was no other way of looking at it.

After the formalities were completed, we stepped outside. The photographer took a few snaps of us standing in front of the town hall, but it wasn't a very picturesque setting and passers-by kept wandering into shot. To top it all, the grey clouds above us were threatening rain.

'Let's go home,' said Edward, when he noticed I was shivering in my sleeveless dress. He took off his jacket and put it gallantly around my shoulders. 'If it brightens up, we can take more pictures in the garden.' He summoned the hired transport – a white fifties Cadillac for us and a vintage bus for our guests.

We slid onto the back seat and the driver shut the passenger door. I waved to Marsha and my parents as the car pulled away.

'We did it,' Edward said, loosening his tie and breathing out. He seemed glad that it was over. 'Not the most romantic of locations, but…'

'It was lovely,' I said.

He leant over and kissed me softly. The real world fell away, and for a few precious seconds, it was only us, two people who'd vowed to spend the rest of their lives together. Then he suddenly pulled back.

'Mustn't spoil your make-up.' He turned away to look out of the window, chewing on his bottom lip.

I wanted to tell him that it didn't matter, that I'd married *him*, not his family, but he'd locked himself away. I sensed him thinking about Clare, maybe even remembering their wedding day. Did they get married in church, or a registry office? Did they have an extravagant reception, or did they just go to the pub? I felt her ghost squeezing in between us on the blue velour seat, snuggling up to Edward, whispering in his ear, jogging his memory, asking him to compare. *Who is the most beautiful bride? Who do you love the most?*

He sighed and reached for my hand. 'I love you, Lily,' he said, still looking at the passing urban scenery. 'Until you came along, I thought I'd never be happy again. I just hope you're doing the right thing, taking on an old duffer like me.'

'Don't be silly,' I said, relieved that he'd come back to me. Clare heaved a disgruntled sigh and lifted herself off the seat. I opened the window and she wafted through the gap into the polluted city air.

CHAPTER FOUR

An hour later, the house was buzzing with chatter and laughter. Downstairs had been transformed with flowers and balloon sculptures, and a delicious buffet was spread out on the dining table. Edward and I were flitting between family and friends, and I could tell that he was charming everyone. Marsha was doing a great job as bridesmaid, making sure nobody was left without someone to talk to, chivvying the caterers to gather dirty glasses and replenish the salad. I was starting to relax and really enjoy myself. So what if Edward's extended family didn't support our marriage? We were surrounded by plenty of people who did.

'Lily! There you are!' Edward's daughters approached me in what felt like a two-pronged attack. Georgia gave me a hug and Tara brushed her lips lightly across my left cheek.

'You look gorgeous,' said Georgia.

'Thanks. So do you,' I said. 'Both of you, I mean.'

Tara smirked. 'Glad you didn't go for the virginal white dress.'

The three of us stood grinning inanely at each other, not knowing what else to say.

Tara glanced over to the makeshift bar, where one of my cousins was wrestling with a bottle of champagne. 'Hmm, looks like I need to fill up before your lot drink the place dry.' She waved her empty flute, then skipped off.

'Don't mind her,' said Georgia, observing my shocked expression. 'She can be a bitch sometimes, but she doesn't mean it. She was very close to our mum. We both were, but Tara was always the favourite. The firstborn, and all that.'

'At least she turned up, unlike the rest of your family. Your grandparents, for example – Edward told me they're on a cruise. Is that true?'

Georgia blushed. 'Don't think so. We don't have anything to do with them.'

'But he sent them all invitations.'

Her eyebrows shot up. 'Believe me, there's no way Dad would want any of them here.'

'Why not? Did they fall out, or something? What about?'

'It's complicated, best not to ask.'

'But I think I should know, don't you?' I persisted.

She was looking very uncomfortable. 'Please don't be cross with Dad for lying, he was probably just embarrassed. And don't tell him I told you, or I'll be in big trouble.' She placed a hand on my arm. 'Look, the past is the past – none of it matters. I'm really happy for you, Lily, honestly. And don't worry about Tara, she'll come around eventually. You're perfect for Dad. He's so happy now he's with you. I worry about him sometimes – he's been through a lot these past few years. Please take care of him.'

I was about to reassure her that I would do my best when my mother came hurrying over. 'Lily!' she said. 'I've been looking for you everywhere. Zoe wants to know when you're going to throw your bouquet.'

'I hadn't thought about it.'

'They've got to head off soon, so it would be nice to do it before they go. Aim it right at her, please, she's desperate for her boyfriend to pop the question.'

'Okay, I'll try,' I laughed.

'I'll gather everyone round.' Mum bustled off to rig the arrangements, and I went to find the bouquet, which had been resting in a bucket of water in the utility room.

Edward caught me on my way back. 'At last I've got you!' He scooped me into his arms and twirled me round.

'Stop! You're crushing my flowers!'

'I don't care.' He put me down. 'I wish everyone would hurry up and go,' he whispered as he kissed my neck. 'I want you all to myself.'

'Don't worry, they're leaving soon. I've had orders to throw the bouquet.'

He released me and I walked into the space that had been cleared for the event. I looked around at the small gaggle of women pretending to jockey for position – Marsha, Tara, Georgia, my cousin Zoe, the girls from the school where I used to work, our neighbour's daughter, whose name escaped me. They held up their arms, ready to catch. Such a silly tradition, I thought, turning with my back towards them. Zoe stood in the centre of the throng and I did my best to aim for her as I tossed the bouquet over my head. Everyone cheered and clapped. I turned around to see who'd won, and there was Tara, clutching the bouquet triumphantly to her chest. My cousin, who was standing next to her, gave her a death stare.

'She almost knocked our Zoe out trying to get it,' said Mum quietly at my shoulder. 'You want to watch that one.'

'It's just a bit of fun,' I replied. 'It doesn't actually mean Tara's going to be the next bride. She doesn't even have a boyfriend, as far as I know.'

It took another hour for the guests to say their goodbyes and leave. Finally, there was just the immediate family left. I could tell that Edward was keen for the girls to go, but they didn't seem to be in any rush. It felt like the end of a normal party rather than my wedding night, and I realised how exhausted I was.

We sat amid the debris. Edward offered to make a pot of tea, and I went upstairs to change into my pyjamas. Tara and Georgia were huddled on the sofa, chatting quietly to each other. Noah was slumped in the corner armchair, where he'd been the entire time, nodding over his tablet screen, refusing to go to bed. As I padded silently back into the room, I caught the end of the girls' conversation.

'Guess what I'm going to do with the bouquet?' Tara said.

'What?'

'I'm going to put it on Mummy's grave.'

Noah looked up from his game. There was a sudden chill in the air.

'Tara,' Edward said reprovingly as he offered around the mugs of tea. 'That's really inappropriate.'

'No it's not. Mummy loved flowers.'

'Yes, but it's Lily's wedding bouquet…'

Tara turned to me. 'You don't mind, do you? It's a nice thing to do, a way of including her in the celebrations.'

'Um… well, I don't know…' I blustered, feeling my cheeks redden.

'Honestly, Tara, you're the limit sometimes.' Edward looked embarrassed.

'What's the problem?' she replied, unrepentant. 'Mummy's not exactly a rival, is she? She's not coming back from the dead.'

Noah jumped up from his chair, putting his hands over his ears and starting to hyperventilate. 'Stop it! Stop it! Don't talk about her like that.'

'Hey, it's okay, buddy, it's okay. Tara didn't mean anything. Shh, now. Calm down.' Edward moved towards him, but Noah shook him off and bolted upstairs.

'Great. Just great,' Edward muttered, breaking the awkward silence that followed. 'Why did you have to say that, Tara? You know how he reacts to any mention of her.'

'Sorry.' She pulled a face. 'I thought he was absorbed in his game.'

'Right,' I said. 'I'll go and check on him.'

'Thank you, darling.' Edward reached out, grabbing my hand as I went to leave the room. He squeezed my fingers and the wedding ring dug into my flesh. 'So sorry,' he said under his breath.

Mixed emotions swirled inside me as I climbed the stairs and stood at the door of Noah's bedroom. I knocked gently.

'It's me. Lily. Can I come in?' There was no reply, so taking that as a reluctant yes, I stepped inside. The room was dark. I picked my way across the carpet strewn with toys and sat down on the edge of the bed. Noah had burrowed under the duvet, but I could still hear his muffled sobs.

I rubbed his back through the mound of bed linen. 'Talk to me... Noah? Please, talk to me.' He didn't answer, but the crying gradually subsided.

His body tensed. I waited nervously, not knowing whether I was making it better or worse. Until that moment, I'd followed Edward's instructions and not mentioned Clare, but now I trusted my instincts. We couldn't ignore the issue any longer.

'Noah? Come out, you can't breathe under there.'

He moved, and a tuft of black hair peeped out from the top of the duvet. I pulled the cover back to reveal his hot little face.

'That's better.' I climbed in next to him. 'Shall we snuggle up?' He nodded, and I put my arm around him.

'It's been a long day,' I said. 'Do you want to sleep or talk?'

'Talk,' he replied after a thoughtful pause.

'Okay. That's good, I like talking. Talking helps, I think, helps get your thoughts straight.' I pulled him closer. 'Okay... so, what shall we talk about?'

He shuffled up close and put his mouth against my ear. 'They're lying to us,' he whispered. 'Me and you.'

My heart sank, but I didn't contradict him. 'Oh dear. Who's lying?'

'Daddy, Tara, Georgia… all of them.' His breath felt hot against my face.

'Hmm, that doesn't sound good. What are they lying about?'

'Mummy.'

'Oh… I see. What about Mummy?'

'Saying she's dead.'

'Noah, darling—' I began, but he put a finger over my mouth.

'They think I've forgotten, but I remember everything. She's not dead, Lily. Mummy's still alive.'

CHAPTER FIVE

I was shaking, but I went straight back downstairs. As I entered the room, the conversation stopped abruptly, making it more than obvious that Edward and the girls had been talking about me.

'How is he?' asked Edward. 'Did you manage to calm him down?'

'Sort of.' I retrieved my tea, now almost cold, and sat back on the sofa. The air was buzzing with tension. I could sense Edward and his daughters sending telepathic signals to each other, cutting me out. Tara sipped her mug of tea defiantly, while Georgia got up and stared out of the window at nothing in particular. Edward looked down, clearly deeply embarrassed, determined to avoid my eye.

'Noah just said a very odd thing to me,' I said.

'Oh, I wouldn't take much notice. He was upset,' began Edward.

'He seems to think everyone's lying to him about his mother.' The three of them exchanged an infinitesimally small glance.

'Lying about what?' asked Georgia.

'That she's dead. He seems to believe she's still alive.'

'Oh my God,' said Edward. 'He actually said that?'

'Yup.'

'Poor kid,' Georgia said. 'I feel so sorry for him.'

'He gets very confused, very upset. That's why we try to avoid the subject,' Edward added, looking towards Tara.

'Sorry, my bad,' she replied – a little grudgingly, I thought.

'I've told you before, you need to be more careful.'

'We *all* do, Dad,' she replied pointedly. There was another meaningful pause I couldn't decipher.

'Why would he think she's still alive?' I persisted.

'No idea,' replied Edward. 'That's a new one on me.' Tara shrugged in agreement.

'He's in denial, can't accept the truth,' said Georgia. 'It's not his fault. When it happened, he was too little to understand. One day Mummy was there, and the next she wasn't. It was really difficult.'

'Yes, I can imagine. How did you explain it to him?' I asked.

Edward looked uncomfortable. 'We, er… didn't.'

'What?' I was unable to keep the incredulity out of my voice.

'He was tiny, Lily. He didn't know what death was.'

'But you must have told him eventually.'

'We never sat him down and explicitly told him, if that's what you mean.'

'Then how did he find out?'

'I don't know, really,' he sighed. 'It just kind of crept up on him. He realised she wasn't around and it was obvious everyone was very upset. He overheard stuff, started to put two and two together. One day he asked me where she was, and I said she'd gone to live with the angels. I don't know if he believed me, but after that, he got extremely agitated every time anyone mentioned her. So we stopped.'

Was it me, or was there a sudden chill in the air? I felt Clare's spirit entering the room on cue, hovering behind the sofa, her hands on Edward's shoulders, leaning into him, kissing his cheek, nibbling his ear. I'd managed to keep her out of my head for hours, but she was back, thrilled to be the centre of attention again. It had been a fantastic wedding party, but now she'd ruined it.

I checked my thoughts. No, that was ridiculous. Clare was dead, she had no agency. It was Tara's fault, nobody else's. She'd been trying to needle me, but the person she'd really upset was Noah. And she didn't even seem to care that much.

'I'm sorry, darling,' said Edward, reaching for me. 'This must be very unpleasant for you. This is our wedding night, for God's sake, we shouldn't be talking about Clare. Let's not say another word about it.'

'I'm fine, thanks.' I smiled weakly and freed my hand. 'It's Noah I'm worried about. I think he should see someone. A child psychiatrist or a grief counsellor. I have some excellent contacts from my old job, I'm sure I could—'

'No, Lily,' Edward replied firmly. 'I'm not having him poked about. I know how to handle Noah. He'll be okay, he just needs time to heal.' He turned to the girls. 'Now then, much as I love your company, how about you two leave us in peace?'

I woke with the dawn. Shafts of soft light seeped through the curtains and I could hear birds in the garden, singing and calling to each other, squabbling around the feeder. My husband – my heart still skipped a beat when I used that word – was lying next to me, fast asleep, his chest rising and falling as he breathed through his dreams. I raised myself onto one elbow and studied his profile for a few moments – the long, straight nose, thick black lashes, soft lips and perfectly rounded chin. He looked so peaceful and calm, without a care in the world.

In contrast, I felt churned up and restless, still thinking about what had happened the previous evening. I wanted Edward to wake up so that we could talk about it properly without Tara and Georgia looming over us. I also wanted to apologise for rejecting him last night. Technically I guessed the marriage hadn't been consummated, although we'd already made love countless times before. But last night was our wedding night, and we'd never have that special moment again. Edward was obviously hurt and disappointed, but he hadn't pushed, hadn't tried to persuade.

Noah's words were still going round in my head. What had he meant when he'd said he remembered everything? Everything about what? I had a strong intimation that Edward and the girls hadn't told me the whole story. I cast my mind back to the only conversation I'd ever had with Edward about the circumstances surrounding Clare's death. I dredged up the memory, turning it over and over, examining it for holes through which the truth might seep.

A few weeks after I'd started in the job, he had asked me to stay after work to talk about Noah's progress. I didn't think anything of it until I was ushered into the sitting room and saw a bottle of red wine, two glasses and a small bowl of crisps on the low table. This wasn't your usual parent–teacher meeting. I sat down nervously on the sofa while Edward poured. He was wearing a fresh white shirt and I could tell that he'd recently shaved, because there was a tiny speck of white foam on his left ear.

'How's it going?' he asked, sitting in the armchair opposite.

'Good, I think.' I raised my glass and we made a distant toast. 'Noah's smart, well behaved mostly. Sometimes he loses concentration, but that's normal for his age. One-to-one tuition is very intense. You can't zone out and you need to take more breaks. But all in all, I'm really pleased with him. He's a lovely boy, just a bit…' I hesitated, unsure how to phrase it.

'Odd?'

'No. He's shy, never wants to chat.'

Edward laughed. 'You mean he's awkward and uncommunicative.'

'Not at all. There's a lot going on inside, but he keeps it all buried. He struggles to show his emotions, or seems to be afraid of them. Sometimes he seems really angry with the world.'

'Angry?'

'It's suppressed. He's probably not aware of it. I think he just has these dark, uncomfortable feelings he can't explain.' Maybe it was the relaxed atmosphere or the wine, but my tongue seemed to be loosening. I paused, wondering whether I dared continue. Then Edward smiled at me encouragingly and I thought, okay, to hell with it. 'Maybe it's because his mother died and he feels abandoned by her.'

He flinched, as if I'd just touched a sore place. 'Abandoned?' he echoed. 'You make it sound like it was her fault.'

I blushed. 'No, I didn't mean that at all. But it's a common response when someone you love… I'm sorry, I didn't mean… If you'd rather not talk about—'

'No, it's fine,' he said. 'Noah is in his room, wrapped up in some video game with his headphones on. He can't hear us.' He rose and came over to top up my glass. The smudge of shaving foam was still there, and I wanted to reach up and wipe it off. A whiff of expensive cologne drifted into my nostrils, making me feel attracted and embarrassed at the same time.

'I hope you don't mind my asking,' I said, trying to recover my professionalism, 'but it would help a lot if I knew more about Noah's mother. The circumstances in which she died. Was it sudden, or expected?'

He sat down, this time on the arm of the sofa, just a few centimetres away from me. I felt his deep blue eyes staring right through me. 'A bit of both, I guess,' he said. 'She had a very severe nut allergy – she knew it could kill her. She lived with the risk every day. We all did.'

'Gosh… So what happened? She ate some nuts by accident?'

'Yes, in a sandwich. There were traces of sesame in the bread. She went into anaphylactic shock.'

'Oh God, that's awful. Didn't she have an EpiPen? When I was working at the school, we had kids with allergies and they always had pens in their bags.'

'So did she, the bloody thing never left her side. But for some reason she didn't use it, or couldn't get to it. The sad fact is, that EpiPen could have saved her life. We think maybe she'd dropped it and couldn't pick it up. It was found later, under the couch.'

I felt a chill rush through me. 'What? You mean *this* couch?'

'Oh no,' he said, noticing my reaction. 'Don't worry, she didn't die in this house. We moved here the following year, you know, to make a fresh start.'

'I'm so sorry,' I murmured. 'How shocking. Was Noah with her when it happened?'

'No, no, he was with me. She managed to call an ambulance, but it took too long to arrive. It was a catalogue of disasters…' His voice broke and he looked away.

'I'm so sorry.' I reached out and put my hand on his arm. It was the first time I'd touched him, and I remember a shock of electricity running through my fingers. I knew he'd felt it too. It was the beginning of our relationship.

Now he stirred, turning over and reaching out for me. I felt a pang of guilt for disbelieving him last night. Should I bring him breakfast in bed as a peace offering? Wake him with soft kisses, ply him with coffee and buttered toast? Maybe it would be better to put the subject aside for a while and start over, behave like everything was fine. He was often up for making love in the morning. We'd reset the clock and erase last night's failure forever.

Feeling more optimistic, I got out of bed, slipped on my dressing gown and went downstairs to the kitchen. The house was quiet, just the three of us left. The cleaners weren't due to arrive until 10 a.m. The caterers had dealt with the leftovers, but everything else had been left just as it was. There were dirty plates and glasses everywhere.

I picked my way through the debris to fill the kettle and put it on to boil.

Finding the last clean mugs, I popped a tea bag into each, then cut four slices of sourdough ready for the toaster. As I poured the hot water over, I heard a sound coming from the hallway. Somebody had just opened the front door.

'Edward? Is that you?' There was no reply. Putting down the kettle, I went to investigate.

The door had been left slightly ajar. Opening it fully, I went out and stood at the top of the steps. There was no sign of him. The entry gates were firmly shut. Pulling the silky gown more tightly around me, I walked gingerly down the steps in my bare feet.

'Edward?' I saw a flash of red moving in the bushes and walked towards it. 'Is that you, Noah? Come out, please… I know you're there – I can see you.'

He emerged from behind a tree. 'Hi,' he said, trying to sound as if it was perfectly normal for him to be in the front garden at half past six in the morning.

'Hi,' I replied warily. 'What are you doing?'

'Nothing.'

'Hmm… doesn't look like nothing.'

'I'm playing, that's all.'

'But why here? You've got a huge garden at the back. It's not safe to be out here on your own, even with the security gates. You know how cautious Daddy is.'

Panic flashed across his face. 'It's nothing. I'm going back inside right now. See?' He darted past me, scooted across the driveway and ran up the steps into the house.

Somehow, I didn't believe him. I stepped into the flower bed, following his footprints in the earth. They took me around the side of the tree and into the corner of the garden, very close to the front railings. It was a jungle of shrubs and plants, damp and dark, the ground littered with last year's dead leaves. Spotting a large, solid shape, I crouched down and pulled back the undergrowth.

A stone ammonite sat in the earth, its spiral ridges covered in bright green moss. It was an ornament, the sort you could buy at any garden centre. The edge of something was poking out from behind it. I reached forward and pulled it free. It was an old flat wooden box, no doubt containing some precious treasure that Noah had collected. Feathers, pebbles, conkers perhaps? Intrigued, I lifted the lid.

Inside was a single piece of paper, on which Noah had drawn a seaside scene. It was packed with careful detail. There was a beach at the foot of a cliff, a red boat bobbing on the wavy sea, a lighthouse in the distance. He'd used every colour in his felt-pen set – blue for the checked picnic blanket, orange for the bucket and spade, green for a ball. And in the centre of the scene, two figures – one big, one small – stood either side of a sandcastle, broad emoji-style grins spreading across their faces. The shorter one was obviously Noah – I recognised his favourite red T-shirt and the black sticking-out hair. The taller figure had brown hair, flicked up at the sides, and she was wearing a pink and green stripy dress.

I turned the paper over. There was a message on the back, written in Noah's neat, childish hand.

Hello Mummy!

Lily and Daddy got married. We had a party. Tara was mean to me. Do you like my picture? I miss you.

Love Noah xxx

CHAPTER SIX

Marsha waved at me from our favourite table, tucked away in the corner of the pub.

I threaded my way through the Friday-night drinkers. 'Sorry I'm late,' I said, taking off my jacket and throwing it over the back of the chair. A large glass of Cabernet was already waiting for me, and I sat down gratefully. 'Just what I needed. Cheers!' We clinked happily.

'I thought maybe you'd forgotten.'

'As if. I've been desperate to see you all week. I've got so much to tell you.'

She wrinkled her nose. 'I know we've always told each other everything, but you're a married woman now. I don't want *all* the details.'

'I wouldn't give you them even if you did,' I bantered.

'So... how's married bliss?'

'Blissful, of course.'

She heard the false note in my voice. 'Hey, girlfriend, what's up?'

'Oh, nothing much. Just...'

'Just what? Come on, you can tell me.'

'Well... remember at the wedding, when Tara caught the bouquet?'

'When she did that goalie dive, you mean?' laughed Marsha. 'She was so desperate.'

'Yeah, and not because she wanted to be the next bride. She wanted it to put on her mother's grave.'

Marsha whistled. 'Wow… that is heavy. She actually told you that?'

'Basically. She was telling Georgia, but everyone overheard. Including Noah, unfortunately.'

'What a bitch.'

'She didn't mean to upset him,' I said. 'I think it was aimed at me. Noah was just collateral damage.'

'Poor kid. Poor you. I wish I'd been there – I'd have slapped her.'

'It got worse. Noah went into meltdown. I went to see how he was, and he told me that everyone was lying. He said they thought he'd forgotten but that he remembered everything.'

'Everything about what?'

'I don't know. Then he said… you're not going to believe this…' I paused to take a sip of my drink. 'He said, "Mummy's still alive".'

Marsha's mouth gaped. 'Shit… How did you respond?'

'I didn't really. I was too shocked. I talked to Edward and the girls about it. Turns out that nobody ever actually sat down with Noah and told him his mother was dead.'

'To be fair, he was only three.'

'Yes, but he's eight now. And there's more.' I went on to tell her about the memory box I'd found hidden behind the ammonite. 'Here's the picture, and the message on the back,' I said, showing her on my phone.

'Is this a picture of him with his mum?'

'I think so.' We stared at the image together. Clare in her triangular stripy dress, Noah in his red T-shirt. Their pink felt-tipped mouths smiled out at us, their dotted eyes seemed to shine with love.

'Aww, this is so sad,' Marsha murmured.

'There was a girl at my old school whose mother died in a car crash,' I said. 'Her grief counsellor encouraged her to make a memory box containing photos and mementos, drawings, poems. She even wrote letters to her mother, imagining she was still alive.'

'Okay, so maybe that's where Noah got the idea from.'

'I doubt it. As far as I know, he's never had any counselling. And there's no way Edward would have suggested anything like a memory box.'

'You think Noah came up with the idea by himself?'

I shrugged. 'Who knows? I haven't talked to him about it. Or to Edward. It's Noah's secret thing. I feel I should respect that.'

'Well, I guess, if it's not doing any harm.' Marsha picked up her glass again, swirling the wine around thoughtfully. 'Just all seems a bit odd, don't you think?'

Suddenly a familiar voice cut in.

'Well, well, well, if it isn't Lily Baxendale!' I looked up, my heart sinking as I saw my ex-boyfriend standing before me, pint in hand.

'Hello, Alex,' Marsha said on a sigh.

'Hi.' He turned to me. 'Long time no see, Lily, how's it going?'

I managed a smile. 'Good, thanks.'

'Yeah, me too, really good,' he replied, as if I'd asked him in return. 'Great to see you. You haven't been around for ages.'

Seeing Alex was the last thing I needed. This pub held a prominent place in our history. We'd met at the bar and hit it off immediately, gradually joining each other's social crowd until they merged into one. After we moved in together, the Rose remained our regular haunt; we came here nearly every Friday night, on birthdays and anniversaries, to meet up with friends. After we split, I wanted to avoid the place, until Marsha reminded me that I had a perfect right to drink here, and if anyone should be embarrassed to bump into each other, it was him.

'So, what have you been up to?' he asked.

'I've been busy getting married,' I replied.

'Yeah, I know, heard all about it from your guests. Vintage limo and champagne all the way. Mind if I sit down? The place is bunged.' Before either of us could object, he planted himself in the chair next to me. 'That's better,' he puffed. 'Been on my feet all day. Cheers!' Marsha and I exchanged a furtive glance, while he took a large slug of his beer. 'Didn't think we'd be seeing you again, not now you've moved upmarket,' he said, wiping foam from his beard.

I took a large sip of wine. This was not turning out to be the evening I'd had in mind.

'So, how's it going?' he said.

'You already asked me that.'

'Sorry.' He tapped his finger absent-mindedly on the table. It was something he always did when he was nervous, and for a moment, I felt a flash of sympathy for him. 'How's the job? Still teaching the boy?'

'Yes. Why wouldn't I be?'

'No reason… just wondering. Not like you need the money any more, is it? Your guy must be minted. Living in that posh house, close to Hampstead Heath… Very nice.'

There was a long, embarrassing pause, then I said, 'How's work?'

'Oh, you know… same old, same old…'

'Still with the same company?'

'Yeah, it's fine. Pay's decent. They let me work from home, suits me. You know how lazy I am.'

'Oh yes,' I said, remembering how he used to spend all day lounging around in his pyjamas.

Marsha cut in. 'Lily and I were having a private conversation, so…'

He held his hands up in surrender. 'Okay. Got the message. Receiving you loud and clear.' He pushed back his chair. 'Sorry.

Just that I saw you from across the bar and I thought I'd come and say hello... seeing as how it's been a long time... I didn't mean to upset you.'

'You didn't,' I replied curtly.

'We're still friends? No hard feelings. You're happy, yeah?'

'Happier than I've ever been,' I assured him.

'That's good to hear. Honestly, I mean that from the bottom of my heart.'

'Alex...' warned Marsha.

'I behaved like a complete shit, I know that,' he blundered on. 'I threw it all away, and for what?'

I stared down at the table, not knowing what to say, wishing he would disappear as suddenly as he'd arrived.

'He's a lucky bastard, I hope he knows that,' he continued, his words slurring. 'He'd better treat you right. If he doesn't, then you come to me, okay?'

I'd had enough. 'Alex, you're pissed. Shut up and go away, before you make an even bigger tit of yourself.'

'Yeah, you're right.' He rose unsteadily to his feet. 'But I want you to know, I'm always there, Lily, any time you need me. We're still friends, remember?' He picked up his glass and tottered away.

'What a jerk,' Marsha said as soon as he was out of earshot.

'At least he knows it.'

'You know what his problem is? He's sick with jealousy. You've married somebody far more attractive and successful than he'll ever be, and he's still on his own. No beautiful, intelligent women are queuing up to marry him. Now that's what I call karma.'

I glanced over to where he was standing at the bar. 'I actually feel a bit sorry for him.'

'What? Don't you dare! You shouldn't even say hello after the way he behaved... Anyway, forget Alex, we've got far more interesting things to talk about.' She whipped her credit card out of her purse. 'Same again?'

It was dark as I exited the Tube station and made my way back up the hill towards the house. I was still feeling troubled by the encounter with Alex. Although the ending of our relationship had been horrible, the previous seven years had been virtually stress-free. We were only a couple of years apart in age. There'd been no dead wife or difficult ex, no stepchildren to deal with, no extended family to win over. Alex's parents were lovely people and we'd got along very well together. They'd treated me as part of the gang, buying me birthday and Christmas presents and inviting me over for celebrations. His mother had been certain we'd get married eventually and was very upset when I finished the relationship.

A memory crashed in, pushing me back in time to just over a year ago. He'd texted me at work, suggesting we meet for dinner. I was intrigued. He knew I didn't normally go out on a school night. Either I was too tired or I had to prep for the following day – often both. While Year 5 did their maths test, I racked my brains, trying to work out what we were going to celebrate. Had I forgotten some important date in our relationship calendar? Had he been promoted? Had he decided, after seven years of being together, that it was time to make it official? I started to tingle with anticipation. Friends and family had been asking for ages when we were going to get married. Before I left work, I reapplied my make-up and scrubbed the marker pen off my fingers. Would one of them be wearing a ring by the end of the evening?

I arrived early, feeling deliciously nervous, like it was a first date. He made me wait for nearly half an hour, and when he finally turned up, he looked like he'd already had a few drinks elsewhere. He didn't kiss me hello, didn't look me in the eye. We made stilted small talk for a few minutes and I stared at my menu without reading it. I knew something was wrong, that he wasn't about to propose.

'What's all this about?' I said finally. 'You're being really odd.'

He leant across the table and took my hands. 'You know how much I love you,' he said. 'I'll always love you, no matter what you think of me. That will never, ever change.' He hesitated, screwing up his face. 'Oh, God… not sure I can do this.'

'Do what?' I said. 'What's the matter, Alex?'

'Look, I know having a family is really important to you, and it's really tough that you can't, you know…' He stopped again, the words sticking in his throat.

'We've talked about this endlessly,' I said. 'There are lots of options – using a surrogate, adopting, fostering. We just have to be positive, decide what to do and get on with it.'

'That's the thing. You see, the truth is, I don't really want kids.'

His words socked into me. 'What? You've got to be joking.'

'No. When we met and you told me we didn't have to use contraception, I was kind of relieved. It seemed like we were the perfect match. You seemed okay about not being able to have children and we had a really good time, just the two of us. But then you started going on and on about these "options", and it made me feel really bad… I didn't know what to say. I love you, but… that's why I've been dragging my feet. I can't do it, Lily. I'm sorry.'

I felt the blood rushing to my head. 'You've never wanted children, is that what you're telling me? You lied, led me on. You're such a coward. Why weren't you straight with me from the start? I've wasted all these years on you!'

'I'm sorry. I didn't mean to… We love each other, don't we? Can't that be enough?'

'That's not the point, Alex. Why would I want to be with someone who can't be honest about their feelings?'

'I don't want to lose you, Lily.'

'Well, tough, 'cos you just have.' I picked up my bag and flounced out of the door.

I pressed the button on my fob and the gates rumbled open. The security lights flashed on as I slipped inside, illuminating the driveway. I felt vaguely guilty, as if I'd been unfaithful to Edward. If he asked about my evening, I would have to erase Alex from the story. In future, I decided, I would meet Marsha somewhere else.

I glanced across to the corner of the flower bed and was just able to make out the white-painted edge of the stone ammonite, glinting in the artificial light. Had Noah put any more pictures in the memory box? I wondered. I was tempted to go and see. But as I started walking towards it, Edward opened the front door.

'Lily?' he called out. 'Is that you?'

I instantly swung around and ran up the steps. 'Hi,' I said.

'What were you doing?'

'I thought I saw something on the ground, but it was nothing.' I kissed him on the lips, hoping to distract him.

We went inside. 'How was your evening?' he asked.

'Good, thanks.' I slipped off my shoes and hung up my jacket. 'It was nice to see Marsha again.'

'You saw her only a week ago. What did you talk about?' There was a note of suspicion in his voice.

I felt my cheeks warming and turned away. 'Oh, nothing much. This and that. Old times.'

'I hope you didn't talk to her about us.'

'Of course I didn't.'

'Our relationship is private.'

'I know. Don't be silly.' I gave him another, longer kiss.

He led me upstairs and we made love. I tried so hard to stay in the here and now, but my mind kept dancing into dangerous territory. The second it was over and we were lying naked and breathless in each other's arms, I thought about Clare. Suddenly she felt very much alive, prowling around the room, picking over our discarded clothes, squirting her wrists with my cheap perfume and screwing up her nose in disgust.

Edward released me and lay back on his pillow, eyes closed, still catching his breath.

'That was amazing,' he murmured.

But I didn't respond. All I could hear was Clare's sarcastic laughter in my ears.

CHAPTER SEVEN

'These times tables aren't sticking today, are they?' I said to Noah the following Monday morning, lowering the flash card in defeat.

'Yeah, I hate maths,' he agreed. 'It's my worst thing.'

'Okay, take a short break and then we'll do something else.'

'Juice and a biscuit?'

'No, it's too near lunchtime. Have a glass of water if you're thirsty.' I packed the cards away while he nipped into the kitchen.

An idea had been circulating in my brain for a few days, but I wasn't sure whether I dared put it into action. Ever since I'd discovered the memory box, my thoughts had buzzed around Clare's death like flies. It felt wrong that Noah was being left to deal with his grief by himself – he was far too young. I wanted to help him come to terms with the truth, but Edward had explicitly told me not to go anywhere near the subject with Noah. I would be breaking the sacred rule, but I felt it was worth the risk. I wasn't going to force anything, but if the boy wanted to talk about his mother, I wanted him to know that I was willing to listen.

A few minutes later, Noah returned from the kitchen and sat down at the desk. There were telltale biscuit crumbs at the corner of his mouth, but I decided not to comment.

'Shall we do some drawing?' I suggested. He nodded eagerly. I went to the shelves and took out some paper, a box of coloured pencils and some felt pens.

'Can I do a T-Rex?' he asked hopefully. 'Or a monster? Or space alien?'

'You're always drawing them. I think we should have a change, something completely different.'

'Like what?'

'Okay, let's think about this,' I said, sitting down again. 'Tell me, how do we get our ideas?'

'I don't know.'

'Sometimes, people draw "from life",' I said. 'That means they're standing there actually looking at the thing they're drawing. It might be a person, or a vase of flowers, or a field of cows.'

'I can't draw cows,' he informed me. 'Anyway, there aren't any in London.'

'It's just an example... Another way is to use photographs. You can take the photo yourself, or download it, or take it from a book...' He was already looking bored, so I cut to the chase. 'But today, I think we should try to draw something from memory.'

He groaned. 'No... that's too hard.'

'It's not, it just takes some thinking about. You said to me the other week you had a good memory.'

'No I didn't.'

'You did. After the wedding. You told me you remembered everything.' He coloured up, and I sensed his muscles tensing immediately. 'What did you mean by that?'

'Nothing. I didn't even say it.' He glared down at his blank sheet of paper, his cheeks reddening. I let him calm down while I sharpened a couple of coloured pencils.

'It's okay, Noah,' I said quietly. 'It's good to remember people, especially if they're not around any more. Memories are very important. They're like having a video channel in your head. You can play them as many times as you want, whenever you want.' He was still refusing to look at me, but I could tell he was taking it in. 'Nobody can take your memories away from you, they're yours to keep. Do you understand me?'

'Sort of,' he mumbled.

'Good. Right, let's do a bit of an experiment. How about we both try to think of a memory and turn it into a picture? It can be something that happened yesterday or a long time ago – up to you, you choose.' I put my hands over my face and he copied me. 'Really try to imagine it, bring it to life. Who else is in your memory? Where are you? What are you doing? What's the weather like…? How are you doing? Anything coming through yet?'

He didn't reply. I peeped between my fingers. He still had his face covered and he wasn't moving. I couldn't tell whether he was trying to conjure a memory or whether he was upset. 'Noah? Are you okay?'

'I'm thinking…'

'Sorry.'

After a few more seconds, he took his hands away. 'I don't want to,' he said.

'Oh… why not? Was it making you feel sad?'

He blinked teary eyes at me. 'Yes.'

'What were you remembering?' I hesitated, nervous of where I was about to tread. 'Were you remembering being with your mummy?'

'Yes,' he whispered. 'But shh, don't tell anyone.'

'It's okay, Noah. You're allowed to remember her.'

'No I'm not. He won't let me.'

'You mean Daddy?'

He nodded vigorously.

'Do you know why?'

'He says it makes me upset.'

'Well, yes, I expect it does, but there's nothing wrong with that, it's normal. It doesn't mean you should try to forget. Your memories are precious, they belong to you. Nobody can take them away, remember.'

'He won't even let me have a photo of her,' he suddenly blurted out.

I was taken aback. Surely that couldn't be true. 'Really? Do you know why?'

'He wants me to forget what she looked like.'

'I'm sure he doesn't.'

'He wants me to forget everything, but I can't. It's here in my head, like you said. I dream about her all the time. I can see her so clearly.'

'That's amazing. You're really lucky to be able to do that.'

'But she's not real. I can't touch her or hug her. That's what I really want to do.' A tear rolled gently down his cheek. 'I miss her so much.'

My heart swelled. 'Oh darling, of course you do...' I so wanted to cuddle him, but I knew it wasn't me he wanted. 'Would you like me to ask Daddy for a photo of her? We could put it in a frame and you could have it by your bed, if you wanted.'

He sniffed up his tears. 'He'll say no. Don't ask him, Lily, please. Don't tell him we've been talking about her. He'll be cross.'

'I'm sure he won't.'

'He will. You don't know what he's like. Please, don't say anything to him. Promise!' His eyes pleaded with me.

'Okay,' I said. 'I promise. Cross my heart.'

He lowered his voice and leant into me. 'Shall I tell you a secret? You won't tell Daddy, will you?' I shook my head. 'Mummy's coming to get me. I'm going to see her very soon.'

I was at a loss to know what to do. If Noah had been a pupil at my old school, I would have gone straight to the head teacher with my concerns. She would have brought the family in, suggested that Noah be assessed by the mental health team. But Noah was being educated privately at home, and I was in the tricky position of being both teacher and parent. As a professional, it was my duty to tell Edward that I thought his son needed help. But if he dismissed my concerns – as I suspected he would – what was I to do then? Go behind my husband's back and contact the local authority? Edward would never forgive me, and Noah would feel betrayed. If I lost the boy's trust, it would damage our relationship and he would end up feeling even more isolated. I didn't know which way to turn. My only option seemed to be to remain in the middle, caught between father and son. Maybe I could turn it to advantage, I thought, and be a secret go-between, a force for good working behind the scenes.

I couldn't believe that Noah wasn't allowed to have a photo of his own mother. Surely there'd been some misunderstanding. I wanted to ask Edward if it was true, but I couldn't, because then he'd know Noah had confided in me. What harm could there be in Noah having a picture of Clare? I decided to try and find one, then give it to him in secret. Obviously I couldn't ask Edward outright, and nor could I approach Tara or Georgia. No, I would have to resort to more covert ways of tracking Clare down.

I was convinced that photographs of her existed somewhere – saved on Edward's computer or mobile phone, stored on a memory disk or in the cloud – but accessing them was going to be a challenge. Edward was very security-conscious and all his devices were password-protected. He hated social media – didn't do Facebook, Twitter or Instagram. In fact, nor did Tara or Georgia, which I found very strange, considering they were in their early twenties. It was as if the family had collectively decided to withdraw from the public gaze. Was it just personal preference, or did they have something to hide?

With my internet searches for the correct Clare Morgan drawing a blank, I started to wonder whether she'd used her maiden name instead. However, I didn't know what that was and couldn't ask. Growing increasingly desperate, I tried searching just with 'Clare' – also 'Claire', as I wasn't sure how she'd spelt it – and various other keywords like 'London', 'Hampstead' and 'events manager'. But nothing came up that fitted. It didn't help that her first name was so common, especially among women of her age.

The internet had failed me. My only other option was to take a more traditional route and look for hard copies. Maybe there was a box of old photos hidden away somewhere. I needed to have a good search, maybe even venture into the loft, but with Edward working from home and Noah not going out to school, I was almost never on my own in the house.

Then a week later, my chance came. Noah had grown out of his trainers and Edward offered to take him to Oxford Street to buy some new ones. 'We could do with some father–son time,' he said. 'I've been so busy lately, what with work and the wedding.'

'Okay, if you're sure,' I replied, trying to stifle my excitement at the prospect of being alone for a few hours.

I waved goodbye to them from the front window as they walked through the gates, then headed straight to Edward's office. It seemed like the best place to start. There was an unspoken rule that this was his private space. Nobody else was allowed to work there, or use his fancy computer. The door was never locked, yet it always felt out of bounds.

Even though I was alone, I still entered the room cautiously. Edward was a very tidy worker. His computer was turned off and the desk was clear. There were no documents for prying eyes to read, no scribbled notes, not even so much as a stray paper clip.

Where might any photos be kept? In the filing cabinet, filed under C for Clare, perhaps? It was a bit obvious, but worth a try. I pulled on the handle, but it was locked, and I couldn't see a key. The desk drawer, then. It opened easily. Inside was a plastic tray of neatly arranged stationery items – pens, beautifully sharpened pencils, a small roll of sticky tape, a staple remover. No photos.

I slowly made a circuit of the room, looking for inspiration. There was a set of tall shelves built into the alcove, lined with books. Not novels, but business manuals and travel guides, a few biographies of sporting personalities and journalists. Then, on the top shelf, I saw a red ring binder, wedged between document boxes and lever arch files. I dragged Edward's black leather chair across the room and stood on it. It swivelled as I stretched up and pulled the binder out.

My hopes surged. I'd found a photo album – the old-fashioned kind with sticky pages and plastic covers. My parents had about ten of them, documenting my childhood and our family holidays. They were probably putting a new album together for the wedding at this very moment, I thought.

I carried it over to the desk and pulled the chair back into position, then sat down, my heart racing as I lifted the cover. And there she was, on the second page, after a cute picture of the girls as toddlers. Clare, sitting on a windswept beach, grinning and holding up what looked like a Cornish pasty. She looked a little older than Tara – mid twenties, I guessed. In fact, if it wasn't for the nineties hairstyle and clothes, I'd have assumed the picture was of Tara herself. Caught in a time trap, mother and daughter looked almost identical. They had the same long brown hair, several shades lighter than Noah's, and the same regular, slightly pointy features. I laughed wryly to myself. I'd been burning with curiosity to know what my rival had looked like, and all the while she'd been hiding in plain sight.

I turned the pages quickly at first, masochistically looking for photos of Clare and Edward together, arms entwined, madly in love, but to my relief, there wasn't a single one. Nearly all the photos were of the girls: Tara in a ballet tutu, Georgia in a pirate costume, the two of them in school uniform. No shots of Noah, but that wasn't surprising. The album had been compiled long before he was born.

There were only a few other pictures of Clare: posing on the beach with her arms around Tara and Georgia, a rather fun one of her licking a soggy ice cream, another of her on a fishing boat holding aloft a string of mackerel. As the photographer, Edward was both absent and ever-present. His three girls smiled at him behind the camera, enveloping him in the shot.

I went back to the beginning of the album, looking more closely at the photos this time, searching for further clues. They were all holiday snaps, most of them taken on the same English-looking beach. The scene tugged at my memory. It was a shingle beach, backed by yellow sandstone cliffs. In one photo, the girls were sitting on a blue and white checked picnic blanket. In another, they were perched on an upturned red sailing boat.

My heart leapt into my mouth. I flicked through the photos yet again, looking for other similarities – the orange bucket, the pink and green dress, the striped lighthouse… None of them featured, but it didn't lessen my conviction. The seaside picture Noah had drawn for his mother was of this very place.

CHAPTER EIGHT

I fetched my phone and brought the photo of Noah's drawing up on the screen so that I could compare it with the pictures in the album. There was no doubt in my mind that they matched. I felt as if I'd discovered something important, something that could be a breakthrough for Noah. He *did* remember. The shapes and colours were lodged in his brain like tiny pieces in a kaleidoscope, revolving and re-forming, making patterns he barely understood. Edward would know the place for sure. What if we took Noah there? Maybe it would help him. Not that I particularly wanted to recreate Edward and Clare's family holidays. Besides, I was sure that Edward would think the idea too risky. He was so frightened of his son feeling upset that he preferred him not to feel anything at all.

Noah's seaside drawing took on a whole new meaning for me. I felt as if I'd had a glimpse of what was going on inside his head. If he had one of these photos of his mother sitting on this very beach, it would validate his memories. Edward would not agree, of course, but he didn't have to know. I peeled back the plastic and carefully removed a photo of Clare in a swimming costume (not such a perfect body after all, I noted), her arms around Tara and Georgia. Then I returned the album to its original place on the bookshelves and left the room.

I immediately went upstairs and hid the photo in my under-wear drawer. I couldn't wait to give it to Noah when he came back from his shopping trip. It would have to be a secret between

us, however. Although I felt uncomfortable about going behind
Edward's back, I felt I was doing the right thing. This was about
meeting Noah's needs, not his father's.

Edward brought Noah home in the early evening. I was lying
on the sofa, flicking through Netflix, trying to choose the next
box set to watch. Edward came into the room and slumped down
next to me. He looked battle-weary.

'How was the shopping trip?' I asked, turning off the TV. 'Did
you manage to find some trainers he liked?'

'Yes, *that* bit went remarkably well.' He rubbed his eyes. 'Then
it all went downhill.'

'Oh. What happened?'

He put his arm around my shoulders and drew me closer.
'Disaster. We went to a burger place and I let him choose what
he wanted. When his burger arrived, it already had ketchup on
and he refused to eat it.'

'Doesn't he like ketchup?'

'Yes, but only a teeny-tiny smear, not a great big dollop. I
scraped most of it off, but he still wouldn't eat it. He wanted me
to order another one so he could put the ketchup on himself.'

I grimaced. 'But you refused.'

'Too right I did. He just sat there with his arms folded while
I ate my burger – wouldn't even touch his fries. I paid the bill
and we drove home in moody silence. He's gone up to his room
for the night.'

'Oh dear, he must be hungry,' I said.

'Serves him right. Don't take anything up to him, Lily, he
has to learn. I don't understand why he's like this over food. It's
ridiculous.'

'It's a power thing, you know that.'

'Huh. You can take him next time. He behaves himself with you.'

'Only because he's used to me being his teacher.'

'Maybe. I try my best with him, but sometimes he's… he's just…' Edward searched around for the word, 'impossible. It's almost like he hates me.'

'Don't be silly, he adores you,' I said. 'I'll talk to him.'

'Be my guest.'

I shuffled off the sofa and went upstairs, making a quick detour to my bedroom to retrieve the photo before gently knocking on Noah's door.

'Hey, Noah?' I whispered. 'Can I come in?' There was no response. 'I've got something for you.'

I squeezed on the handle and entered. Noah was lying face down on his bed. Carefully closing the door behind me, I sat down on the edge of the mattress.

'Guess what I found today,' I said. 'If I show it to you, will you promise to keep it a secret?'

His curiosity was piqued. He turned over and sat up cross-legged. 'What is it?'

I held up the photo. 'This is a picture of your mummy taken when your sisters were younger, about your age.'

He looked startled for a moment, then said, 'Can I see?'

'Of course.' I handed it over. He took the piece of paper and stared down at it.

'She's pretty, isn't she?' He shrugged. 'Of course, it was taken about ten years before you came along, so she probably looks a bit different to how you remember her.' He didn't reply, so I decided to push a little further. 'Maybe you recognise the beach?'

'I want a photo of the two of us,' he said. 'Together.'

'Yes, that would have been lovely, but unfortunately I couldn't find one.'

'Why not?'

'I don't know. This was the best I could do. There are probably hundreds of you with her, but I don't know where Daddy keeps them.'

He stared at the picture for a little longer, wrapped in thought. Then he laid it down next to me, like he'd finished with it.

'It's yours for keeps. You can put it in your…' I checked myself, 'somewhere safe. In a secret hiding place.'

'No. Don't want it.'

'Why not?'

'I want a picture of me and Mummy,' he repeated.

'I know, I'm sorry, but surely this is better than nothing.'

'I don't want it. Take it away.'

'Okay.' I felt hurt. 'What's wrong? Talk to me, Noah. Let me help you.'

'Just leave me alone.'

'All right.' I stood, slipped the photo into the back pocket of my jeans and left the room.

I returned the photo of Clare to my underwear drawer, though I didn't like the idea of her lurking there, hidden beneath layers of my intimate clothing. As I lay in bed that night, I imagined her spirit lying in wait, easing the drawer open and slipping out. She drifted around the room, hovering over the bed, curling herself around Edward's sleeping form. Burying myself under the duvet, I tried to banish all thoughts of her from my mind.

I woke up feeling guilty about upsetting Noah. I'd tried to give him something he wanted, but I'd only made it worse. I should have realised that he wouldn't want a photo of Clare with Tara and Georgia. He was clearly jealous of all the years the girls had spent with their mother. They had countless precious memories to share, but he only had a few fragments.

There *had* to be hundreds of images of Noah with Clare – lovingly mounted in baby albums or stored on Edward's computer – but I'd had enough of nosing around my own house. This was

Edward's responsibility, I decided. Noah needed a photo to bind those fragments of memory together and help him come to terms with his loss. I sensed that he was ready to take this important step, but he couldn't and shouldn't do it alone.

That morning, I gave him a load of maths problems to solve by himself, and went to see Edward in his office.

'Can I talk to you for a few moments?' I asked.

He spun round on his chair to face me. 'Yes, of course. Everything okay, Lily? You were very quiet over breakfast. I couldn't get a peep out of you or Noah.'

'I know I'm not supposed to talk to Noah about his mother, but, um…' I pursed my lips.

'But what?' he said coldly.

'The thing is, Noah would like a photo of her. Preferably of the two of them together. A baby pic, I guess. Or anything really, although not with the girls in it.'

He heaved a troubled sigh. 'Really? He actually asked you for a photo?'

'Yes. It's a natural thing to want.'

'He's never spoken to me about it.'

'He seems to think you won't let him have one… like you're trying to make him forget about her. Obviously you're not, but he's feeling confused.'

Edward pulled a face. 'The problem is, I don't have any.'

'What? You don't have any photos of the two of them together?'

'I don't have any photos of her at all. Not a single one.'

'But what about…' I started, then stopped myself. Edward didn't know that I'd already looked through the photo album. I tried to stop my eyes flicking to the top shelf of the bookcase. 'I mean, you must have some *somewhere*.'

'No. I destroyed them all after she died,' he explained. 'I know it was a stupid thing to do, but I wasn't thinking properly. I was out of my mind with grief, angry with her for dying on us. It was such an unnecessary accident – should never have happened…' He closed his eyes briefly, remembering. 'One night I got blind drunk and smashed all the photo frames in the house, ripped up the albums, put the pictures through the shredder, deleted the files from my Mac. Of course, I bitterly regretted it, but by then it was too late.'

'So you've no photos of Clare at all,' I said, trying to keep my voice neutral.

'No. None.'

'I can't believe they were all totally deleted. Weren't there any stored on the cloud?'

He shook his head.

'The girls must have some on their phones. Or what about Clare's parents?'

'They died long before Noah was born.'

'Other family members then, her friends – why didn't you just ask around?'

'I didn't want anyone to know what I'd done.'

'You didn't have to explain, you could have just said you'd like some more photos of her,' I persisted.

'Yes, I know I could have, but I didn't,' he replied, a little coldly.

'So you're telling me you've absolutely no pictures of her at all… not even old ones, from before Noah was born? Holiday snaps, perhaps.'

Please remember the red photo album, I pleaded silently. *Tell me the truth.*

'I feel like you're cross-examining me here, Lily. I already told you, I don't have any photos. Anyway, I'm not sure it would help Noah, to be honest. It could trigger a panic attack.'

'I don't agree. Having a photo of her and being allowed to remember is all part of the process.'

'What process?'

'Of being able to accept the reality that his mother is never coming back.'

There was a long, pregnant pause. I couldn't understand why Edward was pretending that he didn't have any photos of Clare when the album was right there on the bookshelf. I studied his expression as he turned back to his Mac, hinting that he wanted me to leave. But I wasn't going to let him off the hook that easily.

'Maybe Noah doesn't need photos of his mother,' I said, taking my phone out of the back pocket of my jeans. 'He has such vivid memories of her. He drew this lovely picture of the two of them on the beach. I took a photo of it.'

I swear he flinched. It was the tiniest of involuntary reactions, but I saw it and he knew that I'd seen it, too.

'Look.' I kept hold of the handset as I showed him, making sure Edward couldn't swipe through to the shot of the message Noah had written on the back.

His eyes flickered over the image. 'This is supposed to be her, is it?'

'Yes. Do you recognise the location?'

'Well, obviously it's a beach, but…' He shrugged.

'Look more closely and you'll see that some of the details are very specific,' I pressed. 'It makes me think Noah was drawing from memory. The cliffs, the lighthouse, even the picnic blanket…' I let my words hang in the air, hoping he'd reach out and grab them. But he looked away and turned his attention back to his computer. 'Maybe it's somewhere you took him once.'

'I don't think so,' he said, fiddling with his mouse.

'No?'

'We never went to the seaside.'

'Really?' I affected surprise. 'Why not?'

'Because it always rains and the sea's bloody freezing.'

'Didn't you ever take the girls on a beach holiday?' I asked, unwilling to give up.

'Not in the UK.' He gave me an irritated look. 'What is it, Lily? Am I a cruel parent because I refuse to subject my kids to English summers?'

'Don't be silly.' I sighed. 'I'm just wondering what gave him the idea for the picture, that's all.'

'It's just a generic beach picture. He probably copied it out of a book. It doesn't mean a thing. You're reading way too much into it.'

'No, I'm not. I'm trying to understand how much he remembers—'

He rounded on me. 'Nothing! He remembers *nothing*. That's what upsets him so much, can't you understand?'

'That's not what Noah says.'

'Let's have no more art therapy, okay?'

'I didn't ask him to draw it, he did it all by himself.'

'Then stop encouraging him.'

'What's the big deal, Edward? Who are you trying to protect – Noah or yourself?'

He swivelled round to face me again. 'If you want to help Noah, focus on the future, not the past.'

'His future is out there in the real world,' I snapped. 'He should be at school, meeting other kids, leading a normal life, not stuck on his own like a prince in a tower, dreaming that his mummy is still alive. He's getting older, he needs to know the truth.'

'I'm doing what's best for him, Lily.' He turned back to his work.

I decided to give him one last chance. 'Are you absolutely sure you don't have any photos at all of Clare?'

'I already told you, no.'

I glared at him for a few seconds, then walked out of the office. Flames of anger were licking inside me. My husband was lying to me and I wanted to know why.

CHAPTER NINE

I spent a restless night, churning everything over in my mind, and woke up with a headache. I took a couple of pills, then called Noah down for breakfast. There was no apparent tension between us. He didn't mention our conversation about the photo of his mum, and nor did I. In contrast, Edward was in a strange mood, not engaging with either of us. He ate his toast, then disappeared into his office to work.

Noah and I went into the schoolroom and started our lessons. On the surface, everything was normal, but I sensed that an important development in our relationship had occurred overnight – a tightening of the bond between us. I'd tried to help him, and although I'd failed to give him what he really wanted, he was grateful for my efforts.

At around eleven, the doorbell rang. I left Noah in the schoolroom and went to answer it. To my surprise, Georgia was standing there.

'Oh, it's you,' she said. 'I was expecting Dad.'

'Hi.' I looked at her curiously. 'Something up?'

'Didn't he tell you I was coming over?' She pointed her security fob at the gates and they rumbled shut.

'It doesn't matter,' I said, brushing it off. 'It's always good to see you. Are you here for a particular reason?'

'Hmm, not sure. Dad's taking me out to lunch – just the two of us, I think.'

'Oh. Really?'

'Yeah, he rang me this morning, asked me to come over.' She yawned. 'You don't know what it's about, do you?'

'No.'

'I hope I'm not in trouble.'

'Over what?'

She grimaced. 'I'm over my spending limit on the credit card… Might need you to put in a good word for me.'

'Oh, I'm sure you know how to handle your dad better than I do,' I replied, thinking not for the first time how entitled the girls were, and how they seemed to have Edward wrapped around their little fingers. We lingered awkwardly in the hallway. 'I'd, er… better get back to Noah. We're doing the Romans.'

'Oh, cool.' She lowered her voice. 'How's he coping with the new situation? He was so weird at the wedding – I've been worrying about him.'

'He's fine. Back in his normal routine.'

'Good.' She checked the time on her phone. 'And you're okay? You're not too upset by what Tara did? With the bouquet, I mean.'

'No, water off a duck's back,' I said, squeezing out a smile.

'Great. Where's Dad?'

'In the office.' She started to walk towards it. 'He's in an online board meet—' I started to call after her, but I was too late to stop her barging in.

'Darling!' I heard him cry before the door closed behind her.

I went back to the schoolroom, feeling slightly pissed off – more with Edward than Georgia. He hadn't said anything about taking her out to lunch.

Noah was at the desk, carefully colouring in his gladiator's leather tunic.

'Guess what, Georgia's here,' I said. 'She's with Daddy. Do you want to go and say hello?'

'Not now,' he murmured. 'Need to finish this.'

I strolled over and looked down at the picture. 'I love the fierce look on his face.'

'That's because he just killed a lion,' he informed me solemnly.

'Oh…' I sat down in my teacher's chair. 'Actually, gladiators didn't fight animals, just other gladiators. The animals were very valuable, so their owners didn't want them harmed. They put criminals in the ring and watched the lions tear them apart instead.'

A couple of minutes later, Edward walked in, Georgia yapping impatiently at his heels.

'I'm so sorry, Lily,' he said. 'I forgot to tell you.'

'It's not a problem,' I said, trying to sound more relaxed than I felt.

Georgia waved from the doorway. 'Hi, Noah.'

'Hi,' he replied without looking up from his drawing.

Edward looked over Noah's shoulder. 'Wow! Is that a gladiator or a centurion?'

'Dad…' Georgia warned. 'I haven't got all day. I'm supposed to go to a seminar this afternoon.'

'Yeah, I know.' He ruffled Noah's hair. 'See you later, buddy. You can tell me all about it when I get back.'

After they'd gone, Noah carried on with his picture while I stared out of the window, my head spinning with unanswerable questions. Why was Edward meeting Georgia for lunch? It hadn't sounded like he was going to rap her knuckles for overspending. I tried to think of other reasons. Perhaps he was going to ask her for some photos of Clare. Perhaps he wanted to talk to her about *me*…

I made some cheese toasties for lunch and let Noah eat his on a tray in front of the TV. While he was occupied, I went back to the schoolroom and tried to ring Marsha, but she didn't pick up. I left a long, rambling message saying I needed to talk to her, then told her to ignore it. In a way, there was no point in asking

Marsha for advice, because I knew exactly what she would say: 'Confront Edward with his lies. Don't let him get away with it.' Lying was something Marsha was very hot about. She'd had a couple of cheating boyfriends in the past and was determined never to be tricked again.

Maybe I *should* confront Edward, I thought. It was ridiculous, sitting here stewing, thinking the worst of him. Suddenly inspired, I left the schoolroom. I would take the photo album off the shelves and leave it open on the desk. I could even print out Noah's picture and put it next to the other seaside photos. Then when Edward came back from lunch, he'd be forced to explain himself.

After checking that Noah was still absorbed in his TV show, I went into Edward's office.

But the red photo album was no longer there.

Had I put it back in the wrong place? No, I was sure I'd been very careful to leave the room exactly as I'd found it. But I hadn't been very subtle when I'd questioned Edward about his family holidays. He must have recognised Noah's picture and worried that I'd find the album. Was that why he'd asked Georgia to come over, so that she could take it away?

I went back to the sitting room to see Noah. 'Look, I've got a bit of a headache,' I said. 'I'm afraid we're going to have to stop our lessons for today.'

His face lit up. 'Yay! Can I watch TV?'

'I suppose so. But when Daddy gets back, you'd better turn it off or we'll both be in trouble.' I handed him the remote control and went upstairs to my room.

Checking my phone, I saw that Marsha had responded to the message I'd left earlier. Typically, she'd picked up the strain in my voice and was inviting me over that evening for emergency pizza and wine. Dear Marsha, she was always there for me. I had even more to discuss with her now, I thought. I sent a brief reply, thanking her and saying that I couldn't wait to see her, and it was true, I *couldn't* wait. My head was bursting with so many uncomfortable, incomprehensible thoughts that I felt like it was going to explode.

But I had several hours to get through by myself first. I wandered around the bedroom, smoothing the sheets, puffing up the pillows, rearranging the items on the dressing table, picking up bits of fluff from the floor. I sensed Clare's invisible spirit following me, mischievously messing things up again, because no matter what I did, the room still looked untidy and ill at ease with itself. I didn't belong here.

I heard the sound of the entrance gates rumbling open and went to the window. Edward had returned from his lunch with Georgia. As he got out of the car, I saw that he was on his own. I ran downstairs, calling out to Noah to switch off the television.

Edward entered the house. Noah hurtled out of the sitting room and stood next to me. We looked like a couple of naughty kids, caught in the act.

'Hi, Dad,' Noah said, over-brightly.

'Hi.'

'How was lunch?' I asked.

'Good, thanks. Sorry we didn't take you, but Georgia needed some fatherly advice.'

Another lie, I thought. Georgia had already told me that she'd been summoned to see him, not the other way around.

He studied the two of us. 'Everything okay? I expected you to be in the schoolroom, fighting gladiators.'

'Lily's got a headache,' Noah informed him. 'So we're not doing any more lessons today.'

Edward turned to me. 'Sorry to hear that, darling. Have you taken something?'

'Yes. It's fading now.'

'Good.' He hung his jacket over the end of the banister. 'Still, you should rest. Shall I make you a cup of tea?'

'No, I'm okay, thanks.'

'Better get back to work,' he said. 'I'm way behind now.' He started to make for his office.

'I hope you don't mind,' I said, 'but I'm going over to Marsha's tonight for pizza.'

He stiffened. 'Why?'

'Does there have to be a reason?'

'It's a bit short notice. What are Noah and I supposed to do about dinner?'

'Can't you fend for yourselves? There's stuff in the freezer.'

His jet-black eyebrows drew into a frown. 'You seem to see an awful lot of Marsha,' he said sullenly.

'That's because she's my best friend.'

'*I'm* your best friend now, surely.' He paused, waiting for me to reassure him, but I was still secretly angry with him and didn't feel inclined. There were a few seconds of stalemate, then he stalked off to his office.

Marsha filled our glasses with wine while I rolled the pizza wheel through the roasted peppers, artichokes and Italian salami. I put the slices onto plates, then we sat down at the tiny dining table and raised our usual toast.

'To us,' she said.

'Forever and always,' I added.

She took a drink, savouring the fruity red wine in her mouth before swallowing. 'Okay. Spit it out, girl. You sounded freaked out on my voicemail. What's been going on?'

'So much has happened, I don't know where to start.'

'Try the beginning. We've got all evening – take your time.'

So first I told her about finding the photo album and stealing one of the photos, then about Noah refusing to take it because the picture didn't include him. 'I realise now that I made a poor choice, but it was all I could find.' I suspended my fork. 'Anyway, I decided to ask Edward directly for a photo of her.'

'Good.'

'Except he claimed he didn't have any.'

'Which you knew was a lie.'

'Yup. But it gets worse.' I took another bite of pizza, then told her about Georgia turning up unexpectedly for lunch.

'I'm pretty certain he only asked her over so he could give her the photo album to look after. I didn't see her leave with it, but it's the only explanation I can think of. After they went out, I went to fetch it and it wasn't there any more.'

Marsha looked confused. 'I don't get it. What's the big deal? Why doesn't he want Noah to have a photo of his mother? It's just cruel.'

'Edward maintains it's going to trigger a panic attack, but I'm sure it wouldn't.' I wiped my greasy fingers on a piece of kitchen towel and reached for my wine glass. 'When I showed Noah the picture of Clare with the girls, he didn't turn a hair.'

Marsha shrugged. 'Anyway, Edward shouldn't have lied to you. That's unacceptable. You should have it out with him.'

'I knew you'd say that.'

'So what's stopping you? It's not like you to hold back. You're usually so up front about everything.' She twisted the bead on the end of one of her long braids. 'You're not letting him intimidate you, are you? I know he's a lot older than you, but he's your husband, not your dad.'

'No, no, it's not that,' I replied hurriedly.

'And your own father was a terrible bully.'

'You don't have to remind me, Marsha. I was there. I'm not going to let any man abuse me, mentally or physically.'

'Then why are you afraid of Edward?'

'I'm not! I'm angry with him, but I can't confront him over the photo album because then he'll know I was looking for a photo of Clare, and that'll make me look weak and needy.'

'Hmm… I thought you wanted the photo for Noah,' she said, arching an eyebrow.

I sighed. There was no hiding anything from Marsha, she knew me too well. 'I did, but yes, I also wanted to know what she looked like. Out of curiosity.'

'You were checking out the competition.'

'If you like. Edward thinks I'm obsessed with her, but I'm not. It's Noah I'm concerned about.'

Marsha's face darkened. She collected our plates and put them by the sink. I watched her lean against the counter, head down, thinking.

'What is it?' I asked.

She turned round to face me. 'Edward is deliberately trying to suppress Noah's memories of his mother. Why? What is it he doesn't want him to remember?'

'I don't know.'

'Other things don't add up,' she continued. 'Like, why didn't anyone from his side of the family come to the wedding? Apart from the ghastly daughters, that is. He lied to you about that too, remember? Said his parents had gone on a cruise when he'd never even invited them.'

'He was trying to spare my feelings.'

'Really? Or was he trying to hide something from you? He's got some secret, and I'm sure the girls are in on it.'

'Don't, Marsha, things are bad enough as it is without starting conspiracy theories. I know you've never liked Edward…'

'I've never said that.' She raised her hands in innocence.

'Oh come on, we can't pretend with each other.'

'I know this is going to sound mad, but is there any possibility at all that Noah might be telling the truth?'

A small laugh escaped me. 'What, you mean that Clare is still alive?'

She nodded. 'Yeah. Could he be communicating with her via this memory box?'

'No, of course not. It's a coping mechanism, that's all.'

'I suppose so…'

'There's no way Clare is alive,' I persisted. 'Tara put my wedding bouquet on her grave, remember? And anyway, it says "widower" on our marriage certificate. Edward had to show proof to the registrar.'

'Yes, of course, I'd forgotten that.' She still looked concerned. 'What was the proof, her death certificate?' I nodded. 'And you saw it, did you?'

'Well, he had it in his hand, but I didn't ask to read it. It didn't seem right.'

'He could have faked it, I guess.' She caught my indignant expression. 'Sorry. I didn't mean to offend you, sweetie. I'm just throwing it out there. And you're right about the Ugly Sisters, they'd have no reason to pretend she was dead.' She twisted her mouth, reluctant to let her theory go. 'All I'm saying is, if I were you, I'd keep a close eye on Noah and this memory box.'

'You're barking up the wrong tree, Marsha.' I felt underneath the table for my shoes. The conversation was making me feel uncomfortable and it was time to go home.

CHAPTER TEN

Although I'd dismissed Marsha's outlandish suggestion that Clare was still alive, the idea kept nagging at me. It was a fact that Edward had never actually shown me her death certificate. I hadn't been bothered by it before, but suddenly I needed to see it, just to put any doubts out of my head. The document had to be somewhere in the house, but after my experience with the photo album, I had no appetite for searching Edward's office again. There must be another way of getting hold of a copy. My mum was a bit of an amateur genealogist, and I knew she regularly sent off for birth, marriage and death certificates of our Victorian ancestors. Maybe she could give me some tips.

Once lessons had finished for the day and I had some time to myself, I went into the garden and gave her a call.

'How's married life?' she asked. 'You must be enjoying yourself, otherwise you would have called before.'

'Sorry, Mum, I've just been really busy.'

'I thought maybe you'd gone away on honeymoon without telling me.'

'No, I'm still here, working away.'

'You want to make him take you somewhere exotic and romantic. Like the Maldives.'

'I can't. We follow term times here. Anyway, Edward doesn't want to leave Noah.'

'His sisters can look after him, can't they?'

'Yes, but we don't want him to feel abandoned. The three of us will probably go somewhere in the summer.'

'Hmm… seems a shame not to have a proper honeymoon,' she murmured disapprovingly. 'It's not like he can't afford it.'

I quickly changed the subject and asked about ordering death certificates. 'Is it possible to get them for people who've recently died, or do you have to be a relative? Do you need a proper reason?'

'No, it's public information, anyone can order copies. You can go to the records office in person, but it's easiest to do it online,' she said proudly. 'You just need a few basic details to search – name, date and place of death, age. Why on earth do you want to know?'

'Oh, a friend was asking, that's all,' I bluffed. 'I knew you'd be able to help. Thanks… So, how are you?'

'Not too bad. I'm still waiting for my weekend invitation,' she added. 'We could have a lovely time together going around the designer boutiques in Hampstead. You could take me to lunch in one of those expensive restaurants, or we could have a luxury spa day together. All on Edward's credit card!' she giggled.

'Mum, that's not how it works,' I replied stiffly. 'I'm not a trophy wife, I'm still working.'

'It's not a proper job, though, is it? Teaching your own stepson,' she jibed. I decided not to rise to the bait.

'You must come and stay soon, that would be great.' But I carefully avoided fixing a date with her.

As soon as I got off the phone, I sat down on Noah's swing and started searching online for the record of Clare's death. Mum had made it sound very simple, but I soon realised that I had no hard facts to enter. I didn't know Clare's full name, or the date she'd died, or how old she'd been. Luckily, the website could accommodate this and allowed me to search with approximations. I typed 'Clare Morgan', 'London' and a date five years ago, but to my surprise, there were no results to view. I tried again, allowing for spelling variants, but there was nothing for a Claire Morgan either. I removed the location, and expanded the date range to a year on either side. Still nothing.

I kicked my heels and swung back and forth a few times as I tried to think of a way forward. Maybe she hadn't changed her name when she married. There was no legal requirement to do so. If I could find the record for her marriage to Edward, that would give me her maiden name, and I could search the deaths with that. Suddenly inspired, I went back to the public records website, this time concentrating on records for Edward. At least I knew his exact age, and assuming they'd married before or around the time of Tara's birth, a likely date. Several possibilities came up, including some marriages that had taken place in London, but I couldn't access the bride's name without taking out a subscription. I went to fetch my purse, whipped out my credit card and signed up for three months. My pulse raced as I typed in 'Clare', ticked the box for name spelling variants, then pressed enter.

But there were no matches. I couldn't believe it. I entered all the details again, widening the date ranges and locations, changing Edward's year of birth in case there'd been a mistake. It made no difference. I started to feel dizzy. As far as the public records were concerned, no marriage had taken place. It seemed that I wasn't Edward's second wife after all, but his first.

I knew there had to be a simpler explanation. I was entering the wrong information, that was all. Perhaps Clare's legal first name was something else that she'd hated. Perhaps she and Edward had married abroad. There were countless possibilities. Even so, troubled thoughts gurgled in my stomach. Everywhere I turned, Edward's life seemed shrouded in secrecy.

But I had no more time to pursue the matter. I got off the swing and walked back towards the house.

Edward was still working in his office and Noah was upstairs in his room. I tidied up the kitchen, then added the final touches to the sauce I'd made earlier and put the water for the spaghetti on to boil. While I laid the table, I rehearsed the conversation I was going to have with Edward as soon as Noah was in bed. Honesty was the best policy. I should stop rummaging around in his past and challenge him over his lies.

I shouted out that dinner was ready, then put a bowl of freshly grated Parmesan on the table. Edward entered a few moments later.

'Smells good,' he said, smiling. 'Deserves a bottle of Chianti, don't you think?'

'It's only spag bol,' I replied, carrying the saucepan to the sink and draining the pasta.

'Yes, but it's *your* spag bol.' He fished a bottle out of the rack and unscrewed the lid.

Noah ran into the room just as I was about to call him again. 'Sorry,' he said, jumping onto his seat. He sniffed the air. 'Mmm… yummy… I'm starving.' He seemed to be in a good mood for a change.

We sat down to eat. Edward chatted away about this and that, but I found it hard to listen, let alone contribute. My mind was too wrapped up in other things. I kept glancing at my husband surreptitiously, looking at him with fresh eyes. He was gesticulating as he spoke, as he usually did. It was something I'd always found attractive about him – it suggested confidence, generosity, affability. But tonight I found it irritating, even a sign of arrogance. His features, his voice, even his smell were so familiar, and yet I suddenly felt as if I didn't know him at all.

'Can I get down now?' Noah asked the second he put down his spoon.

'Don't you want pudding?' I said hopefully. Once Noah went back to his room, I'd have no reason not to talk to Edward, and I wasn't sure I was ready for a showdown.

'Nope. I'm full up.' He hovered over the seat of his chair. 'Please?'

'Okay then. If Daddy doesn't mind.' I glanced at Edward, who nodded. Noah immediately bolted out of the room and hurtled up the stairs.

'He must have reached a crucial stage in his video game,' Edward said. 'That boy's obsessed.'

I started to gather up the plates.

'I'll do that. The cook never clears up, that's the rule.'

'Really? Since when?'

'Since now,' he replied smoothly, taking them out of my hand. 'Relax. You seem really on edge this evening.'

'Do I?'

'Yes.' He refilled my wine glass and drew in a breath. 'I've been meaning to talk to you about something for a while, but... it's a little awkward... I don't want you to take offence.'

I felt wrong-footed. This was supposed to be *my* difficult conversation, not his. 'What do you mean?'

'I've, er, been thinking about the current set-up for Noah. I'm not sure it's working as it should.'

'But he's doing really well,' I said. 'He's come on in leaps and bounds.'

'Yes, you've done a brilliant job. But things have changed. You're his stepmother now. I don't think it's very healthy for you to be his teacher as well. He needs somebody outside of the family, who's not so... um... emotionally involved.'

It was as if he'd slapped me around the face. 'Emotionally involved?'

'The two of you have become very close, which is wonderful, means the world to me. But a teacher should be more distanced, more objective.'

'You're saying I let him get away with stuff?'

'No, not at all. But going forward, I think it would be better if he had someone else.'

'But I love teaching him.'

'It's not about your needs, Lily, it's about his,' he said.

His patronising tone was riling me. 'If you really cared about his needs, you'd send him to a proper school,' I blurted out without thinking. 'What he actually needs is to make friends with kids of his own age, to visit other people's houses, play team sports, go out into the world and experience real life.'

'No. He couldn't cope with it.'

'Yes, he could, if he was given a chance. You're the one stopping him.'

'He's my son, I know what he can and can't do.' He threw me a superior look.

'Well, I don't agree,' I huffed. 'But if you want to continue with home-schooling, I can't see any reason why I shouldn't carry on teaching him. Lots of parents do it, they can't all afford—'

He cut me off. 'Also, it doesn't feel right paying you now that we're married.' I rolled my eyes. 'Neither do I think you should work for nothing.'

'I don't care about that.'

'I know, but I do.'

'So that's it, no discussion, no consultation, you're sacking me,' I said. 'Great. You're just like my mother – you don't value what I do. You think I should sit at home all day filing my nails.'

'I knew you'd take it the wrong way,' he sighed. 'But I'm afraid my mind is made up. You're a fantastic teacher, Lily, but you're wasted as a private tutor. You should go back to the classroom.'

'Don't tell me what I should and shouldn't do.'

'If you want to look for another job, something completely different, that's up to you, of course, but there's no pressure,' he continued. 'It's not as if we need the money.'

'Noah won't be happy,' I protested.

'He'll get over it.' He moved towards me, arms outstretched. 'It's the right decision. For his sake and yours too, Lily. You seem very tense at the moment, like you're not coping.'

'I'm coping fine.'

'Please don't be upset. It's for the best. Come on… come here. Let me hold you.' He took me in his arms and stroked the back of my head, like I was a child. 'I love you so much.'

'Love you too,' I mumbled. I was burning with anger, yet my heart felt cold.

CHAPTER ELEVEN

It was late when Edward finally made it upstairs. I'd already got into bed and switched the lights off. I lay still, with my eyes closed. I was hurt that he hadn't come up to check on how I was, and had let me fester here all evening.

He tiptoed around, getting undressed, using the bathroom, then slipped into bed, turning to kiss me lightly on the forehead. 'Love you,' he whispered tenderly, even though he believed I was asleep. I felt myself soften towards him, but I didn't let on that I was still awake. It was too late to talk. He turned away from me and settled down. I listened to his breathing gradually slowing, felt his body sinking into the mattress. Within minutes he was snoring lightly.

I turned onto my back and stared upwards at the looming darkness. My limbs felt heavy but my excited brain wanted to stay up all night. It gave up the fight at some point, however, because something woke me at two in the morning. The outside security light had come on, and was illuminating the room.

I leapt out of bed and ran to the window, pulling back one of the curtains. I stared down at the driveway, scrunching up my eyes, but I couldn't see what had triggered the light. Everything seemed normal. The gates were shut. Edward's car was still sitting there. There was no shadowy movement in the shrubs and trees. I shivered, drawing my arms across my chest, waiting in case somebody or something might emerge. But nothing did. Then the light went off, plunging the scene into darkness. Puzzled, I went back to bed.

Edward was fast asleep, completely oblivious. I pulled the duvet over me and snuggled down, but I couldn't get comfortable. Good sense told me that it must have been a fox crossing the driveway. The area was full of them. They hid in their dens on Hampstead Heath during the day and roamed around the streets at night looking for food. I had no idea how it had got through the railings, and supposed there must be a gap in the side fence somewhere. I would check tomorrow in the daylight.

My brain was exhausted, and despite my best efforts to stay awake for the rest of the night, it eventually forced sleep upon me. I dreamt fitfully. Clare took centre stage, half ghost, half real, my subconscious couldn't decide which. She drifted vaporously through a gap in the railings, then took on a more solid form. I watched her from the bedroom window as she went on a rampage in the front garden, pulling up plants and hurling them across the driveway, scratching a key along the door of Edward's car. She took Noah's box from behind the ammonite and scattered its contents. I was terrified but also impressed by her anger.

When I woke, just before dawn, I lay in the grey-pink gloom trying to analyse what I'd dreamt. The theory was that we were everyone in our dreams. I didn't have any trouble believing that it had been me on the driveway, full of rage and frustration. Careful not to disturb Edward, who was still deep in slumber, I slid out of bed and put on my dressing gown, then crept downstairs to the kitchen, meaning to make myself a cup of tea.

The heating hadn't yet come on and the house was chilly. I put the kettle on to boil and waited, my thoughts flipping between dream and reality. Did Edward really sack me last night? Did somebody or something trigger the security light? I knew all that had happened, and yet it felt unreal, like I'd imagined it.

I poured the bubbling water over the tea bag and stared at the coloured liquid swirling in the mug. I was suddenly seized with the urge to go outside and check behind the stone ammonite. Leaving the kitchen, I went to the front door. I carefully removed the chain and undid the bolts, then opened it and stepped down onto the driveway.

The air was spiked with cold. I looked around. Of course, everything was as it should be. The driveway was clear, Edward's BMW was untouched. I went down the steps and walked to the flower bed. The earth was dry and cool, gritty beneath my bare feet. Crouching down, I felt behind the ammonite for the box, then clasped my fingers around the edge and pulled it out.

When I opened the lid, I saw a small white envelope. Noah had written another note by the look of it. I picked it up and turned it over. To my irritation, it was sealed. Now I wanted even more to know what was inside.

Standing up, I popped the envelope into my dressing gown pocket. The steam from the kettle would unseal it, I thought. I hurried back into the house and switched the kettle on again. Holding the envelope against the vapour, I carefully peeled back the flap, almost scalding my fingers in the process.

There was a small piece of paper inside, folded in two. I opened it up, my heart starting to race as I saw that the message wasn't *from* Noah, but to him. And even more surprisingly, it was typed, not written in his childish hand.

I couldn't believe what I was reading. The paper trembled between my fingers, and I felt weak at the knees and had to find a chair to sit down on. My mouth went dry as I read the short note again and again. I wished I was still dreaming, but I knew that I was horribly awake.

My dear Noah,

How lovely to hear from you! Thank you for the beautiful picture. I am very glad that you like Lily, but please don't tell her our secrets. She is married to Daddy and on his side now, so you can't trust her. Take care. Be a good boy and work hard at your lessons. I love you always and will see you soon. Xxx

The letter wasn't signed from 'Mummy', but clearly that was who Noah was supposed to think had written it. My pulse raced as I read it over and over again. It couldn't be from Clare, could it? *Could it?* I tried to shake the possibility from my head. The woman was dead and buried. My wedding bouquet was withering on her grave. Tara and Georgia were always saying how much they missed her; they would never have colluded in such a deception. Edward wouldn't have been able to marry me if he hadn't been able to provide proof that he was a widower. And yet...

I had searched hard, but found no record of Clare's death. Edward had never actually shown me the certificate – maybe deliberately. None of his family and not a single friend from the past had come to our wedding. He'd lied to me about the photo album. And now there was this note.

If Clare wasn't alive and secretly communicating with Noah, somebody else was pretending to be her. But why would anyone play such a cruel trick on a vulnerable little boy?

I put the note back in its envelope and returned it to my dressing-gown pocket. It was still very early, and neither Edward nor Noah was stirring, but I couldn't risk them coming downstairs and finding me with it. I wasn't ready to face either of them yet. My first instinct was to reach for my mobile and call Marsha, but I knew she would still be asleep. I'd have to wait until later, maybe make up an excuse to go to her flat. I knew what she'd say. *Show the note to Edward. Confront him. Make him tell you the truth.* But I no longer trusted him to tell me the truth, that was the problem. He'd already lied to me too many times.

The envelope felt like a stone in my pocket, weighing me down. It would be easier to talk to Noah first, I decided. In the meantime, I needed to behave as if everything was normal.

Edward was still fast asleep. I studied him for a few seconds before climbing back into bed beside him – his steely hair, long nose, generous lips, those dark eyebrows that had yet to turn grey. He wasn't overweight, but he was as solid as a rock. When he'd held me in his arms before, I'd always felt safe, protected, but now I wasn't so sure.

Two nervous hours passed, during which I didn't sleep a wink. Various plans of action circulated in my brain, but in the end, I decided to talk to Noah before doing anything else. I got up again at seven o'clock and made Edward a cup of tea. While he was in the shower, I transferred the note to my rucksack downstairs. I safely navigated breakfast, then Edward went into his office to start work and I went to the schoolroom, where Noah was waiting for me.

'It's a lovely day,' I told him. 'Let's go for a nature walk.'

'Okay,' he replied, twisting his fingers together. He seemed a little distracted, and I wondered whether he was thinking about the memory box. I'd kept my eyes on him from the moment he'd woken up, and knew he hadn't yet had a chance to check behind the ammonite.

I packed refreshments, a notepad and some pencils and we set off. As I pressed the button to open the gates, I saw Noah's glance flick over to the front corner of the garden.

We walked through the elegant, tranquil streets without talking, absorbed in our own thoughts. How was I going to broach the subject? I would have to take it gently. The last thing I wanted was him storming off and getting lost on Hampstead Heath. The note tucked inside my rucksack felt like a bird, flapping and squeaking as it tried to escape. I wanted to find a good place to set it free, but although we'd entered the heath now, we were still on a main path. Joggers and dog-walkers were out in force; there was nowhere to sit and be private.

'Let's go down here,' I said, pointing to a slender gap that twisted between the trees. The earth was hard and crackly underfoot. Sunlight was dappling through the newly grown leaves, forming pretty patterns on the ground. At last the sound of birds was louder than the hum of traffic.

We reached a small clearing, where a large oak had conveniently fallen to create a natural bench. I gestured at Noah to sit down, and took the small rucksack off my back. I passed him a carton of juice and unscrewed my bottle of water. His eyes lit up when I produced a packet of his favourite chocolate biscuits, and he took one eagerly.

'Noah,' I said. 'We need to have a very important chat.'

His face jerked towards me, blue eyes blinking nervously. 'About what?'

'Lots of things. But mainly about you and Mummy.' I took out the envelope, keeping it folded on my lap. 'I found your secret hiding place behind the ammonite,' I said. 'I know you've been leaving pictures and messages there.' I hesitated, waiting for a response, but he didn't say anything. 'I got up very early this morning and went to look, and I saw that there was this note.'

'It's mine,' he said. 'Give it to me.'

'Before you read it, I want you to know that you really, really can trust me. I'm not on Daddy's side, I'm on *your* side. I haven't told him about the memory box.'

'It's not a memory box. It's a message box.'

He held out his hand, demanding. I passed the letter over and he read it to himself, mouthing the words carefully. I waited for his reaction, my heart in my throat.

'How long has this been going on, Noah?' I asked.

'I don't know. About a year, I think.'

'Who do you think is writing you these letters?'

'Mummy,' he answered without hesitation.

'That's why you told me she was still alive.'

'Yes. Of course. This is proof.'

I bit my lip. 'I can see how you might think that. But just because you've been receiving these letters doesn't mean for certain that...' I tailed off as I saw his little face starting to pucker.

'She's alive,' he said firmly. 'One day she's going to come and get me and we'll be together forever.' He bent his head and starting twisting his fingers together.

I decided to approach the issue from another angle. 'How did it all start? The idea of having this box, you drawing her pictures, her sending you replies, hiding it by the front gates.'

He looked down again at the letter, rereading the warning not to trust me.

'Was it your idea?' He shook his head. 'I see. So Mummy got in touch with you, is that right?'

He breathed out through his nose. 'I can't tell you.'

'How? That can't have been easy. Did she ring the house? Send an email?'

'No.'

'Did somebody help you get in touch with her? Somebody in the family – one of your sisters, perhaps?' He looked away with his mouth tightly closed.

'Was it Georgia?' I waited. 'Or Tara, even? Come on, you can tell me.'

'No, not them,' he muttered.

'Who was it then?' Silence. 'Have you been told not to tell anyone...? Okay, I understand.' There was no point in pressing. I needed to take a different tack.

'How often do you use the memory… I mean, message box?'
I asked. He shrugged. 'Once a week, once a month? Do you have
a special day – say, the first Wednesday of every month?'

'Not telling.'

'You must have some system. Otherwise, how does Mummy
know when you've put something in the box? She can't stand
outside the gates every day, waiting to see – Daddy would have
spotted her.'

His face clouded with suspicion. 'Why do you keep asking
me stuff?'

'I'm just interested in how it all works.'

'Please don't tell Daddy.' His voice cracked with emotion. 'If
he finds out that Mummy's back, he'll make her go away again.'

His words dug into me. 'What do you mean? Make her go away?'

'Nothing,' he replied quickly. 'It doesn't matter. Just don't tell
him about any of this. Promise, cross your heart like before, Lily.
Go on. Do it.'

I crossed my chest, but I already knew that it was a promise
I couldn't keep.

'Let's go home, eh?' I said, rising to my feet. He put the
envelope in his backpack, carefully zipping it up, and we retraced
our steps along the leafy paths, neither of us daring to say any
more about it.

As we crossed the road, Noah took my hand and kept hold of
it the rest of the way home. I sensed he was trying to confirm my
loyalty, to claim me for his side, and it made my heart break that
I was going to have to betray him. This matter was too serious,
too important. My head was spinning with unspeakable thoughts.
Either Clare *was* still alive and my husband was a bigamist, or
somebody else was trying to mess with our little boy's head. But
who could it be? A stranger, or somebody within the family? And
even more puzzling – why?

CHAPTER TWELVE

As soon as Noah and I got back to the house, I bustled him off
to the schoolroom.

'Draw me a picture of Mummy,' I said, pulling the art materials out of the drawer. 'You can use anything you like – felt tips,
crayons, coloured pencils.'

He looked at me strangely. 'You mean, draw her face? I'm not
very good at that.'

'It doesn't have to be a portrait. It could be a picture of the
two of you together, or the last time you remember seeing her.
You could be in the garden, or playing on the beach, perhaps?'

His eyes screwed up even further. 'On the beach?' he repeated,
suspiciously.

'Yes, why not? Or anywhere. Up to you. If you don't want to
draw her, that's fine too.' I could hear the nervous energy in my
voice.

'Why?'

'Maybe you could put it in the message box,' I whispered.

Satisfied with this explanation, he took a large piece of paper
from the pile and sat down. I felt bad for tricking him. The truth
was, I needed to make sure he was occupied while I was talking
to Edward. I went to my desk and switched on the schoolroom
computer. From what I could make out, Noah was drawing a
house. I waited a few more minutes, pretending to read some files
onscreen, then crept out of the schoolroom.

My heart was racing as I walked down the corridor towards Edward's office. I listened at the closed door for a few seconds to make sure he wasn't talking on the phone or in the middle of an online meeting, then knocked.

He called me in, swivelling around in his chair to look at me.

'Hi,' he said. 'What's up? I came to offer you a coffee earlier and you'd gone out without telling me.'

'We went for a walk on the heath.'

'Oh. Nice day for it.' There was a pause. 'So, er… what is it, Lily, only I'm in the middle of writing a report.'

'I need to speak to you. It's important. Urgent.'

'Oh. Really? What's happened?'

I closed the door and took a deep breath. 'But first, I need to clarify something… Is Clare still alive, Edward?'

He jolted, then let out a disbelieving laugh. '*What*? I… er… I'm sorry, but… what did you just…?'

'You heard me. Is she still alive?'

He puffed out air again. 'Darling, what a funny thing to say. Are you okay?'

'Please, Edward, just answer the fucking question.'

He held up his hands. 'Okay, no need to swear!'

I sat on the edge of his desk, waiting. His blue eyes blinked at me several times, and he pushed a lock of grey hair from his forehead. I kept looking at him. My gaze was steadfast, but inside, my whole body was trembling.

Finally he gave in. 'This is absurd. You know full well Clare died five years ago.'

'Do I?'

'Who's been putting doubts in your head? Marsha? That woman's a menace. She hates me, you know.'

'That's not true.'

'She's jealous. You were supposed to be travelling around the world together and you abandoned her for me.'

'This has nothing to do with Marsha,' I said firmly.

'Oh, I know, it was Noah.' He sighed wearily. 'It's because of what he said to you on our wedding night. Please don't tell me you took him seriously. He's a kid! He was upset, overdramatising, trying to hurt you even.'

'No, he really believes it. I'd like to see Clare's death certificate, please.'

'This is ridiculous,' he huffed.

'You never actually showed it to me before, just waved it in front of my eyes. I'd like to read it properly.' I held out my hand.

'I'm not one of your naughty pupils, Lily, I'm a grown man. Your husband, in case you've forgotten. I don't need to prove myself to you. If you want to see her death record, I suggest you look it up online.' There was an edge of triumphalism in his voice, as if he knew I would find it difficult. 'Now can we forget this stupid conversation ever happened, and get back to work? You're supposed to be in the middle of lessons with Noah, aren't you?'

But I was not to be dismissed so easily. 'Okay, so let's assume for now that Clare *is* dead,' I said evenly, taking the pin out of the grenade I was about to throw at his feet. 'Which means somebody else is communicating with Noah, pretending to be her.'

He froze for a second, then his voice juddered. 'What do you mean? Communicating how?'

At last he was taking me seriously. His jaw locked as I related everything I knew about the memory box and its hiding place behind the ammonite, Noah's pictures, the messages, my conversation with him that morning on the heath.

'For God's sake, Lily, why on earth didn't you tell me straight away?' he said. I could almost see the cogs spinning in his brain. His breathing was fast and shallow, and there was a strange look in his eyes I'd never seen before. I couldn't work out what it meant.

'I thought it was some kind of coping mechanism. It's something people get bereaved kids to do, you know, write letters to their dead parent as if they're still alive. I had no idea he was actually getting replies. I only found out this morning. That's why I came straight to you.'

'You really thought it was *Clare*?' He shook his head in despair. 'Are you crazy?'

'I don't know what I thought, Edward, it was very shocking. And... well, you have to admit, you're very secretive about her. Nobody's allowed to mention her, you won't let Noah have a photo. You've been lying to me—'

'No I haven't,' he protested.

'You *have*. You told me you'd sent your family invites to the wedding and nobody was available, but Georgia let it slip that you'd fallen out with all of them. And I know about the photo album.'

He looked down. 'Sorry. I've been an idiot. I was so embarrassed that I wouldn't have anyone on my side at the wedding, I didn't know how else to explain it. And I thought you'd be upset if you knew I'd kept pictures of Clare. You seemed a bit jealous of her, a bit vulnerable. I didn't want to hurt you.'

'It was the lying that hurt, Edward. It was the going behind my back, conspiring with Georgia.' I looked away, swallowing down my tears. I didn't want him to see me crying.

He stood up and took me in his arms. 'I love you, Lily. I *do* think about Clare from time to time, and sometimes I struggle with the grief. But you're the only woman for me. I'm really sorry I lied about the bloody photos. I got it massively wrong. I should have trusted you, told you the truth.'

'It's okay,' I mumbled into his shirt. 'I'm fine. It's Noah I'm worried about. That's way more important.'

He drew back. 'Yes, of course, you're right. It's alarming.'

'Who do you think could be doing it?'

'I've no idea.'

'It has to be somebody in the family, doesn't it?' I pressed. 'Nobody else has access to Noah. I was wondering whether maybe one of the girls—'

'No, it's not them,' he cut in.

'I'm not saying they did it to hurt him. Maybe Georgia started the memory box to help him, and it got out of hand.'

'It's *not* Tara or Georgia, okay? They would never do something like that, at least not without asking my permission.' He looked away from me and stared at a row of files. I knew he was trying to work it out. I wanted to see what was in his head, but he was blocking my view.

'Please share your thoughts,' I said.

'I don't have any,' he replied through gritted teeth, but I knew that wasn't true.

I tried again. 'I know Clare's parents are dead, but what about other family? Did she have any brothers or sisters?'

He shook his head irritably. 'She was an only child – it's nobody in Clare's family.'

'But I can't see how it could be a stranger,' I said, swallowing hard.

He started pacing about, suddenly full of angry energy. 'There are some evil people out there,' he said. 'They have ways of getting to kids. Noah could have met someone online, in a chat room. He's always on that bloody tablet, playing those video games.'

I gasped. 'You mean you think he's being groomed by a paedophile?'

'Looks like it.' He curled his hand into a fist. 'The bastard. When I find out who it is, I'm going to…' He punched a row of books, pushing them to the back of the shelf.

I was stunned. Stupidly, the idea hadn't occurred to me before. I immediately felt guilty for not telling Edward about the memory box earlier. 'In that case, we have to go to the police, don't we?'

He stopped pacing and turned to me. 'No, I don't want them involved.'

'Why not?'

'I just don't, okay?'

'But they can investigate, they'll have specialists. If you seriously think he's being groomed...'

He raised his hand to shut me up. 'No, Lily. No police. Not yet, anyway.' He tried to calm himself down. 'Let's not rush into anything. First thing is to talk to Noah. I'm going to have it out with him right now, demand that he gives me everything he's got. Photos, emails, websites, chat rooms, whatever.'

I started to feel sick. 'Please be gentle with him. Remember, he actually believes his mother is still alive. If you swing in like a wrecking ball...'

'Leave it to me,' he replied firmly. 'I know what I'm doing.' And with that, he marched out of the room, heading off to the schoolroom.

I went to wait in the living room, folding myself into an armchair and hugging a cushion to my chest. What had I done? Noah was vulnerable, he wouldn't cope with a tough approach – either he'd have a panic attack, or he'd go into his shell and refuse to say anything. But it was too late now. Edward wouldn't let me help, and Noah was bound to turn against me. He'd trusted me with his secrets and I'd betrayed him – at least, that was how he would see it. I'd never be forgiven.

But even though it hurt, I knew I'd done the right thing. And although Edward had been furious with me, telling him had somehow drawn us closer together, like a proper couple concerned for the safety of our child. If only I'd gone to him earlier, I thought.

I'd been so stupid, imagining that Clare was still alive. Although I'd defended Marsha against Edward's attack, in a way, he was right. She *had* questioned whether Clare was really dead, and planted doubts in my mind. Now I felt embarrassed for being so high-handed with Edward, demanding that he produce the death certificate. I decided to forget all about it. Compared to what was going on with Noah, my problems paled into insignificance.

Edward wasn't with Noah for long. After about twenty minutes, he came and found me. His expression was grim and he looked frustrated.

'Well?' I asked.

'The little bugger clammed up, completely refused to tell me anything,' he fumed, walking over to the drinks cabinet and taking out a bottle of gin. It was barely lunchtime, but I didn't say anything. 'Would you believe it, he even started saying "no comment",' he continued, 'like he was being questioned by detectives.'

'Oh dear, he must be upset. Shall I try to talk to him?' I offered cautiously.

'No, let him stew for a bit,' he growled, splashing tonic into his glass. He sat down heavily on the sofa and puffed out his cheeks.

'I still think we should contact the police,' I said after a pause. 'They have specialist interviewers—'

'I already said no, didn't I?' He looked at me sharply. 'I'm going to turn his bedroom upside down and go through his devices. I'll check the security camera footage, redirect the cameras to that side of the garden, maybe even set a trap.' He took a large mouthful of G and T. 'Don't worry, whoever it is, they won't get away with it. You have my word.'

CHAPTER THIRTEEN

I felt powerless, not knowing where to go or what to do with myself. I thought about making some lunch, but I guessed nobody had an appetite. Upstairs, Edward was ransacking Noah's bedroom. I wasn't sure where Noah was, but I suspected he was still in the schoolroom. It was horribly quiet and still, like those strange moments after a bomb explodes, when the air is thick with dust and you can't yet see what damage has been done or who's been hurt; those few precious seconds when you think it might be a dream, not real, not bad. I had a sudden desire to escape, to leave the house and breathe in fresh, pure air.

I went into the kitchen and opened the back door, then walked down to the very end of the garden. Taking out my phone, I called Marsha. Her number rang for several seconds, then went to voicemail.

'The shit's hit the fan,' I said. 'I need to talk to you. Please call me as soon as you get this.'

It was a miserable day. Grey clouds were scudding across the sky, and I felt chilly in just my T-shirt and jeans. After a few minutes, I gave up and went back inside. Edward had come downstairs and was fixing himself a sandwich.

'Did you find anything?' I asked.

'No, I bloody didn't,' he replied, almost cutting himself as he hacked at a lump of cheese. 'If Noah won't tell me how this all started, I'm going to take away his games console. And his tablet.'

'I don't think punishing him is going to help… Please let me try talking to him.'

'You won't get anywhere,' he assured me.

I made a tuna mayo sandwich – Noah's favourite – and took it to the schoolroom. He was still sitting at his desk, head down, tucked between his arms. I put my hand on his shoulder. He instantly shook me off.

'Go away,' he mumbled.

'I thought you might be hungry.' I put the plate of sandwiches down next to him, but he studiously ignored it.

'I'm sorry,' I said after a pause. 'But I didn't have any choice. I *had* to tell Daddy.'

He lifted his head. There was a look of hatred in his piercing blue eyes, carbon copies of his father's. 'You crossed your heart and hoped to die. You lied to me, just like everyone else.'

'I know, but sometimes there's a good reason for lying. Please forgive me.'

'I hate you – I wish you'd never come here,' he said bitterly. 'You've spoilt everything. Now I'll never get to be with Mummy.'

I sat down next to him. 'Noah – listen to me, this is important. I hate to have to say this, but the person who's been sending you letters – it's not your mummy. Whoever it is is playing a trick on you, pretending to be her.'

'That's what Daddy said, but he's wrong. You're both wrong. You're lying.'

'No, we're not,' I continued calmly. 'We're telling the truth. This is serious. I know it's really hard to take, but the truth is, your mummy…' I stalled as the words stuck in my throat, afraid to come out. 'Very sadly, your mummy ate something she was allergic to and she died.'

He put his hands over his ears. 'Liar, liar, liar!' he chanted, rising to his feet and kicking the chair away. 'I hate you! Go away, leave me alone!' I reached out to him, but he ducked past me and ran out of the room. I heard him thundering up the stairs then the door to his bedroom slamming.

Not only had I failed to get through to him, I'd made things worse.

Edward came into the schoolroom a few moments later.

'That didn't sound good,' he said.

'He hates me now. Blames me for everything.'

'Yeah... I'm sorry, darling.' He held me. 'But you did the right thing.'

'So what happens next? You can't torture him until he confesses.'

'The important thing is, we've stopped it. I'm going to tighten security, make sure parental controls are installed on all his devices, get some more cameras put in. He'll be banned from playing in the front garden on his own, and we'll make sure he can't talk to anyone from outside.' I didn't like the sound of it. Noah was a virtual prisoner as it was, without the situation getting worse.

'What about his lessons? He won't have anything to do with me.'

'A few days off won't do him any harm. But we should get on with finding your replacement.'

'I suppose so.' I sighed defeatedly. 'It just feels really bad.'

He embraced me and stroked my back. 'Don't worry, I'm dealing with it. Take some time out, put it to the back of your mind.'

'Thanks. I think I might go and see Marsha tonight.'

He pulled away. 'I'd rather you didn't.'

'Why not?'

'I don't want you telling her all about it. It's a family matter, none of her business.'

'Marsha *is* family.'

'No, she's not. Please, don't say anything. Stay here with me.' He gave me a warning look. 'Right... I'm going to check the security footage now, see if I can spot the bastard who left the note behind the giant snail.'

It's not a snail, it's an ammonite, I said to myself.

As soon as he'd left the room and I heard the office door shut, I took my phone out and tried Marsha's number again. This time, she picked up.

'Hi,' she said, sounding a little breathless. 'Just got your message. What's up?'

I lowered my voice to a whisper and told her everything that had happened. 'I don't understand what's going on,' I said. 'If Edward really thinks Noah's being groomed by some paedophile, why won't he go to the police?'

She thought for a few moments before replying. 'Maybe he knows full well it's not a paedophile,' she said. 'Maybe Noah's right and it *is* Clare.'

'Please don't start again, Marsha. I've already made a fool of myself over that.'

'But you said Edward refused to show you Clare's death certificate.'

'I don't blame him, he was offended.'

'Hmm… or was he pretending to be offended?' she questioned.

'Please don't, it's not helping. I can't have my husband and my best friend hating each other.'

'Oh, so Edward hates me, does he?' she said quickly. 'Interesting. Classic controlling behaviour.'

'Stop it, Marsha. I can't take this right now, I've got enough to deal with.' I didn't tell her that Edward had virtually banned me from seeing her that evening. 'Look, I've got to go.'

'Me too. Lunch break over.' There was an awkward pause. 'Take care of yourself, okay?' she added. 'Love you.'

'Love you too.'

*

Over the next ten days, Marsha and I had no contact at all – we didn't meet, or speak on the phone, or even text. It was the longest gap in communication I could remember. It wasn't Edward that was stopping me – if I'd wanted to see her, I would have done so even if it meant going behind his back. I just didn't know what to say to her any more. I felt as if she was making me choose between the two people in the world I loved the most. It wasn't fair.

My lessons with Noah were suspended. He spent all day in his bedroom, mainly playing video games. Fortunately for him, I'd persuaded Edward not to confiscate his console – not that I received any credit for it. Noah was still refusing to have anything to do with me, and when we were together, the atmosphere was thick with tension. He came downstairs for meals, but wouldn't talk to us or answer any of our questions.

Meanwhile, Edward went on a mission to secure the house, installing extra cameras and a brand-new alarm system. He took Noah's tablet away and scoured it for evidence of online grooming. There was nothing suspicious there, but he deleted Noah's email account all the same. He spent hours shut away in his office making phone calls. Sometimes I heard his raised voice, but I couldn't make out what he was saying. When I asked him if he was making any progress with his investigations, he was vague and non-committal. It was obvious that he didn't want to involve me in the matter. I felt hurt and excluded. I was his wife, wasn't I? Surely we were supposed to share our problems and work on solutions together. I could only conclude that after five years on his own, he'd grown used to shouldering responsibilities himself. Maybe it was a macho thing, not wanting to appear weak in front of a woman, especially someone so much younger than him. Or maybe he was still a little angry with me for not telling him about the memory box in the first place. Something wasn't right, that was certain.

I spent the time tidying and cleaning the schoolroom, sorting through my teaching materials and making plans for what I might do next with my career. Edward was still keen to hire a new tutor for Noah, which saddened me, but there was nothing I could do about it. I'd been hoping to persuade him to send Noah to one of the many small private schools in Hampstead, but there was no chance of that now. He wasn't letting the poor child out of his sight.

I went online to see what jobs were going in London, but nothing inspired me enough to make an application. I didn't want to go back to the same type of job I'd left – an ordinary classroom job in an ordinary school. I wanted to do something more purposeful, maybe working with disadvantaged kids or those with special educational needs. My new life with Edward was very privileged and luxurious. I still hadn't got used to not having to worry about money, and when I *did* spend without thinking, I felt pangs of guilt later. Of course, my mother thought I'd already achieved the ultimate success by marrying such a rich man. I didn't confide in her about what was going on, keeping my phone calls with her brief and superficial. We'd never had that close a relationship anyway – Marsha had always been my confidante, the person I turned to in my hour of need. I missed her so much.

Summer was on the horizon and the days were getting warmer. Noah was clearly bored and couldn't bear the stuffiness of his room any longer. He started escaping outside for short periods. I observed him through the schoolroom window as he wandered disconsolately around the garden, kicking divots in the turf or randomly beheading flowers. Sometimes he sat on the swing for ages without moving, just staring into the middle distance. I longed to go out there and try to talk to him, but I'd promised Edward I wouldn't.

Then on Friday evening, while Edward and I were watching a film on Netflix, my mobile rang. My heart leapt when the caller's name came up on the screen.

'Who is it?' asked Edward, frowning.

'Marsha.'

'Don't answer.'

But there was no way I was going to reject her. 'Hi… hang on a sec,' I said to her, swiftly leaving the room. I rushed upstairs and shut myself in the bedroom. 'Sorry about that. Edward and I were watching a film.'

'Right. Are you on your own now?' Her tone was strangely serious.

'Yes. Are you okay?' I climbed onto the bed and pulled a pillow out, placing it behind my back.

'Sorry I haven't been in touch,' she said.

'I haven't been in touch either.'

'I hate it when we fall out.'

'Me too. I don't even know what it was about exactly,' I added with a small laugh.

'Can you come round?' she asked.

'What? Like now?'

'Yeah. Soon as possible, really.'

'Why? What's wrong, Marsha? You sound really odd.'

'I can't explain over the phone. You'll just have to trust me.'

'Can't you give me a clue? Otherwise I'll be worrying all the way there.'

'I'm fine,' she said. 'This is about Edward.'

I groaned. 'Marsha, if you're trying to turn me against him again…'

'Please, Lily, I'm begging you. Just come over.'

CHAPTER FOURTEEN

Something about Marsha's tone was really worrying me. She wasn't the melodramatic type. Although I wasn't happy that she'd been meddling in my life behind the scenes, I had to take her seriously. She was my best friend – I owed it to her.

I went back downstairs and into the living room. 'Sorry, but I've got to go over to Marsha's,' I said.

Edward paused the film and frowned. 'But we're halfway through this. You can't just up and go.'

'She needs me.'

'I need you too.'

'It's urgent.'

He looked sceptical. 'Why? What's happened?'

'Oh, you know, boyfriend troubles,' I lied.

'She needs to stop leaning on you so much. You're not teenagers any more.'

'She's in a terrible state. I can't desert her.' I shrugged helplessly, as if it was a pain but there was nothing I could do about it.

'Okay, but don't be long. Take a taxi both ways,' he instructed.

'Good idea… Thanks. Look, carry on watching the movie. I wasn't really into it, anyway.'

'No, I'll wait until you come back,' he said pointedly.

'Okay, whatever.' I gave him a kiss on the head and left him to sulk in peace.

My mind performed somersaults all the way to Marsha's flat as I tried to guess what bad piece of news about Edward she was going to reveal. As the large, posh houses and elegant blocks of flats gave way to the dirty, jumbled streets of my old neighbourhood, so my anxiety increased. Had Marsha found Clare alive and well, living in London? Had she met her and got her side of the story? Was my husband some kind of abuser, who'd exiled his first wife from the family and forbidden her from seeing her son?

I still had my old keys to Marsha's flat, but I'd forgotten to bring them. I rang the bell and immediately heard her footsteps running down the stairs. She opened the door wide and flung herself at me.

'I was really worried Edward wouldn't let you come,' she said, giving me a long hug.

'He wasn't happy about it, but he's not *that* controlling. I promised I wouldn't stay long.'

'Hmm, well, decide that later,' she replied. I followed her inside, back up the stairs and into the lounge.

A bottle of our favourite Cabernet was already opened and waiting on the table. Marsha told me to sit down while she poured two generous glasses. 'You're going to need this,' she said ominously.

I took a large sip. 'Okay, I'm ready. Hit me with it.'

She picked up an A4 brown envelope from the sideboard and held it to her chest for a second. 'After you told me that Edward refused to show you Clare's death certificate, I felt really suspicious, so I decided to try to find it myself,' she said. 'I started searching online.'

'And? Is that what you've got there?' Hope sprang instantly. Was I here to learn that Edward had been telling me the truth after all?

'Yes,' she said cautiously.

'Oh, thank God, thank God...' Hope gave way to a flood of relief. 'Why didn't you say so on the phone? I've been so worried, thinking all kinds of terrible things. Oh Marsha, you're a wonder. I love you.' I stood up and went to embrace her, but she stepped back. Her face was solemn, almost stern. 'What's the matter? Let me see it, please.'

'I need to explain first,' she said, gesturing at me to sit back down.

'Now what? Oh God, you're killing me.' I returned to the sofa and took another gulp of wine.

Marsha began. 'At first, I had no luck. There was no Clare Morgan death for the right year, right age, et cetera. I know you had the same problem. So I thought, maybe she didn't change her name when she married, only obviously we didn't know her maiden name, so that didn't help much.' She took a breath. 'I asked a friend for advice, and they suggested looking up Noah's birth record, but I couldn't find it.'

'That's odd,' I said.

'Yes. It should be available online by now.'

'So you looked for Tara and Georgia's birth records instead.' She nodded. 'Clever. I hadn't thought of that. And? Her maiden name was...?' I heard an internal drum roll.

'Hope.' Marsha sat down next to me. For some reason, she still wasn't letting me have the brown envelope. 'But that's not the important bit. The only records I could find for a Tara and a Georgia with the same parents in the right years were for births that took place in Birmingham.'

I looked surprised. 'Okay. That's feasible, I guess. I thought they'd always lived in London, but maybe—'

'Please, Lily, let me explain. This is complicated. The mother's maiden name on both certificates is Clare Hope, which is fine. It's the father's name that doesn't make sense.' She paused, chewing on her lip.

'What do you mean?' I stared at her.

'Tara and Georgia were born with the surname Fletcher, not Morgan. The father is called Edward Fletcher. I cross-referenced and found a marriage between Clare Hope and Edward Fletcher, also in Birmingham. Then I found a death record for a Clare Fletcher, correct year, yet again in Birmingham. I sent off for the certificate and I've got it here. The cause of death is given as "anaphylactic shock due to adverse food reaction", so I'm confident it's the right one.'

I was stunned for a few seconds, then the words creaked out of me slowly. 'So… what you're saying is… Edward is using a false name?'

'Not necessarily. He could have changed it legally. I think he probably did it after Clare died.' She watched me as I let the information sink in. 'I take it he didn't tell you?'

I shook my head, bewildered. 'No… never even hinted at it. I don't understand. Why would he change his name? There's nothing wrong with Fletcher.'

'I checked the sold house prices index,' Marsha added. 'He bought the Hampstead house three and a half years ago, which ties in with the move from Birmingham.'

'Let me see the certificate, please,' I said. 'I need to read it in black and white.' She handed me the envelope and I took it out. It was a simple document, but also the most important piece of paper I'd ever cast my eyes over. I went through the details one by one, trying to get my head around all these new, puzzling facts – names, addresses, dates. My heart was beating so fast I felt dizzy.

'But *why*?' I asked, finally looking up. 'I don't get it.'

'Maybe he wanted to make a fresh start?' Marsha fiddled with the bead on the end of her braid. She didn't sound that convinced of her own theory.

I thought back to my wedding – the lack of guests on Edward's side. 'I know he fell out with his family over something, but why did he change his surname? That's serious, you don't do that just because you feel like it. You do it because you want to hide from people.' I put the document down on the coffee table and reached for my glass.

'Yup. Afraid so.' She shuffled up closer and gave me a hug. I felt myself go weak in her arms. 'It's okay, let it out,' she murmured. 'Have a good cry.'

'It's true what Noah said on our wedding night,' I mumbled into her shirt. 'The whole family have been lying to me. Not just Edward – Tara and Georgia too. They're all in on it, making me look an idiot.'

'I know… I know. I could kill the lot of them.'

I pulled away, wiping my tears with the edge of my sleeve. 'It's all connected to what's going on with Noah and the memory box,' I said. 'It's got to be. Edward's hiding from someone. That's why he changed his name, and why he's so security-conscious. But whoever it is, they've tracked him down and now they're trying to get to him through his son.'

'Seems like it's something along those lines,' Marsha agreed. She allowed herself a small wry smile. 'At least you know it's not his first wife. Edward's not a bigamist.'

'Yeah… small comfort, eh?' I'd needed to prove that Clare was dead, but in burying one skeleton, I'd dug up another. 'Thank you so much, Marsha,' I said.

'It doesn't bring me any pleasure,' she replied. 'I wasn't trying to hurt you – I just knew Edward wasn't telling you the truth and I couldn't bear it.'

'I know.' I squeezed her hand. 'It's okay. Better to know, even if it hurts.'

'What are you going to do now?'

'There's no point in challenging him,' I said ruefully. 'He's lied to me too much already. I can't trust him any more.'

'But you can't let him get away with it.'

'Don't worry, I'm not going to.'

I picked up the death certificate again. The facts told a story – or at least the tantalising outline of one. Either way, it was all I had to go on.

'The deceased's usual address is given as 37 Roosevelt Road, Harborne, Birmingham,' I said. 'I've got to go there, Marsha. I need to find out what really happened.'

She nodded in agreement. 'Okay. Makes sense.'

'I know it's a lot to ask, but will you come with me?'

I didn't have to wait for her reply.

CHAPTER FIFTEEN

We finished off the bottle of wine, then I rang Edward.

'I'm going to stay over. Marsha needs me.'

'Is that really necessary?' he replied, his voice ringing with irritation. 'What's wrong with her?'

'I can't tell you now. I'll explain when I get home.'

'She makes too many emotional demands on you,' he moaned. 'I need you more than she does.'

I tensed. 'No, you don't, Edward, not really. And I'm not teaching Noah any more, to be honest. I'm just hanging around the house with nothing to do. Things have been pretty tough recently. It'll do him good to have a break from me.'

'Hmm… it's Marsha you need a break from.'

I decided not to answer that one.

'I'll call you tomorrow,' I said, struggling to keep my tone even.

Marsha had some holiday owing, and after a pleading phone call with her boss, she managed to get two days off at short notice. The following morning, she lent me some clothes and we each packed a small suitcase for the trip. From Euston, we immediately managed to catch a fast train to Birmingham. On the way, Marsha booked us a hotel room for the night and orientated herself with Google Maps.

It was a good job she had everything under control – I was useless. She tried to jolly me along with conversation, but I didn't want to chat. I just stared out of the window at the passing scenery, trying to process all the information she'd uncovered. I kept going back to what Noah had said on my wedding night. He'd been wrong about his mother – but then I'd never really believed she was still alive. Now it was the other phrase he'd used that was nagging me, demanding an explanation. *They think I've forgotten, but I remember everything.* Everything. What had he meant by that?

The train arrived in Birmingham at around lunchtime. The day was warm, the streets seething with people. We bought filled crêpes from a stall and ate them in a large piazza, sitting on the wall of a fountain. Neither of us had ever been to the city before, and we were surprised by how attractive it was.

We trundled our wheelie cases to the hotel, which was in the canal quarter – a mix of boutiques and restaurants with long balconies overlooking the water. The woman on reception greeted us like old friends and let us check in early. The hotel was basic but fairly new. I was paying for our trip, but Marsha had booked the room so that it didn't go through my account. We'd decided to share – mainly to keep the cost down, but also for sentimental reasons. As teenagers, we'd had countless sleepovers, and shared beds when visiting each other at university. And most importantly, I didn't want to be on my own.

'I hate this,' I said as soon as we swiped into our room.

'Really? I don't think it's too bad.' Marsha waved at the bland decor – grey and plum with monochrome photos of Birmingham landmarks on the wall. 'At least it's clean.'

'No, I mean I hate having to go behind my husband's back like some private detective.'

'It's not your fault. If he'd been straight with you from the beginning, you wouldn't have to.' She sat down in the tub armchair and flicked through a hotel information booklet. 'So, what's the plan? Do you want to go to the address now, or leave it until later?'

'Now,' I replied quickly. 'Get it over and done with.' I drew in my breath as I tried to suppress the tide of emotion in my gut.

'Are you okay, Lily?'

'Yeah… sort of. I was just thinking how I should have listened to you in the first place. You warned me about marrying him too soon. *You don't really know him*, that's what you said.' I sighed. 'How right you were. I didn't even know his bloody name.'

'I'm not sure what you're hoping to find out today,' she said slowly.

I shrugged. 'Nor do I. I just know I have to go there.'

We ordered a taxi from the hotel lobby, which came within a couple of minutes. Marsha gave the driver the address and we set off. I looked out of the side window as the high-rise city buildings gave way to suburbia, trying to insert Edward into the landscape. I imagined him living here – driving his car around the one-way system, shopping in the malls, walking in the parks, breathing in the Birmingham air. It was entirely possible.

The driver was chatty and had a strong Brummie accent. I realised there wasn't a trace of it in Edward's voice, although now I came to think of it, there was a faint whiff of Midlands vowels when Tara and Georgia spoke. They must have grown up here before moving down to London with their father. I presumed they'd also changed their surname – Noah too. It was strange to think that he'd been born Noah Fletcher. Now we were the Morgans, myself included. Edward had been keen for me to change my name when we married and I'd willingly agreed. At the time it hadn't bothered me too much. I wasn't attached to the name Baxendale – it was my father's surname, and I felt no allegiance to him. But now, being Lily Morgan made me feel like an imposter.

After about fifteen minutes, we left the main road and drove up a hill, finding ourselves in a well-heeled area. The streets were lined with large detached houses ranging from elegant Victorian villas to chunky properties built in the 1930s. They all had generous front gardens and driveways. Tall leafy trees stood guard kerbside.

The driver drew up outside a smart detached house with pale red bricks, white roughcast and black gables.

'Is this it?' I said, leaning forward.

'That's what the sat nav says,' he replied. We paid him and got out of the cab.

I looked up at the house. It was in very good condition and looked like it might have been recently refurbished. The paintwork on the bay windows was gleaming and the brickwork had been repointed. Had Edward really lived here once? I tried to imagine him parking his car on the driveway, walking up to the stained-glass front door and inserting his key in the lock.

'It's a nice place,' I said to Marsha. 'But the house he's got now must be worth several times more, like millions.'

'Birmingham prices are far lower than London,' she agreed.

'How come he made such a leap after she died?'

Marsha pulled her shoulders up to her ears. 'Perhaps Clare was worth a lot of money in her own right. An heiress.'

'Hmm…'

She took my arm. 'Well? Are we going to knock or what?'

We walked onto the block-paved driveway and up to the front door. I rang the bell but nobody answered, so I used the large brass knocker instead.

'Perhaps they're out at work,' Marsha said, peering into the downstairs bay window. White shutters prevented us from seeing inside. She turned to me. 'Do you want to wait? It could be hours before they come home.'

'No. Let's try the neighbours,' I decided. 'They'll probably know more than the new owners anyway.'

We retreated and went next door to an almost identical house. A car was parked in the driveway, which was more promising. I rang the bell and we waited again. Eventually we heard somebody put the chain on before opening the door. The face of an elderly woman peered through the gap.

'If you're Jehovah's Witnesses, I'm not interested,' she said in that same undulating accent.

'Oh no, we're nothing like that!' Marsha beamed one of her best smiles. 'We were just wondering if you could help us.'

'What with? I don't do surveys.'

'My name's Lily,' I said. 'My husband Edward used to live next door with his first wife, Clare.'

I felt her gaze on my face. I could see that she was deciding how to reply. 'Clare lived here, yes, but not with *him*,' she said at last, her lip curling at the end of the sentence. 'Chucked him out, didn't she?'

My heart fluttered in my ribcage. 'Sorry? Are you saying they weren't together? Are you sure?'

'Of course I'm sure. Lovely woman, she was. Didn't deserve to die like that. Now if you'll excuse me…'

'Please don't go,' I said, stepping forward. 'I really need to talk to you about this. It's difficult, doing it on the doorstep. Would it be possible to—'

She cut me off. 'I wouldn't speak to journalists then and I won't now neither. Nor will anyone around here, so you can get lost.'

'We're not journalists,' Marsha said.

'Huh! You must think I came down with the last shower of rain.' And with that, she shut the door in our faces.

We stood there in stunned amazement for a few moments, then Marsha took my arm and led me gently back up the front path.

'What did she mean?' I was starting to feel a bit shaky. 'Why did she think we were journalists?'

She bit her lip thoughtfully. 'Because there's obviously more to this story, hon.'

'Edward never said anything about being divorced. He's always behaved as if Clare was the love of his life. I don't get it, Marsha.'

She started calling for a taxi. 'We won't find out any more here. Let's go back to the hotel.'

CHAPTER SIXTEEN

As soon as we arrived back, we went to the guest lounge, finding a place to sit by the window overlooking the canal.

Marsha summoned the waiter and ordered a pot of English tea and two large slices of chocolate cake.

'I don't feel in the least bit hungry,' I said. 'In fact, I feel a bit sick.'

'You need something to keep your blood sugar levels up,' she insisted.

My phone pinged, announcing the arrival of a text. As I suspected, it was from Edward, wanting to know when I was coming home. He seemed to have calmed down after last night, and although not actually apologising, was offering to cook one of his famous chicken curries for dinner. I stared at the message for a few seconds, noting the long line of kisses, wondering how on earth to respond. Who was this man? He felt like a stranger to me. I closed the window and put the handset face down on the table.

The waiter arrived with our order and spent ages arranging the teapot, milk jug and plates. We waited in silence for him to finish.

'Okay, what do we know so far?' Marsha said as soon as he'd gone. She sounded like a TV detective, adding to my sensation that I'd accidentally stepped into a piece of drama about somebody who happened to look like me and share my name.

'Well...' I began. 'Clare lived in that great big house on her own, presumably with the children. The neighbour seemed to think she and Edward were no longer together, which is odd because there's no mention of them being separated or divorced on the death certificate.' I reached into my bag and took it out. 'See? Her status is given as "married". That can't be a mistake, it's a legal document.'

Marsha stirred the pot, then poured our tea. It looked very weak, and I started to think maybe a couple of stiff whiskies might have done a better job.

'Maybe they'd only recently split up and hadn't got around to making it official,' she suggested. 'Or maybe one of them was blocking the divorce. There could be all sorts of reasons.'

'I should have asked that neighbour more questions,' I said.

'Nah, she clearly didn't want to get involved. We got as much out of her as we could.'

We drank our tea quietly for a few moments, our heads too full of thoughts to speak. I played with my cake, chasing crumbs around the plate. I wasn't eating, I was re-evaluating my marriage, seeing it for the flimsy, superficial thing it was. Edward clearly hadn't trusted me enough to tell me the truth about his past, and that saddened me. If he'd admitted that his marriage had been a failure, it wouldn't have bothered me one bit. I'd told him all about Alex and he'd been really sympathetic and supportive. If I'd known the real situation, I would have felt more confident that I was the right one for him, that what we had was better and stronger. Instead, I'd believed he'd been deliriously happy with Clare; that she was the love of his life and that I could never take her place, no matter how hard I tried.

Marsha refilled my cup. 'Like I said, maybe there's more of a story to this.'

'Yeah, but how the hell do we work it out? I'm so angry with Edward, I can't tell you. But I don't want to challenge him until I have all the facts at my fingertips. I'm sick of the bullshit and the lies.'

'I don't blame you.' Marsha licked chocolate icing off her fingers. 'Here's a thing. Why did that neighbour think we were journalists?'

'Because Clare's death was reported in the local press? Not many people die of anaphylaxis.'

'Yeah, but it happened five years ago. That's ancient history as far as the media are concerned. Hmm… I have a hunch she was referring to something else.' She picked up her phone. 'Let's see what happens when we search with the name Edward Fletcher, Birmingham, UK…'

'Okay. Go ahead.'

I glanced out of the window as a barge went past. It had been turned into a floating restaurant, and there was a group of people on board, partying, looking like they didn't have a care in the world. Marsha tapped speedily with her sharp manicured fingernails and my heart raced along. I wanted her to find out more information but I also wanted her to stop. It was like picking off a scab, piece by tiny piece, and revealing the red, raw, unprotected flesh beneath.

She scrolled through her results, then stopped and stared at the screen.

'Well? Has anything come up?'

'Do people call Edward "Ned"?'

'No. Never. Not that I've ever heard. There again, I haven't met any of his friends or family, so I couldn't say for sure.'

'Maybe it's not the same guy,' she murmured. 'Jesus, I hope not.'

All my senses suddenly pricked. '*What*? What are you looking at?'

'Oh my gosh,' she gasped. 'This is unbelievable.'

'What is it? What are you reading? Is it about Edward?'

'I'm not sure. I think maybe… Oh shit… Yes, it is, it's definitely him.'

'What do you mean? Please. Tell me!'

She looked up at me, her beautiful brown eyes open wide. 'Ned Fletcher... Ring any bells? About five years ago? All over the tabloids?'

My stomach lurched. 'Um... I'm not sure... Yeah, maybe, I don't know. For God's sake, just read it out, Marsha.'

She cleared her throat and started to read aloud, her voice quivering with emotion. '*Ned Fletcher separated from childhood sweetheart Clare after she discovered the affair with Francesca Harris. Clare Fletcher died last year, but police say there is no reason at this stage to...*' She gulped, unable to finish.

'To what? You can't stop there, carry on.'

'Oh Lily,' she said. 'Oh Lily.'

I snatched the phone from her and read the piece myself.

...police say there is no reason at this stage to connect her tragic death to the mysterious disappearance of Ms Harris. Fletcher continues to be questioned on suspicion...

I dropped the phone into my lap. 'No... no... This can't be true, it can't be *my* Edward.'

Marsha gently took it back and carried on searching, her fingers flying across the screen as she dug deeper and deeper into my pain.

'There's more here,' she said quietly. 'Heaps of it. Oh Lily, this is horrific. Do you want me to read it to you, or would you rather...?'

'You read it.' I could feel myself starting to hyperventilate. 'Just keep your voice down, okay?'

Marsha leant across the table and bent her head over her handset. 'The headline is *Police search for missing babysitter.*'

'Oh God.' My extremities were tingling, I felt weightless, as if my body was floating away from me on the canal. 'Go on,' I rasped. 'Tell me.'

She whispered, '*Forensic teams descended on murder suspect Ned Fletcher's city-centre apartment, which he shared with his lover Francesca Harris. The attractive twenty-six-year-old has not been seen since the evening of 16 July, when a witness saw her arriving home with Fletcher. She has not used her mobile phone and there has been no activity on her bank accounts. Fletcher, a hedge fund manager, was arrested yesterday on suspicion of murder and remains in custody for questioning. He claims his young lover walked out after a row and fears she may have taken her own life. But Fran's mother Elaine, who first reported her daughter missing, said, "She wasn't depressed. It's very unlike her not to be in touch, and we believe she has come to great harm."*

'I need some fresh air,' I said, clutching my chest. We abandoned our table and rushed outside. I leant over the balcony and tried to breathe deeply.

'I'm sorry, Lily,' whispered Marsha, holding me and rubbing my back. 'I wasn't trying to cause trouble – I had no idea.'

'It's okay, not your fault. Better to know.' I stared down into the dark green water, letting the news permeate my skin. 'What do you think? Is Edward a murderer?'

'I don't know… He was never found guilty, not even charged.'

'That doesn't mean…'

'I know it doesn't, but…'

We paused, each developing our own case for or against him. I didn't know what I thought. My jury was out.

'Let's go back to the room,' I said. 'I want to know everything now. Every single little thing.'

Marsha took care of the bill and we went upstairs together. I must have been in a state of shock, but I actually felt calm, more in control than I'd felt for a while. Now I had an explanation for the secrecy, the lies, the omissions and anomalies, the odd behaviour. Edward had done everything in his power to prevent me from knowing who he really was.

As we went up in the lift, I tried to recall what I already knew about the Babysitter Murder, as the media had christened it at the time. I'd seen a few juicy headlines on newsstands and my online feed. I hadn't followed the story closely, but I remembered feeling disgusted, automatically assuming that the guy must have done it. The phrase 'Fletch the Lech' dragged itself forward from the dusty corners of my memory. I shuddered. How could this be the same man I'd fallen in love with?

Back in the room, we immediately got to work with our phones, keying in search words, following threads, digging into online press archives, pulling up images. Every so often we read things out to each other and compared what we'd found. I started to feel increasingly sick as I dredged up more and more awful stuff about Edward. The tabloid headlines shouted out at me in big black angry capitals.

WHERE'S OUR FRAN? Lover Ned denies all
FAST CARS, SEX AND DRUGS – Fletcher's mates speak out
LIAR! LIAR! Mother points finger at Fran's middle-aged lover

There was surprisingly little information about Francesca, sometimes shortened to Fran. She was in her early twenties (although the media couldn't quite decide exactly how old she was) and had babysat for the family until Edward 'seduced' her. There only seemed to have been one photo of her, because it cropped up again and again, fixing her forever in the public mind as a two-dimensional blob. She was brown-haired and averagely pretty, eyes bright, smiling demurely to camera. Exactly the kind of 'innocent victim' look the tabloids went for.

There weren't many proper shots of 'Ned' – he was always trying to hide from the camera, ducking behind his coat or holding his hand over his face. One article featured an old photo of him, provided by some erstwhile friend no doubt. A fuzzy red-eyed headshot taken about fifteen years ago. He was laughing and waving a champagne glass, looking pissed and vaguely danger-ous. The headline included the name tag I remembered: Fletch the Lech. I stared at it for ages, trying to reconcile this 'killer' with the loving, slightly vulnerable silver-haired man I knew. Or thought I knew.

'This is unbearable,' I said.

'The media was totally convinced he'd killed her, but he was never charged with murder. It never went to trial.' Marsha looked up from her screen. 'I vaguely remember reading about it at the time. Edward sued half a dozen tabloids for libel. They settled out of court for a massive undisclosed sum – six figures apparently.'

'That's why he changed his name and moved the family to London,' I said. 'He used the pay-off to buy a posh house with lots of security. And it explains why he won't send Noah to school. He's still hiding from the media.'

Marsha stood up and walked across the room to the window. She stared out for a few moments, then turned back to face me. 'They still haven't found her body.'

'I know,' I sighed. 'Strange, isn't it?'

'Something must have happened to her. She can't have just vanished into thin air.'

'Unless she didn't want to be found.'

'Hmm… I guess.' Marsha went back to her phone. 'The murder investigation is still open,' she told me after some more searching. 'Edward is the only suspect.'

I grabbed at my hair. 'I don't understand. What's the timeline here? Edward and Clare were married, then Francesca started babysitting and they had an affair. Clare chucked him out, then what?'

'Edward moved in with Francesca, I think. They had a flat together.' She tapped away again on her screen. 'Yeah, yeah, here we go… This is so typical. The tabloids made out that Francesca was babysitting for the family when she went missing, but that's not the case at all. She and Ned were a proper couple. They'd been living together for about four years when Clare died.'

'Four years?' I repeated. 'Are you sure?'

'That's what it says here,' Marsha said.

'You know what that means, then?' She stared at me blankly. 'Think about it. Noah must be Francesca's son.'

CHAPTER SEVENTEEN

Marsha put her phone down and gaped at me. 'Of course. That's why there's such a big age gap between him and his sisters.'

'Half-sisters,' I corrected. 'But Edward has gone to great lengths to make Noah believe that they have the same mother. And Tara and Georgia have gone along with it.'

'Why?'

I paused, closing my eyes for a few seconds. My brain was suffering from information overload and I couldn't think straight. 'I guess it was all part of making this new life for himself – changing the family surname, moving to London. It's certainly made life easier, erasing Francesca from the story.'

'Easier for Edward, maybe, not for Noah,' Marsha huffed. 'The man's a pathological liar. How dare he manipulate a child like that? He's been trying to suppress Noah's memories – that's disgusting. It's actually abusive.'

'Yeah, it makes me feel sick,' I agreed. 'No wonder the poor kid's been so confused. He knew something wasn't right.'

Snatches of past scenes and conversations started popping into my head. Things that had puzzled me before now made more sense: Edward's order that I wasn't to talk to Noah about his dead mother because it would trigger a panic attack; Noah's strange reaction when I tried to give him the photo of Clare; Edward's refusal to accept that Noah's seaside picture was drawn from memory. And most significant of all, Noah's angry words on the evening of our wedding. *They're lying to us. They think I've forgotten, but I remember everything.*

'The whole family is deeply messed up, Lily,' Marsha said. 'I'm sorry to have to say this, but you're better off out of it.'

'But it's *my* family now. I'm part of it.'

She stared at me, staggered. 'What? You mean you're going to go back to that man and carry on like nothing's happened? He's lied to you over and over again. And not just small lies, Lily, big massive ones. He and his daughters have deceived you from start to finish. And that's forgetting that he might actually be a murderer! Are you crazy?' She stood up and marched over to the minibar, opening the door and rummaging for something stiff to drink. 'I don't get it. You really worry me, you know that?'

'Look, I know Edward's behaved appallingly towards me – worse than appallingly. Right now, I don't know if I'll ever be able to forgive him. But Noah's my stepson. I can't walk away and leave him to suffer. What other choice do I have?'

'You could try calling social services,' she barked.

'Really? And have him taken into care?'

'No, no, I didn't mean that.' She took a can of pre-mixed gin and tonic out of the fridge. 'Do you want anything?' I shook my head. She snapped it open and poured its contents into a glass.

'We've been ignoring something incredibly important,' I said slowly.

'What?'

'The message in the box. From *Mummy*.'

Marsha paused with the glass halfway to her lips. 'Oh. You mean... you think it actually could be...'

'Yes. It makes sense, doesn't it? Noah's been right all along. His mummy – his *real* mummy – is still alive.'

She nodded thoughtfully. 'Which would mean that Edward is innocent.'

*

We checked out of the hotel almost immediately and caught the first train back to London. I was full of a strange nervous energy; it was as if my brain was on fire. Marsha spent the whole journey trying to dampen down the flames, warning me to be careful, to stay focused and not let Edward weave another web of lies around me.

'I wish you'd come back to my place and just calm down, think it over. We can plan what to do next.'

'No, I have to go back tonight and confront him.'

'You'll let me know how it goes – promise? I won't be able to sleep until I hear from you.'

I gave her what I hoped was a reassuring smile. 'Trust me, Marsha, I know what I'm doing. I'm quite safe.'

It was just before 10 p.m. when I buzzed open the gate, triggering the lighting as I walked towards the front door. Although I'd put a brave face on in front of Marsha, I was feeling nervous.

He called out as I entered the house. 'Lily? Is that you?' I was taking off my jacket when he appeared in the hallway. He looked tired and vaguely pissed.

'Hi,' I said, slipping off my shoes.

'You didn't answer my texts or pick up my calls,' he said grumpily. 'I thought you'd be back in time for dinner. I made a curry and everything.'

'Sorry.'

'Too busy running around after Marsha, I suppose.' He scowled. 'I'm surprised she let you come home at all.'

'Can we stop the Marsha-bashing, please? I'm not in the mood.'

He peered into my face. 'What's wrong? You look really tense.'

'I've had a really stressful day, actually. One of the worst days of my entire life, in fact.'

He stared at me. 'What do you mean?'

'I went to Birmingham, Edward.' I let my words float through the air and settle on him. 'Or should I call you Ned?'

There was an exquisite pause as his brain caught up.

'Oh God, oh God… You know.'

'Yes, I'm afraid I do.'

'I'm so sorry.' He went to embrace me, but I stepped back.

'Please, Edward, don't. I can't bear the thought of touching you right now.'

'Everything they wrote about me was lies. I proved it. The media tried to destroy me, but I sued and won.'

'We mustn't talk here,' I said. 'We might wake Noah up.'

'Of course, of course.'

He walked into the sitting room and I followed. The room was a mess – his dirty dinner plate was on the carpet next to his discarded socks. A bottle of red wine was sitting on the coffee table next to an empty glass. He switched the television off and turned to me.

'Oh God, I can't believe you actually went to Brum. Let's sit down, get ourselves a drink.' He beckoned me to sit next to him on the sofa, but I took the armchair instead. 'I'm so sorry, darling,' he rattled, 'you shouldn't have had to find out this way. It's my fault. I'm a coward.' He picked up the bottle. 'Wine, or something stronger?'

'Nothing, thanks,' I said coolly. 'I want to keep a clear head.'

'Sure. Anything else you need? A glass of water? Something to eat? I could heat the curry up.'

'Please don't fuss over me. I'm not hungry.'

'You poor darling, you must be so upset.' He sat down on the sofa, clasping his hands together, jiggling his knees.

'I'm not upset, Edward, I'm shocked. And extremely angry.'

He hung his head. 'Yes, yes, of course you are. I don't blame you.'

'You made a complete fool of me. You, Tara and Georgia. The three of you conspired together to deceive me. And as for the way you've treated Noah…'

'It wasn't deliberate. I never meant to hurt anyone.' There was a pause. 'Who tipped you off?' he asked eventually. 'Some nasty little journo, was it?' I shook my head. 'I bet it was my sister. She still thinks I did it, you know. She's turned the whole family against me.'

'No. Marsha did some digging around in the public records and discovered you'd changed your name. It kind of snowballed from there.'

A small, ironic laugh escaped his lips. 'Huh. Marsha... my rival. I might have known. Must have made her day. No doubt she thinks I'm guilty as hell.'

'It doesn't matter what she thinks. This is about us.'

'Yes, of course. Sorry, that was cheap.' He picked up the wine bottle and refilled his glass. 'Well, at least you came back. That's a positive sign, I guess.' He cast me a boyish, optimistic glance.

Normally I would have melted under his blue-eyed gaze, but not now, not any more. 'I came back to hear your side of the story,' I said. 'That's all I'm prepared to commit to at the moment.'

He gulped. 'Okay. Go on, put me on trial, ask me the question.'

I drew myself in, summoning all my strength, even though I felt utterly exhausted and racked with emotion. I thought – or at least hoped – that I already knew the answer, but I had to hear it from his lips.

'If there's any future for us, Edward, any future at all,' I said, 'you're going to have to be completely honest with me. No more lies. No more cover-ups. I want you to look me in the eye and tell me the absolute truth.' I waited until he lifted his head and met my gaze. 'Did you kill Francesca Harris?'

'No,' he responded without a second's hesitation. 'I swear on my life, on my children's lives. I didn't kill her, Lily.'

I studied him for a few moments. He'd seemed so strong to me before – a silver fox, mature and confident, a wealthy man with the world at his feet. But now he looked weak and desperate, older than his forty-five years. His hair was thinning on top and the creases around his eyes and mouth looked like wrinkles rather than laughter lines.

We stared at each other. I tried to peer into his soul, searching for a sign that would convince me beyond all doubt that he was telling the truth, but of course, it was impossible to know. It had become a question of faith.

'Tell me about Francesca,' I said finally. 'From beginning to end. Don't try to spare my feelings. I want to know everything.'

PART TWO

CHAPTER EIGHTEEN

Fran pushed the doorbell again, then stood back to survey the house. It was large and detached, built in mock-Tudor style with fake black beams, white walls and leaded windows. Two cars – a black BMW and a silver Fiesta – were parked on the pristine block-paved driveway. The hedges were trimmed and the flower beds beautifully tended. It was very smart. Very 'executive'.

It was her first time babysitting for Clare. The job involved looking after two girls, twelve and ten years old. On top of that, she lived two bus rides away, and once you added travel time, the hourly rate was barely worth the bother. But Clare had a knack of making people feel honoured to do her a favour. Fran wanted to keep in her good books, so hadn't dared refuse.

She pressed her nose against the stained-glass window, looking for signs of life within. All seemed quiet. Maybe she'd got the wrong day, or the wrong house, or Clare had cancelled and she hadn't picked up the message.

At last the door swung open and she was greeted by a tall woman wearing a slinky black party dress, huge sparkly earrings and a lot of make-up. For a split second, Fran didn't recognise her.

'Oh, it's you!' Clare said, surprised. 'You're rather early. Didn't I say seven?'

'Sorry.' Fran blushed. 'I didn't know how long it would take to get here. Shall I go away and come back?'

'No, don't be silly. Come in and meet Tara and Georgia.'

A shiver of anticipation ran through her as she crossed the threshold. She glanced around, trying to take in everything at once. The hallway was wide, its floor polished parquet. The decor was neutral, but there were some interesting pieces of furniture and lots of colourful prints on the walls. A wide staircase with an oak banister wound up to the first floor. It was both organised and relaxed – like Clare Fletcher herself.

Fran felt privileged to be allowed an insight into her boss's home life. She liked Clare a lot. She was in her late thirties, at the top of her game and well respected within the events industry. Working for her was exhausting but fun. Clare was very demanding of her teams but had a wicked sense of humour. For some reason she'd picked Fran out and taken her under her wing. She was twenty-one, fresh out of university, eager to learn.

'They're in the snug, watching a video,' Clare said, waving towards the back of the house. 'Just go and say hello. They won't bite – not until they know you better, anyway.' She stopped, noticing Fran's alarmed expression. 'Joke. They're looking forward to meeting you. I've told them you're cool.'

'Cool? Me? Don't think so.'

'You're cooler than their parents, that's all that counts. Right. Got to go and put a rocket up Ned.' She ran barefoot up the stairs, leaving Fran standing on her own in the hallway.

She found the snug next to the sitting room. The girls had a sofa each, arranged at right angles to each other, and were lying with their legs stretched out. They were snuggled under blankets like invalids, even though they looked perfectly healthy and the room was warm. A chick flick was playing on the television, and either they were too engrossed to notice Fran's entrance or they were being deliberately rude. She suspected it was the latter.

'Hi,' she said. 'How you doing?' They swung around simultaneously to look at her. 'I'm Fran. The… um…' Two pairs of eyes narrowed. 'I've come to chill with you while your mum and dad go out.'

'Yeah, we know,' said the younger, slightly dumpy-looking one, who she assumed was Georgia.

'You're one of Mum's minions, aren't you?' said the other. Tara, presumably.

'I'm a production assistant, if that's what you mean.'

'Is she paying you for this?'

'Tara!' interjected Georgia.

'So? I can ask if I want.'

'Yes, your mother is paying me,' Fran replied neutrally. 'Why wouldn't she?'

Tara, who was very pretty and probably knew it, shrugged. 'Just that there's like literally nothing for you to do. We're not babies. We can wipe our own bottoms, clean our own teeth, put our own pyjamas on...'

'Read our own stories,' Georgia chipped in.

'So actually, you can ignore us and do whatever it is you have to do. Like watch TV in the other room, or study, or talk to your boyfriend, if you've got one.' Tara smirked.

'But don't raid the drinks cabinet like the last one did. You can guess what happened when Mum found out.' Georgia made a throat-slitting gesture and both girls giggled.

Fran kept her voice even. 'Thanks for the tips, guys. I won't interrupt your movie. I'll be next door if you need me.'

'As if,' muttered Tara as she left.

She went into the sitting room. Like the rest of the house, it was comfortably furnished and tastefully decorated. She spent a few minutes browsing the books on the shelves and chose one to look at – a historical romance set in Renaissance Italy. Sitting down on the luxurious velvet sofa, she started to read, but her thoughts kept straying to the entitled little brats in the next room. As she'd suspected, they didn't want to be babysat and hadn't been afraid to show it. Not that Fran cared too much. She wasn't going to waste time trying to become their friend, or making them obey the rules. As long as they were in their rooms and at least pretending to be asleep by the time their parents came home, that would be fine by her. It was Friday, not a school night; if they stayed up late, there would be no harm done.

'Ned? Have you called the taxi yet?' Clare called over her shoulder as she hurried into the room. She was wearing a fluffy black bolero thing over her dress and a pair of ferociously high heels.

'God, I hate these do's,' she said, puffing up her hair in the mirror over the fireplace. 'Everyone gets smashed and the music's so loud you can't hear a word anyone's saying.' She looked at Fran's puzzled face and laughed. 'Ned works in financial services – it's his firm's annual piss-up. I *have* to dress up like an ostrich, it's expected.'

'I think you look great,' Fran ventured, instantly regretting the familiarity.

'Very sweet of you, but I know I look ridiculous.' Clare went to the door. 'Ned! You didn't answer me about the taxi!'

'Sorry, darling. It's on its way,' came the disembodied reply. The voice sounded oddly familiar.

'Keep an eye on the girls,' said Clare. 'If they're still watching TV at eleven, remind them that they have drama group tomorrow morning and I expect them to be fully awake and ready to leave the house at nine.'

'Okay, I'll do my best.'

'Help yourself to tea, coffee, soft drinks. Toast, whatever. We should be back by one o'clock. The taxi will take you home.'

'But it's way on the other side of Birmingham. I can probably get a night bus.'

'I wouldn't dream of it.'

Clare's husband entered the room. She noticed immediately that he was very good-looking – strong nose, jet-black hair, intense blue eyes, smooth skin. He was wearing what looked like a very expensive suit.

'Hi, I'm Ned,' he said, his warm, liquid tones seeming to soak through her skin. 'Thanks for helping. Clare usually tries to duck out of these things, but this year she's got no excuse.' He gave his wife a cheeky wink, and she rolled her eyes in response. It appeared to be an established routine.

'Any problems, just text,' Clare said. 'We'll be at the Hyatt.'

A car beeped outside. 'Best of luck with the gruesome twosome,' added Ned mischievously.

The taxi whisked the glamorous couple away to the city centre. Fran returned to the historical novel, but it couldn't hold her attention. Her autonomic nervous system was already clicking, or flipping, or pinging, or whatever happened when you fell in love at first sight. She put the book back on the shelf and tried to watch the television, but it was just a noisy blur. Tara and Georgia ignored her, and she eventually heard them climbing the stairs to their rooms just before midnight.

It was nearly two o'clock in the morning before the Fletchers came home, an hour later than they'd promised. Fran had fallen asleep in front of a film and was feeling a little grumpy because they hadn't even texted to apologise.

Clare looked exhausted, but Ned was definitely drunk. He grinned at Fran rakishly as he took off his jacket and threw it at the couch. It missed and fell at her feet instead.

'Shit,' he said. She picked it up, and as she handed it to him, their eyes locked. 'Sorry we're so late.'

'That's okay,' she murmured, unable to tear herself away from his gaze.

'Had to wait forever for a taxi.'

'Speaking of which…' said Clare snippily. She started removing pins from her hair and shaking it out.

'Oh, sorry.' The spell was broken and Fran stood up quickly, shoving her feet into her shoes and gathering up her things. She slung her bag over her shoulder. There was an embarrassing moment while she waited for somebody to pay her, but then Clare gave her husband a nudge and he took out fifty quid. Their fingers touched briefly as he handed the money over.

'That's too much,' she said. 'I don't have any change.'

'No problem. Keep it.'

Clare followed her into the hallway and opened the front door. The taxi was humming on the driveway. 'We've been invited to a dinner party next Thursday. Are you free? It won't be such a late one. Hopefully Ned won't be so drunk and can give you a lift home,' she added pointedly.

Fran's insides quivered inexplicably. 'Okay. Yeah, I can do that. Great.'

'See you on Monday. And thanks again.' Clare nodded at her and she stepped into the darkness.

She thought about Ned all the way home, and then later when she was lying in bed, unable to sleep. She knew she hadn't imagined the instant connection between them – like an electric current being switched on. He'd sensed it too, she was sure of it. She felt exhilarated yet at the same time wonderfully calm. It was as if this man already belonged to her but had been absent for a long, lonely time. She'd been missing him for years, decades, centuries – maybe even other lifetimes – without knowing it. Now, miraculously, they'd found each other again. It was crazy, but she was certain that their meeting tonight was the beginning of something wonderful and yet utterly terrifying. Next Thursday could not come soon enough.

CHAPTER NINETEEN

We talked long into the night, although I mainly listened. I'd told him not to pull any punches, and he took me at my word. But it was so hard to hear him talk about how much he'd loved Francesca, when only a few hours earlier, I hadn't even known she'd existed.

'I was crazy about her,' he said. 'Couldn't help myself. She was beautiful, funny, extremely intelligent. I could talk to her about anything. It was like a miracle that she came along. My marriage was in the doldrums, I was miserable and dissatisfied, but I couldn't work out why. Then I met Fran and realised I'd spent the previous fourteen years of my life with the wrong woman.'

It was not the angle I'd been expecting. On the journey back to London, I'd concocted a number of defences that he might make: *she seduced me and like a fool I fell for it*; or *Clare was a complete cow, she drove me into the affair*; or *I only stayed with Francesca because she was pregnant*. But now I could see that he had genuinely adored her, that he was grateful to be able to talk about her at last.

He carried on, unaware that he was tearing me apart. 'The press dubbed her "the babysitter" like she was some dumb teenager, but she actually had an English degree. Fran was very smart – too smart.'

I frowned. 'What's that supposed to mean?'

'Oh, I don't know… She thought too much, got worked up about things, came down on herself too hard. I blamed her parents. They'd had such high expectations of her and they thought she'd thrown it all away.'

'By going off with an older, married man?'

'Exactly. She was only twenty-two when she got pregnant, you see. Fresh out of college.'

'I'm presuming Noah was an accident.'

'Yes, but a happy one. We were both thrilled.' He looked away, tears in his eyes. 'But it turned out she wasn't ready for it. She loved Noah, don't get me wrong, she was a fantastic mother, but…' he exhaled heavily, 'I think she regretted giving up her job. She was bored, unfulfilled. Noah wasn't enough for her, and that made her feel guilty.'

'Sounds like postnatal depression,' I suggested.

'Yes, I guess. It wasn't easy for either of us. We were renting this poky little flat in the city centre – it was all I could afford. I wanted to buy her a proper house with a garden, but Clare wouldn't give me a divorce, wouldn't agree to selling the family home. I was still paying the mortgage and giving Clare money for the girls, working my butt off day and night. Looking back, I realise how depressed Fran was, but she hid it from me, you see. She hid it from everyone, family, friends. If only I'd known at the time, I could have done something.' He stared into his glass for a few seconds, then downed the rest of the wine. 'If she'd seen the doctor about it, if she'd made a call to the Samaritans, if there'd been some evidence…' He tailed off.

'What happened on the day she disappeared? Did she have a breakdown? Did you have a row? Something must have triggered it.'

'No, it was just an ordinary day. I took Noah out to the park in the morning, and when I got home, she wasn't there. A small suitcase was missing, a few clothes, mobile, handbag, toiletries, a baby photo of Noah. She didn't leave a note. I assumed she'd gone to stay with her parents, or Lauren, her best friend… I was worried, but I didn't chase after her because I was trying to give her some space. It was her parents who reported her missing, a week later. Of course, that made me look bad.'

'What do you think happened to her?'

Pain swept across his face. 'I don't know… She hasn't been seen or heard of for five years. Hasn't used her phone, or her credit card, or turned up at A&E, or travelled abroad. I think she must have killed herself. It's the only explanation that makes any sense.'

'But they never found her body, did they? Usually when someone commits suicide…'

'They're found quite easily, yeah, I know… Suicide, murder – without a body, there's no proof either way. That's why this shadow is still hanging over me.' He started to cry. 'Sorry… It's just been so hard, you can't imagine,' he blurted, wiping his tears with his fingers. 'To lose the person you love and then be accused of killing them.'

I finally left the safety of my armchair and went to sit next to him. 'All sorts of things could have happened to her. She could have had a breakdown, cut herself off from her family, become homeless… Maybe she's recovered, got her life back on track. These messages that Noah's been receiving, they could be from her, couldn't they?'

'They *could*… It occurred to me straight away, of course,' he said. 'It's always been a dream, that one day she would turn up and prove to the world that I didn't kill her.'

'But you don't think it *is* her?' He shook his head. 'Why not?'

He sighed. 'Because it's far more likely to be a con, set up by one of the tabloids. Believe me, they get up to these kinds of tricks all the time, trying to flush me out, hoping I'll make some slip, drop myself in the shit. That's why I changed my name and came to London, why I have all this security, why I won't send Noah to school, why my girls are too scared to use social media, why I live like a bloody prisoner in my own house.'

'But what if it's not a journalist?' I pressed. 'What if it *is* Francesca? Surely we have to investigate.'

'Yes, you're right, darling, and I *am* working on it, don't worry. There's nothing I want more than for Francesca to be alive, but I'm frightened of getting my hopes up. And I don't want some bloody tabloid making a fool out of me. I fought them before and won. They're desperate to get their own back.'

'It's got to be worth the risk. If we can find Francesca, you'll be proved innocent once and for all. We won't have to live like this any longer. We'll be free.'

He looked up at me, a flicker of hope lighting up his face. 'You said "we" just then. Does that mean you're going to stay?'

'I don't know. Maybe…'

'I love you so much,' he said. 'I couldn't bear to lose you too.'

I felt myself weakening. He took my hand and led me upstairs to our room. We got into bed without undressing and lay in each other's arms with our eyes open, not moving, not saying anything, just listening to each other breathing as we watched the sun rise on a strange new day.

I must have fallen asleep eventually, because when I woke up, I saw that I'd received a string of anxious texts from Marsha asking how I was. I sent her a short reply telling her that I was okay, but shattered, and that I would call her later for a proper chat.

In all honesty, I didn't know how I was feeling. My emotions had buried themselves somewhere deep inside me, leaving behind a dull pain. I was worn out. Although I was relieved finally to know the truth about Edward's past, I was also deeply shocked by it. The ghost of Clare had been difficult enough to deal with, but now she seemed like a minor player, an irrelevance. I made her vanish with a click of my finger. I had a new spectre to torment myself with: Francesca, who I now realised was the *real* love of my husband's life.

What made it worse was that the two of us were close in age, and we'd met Edward in a similar way, as his employee. All I'd seen was the grainy photo that had been repeatedly used by the media, but it was obvious to anyone that we looked similar. If I left off my make-up, scraped my hair back and stared blankly into the mirror, the likeness was unnerving. I knew, because I tried it that morning when I went to the bathroom. Was that why he'd fallen in love with me? I wondered, staring at my reflection. Was I a prop in a magic trick to turn back time and start all over again?

Over the next few days, Edward tiptoed around me nervously, trying to please me in little ways. He kept asking if I still loved him. I told him I did, but I didn't really know, not for sure. It was too soon to tell. I wasn't angry any more, but I was bitterly disappointed. Not only in him but in that human entity that was us. Our relationship should have been able to bear the weight of the truth, but he hadn't trusted it enough to put it to the test. In that respect, we'd failed before he'd even put the ring on my finger. I felt bereft. It was as if we'd lost something way back at the beginning and were having to retrace our steps to find it. Although I was no longer sure what we were looking for or whether it would ever be found.

'Let's invite the girls over for Sunday lunch,' he said, trying to be cheerful. 'I already told them that you know. They're really keen to see you.'

'Good idea,' I agreed. 'It'll be great to clear the air… Not that we've fallen out or anything, it's just that…' I drifted off, unsure how to finish the sentence.

'It'll be easier to get on now it's all out in the open,' he finished for me.

'Yes… but what about Noah?'

'Obviously we can't talk in front of him, but he'll go back to his room at some point – we'll have plenty of opportunity. I'll sort it, you just relax. If the weather holds, I'll do one of my special barbecues.' He made it all sound so easy.

The warm weather did indeed hold until Sunday. Tara and Georgia arrived together shortly after 1 p.m. Tara was cool towards me and went straight into the garden to see her father, who was already at the barbecue wearing a large manly apron and wielding an alarming number of tools.

In contrast, Georgia gave me a warm hug and followed me into the kitchen.

'Are you okay?' she asked quietly. 'It must have been such a shock.'

'Yes, it was, but I'm fine, thanks,' I answered half truthfully. 'I'd rather have known from the start, but… better late than never, I suppose.'

She ran the tap, then filled a glass with cold water. 'I kept on at Dad to tell you before the wedding, but he was too scared, he couldn't do it.'

'Yes, I know.'

'It's such a relief now you know what he had to go through. It was hell for him, really, I'm not kidding.' She lowered her voice. 'I know it's wrong to speak ill of the dead, but it was all Fran's fault. She was seriously messed up.' I carried on preparing the salad – a job I'd been allocated at the last minute because Edward had forgotten. 'If only she'd left a note, or at least died somewhere conspicuous. I mean, the trouble she caused us!' Georgia shuddered. 'I think killing yourself is the ultimate selfish act, don't you?'

I shrugged as I sliced a cucumber. 'Nobody knows for certain that she committed suicide. Her body still hasn't been found.'

She carried on as if I hadn't spoken. 'We never liked her, not even when she was just the babysitter. She and Dad were totally wrong for each other, that was obvious to everyone. Except him… idiot… it was like she'd enchanted him.'

'They were together several years, weren't they? That's a long time to keep a spell going.'

'Dad only stayed because of Noah. If he hadn't come along, it would have finished way earlier. Not that Mum would have forgiven him or had him back, but at least he wouldn't have been arrested on some fake…' She stopped herself as Noah came into the room. He scowled at me, then went to the fridge and took out a carton of juice.

'Hello, Noah. Good to see you too,' said Georgia pointedly.

'Hi,' he mumbled as he poured himself a glass, then carried it carefully outside.

She raised her eyebrows. 'What's got into him? He gave you a really hateful look.'

'Oh, nothing, just kids,' I said, not wanting to explain further. 'Right,' I said, picking up the salad bowl. 'Shall we join the others?'

In the garden, the barbecuing was well under way and Edward had worked up the traditional sweat. He mopped his forehead with a hankie and took a swig of his Italian beer. 'Salad! Marvellous!' he cried as I set the bowl down on the table.

He piled our plates high with steaks, sausages and huge tiger prawns. We helped ourselves to salad and sat around the garden table. The sun was blazing down and there was no shade. Edward kept refilling my wine glass, and soon I was feeling slightly pissed. Everyone was giving a good performance of normal family life, although Edward was overacting. He laughed too loudly when anyone made anything even vaguely approaching a joke, and waxed lyrical about plans for our delayed honeymoon. Georgia regaled us with funny anecdotes about her fellow students, and Tara told us about her forthcoming work placement with a London design house.

Noah said almost nothing. He ate his sausages while they were still too hot, then spent the rest of his time playing with the bits of salad I'd put on his plate. Eventually Edward gave in to his requests to leave the table. Noah climbed down from his chair and went into the house. Georgia helped Edward gather up our empty plates and they took them inside, while Tara took out her phone and started playing some game with irritating sound effects. I felt as if she was deliberately blocking me out, but I chose not to rise to the bait.

A couple of minutes later, Edward brought out a tray laden with desserts he'd bought from the wildly expensive local patisserie. 'I let Noah take his cake to his room,' he said.

'Ooh, yummy,' Tara enthused. 'Can I have the chocolate bomb thing?'

'Thanks, both, for coming today,' I said as Edward handed round the plates. 'We've been having a bit of a torrid time recently, and it's great to have your support.' The girls looked at each other, then at Edward.

'Yes, but we're all right now, aren't we, darling?' He reached for my hand, squeezing it tightly. 'We've weathered the storm. Now it's upwards and onwards.'

'Thanks for standing by Dad,' said Georgia. 'Means a lot to us, doesn't it, sis?'

'Of course.' Tara gave me a thin crocodile smile. 'You're properly one of us now.'

I swallowed her words, wondering what they really meant. They roiled in my stomach, mixing uneasily with the alcohol and Edward's surf and turf.

'I'm okay. It's Noah that's still in the dark,' I said. 'I think he's ready to know about Francesca. It won't be easy for him, but in the long run it will lessen the pain. Once he knows the truth, he can start having the therapy he so badly needs.'

There was silence. I sensed the three of them trying to use telepathy to work out what their response should be.

'Lily's right,' said Edward finally. 'I've been putting it off, terrified of the impact it's going to have, but it can't go on indefinitely. Noah's old enough to be told now. Not about the police investigation or the libel case, just the bare essentials. I'll work out what to say to him. Lily's going to help me.'

'I'll do my best,' I said.

He leant across and planted a kiss on my cheek. 'Then we can stop pretending and be like any normal family.' He looked towards his beloved girls. 'Agreed?'

'Agreed,' smiled Georgia.

'Whatever,' said Tara, smashing the chocolate bomb with her fork.

CHAPTER TWENTY

We called Noah downstairs not long after Tara and Georgia had gone home. Edward had wanted to put it off until bedtime, but I said it wasn't fair to open up such a delicate subject and then expect a child to go straight to sleep afterwards. We stationed ourselves in the living room, sitting close together on the sofa to present a united front. Edward's knee was jerking nervously and I reached out to steady it.

'It's going to be okay,' I whispered. 'We're doing the right thing.'

'But what if he totally freaks out?'

'We just support him through it – let him feel what he needs to feel.' I heard footsteps on the stairs. 'Shh… he's coming.' Edward kissed me on the cheek.

'Am I in trouble?' asked Noah, lingering in the doorway. His big blue eyes looked out anxiously from beneath his scruffy fringe.

'No, buddy, not at all.' Edward beckoned him forward. 'There's nothing to be scared of. Come in, take a seat.'

Still uncertain, Noah sidled into the room and deposited himself in the armchair opposite us. He tucked his legs up and shielded himself with a large cushion.

Edward leant forward, clasping his hands together. 'We just want to have a chat with you about, um…'

'We want to talk to you about Mummy,' I said.

Noah narrowed his eyes. 'What about her?'

'Daddy didn't tell you before because it's a difficult thing to explain and you were too little.'

'But you're much older now, big man,' Edward added. 'You're smart and really strong.'

Noah frowned. 'Why do I have to be strong? Is it because it's bad news?'

We hesitated, unsure of how to answer. 'No, not really,' I said. 'But there *has* been a misunderstanding going on and Daddy wants to clear it up.'

'Yes, Lily's right, it's a misunderstanding, that's all. An easy fix.'

Noah's brow creased. 'What do you mean?'

'You see, the thing is…' Edward stalled.

'Go on,' I whispered.

He cleared his throat. 'The thing is, what we didn't explain properly before is that you and your sisters have different mummies.'

Noah froze. I thought he might even be holding his breath. Edward and I glanced at each other anxiously, then I nodded and he carried on.

'You see, a long time ago, I was married to Tara and Georgia's mummy, who was called Clare. Then we split up and I met *your* mummy, Francesca. We fell in love, and a little while later, you were born.' It wasn't an accurate description of the order of events, but I could see that at this stage, it was better to keep the story simple.

'Okay,' Noah said, retreating further behind the cushion.

I didn't like the flatness in his voice. 'Do you understand what Daddy's saying?'

After a while, he said, 'Yes. Their mummy is dead.'

'That's right,' said Edward. 'You know what happened. She died because she ate some bread with nuts in it. She was very allergic and when she ate the nuts she couldn't breathe. It was a terrible accident.'

Noah lowered the cushion, but kept hold of it. 'But she's not my mummy, so…' He looked up at the ceiling with a faraway expression on his face, as if he was trying to puzzle out some mental arithmetic.

'We'd like to talk to you about *your* mummy now,' I said, trying to get his attention back. 'I know it makes you feel uncomfortable, but I want you to try to be brave and listen, because it's really important—'

'There's no point,' Noah interrupted. 'Dad just lies. He does it all the time.'

'Now, now, that's not fair, buddy.'

'You and Georgia and Tara and everyone, you've lied to me my whole life. You think I'm stupid, but I'm not. I know you lie because I remember her. I remember *everything.*'

'You might think you do, but you don't,' Edward responded, his tone sharpening.

'He clearly remembers something,' I said. 'Is that right, Noah? Do you remember Mummy's face? Or her voice? Do you remember her looking after you?'

He looked down. 'Not telling.'

'He doesn't remember, Lily,' said Edward impatiently. 'He was too young.'

'I *do*, so there,' Noah flared. 'I'm just not telling *you.*'

'Well, buddy, you may think you remember, but it's impossible. Children forget their early memories – it's how their brains work.'

'I'm not your buddy, okay? Stop calling me that.' Noah threw the cushion onto the floor. 'And my brain works differently because I *do* remember her. I dream about her all the time.'

'There's no point in arguing about it,' I said.

'You lied, Dad,' he repeated. 'You pretended she was dead. That's like something a really evil person would do. Why did you do that?'

'It wasn't deliberate. It was a misunderstanding.'

'Liar.'

'*Your* mummy… Fran… she…' Edward gulped. 'The truth is… the very sad truth is that she left us, a long time ago, when you were just a little boy. Nobody knows why, or what happened to her or where she is.'

'*I* know,' Noah replied confidently. 'She's here, in London. Soon she's going to come and get me, and then I won't have to live with you two any more.'

Edward looked frustrated. 'Noah, I can see why you might believe that, but—'

'She's coming to get me and you can't stop her. Even if you lock me up, she'll find a way.' He stood up and folded his arms defiantly.

I rose and went over to him. 'Please listen to what Daddy's saying.'

'Why should I? He's a liar. You're both liars. That's all you ever do, lie, lie, lie. Go away, leave me alone. I hate you both!' He ran out of the room, and I followed him.

'Noah! Come back! Please!' But he was already at the top of the stairs. I heard his bedroom door slam shut.

Edward joined me in the hallway. 'You okay?' he asked. We held each other for a few seconds, then he took my hand and led me back into the living room.

'Oh God,' I said. 'That was terrible.'

'Hmm… couldn't have gone worse,' Edward agreed. 'It was my fault. I said everything in the wrong order, went into way too much detail about Clare. He didn't need to hear that, it was irrelevant.'

'You were feeling your way into it.'

'I should have taken the bull by the horns and gone straight in with Fran.'

'Possibly… It's easy to know after the event.'

'I didn't even get the chance to explain that someone was pretending to be his mother.' Edward went to the sideboard and took out a new bottle of whisky.

'But we don't know for sure, do we? It could actually be Francesca.'

'It's not. As I suspected, it's an investigative journalist.' He poured himself a double shot and slumped back onto the sofa.

'God, why didn't you tell me?' I gasped.

'I wanted to be sure before you got too excited, but I've been doing some digging. The five-year anniversary of Fran's disappearance is coming up, and apparently one of the tabloids is planning a "special".' He pulled a face of disgust.

'Which one?'

'I don't want to say until I know for certain, but it's not one of the papers I sued last time around. They wouldn't dare, not after what it cost them before.'

'How did they get to Noah?'

'I don't know. They're still holding out on me. But I'll find out somehow, and when I do, there's going to be hell to pay.'

'Gosh… that's a significant piece of news,' I said after a pause. 'But we should wait until we have absolute proof before telling Noah. He'll be devastated.'

'You sound pretty devastated yourself.'

'Of course I am. Aren't you? I'm desperate for Fran to be alive. She's the only one who can prove your innocence.'

'It makes me so happy to hear you say that, Lily. I know we've still got problems with Noah, but we're stronger than ever.' He raised his glass to me. 'I love you so much. More than anyone.'

A couple of weeks passed. Noah was refusing to talk to either of us now, once again hiding in his room for hours on end, hardly eating at mealtimes. His schooling had been completely abandoned. I was really concerned about his mental health and begged Edward to take him to the doctor, but he wouldn't have it.

'I can do without so-called experts interfering,' he said. 'They'll only make things worse.'

'But they can't get much worse, can they?' I replied. 'Noah needs therapy. There are some fantastic people out there, specially trained to help kids like him.'

'No. Please don't keep on about it, Lily. He's my son, I know how to handle him.'

I didn't agree. As far as I could see, Edward had made a mess of things from start to finish. I kept thinking back to what Noah had said about remembering everything. Maybe he'd witnessed traumatic scenes involving his parents – arguments, perhaps, maybe even fights. Although Edward was finally opening up about the past and his relationship with Francesca, I sensed that he wasn't telling me everything. He painted a rosy picture – too rosy at times, I thought. It didn't tally with his insistence that she'd been depressed to the point of being suicidal.

I talked to Marsha about it on an almost daily basis, secretly on my mobile when I knew Edward was busy in his office. She listened politely and hardly ever disagreed with my point of view, but I could tell by her tone of voice that she was still worried about me.

'Why don't you come over for a proper chat?' she asked. 'I haven't seen you for ages.'

'I'm sorry, I can't. I don't want to leave Noah,' I said. 'He's not in a good way, Marsha. I'm really worried about him.'

'Hmm…' She didn't sound convinced by my excuse. 'Has Edward banned you from seeing me? I know he thinks I'm the bitch from hell.'

'Don't be silly. That's not true. It's just that things are still very delicate between us. We're doing okay, but I don't want to rock the boat.' Her silence said it all. There was no fooling Marsha.

'Look, I'll come over soon, promise.'

'Okay,' she said. 'You know where I am if you need me.'

Despite our problems with Noah, Edward still wanted to go ahead with recruiting a new tutor. He felt it was important to restore some normality to Noah's life and get him back into the classroom. Reluctantly, I had to agree that he would be better off being taught by somebody outside the family, who wasn't so emotionally involved.

The interviews that had been postponed were rescheduled for the following week. We'd already lost two of the strongest contenders, so the agency was asked to produce some more applicants. There were no male candidates. Three of the four women proposed were close in age to me, and they were all single. I studied their CVs thoroughly, looking for spelling mistakes or unexplained gaps in their employment. Noah deserved somebody really good. I was determined to be much harder on them than Edward had been on me.

By Friday morning, we only had two candidates to interview. Of the two dropouts, one had accepted a post elsewhere, and the other – the older woman, who'd been my favourite – had withdrawn without giving a reason.

'I didn't like the look of her anyway,' admitted Edward. 'She reminded me of your predecessor, Kim. I didn't trust *her* one bit. Noah needs somebody young and sparky.'

'What, like me?' I joked as we tidied up the sitting room in preparation for the interviews.

'Yes,' he smiled. 'Exactly like you.'

'What are we going to tell them about the set-up here? They're bound to assume I'm Noah's mother.'

'So?' Edward frowned. 'Does it matter?'

'Noah doesn't even accept me as his stepmum at the moment – he's not going to take too kindly to me being called his mummy. I don't want to lie. I'm just trying to avoid any scenes.'

'I'm sure you can find a way round it, darling,' he said. 'Just tell as much of the truth as you need to, but no more.' It sounded like a technique he was very familiar with.

I put a notebook and pen on the coffee table and sat down. Edward sent a few work texts, then turned off his mobile. The first candidate was a few minutes late – a black mark against her as far as I was concerned, until I recalled that I'd also arrived late for my interview. When the doorbell finally sounded, I had a sudden flashback to almost a year ago. How naïve I'd been. Tutoring an eight-year-old boy by himself had sounded like the easiest job in the world. Of course, I hadn't anticipated the depth of Noah's problems, or that I would fall in love with his father. And now here I was, the mistress of the house, choosing my replacement. Not that I felt like I was in charge. I smoothed my hair and pulled my skirt over my knees.

'This is Daisy,' introduced Edward, leading a young beanpole of a woman into the room. 'Daisy, this is my wife, Lily.'

'Hi, lovely to meet you,' she said, holding out her hand. I stood up and shook it, then gestured at her to sit down in the armchair opposite. 'Sorry I'm late, I got a bit lost.'

So did I, I thought privately.

Daisy was pretty and dark, with large brown eyes and beautiful white teeth, which I noticed immediately. I already knew from her CV that she was twenty-four, six years younger than me, but her skin was so flawless and fresh I would have believed she was sixteen. She was wearing a blue floral buffet dress that fell almost to her ankles, with billowing sleeves and a gathered flounce at the hem. Somewhat incongruously, she had a pair of white trainers on her feet. I guessed she was a little embarrassed by her height and didn't like heels.

Edward offered her tea or coffee, just as he had offered me, and she refused, just as I had done. Although we were physically unalike, I had the strange sensation of watching my interview replay itself. Edward took charge of the conversation. As before, he focused on Daisy's personal interests rather than her teaching experience, and waved aside her certificates. I tried to interrupt with more challenging questions, but he batted them away apologetically.

'I'm sure Daisy knows what she's doing,' he said, then turned to her. 'So, when could you start?'

'*If* we offer you the job and you decide to accept,' I interjected.

'Yes, of course, understood.' She pushed a lock of her glossy black hair behind her ear. 'I could start straight away if you want. I'm, like, totally free at the moment.' She ended each sentence with an upwards inflection, as if replying with a question. I knew it would irritate me if I had to listen to her every day.

'Great,' said Edward. 'That's fantastic. Noah's been having a break, but we don't want him to get behind.' He beamed at her. 'Now, I expect you'd like to see the schoolroom. It's actually a conservatory, but we use it for lessons.'

'Oh, cool.'

'I'll call Noah down, then you can meet him.'

'That'd be amazing.'

'He's very shy with strangers,' I said. 'He's a lovely boy, but he needs time to get to know people.'

She put her head on one side. 'Oh bless.'

Edward led her out of the sitting room and into the schoolroom at the back of the house. I stayed put and wrote a few notes. *Sweet girl, bit young. Noah will like her. Strict enough? Check experience.* Laughter tinkled down the hallway. I didn't like it. But I already knew that no matter what objections I made to Daisy or how strong the second candidate was, Edward had already made up his mind.

CHAPTER TWENTY-ONE

Fran had been babysitting for the family for about three months. Clare had decided that she and Ned needed to spend more quality time together as a couple, and was pleased to have found somebody who was 'so available'. She had no idea that the babysitter was available for her husband, rather than her; that Fran only endured the long evenings of sarcastic non-cooperation from Tara and Georgia to spend twenty minutes in the car with Ned while he drove her home. They'd chat like old friends on the journey, and when they reached her place – a dilapidated student house share – he'd turn off the engine and they'd carry on talking until the car grew cold and the windows steamed up with their breath, neither wanting to say goodbye and part company. It never felt like flirting, but that was exactly what it was, on a very deep, subconscious level.

She was twenty-one and he was thirty-five, but he never treated her like a kid. Their conversations were serious, reflective, soul-searching. They shared their life stories, told each other things they'd never dare tell anyone else, poured out emotions they didn't even know they'd been suppressing. The car was their confession box and they were each other's priest. Every time Fran got out, she felt understood and forgiven. He said he felt exactly the same.

One time she babysat while Clare and Ned went to the cinema on a 'date night'. He'd got bored and fallen asleep, missing most of the movie. When they arrived home, they fell out in front of her. Ned was very emotional as he drove Fran home that evening, emboldened by the darkness and the rain.

'I was only twenty-three when Tara was born,' he told her. 'I was way too young, not ready at all. I was working in the City back then. We worked bloody hard and played even harder, drank ourselves stupid every weekend, did some drugs, played around, you can imagine... Clare was a bit of a wild child too – not that you'd think so now. We had a lot of fun together. Then she took that pregnancy test and grew up overnight.'

'But you didn't want to grow up,' she surmised, twisting around sideways in her seat to get a better look at the expression on his handsome face.

He pouted. 'No, I guess not, but I did want to do the right thing. At least, what I thought was the right thing. We got married straight away, moved to Birmingham to be close to Clare's family, and I got a job with an investment bank. Tara was born, we bought our first house, Georgia came along soon after. Clare returned to work, we moved up the property ladder, life was ticking along nicely.' Water was streaming down the windows and pattering on the roof of the car, sealing them in. Ned drummed his fingers on the steering wheel. 'But I was bored. I felt like I was missing out, convinced there were constant wild parties going on in London without me. My old friends seemed to have forgotten I existed.'

'You must have made new friends.'

'Not really,' he admitted. 'I felt resentful about being here, didn't want to put down roots. I loved the girls, but the truth was, I wanted out of the marriage. I was going to tell her when her parents were suddenly killed in a horrific car crash. It knocked her for six. I couldn't leave her in that state, it wasn't fair.'

'But you had a right to happiness too,' she said, filling up with sympathy.

'Yes, and I kept telling myself I was happy, or *should* be happy. I had nothing to complain about. I had a good job, a lovely big house, a great wife, two gorgeous daughters…' He turned to her. 'But somehow, it's not enough. *Clare* isn't enough. That makes me sound like a complete shit, doesn't it?'

'No, you're just being honest.'

Emotion welled up inside him. 'I don't love her any more. I don't think I ever loved her. Oh my God, I don't know why I'm telling you this.' He dived into the glove compartment and took out a small packet of travel tissues. 'Promise you won't breathe a word.'

'Of course not.'

He suddenly reached across and hugged her. 'Thank you. I knew you'd understand.' They held onto each other for a few seconds longer, neither of them wanting to break away. As he withdrew, their cheeks brushed, and then they found each other's lips…

Their relationship owed a lot to that BMW. It witnessed their first touch, their first kiss. They even had sex for the first time on the back seat, in the far corner of an empty supermarket car park near to where Fran lived. Despite it being a top-of-the-range model with heated leather upholstery, the whole experience was uncomfortable and demeaning. 'I'm sorry,' he said. 'You deserve better than this.'

He'd drawn the line at going to Fran's place and she hadn't tried to persuade him otherwise – the walls of her bedroom were paper-thin, the heating unreliable, the mattress lumpy and stained from previous occupiers. Spending time together at his house was obviously out of the question – even if they'd been able to engineer it, it was unthinkable for them to make love in the marital bed. Fran was also terrified of Clare finding out and giving her the sack.

She stopped babysitting as soon as the relationship became sexual. Ned told Clare he was fed up with giving Fran lifts home because it meant he wasn't able to drink when they went out. It was his idea, a good way – or so he thought – to put her off the scent. Fran realised that Clare felt guilty about letting her go, because she was extra friendly at work after that, as if she was trying to make up for it.

Now they had to find other opportunities to meet, other places to go. Fran didn't want to use hotels, especially when they couldn't stay overnight and sometimes only used the room for a couple of hours during the day. She told Ned it made her feel like a prostitute, but he promised her nobody would bat an eyelid, and he turned out to be right.

Their favourite hotel was in the city centre – part of a chain that offered excellent midweek discounts. They saw each other about once a week. All the rooms were identical, so it seemed like they were always given the same one. It was their haven, sealed off from the rest of the world, where the realities of wives and work didn't exist. The bed was extra wide and the sheets were clean and crisp. Fran loved the bathroom, and always took advantage of the power shower to wash her hair. They used room service – white wine chilling in buckets, smoked salmon sandwiches cut into dainty triangles, sometimes a pot of tea and a large portion of chips. They had intense, important conversations. They watched movies. And as for the sex… well, it was unbelievable.

'Promise me you haven't told anyone about us,' Ned said one evening, lying back on the pillows. 'Not even your closest friends.'

'Especially not my closest friends. I work with some of them,' she reminded him. 'I need to keep it a secret just as much as you do.'

'True.' He drew her into the crook of his arm. 'It's insane… I've never done anything like this before. Never so much as kissed anyone at an office Christmas party.'

'Really?'

'Yes, really. You're the first.'

'The first?' She pinched him playfully. 'That sounds like there'll be others in the future.'

'Okay, first and last. How's that?'

'Perfect,' she said.

It wasn't perfect, though, not even at the beginning. Fran was madly in love with Ned, but at the same time she knew what she was doing was wrong. She'd never set out to wreck her boss's marriage, or *anyone's* marriage. She hadn't even been looking for a new relationship. And worst of all, she liked her job and didn't want to lose it. Clare was good to work for: open-minded, inclusive, keen to listen. Ned said she was too conventional, but Fran thought her very creative. Sometimes, when Clare was delivering the team briefing on the eve of an event, she shuddered with guilt as she remembered intimate things Ned had revealed about their sex life.

The affair was growing more serious and more complicated. In between encounters, Fran felt as if she barely existed. She was like a mechanical doll waiting for her owner to come and wind her up. She stopped meeting up with friends and avoided any social gatherings with colleagues, especially if Clare was involved. They worked together closely on projects, but Fran could no longer look her boss in the eye.

On weekdays, Fran and Ned skulked in awful pubs after work for a quick drink before duty or supper called him home. At weekends, he structured his lover into his domestic life. They 'bumped into each other' in various unromantic locations like shopping centres and car washes, even the municipal dump. He took up jogging – or pretended to – and they'd go for walks along the canal. The hotel bills were mounting up, so they reverted to making love in the car, or driving to woodlands and having risky, frantic sex up against a tree.

Fran's work was suffering. Event management had been her dream career, but she found she could no longer be bothered to put in the extra hours it demanded. Once she'd been the sparky one of the team, but now she did the minimum. Unsurprisingly, Clare noticed her protégée was losing focus. She called Fran into her office, asked if she was having personal problems and whether she could help in any way. Fran felt so bad she nearly broke down and confessed the affair there and then.

'This is no good. You'll have to get another job,' Ned said when she told him later.

Or you could leave her, Fran said to herself. They'd touched on that possibility a few times, but he'd always come up with compelling reasons for not doing it at that precise moment: Clare was working towards a promotion, Tara was struggling with puberty, Georgia had fallen out with her friendship group, they had a holiday booked, he was on the verge of closing some big deal. He insisted that he loved her and longed for them to be together, but he didn't want his family life to be affected.

Then she got pregnant and everything changed.

CHAPTER TWENTY-TWO

Daisy was able to start work the following Monday. She arrived early, all bright-eyed and bushy-tailed, as my mother would say, brimming over with nervous enthusiasm.

'I was so excited, I could hardly sleep last night,' she said.

Edward went to make her a cup of coffee while I showed her to the schoolroom.

'I've left some notes for you,' I said. 'Topics we've covered already, Noah's most recent assessments, where we've got to in the syllabus… I've also given you some thoughts about his strengths and weaknesses, approaches he responds well to, or doesn't – that kind of thing. Obviously you'll find out for yourself, but I thought it might help to give you a head start.'

'Thanks, that's great,' she beamed. 'I'll read every word.'

I felt a pang of jealousy as I showed her to her desk and handed over the password for the computer. 'Feel free to reorganise things if you want,' I said. 'It's your space now. Any questions, just ask.'

'Oh, it all looks perfect just as it is,' she enthused. I hovered while she took a plastic lunchbox out of her bag, then a large notepad and a pencil case. She picked up the folder I'd prepared for her and started flicking through it.

'If you need any materials, ask Edward and he'll order them for you.'

'Okay, thanks.' She looked up. 'Actually, I do have one question. I hope you don't mind my asking, but why aren't *you* teaching him? You seem way more experienced than me.'

I tried to keep my tone neutral. 'We thought it was better for Noah to have somebody from outside. It doesn't always work, teaching your own kids. Gets a bit intense – you know?'

'Intense, yeah,' she repeated. 'Um… sorry, I'm a bit confused. Are you Noah's mother? Only when I met him the other day, he called you Lily.'

'I'm his stepmum,' I told her.

'Oh, right… But he lives with you and Edward full-time?' I nodded. 'So, um… where's his birth mum?'

Good question, I thought. Fortunately, I'd already prepared an answer. 'He doesn't see her. She's not part of his life any more.'

She opened her mouth to ask me a third question, but I was saved by Edward, who entered with her coffee.

'Noah not down yet?' he said. 'Tut-tut. I'll call him right now.' He went straight out.

'Is Noah okay about doing lessons?' Daisy asked anxiously.

'Absolutely. He had a break and got very bored. It might take him a little time to settle back into it, but I'm sure it'll be fine. If all else fails, draw a picture with him. He loves art, he's really good at it.'

'Sounds like a top tip,' she replied.

At that moment, Noah came running into the room. He halted when he saw me and threw me one of his filthy looks. If Daisy spotted it, she didn't let on.

'Hi, Noah,' she said. 'Ready to have some fun?'

'I'd better leave you to it,' I said, and made my retreat.

I went into the kitchen and stacked the dishwasher with the breakfast things. Now what? I thought, wiping down the surfaces. I had the rest of the day to myself – the rest of the week, in fact. The month. Year. I was a free woman. I could go shopping and buy myself a load of clothes, join a gym, watch a movie, have my hair done and my nails manicured, or just sit in the garden and read a book. But I didn't want to do any of those things. I wanted to be back in the schoolroom, helping Noah get his head around long division or some English comprehension.

Edward had already gone into his office to start work. I went upstairs and made the beds. There was a pile of dirty laundry that needed seeing to, so I sorted out a load and put it on. Should I call my mother and invite her for that visit I'd promised? I'd sent her a few brief emails but hadn't rung for a couple of weeks. Mum was very good at picking up signals, and I'd been scared that she would hear the strain in my voice. I felt a lot calmer now, but not yet confident enough to tell her what had been going on. She read the tabloids and was bound to remember who 'Fletch the Lech' was. After her own experience with men, she would have no doubt at all that he was guilty. I had visions of her mounting a rescue mission to get me away from him. No, I decided, I couldn't deal with my mother just yet.

I went back downstairs and wandered around, trying to find something useful to do. We had a cleaner twice a week, so there was no point in doing any hoovering. Edward's office door was closed, a sign that he was busy and mustn't be disturbed. Laughter was skipping down the hallway from the schoolroom – it sounded like Daisy and Noah were playing some fun game together. I was pleased that the lessons were going so well, but I felt excluded and irrelevant.

Pull yourself together. I made a cup of tea and went into the sitting room, taking out my phone and starting to search for job vacancies online. Edward was right. Rather than moping around with nothing to do, I should go back to working in a primary school. There were a few vacancies worth applying for, so I downloaded the application forms. But I needed access to my laptop to fill them in properly, and that was in the schoolroom. Edward wouldn't let anyone borrow his Mac. It would have to wait for the evening or the weekend, I realised. Which still left me with nothing to do.

The person I really wanted to see was Marsha. Edward hadn't banned me from seeing her as she'd claimed, but he'd made it clear he wasn't happy about our friendship. He was jealous, that was obvious. I understood that he was feeling vulnerable right now – neither of us knew whether our marriage – so new and delicate – was going to survive the current storm. However, I couldn't let him stop me seeing my best friend.

We hadn't spoken for a few days, which was unusual. I knew she'd be at work, but I chanced sending her a text. *Sorry for short notice. Can you meet for lunch?*

Luckily, she replied immediately and said she'd love to see me. I arranged to meet her at the British Museum, where she worked. She would only have an hour to spare, but it was better than nothing, and infinitely more attractive than drifting around the house all day like a disgruntled ghost. I rushed upstairs to change into something smarter and put on some make-up, then wrote a brief note to Edward, which I left next to the kettle, hoping he'd find it when he emerged at lunchtime. I didn't mention that I was meeting Marsha, saying instead that I was going shopping in the West End. Finally, I put my head around the schoolroom door and explained to Daisy that I was popping out.

'Anything you need before I go?' I asked.

She flicked her hair over her shoulder. 'Don't think so. What time's lunch?' She picked up her plastic box. 'Don't worry, I brought my own.'

'Usually we break at around one and have lunch with Edward. But it's up to you.'

'One o'clock sounds perfect. Have fun!' she cried.

My shoulders dropped as soon as I left the house, and I found I was walking extra quickly down the hill to get to the Tube station.

The museum was buzzing with visitors – milling around the Great Court, queuing to get their belongings from the cloakroom, dithering in the shop. The various cafés were full, and there was nowhere to sit down. I waited by the ticket office while Marsha handed over to a colleague and went to collect her bag.

A few minutes later, she emerged from a door marked *Staff*. She was wearing a pair of bright red dungarees over a floral shirt and new Converse trainers.

'Lily! I can't tell how good it is to see you.'

'Me too.'

We hugged, holding onto each other for longer than usual. I inhaled the familiar smell of her hair oil and felt suddenly at home.

'Sorry I haven't been in touch for a few days. Shall we go to Leyla's? It's a little Lebanese café just around the corner.'

'Suits me,' I replied.

She took my arm and we walked out of the building. It was a warm day, and everyone seemed to be spending their lunch break outside. The pavements were littered with tables and chairs, and office workers were standing outside pubs, chatting with pints of lager in hand.

'Any news on the investigations?'

'Edward says he's getting close. He's almost certain it's one of the tabloids, or maybe a freelancer trying to make a name for themselves.'

'What's he going to do – sue?'

I sighed. 'No idea, Marsha. He doesn't want me involved. I think he's trying to protect me.'

'Hmm... or himself, more like,' she grunted.

The tables outside Leyla's were all full, but we found a free one inside, tucked into a corner by the toilets. Marsha immediately ordered a plate of cold meze, some pitta bread and two Diet Cokes. While we waited, I looked around at the dated decor – the green and blue patterned tiling, the patchy orange walls, the faded posters of Lebanese tourist attractions framed as if they were works of art. The bench seat was hard and the tapestry cushion behind my back was lumpy, but I didn't care. I was just pleased to be with my best friend again.

'How do you feel?' she asked, searching my face for clues.

'Fine.'

'Things are okay between you, then? He's told you everything that happened and you're satisfied that he's innocent?'

'Yes… I think so.'

An elderly man – Leyla's husband, apparently – set our food on the table, together with a jug of water and two glasses. Marsha started ladling up a piece of bread.

'You don't sound very sure,' she said.

'No, I am. Don't worry, Marsha, if I thought Edward was a murderer, I wouldn't still be with him. No way. He's told me the whole story. He was put through hell by the police, not to mention the media. They didn't have one shred of evidence against him – he was never even charged, let alone put on trial.'

'I know,' she murmured. 'Try the kibbeh, they're delicious.'

I paused to load up my plate. 'They arrested him in front of the media and questioned him for forty-eight hours. They let him out on bail but didn't drop the charges for months! It was outrageous. And all that time he wasn't allowed to see Noah. Francesca's parents were looking after him, but even when the police said he was no longer a suspect, they refused to give him back. They kept on accusing him of murder. Edward had to take them to court. There was a nasty battle and he ended up taking an injunction out against them, so now they can't see Noah at all.'

Marsha twisted her mouth thoughtfully. 'It must have been a terrible time for them, though – with their daughter missing.'

'Of course it was, but Edward went through hell too. He really loved Francesca.' I swallowed. 'Probably still does. The way he talks about her, it's hard to listen to sometimes. But I told him to be honest, so I can't complain.' I carried on talking, and she listened carefully, not interrupting at all. 'I want Francesca to be alive so that Edward will be free of suspicion, but on the other hand, I'm terrified that she's going to take Noah away, or even worse, that Edward will go back to her.'

'That's not going to happen,' Marsha said firmly. She started fidgeting with a bead on the end of her braids. It was a nervous gesture I'd seen a thousand times; it meant she was about to broach a difficult subject.

'I've been doing some research,' she began. 'Reading up about the case.'

I held up my hand to stop her. 'Most of what they wrote about Edward was complete garbage. It was accepted in the courts. That's why he was paid a massive sum in compensation.'

'Yes, I know, I understand, I didn't take any notice of that. I dug a bit deeper, went more local… I found an interview with a woman called Lauren Davis. She and Francesca were best friends, like us, so she knew her well. I think it's well worth a read.'

I immediately felt a sickening lurch in my stomach and put down my fork. 'Why? What does it say?'

'Well… Lauren insists that Francesca never talked to her about feeling suicidal.'

'That's understandable. Edward told me she was too embarrassed to ask for help.'

'Yes, that's what he claimed, but there was no evidence of that, and quite frankly, nobody believed him. Lauren says Francesca wasn't the depressive type, and even if she *had* been feeling down, she would have confided in her. They were incredibly close.'

I looked down at my plate. The food was swirling into a blurry mess, and I realised I had tears in my eyes. Marsha leant across and took my hand.

'And in another interview that I read, Francesca's parents said the same thing.'

'But Edward told me she had postnatal depression.' I stopped myself, remembering that *I'd* suggested that term, not him.

'I'm sorry, this must be so hard to take. But you have to listen to me. I managed to track down Lauren via social media.'

'You did what?' I looked up. 'You mean, you went behind my back? I didn't ask you—'

'She's a GP now, a really nice woman, incredibly down to earth. She agreed to talk to me and we had a long phone call yesterday evening. She said Edward was controlling, he wouldn't let Francesca see any of her friends or family. She wanted to leave him but she knew he wouldn't let her take Noah. She was frightened of him, Lily.'

'No, they were happy together. Edward told me.'

Marsha continued. 'She was really worried when I told her that he'd remarried, especially when she heard you were so young.' She looked at me pleadingly. 'She wants to talk to you.'

'No, no, I can't. It would be disloyal. Edward's told me the truth and I... I believe him.'

'Really? After what I just told you?' Marsha folded her arms across the bib of her dungarees. Her dark brown eyes were blazing, and she looked determined. 'I want to talk about the police investigation now.' She spoke slowly and deliberately, almost as if she were in court, giving evidence. 'Francesca was last seen in Birmingham by a neighbour as she got out of Edward's car late one evening. She went into the flat they shared and never came out. Not alive, anyway. He didn't report her missing. When the police turned up, he said she'd gone away for a few days, and only mentioned her depression much later, when he was arrested. Apparently the detectives in charge of the case are still convinced she was murdered.'

'Okay, I get that, and maybe they're right. But that doesn't mean it was Edward that killed her. He was never charged. He was put on trial by the media, not the courts.'

'The police haven't given up, Lily. They're still investigating, and Edward is the only suspect. He's lying to you, just as he's lied all along. Please, talk to Lauren.'

'I can't listen to this any more,' I said, getting up from the table. 'You're just trying to hurt me.'

'I'm not, I'm trying to save you. Don't go, please.'

'I thought you were on my side.'

She looked to the heavens, exasperation writ large across her face. 'I *am* on your side, you idiot, that's why I'm doing this. I don't care if you hate me and never speak to me again – I just want you to be safe.'

CHAPTER TWENTY-THREE

I walked out of Leyla's feeling angry and upset, but most of all confused. I'd spent the last few weeks adjusting to my new, honest and open relationship with Edward. We'd virtually had to go back to the beginning and start all over again. I'd listened to him for hours, talking about Francesca and recounting what had happened around the time of her disappearance. I'd searched my heart and finally concluded that he was telling me the truth. If he *had* killed her, I would have sensed it, wouldn't I? I would have seen it in his eyes, tasted it in his kisses, felt it in his touch…

But now Marsha had thrown all my beliefs into the air, and I realised how fragile some of them were. She must have known that a best friend's account of what had been going on in Edward and Francesca's relationship would have a powerful impact on me. I was annoyed with her for going behind my back, but I also knew that she loved me and had my interests at heart.

My mind was in turmoil. After leaving the café, I walked around Bloomsbury for ages, not really looking where I was going, just taking random turnings this way and that, until I realised I was totally lost. I took out my phone and reorientated myself on the map, then threaded my way back in the direction of Oxford Street.

The pavements were seething with shoppers, mostly tourists by the sound of their conversations. I tried to lose myself in the crowds, wandering in and out of boutiques and department stores, flicking through rails of clothes, staring at displays of kitchenware and home accessories, sitting on sofas and beds in the furniture sections and trying not to catch any assistant's eye. After I'd exhausted Oxford Street, I walked to Regent's Park. It was a warm afternoon, so I found a bench under the shade of a tree and sat there just staring into space. School was out and the park was filling up with children. I picked up a tabloid newspaper that somebody had left behind and flicked through its pages. It was littered with sensationalist stories.

In the past, I would have believed the old adage that there was no smoke without fire. In cases of murder, I would have automatically taken the woman's part, condemning the man without a second thought. Now I realised that it was all too easy to judge strangers; once you knew the actual people involved, it became far more difficult. The truth was far more nuanced than it seemed, if it existed at all. In the final analysis, the only person who knew what had happened to Francesca was the woman herself. I was still clinging onto the hope that she was alive after all; that she was out there somewhere, holding the key to Edward's freedom tightly in her fist. If only I could entice her out of the shadows and encourage her to let it go. But how?

I stayed in the park until the light softened and I felt chilly in my light jacket. Edward had sent me several texts during the day asking where I was and what I was doing, and I'd palmed him off with half-truths. Now I had to go back and face him.

It was getting on for eight o'clock when I buzzed open the gates and let myself in to the house. As soon as I stepped into the hallway, I heard the sound of conversation and a burst of girlish laughter. My jaw tightened. I quietly stepped out of my shoes and shrugged off my jacket, then walked into the sitting room.

Daisy was sitting in the armchair, a large glass of red wine nestling in her lap. An almost empty bottle of Rioja was on the coffee table. Edward was sprawled on the sofa, cheeks flushed with alcohol. He'd taken his socks off and was looking very relaxed.

'Hi there,' I said coolly as I surveyed the scene.

'Lily! You're back! At last!' he said, immediately sitting up straight. 'Let me get you a drink.' He jumped off the sofa.

'Has Noah eaten?'

'Yes, yes, ages ago. I heated up that risotto. I assumed you'd eaten out, so I gave your portion to Daisy. Hope you don't mind.'

I hadn't eaten since lunch, but I nodded and said, 'Sure, fine.'

'Thanks, it was amazing,' said Daisy.

Edward emptied the rest of the bottle into a glass and handed it to me. 'I asked Daisy to stay behind to tell me how she got on today,' he explained.

Ah yes, I remember that ruse, I thought.

'We had a great time,' she said. 'He's a lovely kid, so easy to teach.'

'We've been quite worried about him recently, but he seems to have settled back into it very easily.' Edward beamed.

I smiled at Daisy. 'Well, we shouldn't keep you,' I said. 'I'm sure you've better places to be.'

'Not really,' she admitted.

'Why don't you stick around? I'll open another bottle.' Edward made for the wine rack.

I shook my head very slightly, trying to signal to him. 'Noah should be getting ready for bed,' I said. 'Your turn to supervise the dreaded teeth-cleaning, darling.'

'Yes, you're right. Sorry.' He pulled an apologetic face.

Thankfully, Daisy took the hint. 'I'll be off. Thanks for the drink. It was good to have a chat about Noah, really helpful. I'll, er, see you tomorrow.' She gathered her long limbs together and stood up.

Edward showed her out. I stayed on the sofa, seething with annoyance.

'What's going on?' I said as soon as he came back into the room. He looked at me blankly. 'Don't play the innocent, I know how you operate.'

'Don't be ridiculous,' he replied. 'I genuinely wanted to find out how he was getting on. It's not my fault you weren't here. Besides, I didn't fancy drinking alone.'

'You were flirting with her.'

'I wasn't! I'm the one who should be feeling jealous. What on earth have you been doing all day?'

'Nothing. It doesn't matter.'

'Were you with Marsha?' His gaze drilled into me. 'You were, weren't you? I already told you I'm not happy—'

'Oh, so I'm not allowed to see my friends now,' I retorted.

Edward frowned. 'No, but every time you see her, you come back in a strange mood. I don't trust her. She's trying to turn you against me.'

'Don't be ridiculous,' I replied, thinking he wasn't far wrong. 'Although she's not very impressed by the way you lied to me.'

He groaned. 'It's got nothing to do with her. Anyway, I thought we'd got over all that.'

'Not completely.' I lowered my eyes. 'It's a lot to come to terms with, Edward. It still hurts, right here.' I pointed to the centre of my chest. 'All the time. It's like a stone is lodged in my heart. I keep hoping it's going to soften gradually, that one day it'll just dissolve away, but right now, it's rock-hard. And finding you with Daisy tonight, laughing and joking…'

'Okay, I was a bit overfamiliar. I'm sorry. I understand your fears, but you mustn't worry – from now on I'll keep things strictly professional with her.' He gave me a puppy dog look. 'You and me, we're going to be okay, aren't we? It doesn't matter what anyone else thinks. We love each other and that's what counts.' He reached out. 'Please, darling, don't dwell on the past. It's dead and buried. There's only one woman in my life, and that's you.'

*

That night I dreamt that Edward was on trial for Francesca's murder. I was on the jury and we were listening to various people give evidence against him. Clare made an appearance – bizarrely, wearing the swimming costume from the photograph – and so did Lauren, Francesca's best friend, only she looked exactly like Marsha. My mother was one of the barristers, dressed up in a wig and gown. Even Noah was there. He stood up from the gallery and shouted, 'Liar, liar, liar!' at the top of his voice until the judge – who was Alex, my ex – barked at him to sit down.

I woke up in a sweat, exhausted but too scared to go back to sleep. I lay next to Edward for what felt like hours, trying to settle my nerves. Then, at about three in the morning, the security light came on outside. Alarmed, I leapt out of bed and ran to the window, just in time to see Noah creeping across the driveway in his pyjamas. He ran into the bushes, where the stone ammonite was, and disappeared.

I grabbed my dressing gown and ran down the stairs. The front door was open. I stood on the steps, arms folded, waiting for him to return. The light had gone off, but it came on again as he emerged from the flower bed. He was carrying a small white box. The second he saw me, he stopped, his face bathed in guilt.

'Noah!' I hissed. 'What the hell are you doing? Come inside. Now!' He hesitated, as if contemplating escape, but there was nowhere to go. 'If you don't, I'll wake Daddy up. Is that what you want?'

He shook his head vigorously. I beckoned him forward, and he scuttled into the house. I shut the door quietly behind us.

'What's that you've got?' I whispered, pointing to the box he was clutching as if his life depended on it. 'Show me.' He shook his head again. 'Either you show me or I go and get Daddy. Your choice.'

Reluctantly he handed it over. I took him into the sitting room and told him to sit down while I opened the package. He sat there sniffing up tears, twisting his fingers anxiously as I peeled back the sticky tape and opened the flap.

Inside was a small, cheap mobile phone, together with a charger and a basic instruction leaflet. I pressed the on switch and it sprang instantly to life.

'Who left this for you?' I asked.

'Mummy,' he mumbled. 'I told you she would find a way… Please, please don't tell Daddy.'

'How did you know it was going to be there?'

'I just did.'

'Sorry, not good enough, Noah. I don't believe you go out there every night on the off-chance. You must have known in advance.' No response. 'How did she get in touch? Did she send an email?'

'No.'

'So how, then? Did she ask Harry Potter to send an owl, perhaps?' He looked up, almost smiling. 'Come on, you've got to tell me, Noah.'

'I can't.'

I returned to the phone. It was already set up ready for use. I looked at the home screen.

'You've got a text,' I said.

He reached out. 'It's for me, you can't read it.'

'Sorry, but I have to.' I clicked on the icon, my pulse racing as I opened the message and read it aloud.

'*Well done, Noah! Now we can text and talk to each other whenever we like. Call me on this number when nobody can hear you. Any time of the day or night. Love you, xxx*'

'Please give it to me, Lily. Please-please-please-please-please. Let me talk to her, let me hear her voice. She is my mummy.'

I sighed. 'We don't know that, Noah, not for certain. This could be someone playing a nasty trick on you.'

He looked at me, bewildered. 'Why would they do that?'

'I don't know. To get at Daddy, maybe? There are some horrible people who are trying to harm him, and they could be using you.'

'No, no, it's Mummy.'

'I really hope it is, Noah, believe me, I want it to be her more than anything else in the world. But we have to be super careful here.'

There was a long pause. 'Are you going to show Daddy the phone?'

'Yes. I'm really sorry, but I have to. Now go back to bed. Don't worry, you're not going to get in trouble over this, okay?'

'But Daddy—'

'I won't let him even tell you off one little bit.'

To my surprise, he didn't protest or accuse me of being evil. We went back upstairs together. Noah went into his room and I woke Edward.

'What's up? What time is it?' he grumbled sleepily, hauling himself up. I sat down next to him.

'"Mummy" isn't giving up,' I said, plonking the handset into his lap. He stared at it, blinking. 'They hid it behind the ammonite. I just caught Noah collecting it. There's a text, asking him to get in touch.'

'Good God...' he murmured, picking the phone up and examining it. 'It's not a smartphone. Looks like a pay-as-you-go. Untraceable.'

'Maybe the police will be able to track down who bought it. Or work out where the caller is.'

'I'm not involving the police – we've already been through this.'

'But this is serious, Edward.'

His blue eyes flashed at me. 'Yes, I know that!'

'It could be Francesca.'

'I don't think so.'

'But it *could* be. We should call the number, start negotiating, make a deal. Access to Noah in return for your exoneration.'

'No. If this turns out to be a journalist, I'll end up all over the tabloids again. They'll twist my words to construct false arguments against me. *How did Fletch the Lech know it wasn't Fran behind the secret messages? Because he killed her.* That kind of shit. I can't take the risk.'

'Okay, I get that. But what about Noah? He's the victim here. He's utterly convinced this is his mother and that we're trying to prevent him from seeing her. It could rip the family apart.' I paused. 'Whatever the risk, we owe it to him to find out the truth.'

Edward nodded. 'That's what I'm trying to do, carefully, behind the scenes. As soon as I have firm proof, we'll talk to him, explain everything.' He leant forward and embraced me. 'Thanks, darling, you've done a great job here. I'll handle it from now on.'

I wriggled free of him, feeling unsatisfied. 'What are you going to do about the phone?'

'Nothing.' He got out of bed. 'Just lock it away where Noah can't get to it.'

He left the room carrying the handset. I thumped the mattress. Why was he always shutting me out, treating me like a kid? Now I was cross with myself for rushing straight to him. If only I'd made a note of the number, I thought, I could have called her myself.

CHAPTER TWENTY-FOUR

Fran didn't want to tell Edward she was pregnant, terrified that he'd blame her for wrecking his life, that he might even demand she have an abortion. But when she finally plucked up the courage, his reaction was entirely opposite and unexpected.

His mouth fell open in shock and he covered his face with his hands, but only for a few seconds. Then he was kissing and hugging her, declaring that their baby had been conceived in love and was cosmic proof that they were destined to be together forever.

'I'll tell Clare straight away,' he said excitedly. 'I'll get a divorce and we'll get married, maybe even before it's born.' He made it sound so easy, as if his marriage was a coat that no longer suited him and all he had to do was cast it off and buy a new one. 'I hope it's a boy this time,' he added. 'I always wanted a son, never thought it would happen. Clare wouldn't have any more kids – too interested in her career.'

Fran was thrilled that he was thrilled, although secretly she was also slightly alarmed. Was this really such unequivocally good news? She was fresh out of university, trying to make progress in her first proper job. Although she'd always loved the idea of having children, starting a family this early was not part of her life plan. But then, nor had been falling in love with a married man...

To her surprise, she found that she was the pragmatic, down-to-earth one. 'Don't tell Clare yet,' she said. 'Once she knows, she'll probably chuck you out. I'll have to leave the job and I won't get another one while I'm pregnant. We need to get ourselves organised first. You can't move in here, there's not enough room. We'll have to find somewhere new to live.'

'Not necessarily,' he said. 'Clare's the one who should go. After all, it's my salary that pays the mortgage.'

'Yes, but the house is in your joint names, isn't it?' He waved it aside as if it were a minor detail. 'So, she owns half regardless. And what about the girls? They're still young. You can't chuck them out of their own home.'

'Hmm…' He pushed out his bottom lip. 'Let's not worry about that now. We have to celebrate. Bottle of champagne?'

She laughed. 'Not unless you want to drink it all yourself. I can't have alcohol for the next eight months, remember?'

She felt sick; God, she felt so sick. From the moment she woke up until mid afternoon, her stomach heaved and roiled and cramped until she was ready to throw herself out of the nearest window. Then there was the utter exhaustion that came in long, rumbling waves, submerging her for hours. And all this while she was still going to work and desperately trying to keep the pregnancy secret, especially from Clare.

It was May. The months of event planning were over and the summer season was about to start. Fran was working on several outdoor concerts – classical and pop – and an experimental new opera that was premiering in one of Birmingham's prestigious parks. Work started early, often at six in the morning. She'd turn up in her high-vis waistcoat and flat shoes, constantly yawning and looking like she had a terrible hangover. As a junior, she was given the more menial tasks – supervising the positioning of catering mobiles, or checking that the signs to the toilets were pointing in the right direction. Proximity to the row of chemical loos was useful, but the burger vans made her want to throw up there and then on the grass. She took to secretly nibbling dry crackers in an effort to control the nausea. Having once been a coffee junkie, she now found she couldn't even stomach the smell, let alone the taste. Caterers were always offering her free cups – sometimes she accepted them then poured the coffee onto the ground when nobody was looking.

The first event of the programme – a classical concert with fireworks – was a resounding success. The weather was good and thousands of people turned up with their picnics. They swayed and danced to the music, then whooped and cheered as the fireworks lit up the sky. Apart from a couple of briefly mislaid children, a twisted ankle, a foot badly cut on some broken glass, some drunk teenagers and a prang in the car park, everything went exceptionally smoothly. Fran did her best, but she was struggling to keep up with the pace. Luckily, she hardly saw Clare, who divided her time between high-level troubleshooting and entertaining sponsors in the hospitality tent. She thought she'd got away with it.

On Monday morning, there was a team debrief. She'd already thrown up twice since breakfast, was as white as a sheet and could hardly keep her eyes open. Afterwards, Clare asked her to come to her office.

'Are you all right, Fran?' she said. 'You look so washed-out. Are you ill?'

'No.'

'You were seen throwing up behind a tree yesterday afternoon.'

'I'm fine,' Fran insisted, trying to stifle a yawn. 'Slight stomach upset, that's all.'

Clare studied her sceptically. 'You've been very distracted lately. You're a different person compared to the ball of energy you were when you first started the job. Is something going on in your private life? I don't want to interfere, but if there's anything I can do to help…'

Fran looked down at the carpet. 'No, no, it's nothing, sorry. I'm just a bit tired.'

'The season has only just started. If you're tired after only one event, I dread to think how you're going to cope once we're at the peak.' Clare drew herself up like a headmistress. 'Early nights and keeping off the booze might help.'

'Oh, I'm not drinking,' Fran assured her, then instantly regretted it.

'Ah…' Clare gave a knowing smile. 'Look after yourself, Fran. And remember, any problems, come straight to me.'

Fran met up with Ned in a dowdy pub after work. 'You have to tell her now,' she said. 'I can't keep going on like this. I've got to leave the job anyway, so we might as well get it over and done with.'

'Hmm…' he replied, playing with a beer mat. 'Not great timing at the moment. I'm in the middle of a crucial deal.'

'The baby won't wait. We need to make some plans for the future.'

Having at first been gung-ho about telling Clare their marriage was over, Ned was now dithering. It was becoming clear that he didn't want to move out of the family home. How was this going to work with his desire for them to be together forever? she wondered. There was no way Clare would leave voluntarily; besides, any court would uphold the girls' right to stay in the family home while they were still in full-time education. Was he planning to move Fran into the spare room? She couldn't believe how unrealistic he was being. He was the one who wanted the marriage to end, not Clare. As far as they knew, she didn't have a clue about the affair.

But they were wrong. That evening, Clare confronted Ned and forced him to tell her the truth. Apparently, she'd suspected for a while that something was going on. He was always having to work late, had been going to a lot of conferences and having an unusual number of dinners with clients. She'd found a couple of odd payments on his credit card statement, and a friend of hers had reported seeing him walking hand in hand with a younger woman by the canal. Fran's odd behaviour towards her boss since she'd stopped babysitting, combined with the obvious pregnancy symptoms, had clinched it.

'You're pathetic,' Clare said. 'Throwing everything away for a stupid little girl you hardly know. Did she make you feel young and sexy? Did she listen to your tales of woe about your awful wife who was too busy with her career to give you the attention you deserved?'

'It wasn't like that,' he protested. 'We didn't want it to happen, we couldn't help it. We love each other – it's not a fling, it's real. I've been wanting to tell you for months, but I didn't want to upset you or the girls.'

'Oh, just get out, Ned, and leave us alone,' she cried.

At first, he stood his ground. 'Why should I be the one to leave? This is my house too. I pay the mortgage.'

'You've got half an hour to pack,' she said firmly. 'If you're not gone by then, I'm calling the police. I'll tell them you threatened me.'

'I'll tell them you threatened *me*!'

Clare looked at him, astonished by his attitude. 'Did you really think I was going to make it easy for you? That the girls and I would move out so you could move her in? What planet are you on?'

'Okay, I'll go now, but only for the sake of peace,' he agreed, throwing a few items into a suitcase. 'I don't want an ugly scene in front of Tara and Georgia. But this is not a surrender.'

By the time Ned arrived at Fran's house, it was two o'clock in the morning. He was spitting blood.

'That house is just as much mine as hers,' he said, storming around her tiny bedroom. 'More mine actually – I pay the mortgage.'

'It doesn't matter about the house,' Fran replied. 'We're together now. We can stop creeping around, lying and pretending. We're free.'

She never went back to work, not even to collect the stuff from her desk. She got a sick note from the doctor to cover her notice period, and that was that. Her brilliant career over. Ned quickly realised that living in her flat-share, squeezing into her lumpy bed and sharing a bathroom with three strangers, was way beneath his dignity. With Clare firmly dug in at the house and the girls refusing to have anything to do with him, he had no choice but to look for somewhere more permanent. He rented a two-bedroom apartment in the city centre, a short walk from his office. It was tiny and characterless, with a balcony overlooking the railway tracks, but Fran eagerly moved in with him and started trying to turn it into a home.

Her parents were furious with Ned for getting her pregnant, as they put it – as if she'd had nothing to do with the procedure. 'You stupid fool, you've wrecked your life,' her mother told her. 'He won't stand by you, they never do. It won't last. You'll be left to bring up that baby by yourself.'

'No I won't. He's getting a divorce,' she insisted. 'We're going to get married as soon as possible.'

'Huh. If he can cheat on his first wife, he can cheat on his second,' was the reply.

Mother and daughter didn't speak for a few weeks, then Elaine softened – started knitting little cardigans and hats. Fran's aunt crocheted a blanket; her best friend Lauren embarked on a patchwork quilt. Meanwhile, the sickness abated and Fran started to bloom. She was happy drifting around the flat all day, doing little chores, browsing for baby equipment online, drawing up lists of possible names, teaching herself how to cook proper food – filling the long hours while she waited for Ned to come back from work.

In the evenings, they would lie together on the sofa, his ear pressed against her swelling belly, listening for the baby's heartbeat, feeling for a foot or an elbow. He kept saying how happy he was, but Fran knew, deep down, that he missed his five-bedroom house in one of the best suburbs of Birmingham.

'I can't run two homes,' he moaned. 'There's a huge mortgage on the property, and the rent for this cubbyhole is ridiculous. We need to divorce as soon as poss, sell up, pay off the debt and divide the spoils – move on with our lives. But she's refusing point-blank. I mean, why? When she obviously hates my guts.'

'Because it's the only weapon she has,' Fran replied. 'You've hurt her, humiliated her, made her feel unattractive and past her sell-by date. Why should she make life easy for you? Clare's a smart woman. She'll dig her heels in and make you suffer as much as she can.'

'The cow…' Ned muttered. 'It's not fair. There's a lot of capital in that house, and I need it to buy somewhere decent for us.'

She stroked the back of his head, trying in her simple way to comfort him. 'Money doesn't matter, we can manage. Who cares if she makes you wait five years for a divorce? It doesn't bother me. We love each other, and in a few months' time we're going to have a beautiful little baby. That's all that really counts, isn't it?'

'Yes, you're right, of course it is, darling,' he replied, but she didn't completely believe him.

Noah was two weeks overdue and blatantly didn't want to leave the womb. Fran had to be induced, and he was dragged out of her kicking and screaming. He was a long, skinny baby with a shock of spiky black hair that wouldn't lie down and behave. His blue eyes were alert from the beginning, and he had a solemn, knowing gaze.

Fran's mother declared that he'd been on earth before. Everyone said he was the spitting image of his father.

They were happy. Ned had the son he'd always wanted and Fran felt complete, like she finally knew what she'd been put on earth for. During that period, Clare receded into the background, her power somehow diminished by the arrival of this helpless human being. She was still refusing to sell the house or divorce Edward for adultery, but it seemed to matter less and less. Fran wished the woman would get on with her life, concentrate on her career and meet somebody new, but Clare seemed determined to cling to her bitterness. Fran felt sorry for her, but there was nothing she could do. She wasn't going to give Ned up – not that Clare wanted him back anyway.

Understandably, Tara and Georgia took their mother's side. They told Ned he was the worst father in the whole world, and at first refused to meet their baby brother. Ned was very hurt. He couldn't understand why the world wouldn't turn on the tip of his finger. He wanted everything to be lovely and normal again, all sins forgiven, everyone's wounds healed over without a scar. It was either naïveté or egoism, Fran thought. At that time, she couldn't work out which.

CHAPTER TWENTY-FIVE

Edward had locked the phone away, presumably in his office. Over the next few days, I fantasised about retrieving it and secretly ringing the number. Although I understood my husband's determination not to fall into a trap laid by the media, I couldn't stop hoping that Francesca would be on the other end of the line. Why didn't we just call and find out? It had to be worth the risk, didn't it?

I'd asked Edward not to interrogate Noah or to tell him off, and for once, he took notice of me. But he refused to share his investigations with me, or even discuss the matter at all, which I was finding increasingly frustrating. We were supposed to be a team, weren't we?

One good thing had come out of the phone drama, however. Noah was more positively disposed towards me. We didn't talk about Mummy or what had happened that night, but he seemed far more comfortable in my company. I felt as if he was starting to trust me again. His lessons with Daisy were going well, and Edward was keeping his distance, leaving it to me to liaise with her. I busied myself around the house and even made a couple of job applications to primary schools in the area.

We tried to settle into our new domestic routine, but I could tell we were all finding it difficult. The three of us played our allotted roles in the family and pretended to go about our daily business as before, but in reality, we were each leading a separate inner life. Our secrets hung in the air like motes of dust, settling on every surface.

A week went by, but try as I might, I still couldn't get the mysterious mobile phone out of my head. How had Francesca (or whoever it was pretending to be her) managed to tell Noah that it was behind the ammonite? Noah had denied that they'd used email, but it seemed the obvious method. In fact, I couldn't think of any other way – considering that Noah never left the house unsupervised.

It seemed like a sound theory and certainly worth pursuing. This time, however, I had no intention of discussing it with Edward. He would only palm me off and tell me he was already dealing with the matter. I was no computer expert and didn't know how to find deleted files. But luckily, I knew somebody who did…

The following morning, I waited until Edward had gone into his office and Daisy had started teaching, then sneaked upstairs to Noah's bedroom. I found his tablet under his pillow and put it in my bag. Then I went back down to the kitchen and left a note by the kettle, as I'd done before. *Gone shopping, back for lunch*, it said.

I didn't call ahead to say I was coming over. There was no need. My ex-boyfriend worked from home, and I knew he'd be there, holed up in the box room, staring at his computer screen. Alex was a cyber-security engineer, working for a company based in Germany that had clients all over the world. He was vastly overqualified for this tiny job; it would take him no more than a couple of minutes to find out what, if anything, was going on.

It felt strange to be walking down a street I'd lived on for nearly seven years. I knew every house, every front garden, every roadside tree. I'd put letters into that postbox, jumped over that dip in the pavement when it rained. My head felt like a cocktail shaker, mixing a heady concoction of memories, some bitter, some sweet.

For most of the time, I'd been happy living here. Flat 32a had felt like home, even though legally it only belonged to Alex. He'd taken out a loan from the Bank of Mum and Dad to buy it about a year before we met. It made complete sense for me to move in. He paid the mortgage and I covered everything else – utilities, broadband, council tax. It seemed like the most sensible way of organising things at the time, but I had no stake in the place. I assumed that when we got married, he would put the flat into our joint names, although to be fair to Alex, we never discussed it. I made a lot of assumptions back then – like thinking we were going to adopt children – and most turned out to be false.

As I walked up the front path, my hand instinctively went to my pocket for the door key. I withdrew it, wondering at myself. I hadn't been back here since the day I moved out. Marsha and I had hired a van and between us we'd hauled my belongings, haughtily refusing Alex's assistance. There were only a few items of furniture I could claim to be indisputably mine – a desk I'd had since university, a coffee table I'd found in the road and refurbished, a lamp stand passed on by my grandmother. It was a poor show for seven years of adult domesticity.

Alex answered the door, his dark curly hair unbrushed. He was wearing his typical work clothes – a pair of long tartan pants and a T-shirt I'd put in the wash a hundred times.

'Lily?' he said, rubbing his eyes as if they were deceiving him. 'What are you doing here?'

'Um… it's a bit complicated to explain. Mind if I come in?'

'Yeah, sure.' He stepped back so I could enter the small hallway. The familiarity of the surroundings was so sweet it hurt. I made an automatic beeline for the lounge, and he followed me anxiously, his mules shuffling across the laminate floor.

'Are you okay?' he asked.

'Yes, fine. I'm not moving back in, if that's what you're worried about.' We shared a clumsy laugh. 'I need a favour, that's all.'

'Oh.' He looked relieved, then puzzled. 'Want a coffee?'

'Please.'

He picked up an empty pizza box. 'Sorry about the mess. Wasn't expecting visitors.' He went off to the kitchen, leaving me alone.

I knew every inch of this room. Alex had encouraged me to put my stamp on the flat when I moved in. I'd chosen the teal and mustard colour scheme, daubing the walls with match pots before deciding on the perfect shade. I'd picked out the sofa and ordered the roller blind. I'd stood on a stepladder and hung the bamboo lightshade that was still hanging above my head. I'd thought Alex would have had the place redecorated, or at least added some new items, but he hadn't changed a thing. The room was like a museum of our relationship, curating our holidays, social gatherings, takeaways in front of the telly, birthday celebrations, dinners with friends, bad arguments, sweet reconciliations... There was even a photo of the two of us on the mantelpiece. It was all too much.

He came back with two mugs of coffee. 'So, what's this favour?' he said, sitting down next to me.

'Edward and I think Noah might be being groomed online,' I said, deciding to keep it as simple as possible. 'Somebody left him a mobile phone in a hiding place in the front garden. We need to know how he knew it was there.'

Alex grimaced. 'You're thinking it might be a paedo?'

'Possibly. I was hoping you might be able to help track them down.'

'I can try. But why don't you go to the police?'

'Edward's reluctant... He thinks we need more evidence.'

He raised his eyebrows. 'So he knows you're here, does he?'

'Of course,' I lied.

He drank some of his coffee. 'It does happen, unfortunately. Noah could have met them via some gaming platform, or in a chat room, or on a kids' website. Perverts pose as other kids. They look out for vulnerable, lonely children.'

'That's Noah,' I said. 'He spends hours gaming on his own in his room. We don't really know what he's up to half the time.'

'What sort of parental controls are on his devices?'

'I don't know. Edward would have set them up. He's very protective, I'm sure he would have thought of that.'

'Hmm... trouble is, some of these gaming platforms can circumvent parental controls.'

'Really?'

Alex smiled reassuringly. 'Yeah, but luckily, I'm an expert in digital forensics.'

I unzipped my bag and took out the tablet. 'If there's anything to find, it'll be on here.'

'Just this? No smartphone?' Alex looked surprised.

'No. He doesn't need one. He has no friends, no social life, nobody to call.' I put the tablet on the coffee table. 'Would you mind just taking a quick look?'

'I can do better than that,' he replied. 'I'll run a web browser forensic investigation.'

'Sounds great, but what does it mean?'

'I'll use forensic tools to access all his files, existing and deleted. Then I'll carve out information from his cache, history, cookies and download lists and do a full analysis of his web usage. I'll create a timeline of his activity, run a string search of keywords, obtain artefacts including images and videos, downloaded and uploaded, and give you the entire picture of what he's been up to.'

'I doubt all that will be necessary. Noah's only eight years old. He's not a tech genius.'

'No, but he may have been given instructions on how to hide stuff.'

'Oh yes, I hadn't thought of that. Okay, but how long will it take? I can't leave it with you.'

'Not a problem. I'll take a forensic image and work from the copy. Trust me, if there are any dodgy artefacts there, I'll find them, no matter how well they've been hidden.'

'Thanks, Alex. I really, really appreciate this.'

'Any time. I'm glad you came to me.' He shifted towards me and squeezed my shoulder. I felt a frisson of something pass through my body – not sexual attraction, but the memory of it, perhaps. It was time to leave.

CHAPTER TWENTY-SIX

As soon as I got home, I went straight upstairs and put Noah's tablet back where I'd found it. Hopefully, he hadn't had a chance to miss it. I found Noah in the kitchen. He was with Edward, who was making him some cheese on toast. I noted that Daisy was absent, and suspected she was having lunch in the schoolroom or sitting outside on the patio. That was where I'd spent my breaks until Edward had invited me to join the rest of the family. Then he'd started making lunch for me too. Seeing the two of them together suddenly brought it all back, and I felt a pang of nostalgia for those happy, simple days when I was just Noah's tutor and Edward my kind and rather attractive employer.

'Well? Did you find anything?' he asked me as I went to the fridge to get something to eat.

I started. 'W-what?'

'In Hampstead. I presume you've been clothes shopping.' He gestured to the note I'd left earlier.

'Oh, yes.' I took out some ham and a limp-looking lettuce. 'No… There was nothing I liked.'

Edward cut Noah's toastie into triangles and handed them over.

'Can I eat in front of the telly?' Noah asked.

'Okay, as long as you're careful. Twenty minutes, that's all, then it's back to class.'

Noah ran off to the sitting room. Edward chatted to me about the latest crisis in government while I made myself a sandwich, but I was finding it hard to concentrate on what he was saying.

My ears were on stalks, listening out for the ping of my phone. Alex had promised to get back to me as soon as he could, but he only had one speed setting – slow. In contrast, my brain was charging ahead like an express train. If Alex found an email trail or a phone number, what was I going to do about it? Tell Edward and let him investigate – or not – or take the matter into my own hands?

After lunch, Noah went back to his lessons and Edward retired to his office. 'I've got an important conference call this afternoon,' he told me. 'I mustn't be disturbed.'

I went upstairs to the bedroom and tried to read a book. It was hopeless. I felt like a teenager waiting for my new boyfriend to ring. Strange, I thought, that it was Alex I was dying to hear from.

He finally contacted me an hour later. 'Okay,' he said. 'I've been through everything on his device.'

'And?'

'Not much to report. He only games as a single player. Doesn't do social media at all. Hasn't been in any chat rooms. He had an email account, which was deleted a few weeks ago, but he hardly used it anyway.'

'Edward deleted it,' I said. 'Were you able to retrieve the emails?'

'Oh yes. He exchanged a few messages with somebody he called "Mummy", which I thought was a bit weird. She's dead, isn't she?'

Keep it simple, I told myself. 'Yes,' I replied.

'Okay, so that's your predator. A few days ago, a new email account was set up. Noah sent a message to the same address and got a reply straight away. They told him to keep a lookout in the "old place", whatever that means.' The ammonite, I thought, as Alex continued. 'Then they gave him instructions on how to delete everything and empty the recycle bin.'

'Could there be other stuff that's been wiped?'

'Not a chance. Even a factory reset can't get rid of all artefacts. I promise you, Lily, if I didn't find it, it was never there in the first place.'

'Thanks so much, Alex. You've been incredibly helpful.'

'The police might be able to find out who owns the email address.'

'Expect so,' I said vaguely.

'If you need any more help, just shout…' He paused, then added tentatively, 'It's good to be friends again. I miss you like hell, Lily. I was an idiot, saying I didn't want children. If I'd known I was going to lose you over it…'

'It was for the best all round,' I told him. 'You were honest. I actually admire you for that. Thanks again. See you around, eh? I owe you a drink.'

'I'll take you up on that. Take care,' he added, and we said goodbye.

Alex forwarded me the email exchange and I read the brief messages several times. My body was tingling with excitement. At last I could make contact with the person who'd been causing such havoc in Noah's life. I knew I might be walking into a trap, and that if Edward found out, he would be absolutely furious with me. But on the other hand, if it actually was Francesca, the positive consequences for all of us would far outweigh the risk.

I started composing a message, knowing there was a strong chance that she – or he or whoever it was – would be scared off and wouldn't reply, or would immediately delete their email account. After some long-winded attempts at introducing myself, I changed my mind and wrote only a few words.

Hello. I'm Lily, Noah's stepmother. I know you've been in touch with him. Who are you?

I waited, eyes fixed on my phone screen and the email icon, waiting for a reply to pop into my inbox. But none came. I lay back on the bed, the handset clutched to my chest. The room felt airless. I tried to take some deep breaths, but I couldn't fill my lungs properly. Time seemed suspended. I went through the whole gamut of reasons for her silence. Her phone was switched off, she was busy at work, she thought it was Edward pretending to be me, she was scared of being exposed, she hated me, she had no intention of replying, not now, not ever. She wasn't Francesca anyway, but some cut-throat journalist who didn't care how much they had to manipulate a child to get a good story.

After an hour, she still hadn't answered, so I sent another message.

Please reply. I want you to know that you can trust me. I love Noah and only have his best interests at heart.

When nothing came back, I sent a third message.

Edward doesn't know I'm doing this.

That clinched it. Within a couple of minutes, a reply came flying back.

Good. Keep it that way.

I sat bolt upright. We'd made contact at last. It was time to ask the question that had been burning inside me for ages. I punched it out with a shaking finger. *I think I know who you are, but please confirm.*

No reply.

Noah believes you're his mother. Is that true? There was a long pause, lasting several minutes. I was worried that I'd scared her off and had to find a way to pull her back.

Noah is a lovely little boy, but he is very vulnerable, I care deeply about his safety. It's cruel to lie to him. If you're not Francesca, please leave him alone.

Still nothing. I thought I'd blown it, then…

Thank you for looking after him. Meet me and I will tell you the whole story.

My heart was almost beating out of my chest. *Okay. When and where?*

I will let you know. But you must bring Noah with you. If you turn up alone, or I see Edward, the meeting's off.

I didn't hesitate in my reply. *Understood. I'll bring N. Promise.*

Thank you, Lily. Send me your mobile number and I will be in touch.

I sent it to her then collapsed onto the bed, emotionally wrung out. Tears started to roll down my cheeks. I didn't know exactly why I was crying – relief, perhaps? Or shock that I'd actually been communicating with Francesca, that she was still alive, after all this time? Part of me wanted to tell Edward straight away – the implications for him were overwhelming – but I had to keep my promise. I was sure that eventually it would be possible to clear his name, but for now, I needed to take baby steps. Of course, there were risks involved in taking Noah to meet her, but I calculated that she would be unlikely to try to snatch him if we were in a public place. Overall, I was convinced that I was doing the right thing. My actions would exonerate an innocent man and reunite a child with his mother. Everyone would thank me for saving the day.

A noise from my phone cut into my musings. A new text message had arrived. I saw it was from Francesca, and expecting details of our rendezvous, I opened it eagerly. But instead of a time and place, there were seven heart-chilling words.

Be careful, Lily. You are in danger.

CHAPTER TWENTY-SEVEN

'Come on, buddy, blow your candles out!' Ned shouted orders as he took photos on his phone. Noah puffed out his cheeks. There were only three candles to extinguish, but it took all his strength.

It was a small birthday party: just Fran's parents, her best friend Lauren, and a few children from the toddler group with mums in tow. Tara and Georgia had turned down their invitations, which had upset their father. Fran knew that Ned didn't like being outnumbered by her friends and family. He tended to sulk, or make barbed comments. She didn't want him to spoil the occasion, and it was making her feel anxious.

They all cheered and applauded. Fran hugged Noah and told him he was a clever boy, while her mother took the cake into the kitchen to cut it into slices. Elaine had made it herself and written Noah's name on the top in coloured icing.

For all their misgivings about the pregnancy, Fran's parents adored their grandson. Unfortunately, their enthusiasm didn't extend to his father. They were pleased – not to say surprised – that he'd stood by her, but still didn't trust him. Ned was jealous of Fran's closeness to them. Whenever they visited, she spent the whole time managing the relationship: smoothing over the pointed remarks, changing the subject as soon as anyone wandered into controversial territory, apologising on one or the other's behalf in private. At least she didn't have to deal with Ned's parents too – they'd decided long ago to side with Clare and their granddaughters, so she had very little contact with them. She found it sad that Noah didn't know his paternal grandparents, but Ned declared it was their loss.

The little ones went back to running around, oblivious to Ned's attempts to organise a game of hide-and-seek. The other mums were chatting with each other and Lauren was clearing the debris from the dining table.

Defeated, Ned came over to Fran, putting his arms around her and muttering in her ear. 'How much longer is this going on for?'

'Until everyone's had enough, I guess,' she replied, while retaining a fixed smile.

'I've had enough already.'

'Shh.' She wriggled free of him and went into the kitchen.

'Piece of cake?' Elaine asked, offering a plate. 'I hope it's all right.'

'It looks fantastic.' Fran wasn't feeling hungry, but it was impossible to refuse. She took a bite. 'Mmm, delicious.'

'Really? Do you think it's moist enough?'

'Yes, it's perfect.'

'A triumph,' said Lauren, with her mouth full. 'Far better than shop-bought.'

'Oh, I'm so pleased.' Elaine flushed pink with pleasure.

Fran gave her a hug. 'Thanks, Mum, you're brilliant.'

Lauren loaded the dishwasher. 'So, any news on the divorce?' she enquired quietly beneath the clatter of plates.

Fran shook her head. 'It's the same old, same old… Clare's still refusing to cooperate. We're going to have to wait until the five years are up.'

Her mother sighed. 'I feel sorry for the woman, but really, she should just give in. Why won't she agree to a divorce? She doesn't want him back, does she?'

'No way, she hates his guts. She just wants to make life as difficult for us as possible. He pays the mortgage and gives her a generous allowance for the girls, but it leaves us short. We need a bigger place, somewhere with a garden for Noah, but we can't buy anywhere until the house is sold and divided.'

'You could go back to work,' suggested Lauren as she plopped dirty spoons and forks into the cutlery basket. 'It would help with the isolation and bring some more money in.'

Fran lowered her voice. 'Edward doesn't want me to work.'

'Why not? If you're strapped for cash…'

'He says it's not worth the childcare fees.'

Elaine huffed. 'He wants to control you, that's what.'

'Not now, Mum.'

'It's true, isn't it, Lauren? We can all see it. You're stuck at home all day, hardly ever go out to see friends. And you never visit us. It's a wonder we were allowed to come to the party.'

'Please, don't start on this again,' Fran hissed, although her mum wasn't wrong. Over the past four years, Ned had become increasingly possessive. He didn't like Fran seeing friends or family, and was paranoid that she was going to leave him for someone else. He often listed the sacrifices he'd made to be with her and Noah: he'd fallen out with his parents, wrecked his relationship with his daughters and was financially stretched to the limit. If Fran left him, he said, all those sacrifices would be for nothing. Most of all, he would have lost to Clare, and if there was one thing Ned hated, it was losing.

The sound of crying was coming from the sitting room. She left Mum and Lauren to the clearing-up and went to see what was going on. It turned out that one of the little girls had hit Noah on the head with a wooden xylophone. Her mummy was telling her off, so now she was crying too. It wouldn't take long for the other kids to join in. Ned shot Fran an exasperated look.

'Who'd like a party bag to take home?' she shouted above the din. The mums took the hint, and within minutes, coats were bundled on, party bags, cake and balloons were thrust into grubby little hands, and the customary thanks and farewells were exchanged. Her parents and Lauren stayed on for a cup of tea, then gave Noah a final kiss and cuddle and left.

'Thank God for that,' said Ned, closing the door on them. But Fran was fighting back tears. Spending time with her parents and best friend had reminded her of how confined and lonely her life had become. She loved being Noah's mother, and loved Ned too, but she missed her previous life – working in event management, seeing university friends, going to clubs and music festivals, staying up all night watching films or talking politics, travelling, dancing, sleeping on beaches… She felt middle-aged. Fran had also made sacrifices, but Ned didn't see it that way.

At the beginning, Fran had felt sorry for Clare, and incredibly guilty for having taken away her husband. But over the years, she'd come to hate her. The way Clare was able to hang onto her anger was impressive. She had no qualms about poisoning Tara and Georgia's minds, encouraging them to mess their father around and use emotional blackmail to get what they wanted. Annoyingly, Ned fell for it every time. Tara passed her driving test (lessons paid for by Daddy) a few months after turning seventeen, and turned up at their flat driving a brand-new Mini. Ned swore that he hadn't bought it for her, but Fran later found out that it was an early eighteenth birthday gift. Georgia wouldn't be far behind, and no doubt would also expect her own car. And yet Ned was constantly complaining to Fran about overspending on food and clothes for Noah.

'It's Clare's fault,' he said whenever they rowed. 'If she'd agree to sell the house, we'd both have a nice lump sum to play with. The place has gone up massively in value – there's easily enough capital there. If only I could get my bloody hands on it.' He went to a solicitor to see if he could force Clare to sell the house, but was advised not to even try. Clare had a right to stay in the family home until the youngest child was eighteen – that was two and a half years away. Ned was beside himself with frustration.

His behaviour changed. He started to arrive home late two or three evenings a week, missing Noah's bath and bedtime story. When Fran questioned him, he claimed he was in the middle of a big deal and needed to stay behind for conference calls with clients who lived across the pond. She suspected he was seeing another woman. Her mother reminded her that he'd lied to Clare throughout their affair, so it wasn't surprising that he was now deceiving Fran. She found herself checking up on him – raiding his pockets for hotel or restaurant receipts, examining his dirty washing for lipstick marks. If she'd known the passcode for his mobile, she'd have ransacked his texts and call history, too. Of course, she never found any definite proof – Ned was too smart and experienced an adulterer to leave traces behind. But she caught him lying in small ways. Bit by bit they added up to something, but she couldn't work out exactly what.

'I don't think I can go on like this,' she confessed to Lauren one evening on the telephone. It was late at night and Ned still hadn't come home. 'I love him, but I know he's hiding something from me, and I don't trust him. He keeps talking about getting married the moment his divorce comes through, but I'm not sure any more.'

'You've got to listen to your feelings,' Lauren replied. 'If you have any doubts at all, get out while you can. You're still young, you've got so much potential. You'll easily find a job and be able to support Noah. You don't *need* Ned.'

'But he's given up so much to be with me. If I walked out on him now, he'd have nothing and nobody.'

'That's no reason to marry him.'

'I know, but…'

She had several conversations like that with Lauren over the next few months. She even admitted to her mother that she was having second thoughts, and Elaine told her to leave him straight away. Ned sensed that Fran was pulling away from him, but it only made him hold onto her more tightly. He decided her parents were a bad influence and said he didn't want them to visit so often. Whenever Fran arranged to go out for the evening with friends and asked Ned to look after Noah, he let her down at the last minute, saying he had to stay late at the office. She realised that if she *was* going to leave him, she would have to do so stealthily. He'd virtually lost his daughters and he would not want to lose his son too. There was no doubt that he would come after her and beg her to change her mind, so she would have to cover her tracks.

She made plans in her head, imagining a new life for her and Noah. They'd go somewhere far away, maybe even abroad. Her parents said they would help financially until she managed to get a job. But as soon as she sniffed the possibility of freedom, Ned would start being super romantic and attentive towards her, saying how much he loved her and how he'd die if she ever left him.

'Only a year to go, darling,' he'd say. 'Then we can marry. We'll have something small and discreet, maybe go to the Caribbean and have a ceremony on the beach, just the three of us. I love you so much, I can't imagine life without you.'

One evening, he hired a babysitter and took Fran out to dinner in a very fancy restaurant. He got down on one knee and presented her with an engagement ring – a stunning diamond solitaire.

'How on earth could you afford this?' she asked, taken aback by its beauty. 'You're still paying off your credit cards.'

'Never you mind,' he replied. 'It's the least you deserve for all the trouble I've caused you.' Still shocked, she let him slip the ring onto her finger.

Fran realised she should have rejected him there and then, should have told him that their relationship was over, that she would never be his second wife. But she didn't have the guts, couldn't face his anger or his pain.

If only she'd managed to walk out *before* Clare had died…

They heard the news from Tara first. She rang her father on his mobile, screaming so hysterically that he couldn't make out what she was saying. He was extremely shocked; they all were. Although Fran had known that Clare had a severe nut allergy, she'd never dreamt she might actually die from it. She was too alert, too organised to let such a tragedy happen. And yet somehow she'd accidentally bought an artisan loaf containing traces of sesame seed, brought it home and made herself a sandwich with it. She'd gone into anaphylactic shock and was unable to use her EpiPen. The investigation surmised that it had fallen from her grasp and rolled under the sofa, although nobody knew for certain exactly what had happened.

As Ned was still technically next of kin, he was the first to receive any information. He supported his daughters as much as they would let him, handled all the funeral arrangements, engaged solicitors to handle probate. Fran was pushed to the sidelines and told that her presence was inappropriate. She and Noah were an embarrassment – they gave the lie to Ned's role as grieving husband, although she sensed he was feeling more guilt than grief.

There was no ignoring the fact that he had got what he wanted and more. Full ownership of the family home automatically passed to him; he could sell it when he liked and didn't have to give Clare her share. There was no longer any need for a messy, expensive divorce. He was free to remarry, but out of respect for Clare and her daughters, he decided they should wait until the dust had settled on the grave.

He played his public role well, but didn't know how to behave when he and Fran were alone. He wouldn't meet her gaze, terrified that she might detect a glint of triumph or relief in his eyes. Fran knew he felt bad for having wished harm on Clare. She felt it too.

Six months passed, and life was settling into a new normal. Ned was more relaxed about their financial situation and spending more time at home. He was trying to build bridges with Tara and Georgia, who were still living in the big house. Tara was legally an adult now, and Georgia was sixteen; they insisted they were quite capable of looking after themselves. Besides, there was no room for them in Ned and Fran's flat.

Ned was trying his best to help the girls and working hard at being a good dad to Noah. He told Fran how much he loved her every single day. She told him she felt happier too, but secretly Clare's death still weighed heavily on her shoulders, and she couldn't shake it off.

'We need a break. Let's go away together, just the three of us,' Ned said one day when he came home from work. He'd just completed a lucrative deal and was due a fat bonus.

'I'd really like that,' Fran said. 'Noah would love a holiday.'

'Leave it to me, I'll book it.'

She told herself she would give their relationship one last chance. They'd been through so much, made so many sacrifices, hurt so many people in order to be together. *Take what you want*, said God in the old Spanish proverb. *Take it and pay for it*.

She had no idea the price would be so high.

CHAPTER TWENTY-EIGHT

I was shocked by Francesca's text. Why did she think I was in danger? I'd never felt physically threatened by Edward. When I'd confronted him over his lies, he'd been gentle and full of remorse. Maybe the Ned that Francesca knew was a different man. Maybe he'd been violent towards her and that was why she'd had to run away. I was ready to hear her side of the story, and had so many questions to ask her.

I had no idea what had happened to her over the past five years or why she'd done what she had, but it didn't stop my imagination going into overdrive. I explored every possible scenario, changing my levels of sympathy for her accordingly. Maybe she'd had a breakdown and had only recently recovered. Maybe she'd been in an accident and lost her memory, recovering it again after years of therapy. But in that case, why hadn't she simply come forward? Why hadn't she gone straight to her parents, or her friend Lauren? Why, instead, had she gone to great lengths to contact Noah in secret?

There was of course another explanation. She was mentally unstable and out for revenge on Edward, using me as part of her plan to kidnap her son. What if I were in danger from *her*?

Finally she texted me the details of our meeting. It was to take place in two days' time, at four in the afternoon. The venue she'd chosen was a large park not far away. It was the ideal venue, well used and very public. In addition to the vast lawns, there was a café with an outdoor terrace, a couple of ponds, an ornamental garden and even a children's petting zoo. We were to meet at the playground. I was to find a nearby bench. She would wait until Noah was busy playing, then join me. I replied saying we would be there.

She didn't ask me to send a picture of myself, which made me think she already knew what I looked like. She'd probably looked me up on social media, or had been spying on me from a distance, watching through binoculars from a car parked opposite the house. I'd never seen anyone who looked like her, but then the only image I'd seen was that grainy press photo Marsha and I had found on the internet, her face staring blankly above a juicy headline.

I turned my attention to Noah. There was no way I could tell him in advance that we were going to meet his mother. For a start, she might get cold feet and not turn up – that would have a devastating effect on him. Also, I didn't want to ask him to keep the meeting a secret from his dad. No, I would have to find some other way to lure him. After a lot of thought, I came up with what I hoped was a solution.

'You can take tomorrow afternoon off,' I told Daisy. 'We'll pay you, of course. Noah has a dental check-up.'

'I can take him if you like,' she offered.

'Hmm, thanks, but it's better if I'm there. In case he needs a filling or something.'

Noah was none too pleased when I told him. 'I hate the dentist,' he said.

'If you're good, I'll take you for a treat afterwards.' Some intense bargaining followed, and in the end, I had to promise not only a trip to his favourite burger bar, but a new video game as well. I didn't care. Now he was willing, and that was all that mattered.

We took the bus to Golders Green, a novelty in itself for Noah, who usually went everywhere by car. The weather was hot and the journey was uncomfortable. We hardly spoke, both of us sweating with anxiety, albeit for different reasons. He was anticipating the dentist's drill and I was worrying about putting him in a far worse situation. What if he went into shock when he met his mother and I had to call an ambulance? What if she tried to abduct him and I had to call the police? As the bus groaned and stuttered its way through Hampstead, then skirted the edge of the Heath, I tried to think of a way to break the news. A few gentle sentences washed around my mouth, but none of them tasted right, so I swallowed them down. It was too late to tell him. I would have to stick to my original plan.

I reacted as if I'd just received a text, took out my phone and pretended to study the screen. 'Oh no,' I said. 'Your appointment's been cancelled.'

'Yay!' A broad smile crossed Noah's face and he instantly relaxed back in his seat.

'What shall we do? I know, let's go to that lovely big park instead. We might as well.'

'Or we could just go for a burger,' he suggested hopefully.

'Hmm, it's a bit early. Let's run around the park first and build up an appetite.'

He didn't argue, rising quite readily when we reached the bus stop outside the park gates. As we plodded down the hill, I tried to disguise the fact that my knees had turned to jelly and I could hardly walk. My pulse was racing and I was hyper-alert, eyes darting this way and that, as if we were about to be ambushed. Whenever I spotted a woman with long brown hair, my heart jump-started.

The park was heaving with schoolchildren, small gangs of teenagers, mothers and babies, dog-walkers of all ages, elderly couples snoozing on benches, lovers picnicking under the shade of a tree. The café was doing a roaring trade and there was a long queue at the ice-cream hut.

'Can I have a lolly?' asked Noah.

'Not now,' I said tensely. 'After we've been to the play area.'

He stopped. 'But I'm thirsty.'

I took a bottle of mineral water from my bag. 'Here.'

He shook his head defiantly. 'I want a lolly.'

'You can have one later. If you're good,' I added pointedly. He didn't move, just gazed longingly in the direction of the ice-cream hut. 'Come on, Noah, let's go and play. They've got an assault course, remember? Monkey rings and cargo nets and stuff. You can pretend you're a special ops soldier.'

'It's too hot.'

'Then go on the swings, that'll cool you down.' I looked at him imploringly. 'Please? Come on. If you want that video game...'

I set off and he grudgingly followed, muttering to himself. Taking a sneaky glance at the time, I realised that we were a few minutes late. Francesca was probably already there, waiting for us. My mouth dried and I took a swig of water, then picked up the pace.

The playground was busy with kids of all ages. They crawled and toddled and ran and climbed over the equipment like manic ants, while their various carers – mothers, fathers, grandparents, nannies, au pairs – chatted in small groups or lost themselves in their mobile phones. Unsurprisingly, all the benches were taken, so I found a spot at the edge of the area and sat down on the grass.

'I'll stay here,' I said. 'You go and have fun.'

Noah wandered off in the direction of a large construction of ladders, bridges, towers, tunnels and slides. I took a deep breath and looked around, half expecting Francesca to appear at my side in a puff of smoke. But ten long minutes passed and there was no sign of her. I started making excuses. She'd been delayed, she'd lost her nerve, she'd decided she didn't trust me... I checked my phone, but there were no messages.

Seventeen minutes had ticked by now. I started to feel like a fool. What if I'd been texting with a journalist, who'd lured me here under false pretences? Somebody could be snapping photos of Noah right now. Edward would be flaming mad when he found out.

We needed to go. I stood up and called out to Noah, but he was crawling through a tunnel and couldn't hear me. I was moving forward to extract him when a finger tapped me on my shoulder and a voice said softly, 'Hello, Lily.'

I instantly spun round. An older woman was standing there – in her fifties, plump and short, with cropped brown hair. Weirdly, I'd already spotted her wandering around the play area observing the kids, but hadn't imagined, not even for a moment...

'I'm sorry I kept you waiting,' she said. 'I needed to check Ned wasn't with you, and I wanted to spend some time watching Noah. Couldn't take my eyes off him. He's grown so much.'

'Who are you?' I croaked.

'Sorry, I should have said. I'm Elaine, Noah's grandma.'

I stumbled back. 'But I thought... I was sure... you said you were Francesca.'

'No, love, I never said. You assumed and I didn't correct you, that's all.' She smiled at me apologetically. 'I felt bad about tricking you, but I didn't think you'd meet me otherwise.' I stared at her, confounded. 'Shall we sit down?' I nodded, but only because I felt too weak to stand. I sank back onto the grass and she lowered herself next to me.

'So... it's been you all along,' I said, my voice still hoarse.

'Yes.'

'I really believed you were Francesca.'

'My daughter's dead,' Elaine replied unflinchingly.

'You don't know that for sure.'

'I do. I've always known it, deep inside, I knew it from the moment we realised she was missing. She would never have left Noah, you see, no matter how bad things were at home. She loved that boy so much.' She paused and looked across to the assault course. At that moment, Noah emerged from the tunnel and started climbing down the rope ladder. 'He's so beautiful,' she said. 'Her hair was like that when she was his age. Different colour, but it had a life of its own. I couldn't do a thing with it.'

'He's a very special child,' I agreed. We watched him play for a few moments, then I turned to her and said, 'Edward told me he'd had to take out an injunction against you, forbidding you from seeing Noah.'

'That's right. Easy when you've got money.'

'How did you manage to keep track of where he was?'

'Private detective,' she said. 'Cost us all our retirement savings, but it was worth it. Ever since they moved to London, I've been coming down about once a month, hanging around Hampstead, walking past the house, just hoping for a glimpse of him, that's all. I realised he wasn't going to school and was being taught at home. He had no life – he was being kept a prisoner. It was breaking my heart. I knew I had to make contact somehow.'

'So how did you do it?'

She smiled, remembering. 'One day last summer, I followed Noah and his teacher to the lido on the Heath. She was an older woman and I had a feeling she might be sympathetic to my situation. I decided to risk it. While Noah was having his swimming lesson, we got into conversation. I told her I was his grandma, and how I'd been prevented from having contact. Kim remembered the case. She was very sympathetic. It turned out she really disliked Ned, so she said she was happy to be a go-between. But she didn't want to get in trouble over the injunction. We decided to pretend I was Francesca. I wasn't happy about it, I hated deceiving Noah, but there wasn't much choice. Kim set him up with an email account and we exchanged a few messages. Then he told Kim he didn't like writing emails. He wanted to send me pictures instead.

That's when she came up with the idea of the secret box in the garden. She did all the toing and froing. I sent her letters and gifts for Noah and she put them in the box for me. Then she collected his pictures from the box and put them in the post.' Her eyes misted over. 'I'm so grateful to Kim, she's a wonderful woman. I was desperate and she saved my life.'

'But then she was sacked,' I said. 'Was that because Edward found out?'

'No. He said she was too strict, but the real reason he got rid of her was because she was getting too close to Noah.'

'And after that?'

'We carried on, although it hasn't been easy. Kim's been fantastic, she comes and checks the message box when she can. She thought you might take over from her, but then Noah told me you'd married Ned.' She grasped my hand and held onto it tightly. 'Don't be a fool like my daughter,' she whispered. 'Get out while you can.'

'I accept that something terrible happened to Francesca, but there's no proof that Edward killed her,' I said, trying to wrestle free. But she wouldn't let me go.

'Fran sent a text to Lauren shortly before she disappeared,' she said. 'She told her she was going away for a few days.'

'Yes, Edward told me that. He said she was depressed and she needed a break, away from Noah, away from *him*. He didn't report her missing because he was trying to give her some space.'

'Lauren got the impression the three of them were going somewhere together. For a holiday,' Elaine continued. 'The police couldn't find any record of a booking, but I think they did go somewhere. Noah knows what happened,' she said. 'Wherever they went, I'm sure he was there, that he witnessed her death.'

'But wasn't Fran last seen alive in Birmingham, going into her flat?'

'Yes, but I keep thinking that neighbour was mistaken. When Fran disappeared and Noah came to us, he was very withdrawn, wouldn't speak for weeks. He had terrible nightmares, woke up screaming. The police brought in people trained in interviewing children. They tried all sorts of tactics – dolls, pictures, games – but they got nothing out of him. Has he ever said anything to you? *Anything* that might give us a clue?'

Her words dug deep into me. 'No, but he remembers something,' I said. 'Edward insists he can't possibly, that he was too young. I've had this horrible feeling that he's been trying to suppress Noah's memories.'

'I knew it, I knew it.' Elaine looked at me appealingly. 'Look, all I'm asking is for you to take him to see a specialist.'

'Edward won't allow—'

'Then do it behind his back. Please. Help me, Lily,' she begged. 'For Noah's sake. The truth is inside him and it needs to come out before he gets any older, before he forgets forever.' She stood up. 'Please think about what I said. You know how to get in touch.' She took a last look at Noah. 'Give my darling a special kiss for me, will you? And be careful. I meant what I said about you being in danger.'

She walked away, up the hill towards the park gates. Emotion welled up inside me. I wanted to scream and thump the ground, but I had to put on a face of calm. After a couple of minutes, Noah jumped off the swing and ran up to me.

'Who was that lady?' he asked.

CHAPTER TWENTY-NINE

I couldn't tell Noah that I'd just been speaking to his grandmother. It was out of the question. For a start, it was illegal for her to have contact with him, and I didn't want to land her in any trouble. But I was more worried about how Noah might react to hearing such extraordinary news. He might be upset, or overjoyed, or angry; there was no predicting or controlling it. So I replied to his question with some bland remark about her being a stranger passing the time of day.

I hadn't detected a glimmer of recognition in his eyes and was sure he'd enquired out of curiosity, no more. That was sad in itself, although not surprising. Five years had passed since Elaine had looked after him during those strange, stressful months. In the intervening time, Edward had deliberately erased any memories Noah would have had of her. There'd been no mention of her existence – no meetings, no calls, no photos of her in the house, no birthday cards or Christmas presents arriving in the post. I could hear Edward rationalising his actions, insisting Francesca's parents were evil people and that he'd had no choice but to cut them off. He always framed himself as the main victim in the tragedy, but there was no getting away from the fact that Noah had been treated cruelly.

I watched Elaine as she walked back up the hill towards the park entrance, sighing with relief as her diminishing figure finally vanished from sight.

'Can I have my lolly now?' Noah asked, cutting into my thoughts.

'Of course,' I said.

We left the playground and walked back up the hill. I was all shaken up inside, as if a giant had picked me up and swung me around by my ankles. As we stood in the queue at the ice-cream hut, I longed for some alcohol to dull the sensation. A gin-, vodka- or whisky-flavoured lolly would do, but sadly none were on offer. I bought a vanilla cornet with a chocolate flake, but one lick made me feel sick, so I tossed it into the nearest bin.

Noah was rotating his dripping lolly, his tongue flicking over it like a lizard. 'Burger bar next,' he announced.

'You haven't finished that yet,' I said.

'I have nearly. Look!' He held up the almost empty stick. The edges of his mouth were stained red. It looked like badly applied lipstick and I wanted to rub it off with a baby wipe. I also wanted to cuddle him and tell him that everything was going to be all right, even though I knew with more certainty than ever that it wasn't.

I let him drag me to his favourite fast-food restaurant and allowed him to order a super-whooper burger and a large chocolate milkshake, knowing he wouldn't finish either. I bought a black coffee, sipping at the burning liquid as I observed him trying to get his small jaws around the overstuffed bun. Ketchup dribbled down his chin and bits of pickle and tomato fell onto the table. I stole a chip, much to his consternation, then realised I couldn't stomach it. We didn't talk much, but I sensed that our relationship was healing.

'I can still get my video game, yes?' he asked, rubbing his fingers with a small paper napkin. He was determined to make me deliver on every one of my bribes, despite the fact that he hadn't gone anywhere near the dreaded dentist's chair.

'Suppose so,' I replied. 'But when I make the new appointment, there won't be any extra treats, okay?'

He pulled a grumpy face. 'It's not fair, I hate the dentist.'

'Clean your teeth properly and you won't have anything to worry about.' I gathered up our debris. 'Come on, let's go home.'

We walked back to the bus stop, a new atmosphere of calm between us. On the journey home, Noah stared out of the window and I relived the encounter with Elaine. She hadn't revealed anything I didn't already know or that Marsha hadn't told me, yet it had felt like I was hearing it for the first time. Elaine's was a mother's truth, spoken from the heart. She knew her daughter wouldn't have taken her own life, or voluntarily abandoned her little boy, or stayed away for all those years without getting in touch. I'd tried to defend Edward, but my argument had sounded hollow and false. I no longer believed in his innocence, and the realisation shocked me.

I'd walked out of the trenches, crossed no man's land and entered enemy territory. I was on the other side now. The only way I could go back to Edward was as a spy.

Going undercover in my own marriage was hard. Part of me wanted to pack a bag and leave immediately, to get as far away as I could. I didn't want to see Edward or let him touch me, and the prospect of sharing his bed made my toes curl. But I would have to stay and pretend that everything was fine, for a while at least. I had to try to find out what had happened to Francesca, and I could only do that by remaining on the inside. Edward had managed to elude a team of detectives, so there was no logical reason why I, a complete amateur, should have more luck. But as his loyal and trusting wife, I was at least better placed. It wasn't a role I relished playing, nor was I sure my acting skills were up to the task, but I was going to give it my best shot. I owed it to Francesca and the people who loved her.

My transformation was complete. A new woman went home that evening and kissed her husband on the mouth. She cuddled up to him on the sofa, steadying her trembling hand when he gave her a glass of wine. She lied about the cancelled trip to the dentist, then faked a headache and went early to bed. When he followed an hour or so later, she pretended to be asleep so that he wouldn't disturb her, but in fact she was wider awake than she'd ever been in her life.

The next morning, I rose early and went for a walk on Hampstead Heath. I'd hardly slept and my brain was feeling both sluggish and on fire. One restless night lying next to Edward was enough to convince me that I didn't want to stay with him a moment longer than was absolutely necessary. He was a smooth operator, cold-blooded and extremely smart. There was no point in my hanging around hoping he might accidentally let something slip, or get drunk and confess all. It just wasn't going to happen. However, there was a chink in his armour. Noah.

So far, Edward had managed to control his son by hiding him away and feeding him lies. He pretended to protect him, but in fact the only person he was protecting was himself. That was why he was so against Noah having therapy – he was frightened of what might come out. Noah was like a safe: seemingly impenetrable from the outside, but if someone could get close enough to listen to the clicks, they might crack the combination and open him up.

I wanted to help Elaine, but I couldn't send Noah to a specialist interviewer without Edward finding out. To begin with, I'd need parental consent, and I doubted that a stepmother's permission would be accepted. The police had such people, of course, but there was no point in going to them unless I had fresh evidence of Edward's guilt.

As I trod the familiar paths of the heath, I racked my brains for a sign, a clue, a lead. Any little thing. It was warm for so early in the morning. The leaves were cracking in the heat and the grass had yellowed, yet amazingly it was still only June. Soon the summer break would be upon us. Edward didn't seem interested in taking vacations. I remembered the luxury honeymoon I'd been promised that had never materialised. We didn't even have a family holiday booked.

I sat down on a bench. Why was I even thinking about that? The last thing I wanted was to go away with that man. Then suddenly an image swam into my inner vision – I could see it so clearly it startled me.

Noah and Mummy enjoying a picnic on the beach. Sand, sea, yellow cliffs, a stripy lighthouse, a red boat...

Noah had drawn the picture from memory, I was sure of it, but when I'd shown it to Edward, he'd insisted he didn't recognise the place. However, I'd already seen similar photos in the family album. That was the first time I knew he'd lied to me. When the album mysteriously disappeared, I'd believed it was the photos of Clare he was trying to hide, but it was nothing to do with her. It was the location he didn't want me or Noah to see. Was this where Francesca had been before she went missing?

I felt briefly exhilarated by my powers of deduction, only to come back down to earth with a thump. There hadn't been any photos of Francesca and Noah in the album, and she hadn't gone missing at the seaside. As I'd reminded Elaine, she was last seen alive going into her flat in Birmingham, which was about as far from the coast as you could get. Yet I still had this nagging feeling that the seaside was somehow connected to her disappearance, maybe even her death.

I stretched out my legs, feeling the warm morning sun on my bare skin. Where was this place? We lived on an island with thousands of miles of coastline, and although Noah's picture seemed detailed and specific, in reality there were hundreds of locations that might offer a match. I needed to narrow the search, find out more information. Maybe there were other family photos that hadn't been destroyed, old holiday brochures, hotel bills, petrol or restaurant receipts, credit card statements...

I needed to get back into that office.

Another torturous week passed before I found myself alone in the house. Edward had bought tickets for the three of us to go to a basketball showcase in London. Maybe he sensed that the atmosphere between us was strained and was trying to bring us back together as a family. Noah, who'd been shooting hoops in the back garden with Daisy and watching games online, was excited. He'd never been to a professional sporting event before.

I pretended I was looking forward to our outing, although I had no intention of going. That afternoon, a few hours before we were supposed to leave, I developed one of my 'migraines' and declared that I was too ill to attend.

'Can Daisy come instead?' asked Noah. 'She loves basketball.'

'That's a great idea,' Edward replied instantly, then backtracked a little. 'Only if that's okay with you, Lily.'

'Absolutely,' I said. 'It would be a pity to waste the ticket.'

Daisy was only too eager to drop her plans for the evening, which didn't surprise me. Although Edward was trying hard not to flirt with her in front of me, it was obvious that there was a spark of attraction between them. I'd found them chatting in the hallway at the end of the day, and sometimes Edward went into the schoolroom for no apparent reason. Usually I found it annoying, but tonight it served my purpose that Daisy would take my place.

Brandishing a packet of painkillers, I went upstairs to my room and drew the blinds. I sat on the edge of the bed and waited, alert as a cat watching for a mouse to venture out of its hole.

They seemed to take forever to leave the house, but eventually I heard the front door slam and went to the window. Edward opened the passenger door of the BMW for Daisy, and put his hand on her shoulder as she sat down. I watched as the electronic gates opened and the car glided through. The gates rumbled shut and the car disappeared from view. Even though I would have hours to conduct my search, I immediately left the bedroom and ran downstairs.

I stood in the office and surveyed the possibilities. The filing cabinet seemed like the best place to start. I pulled on the top drawer, and to my surprise, it opened. Edward had either forgotten or been in too much of a hurry to lock it. It was the stroke of luck I needed.

The top and second drawers were full of work folders, all meticulously labelled. I clearly wasn't going to have any joy there, so I tried the bottom drawer instead. This was where Edward kept his personal and domestic files – folders labelled *Doctor*, *Dentist*, *Insurance*, *Useful Info*, *Family*, *Leisure*. Hoping to find some holiday information, I took the leisure folder out first and, kneeling on the floor, trawled through its contents. There was an application form for a gym that I didn't even know Edward belonged to, some details about kids' holiday camps I was sure Noah had never attended, and a glossy brochure for luxurious tours of South Africa, India and Japan. Disappointed, I put the folder back in its place.

I delved back into the drawer, pulling it out as far as it would go. There was an unlabelled folder right at the back with a purple envelope file inside. Sensing this might contain something Edward wanted to keep private, I took it out. It contained correspondence between himself and some lawyer, and after reading a few of the letters, it became clear that they concerned Clare's estate. She had died, it seemed, without making a will, and as she and Edward were not legally divorced or even separated, all her assets had passed automatically to him.

It had been a while since I'd even thought about Clare, but the letters revived my curiosity. I sat back on my heels with the pile of paper on my lap, reflecting how unjust it had been for Edward to inherit everything when he'd run off with another woman.

I started to skim-read the correspondence, most of it boring and irrelevant. But then I found a typed list detailing Clare's various bank accounts together with details of her assets. I studied the poignant inventory of items that had been placed in storage – clothes, make-up, bedding, ornaments, books, furniture, garden tools, kitchen equipment – and felt incredibly sad.

When I turned over the page, I discovered that Clare had also left a property, which she owned outright with no mortgage. It was called The Lookout, and the address was Watcher's Rock in East Sussex. I took out my phone and typed in the postcode. My heart performed a double somersault as I stared at the pin in the map.

The house was right on the coast.

CHAPTER THIRTY

'Hey, Noah, guess what – we're nearly here!' There was no reply, so Fran twisted around to look at him. His head had lolled forward onto his chest and was bouncing gently to the rhythm of the car. 'Typical! He's been demanding to see the sea ever since we left home, and now we're finally here he's fallen asleep.'

'I'm not surprised.' Ned yawned. 'I could do with a nap myself.'

'I did offer to share the driving.'

'Yes, but you know I get carsick if I'm in the passenger seat.' He changed gear as he carefully rounded a sharp bend, then speeded up again as the road straightened out. 'Not to worry. We're nearly there now.'

She'd been dreaming of an island in the Mediterranean, a villa with a pool or a hotel with a kids' club and babysitting service, so when Ned announced he'd booked an old coastguard cottage on the East Sussex coast, it had been hard to hide her disappointment. She knew the English Channel would be rough and cold, that the beaches would be painfully shingly, that the wind would whip around their ears and it would probably rain every day.

'It's beautiful down there,' he'd said, trying to reassure her. 'Noah will have a whale of a time, I promise.'

They passed a row of bungalows, all shapes and sizes, some smart and gleaming but many in need of a lick of paint. Fran stared at them curiously – retirement homes or holiday lettings, she guessed. There was a small supermarket and a run-down pub, no other shops.

After about a quarter of a mile, the houses petered out, giving way to a holiday park full of static caravans and an outdoor café, beyond which there were no buildings at all, just the long, straight road with the sea wall on their left and marshland to their right. The land was astonishingly flat, dotted with natural pools. Sheep and cows grazed peacefully in the open fields, while birds circled noisily over the water.

Ned had been right, it *was* beautiful, in a bleak kind of way, but Fran still thought it was a strange choice of location for their getaway. He usually had far more sophisticated tastes. This place was defiantly unpretentious; it was like being back in the 1950s, when English seaside holidays were all that were available to most people.

'It's a pity,' she said, gazing at the steep grassy bank. 'We must be only a few metres from the sea, but we can't see it.'

'If the wall wasn't there, the whole area would flood,' he replied, swerving to avoid a pothole. He'd been driving increasingly irritably since they'd left the motorway, revving at traffic lights, overtaking slow drivers, swearing when they got stuck behind a tractor for a couple of miles. As Fran gazed out of the car window, absorbing the new surroundings, she felt puzzled. Why had he brought them here?

Cars were parked nose to tail in the lay-bys. A catering mobile was selling burgers, and an ice-cream van purred as customers queued for cones. Elderly couples were strolling along the top of the sea wall, their dogs scampering back and forth. A bare-chested guy in tiny shorts jogged past. Ned veered to the right as a group of kids wandered into the road, wrapped in towels, wet hair plastered against their faces, lips blue with cold.

'It's busy now,' he said, 'but everyone's gone by six o'clock. That's when the locals go down to the beach. When the tide goes out, it's amazing. So beautiful.'

'You seem to know a lot about the place,' she said after a pause. 'Have you been here before?'

He bit his lip and she sensed him cursing inwardly. 'Um… yes. Many times, actually.'

'Oh, I see.' She processed the news slowly. 'With Clare?' He nodded. 'Stop the car, please,' she cried. 'Stop right now! NOW!'

He slammed on the brakes, pulled into a space behind a motor home and turned off the engine. Toxic silence filled the inside of the car. Fran glanced over her shoulder, anxious that her shouting had woken Noah, but thankfully he was still asleep.

'Okay,' she said, lowering her voice to a hard whisper. 'Would you like to tell me what the hell is going on?'

Ned sighed. 'I'm sorry. I was going to tell you in advance, but I was worried you'd refuse to come.'

'Too right I'd have refused. I thought the whole point of the holiday was to try to put her out of our minds and move forward. I can't believe you'd do this. What's wrong with you?'

'I know, I'm an idiot. I should have warned you.' He banged his head on the steering wheel. 'It's just so hard to talk about it. I thought maybe once you saw the place, you'd understand.'

'This cottage you've booked,' she said slowly. 'Is this somewhere you used to go with her?' He looked away as his silent reply sliced into her. 'It is, isn't it? Oh God! How could you do this?'

'It's her cottage. *Was* her cottage, I should say. She inherited it from her parents.'

'Right… so now it belongs to you?'

'Yes. Much to Tara and Georgia's annoyance.'

'But you've never mentioned it. Not once, in all the years we've been together.'

'Haven't I?'

'You know full well you haven't. You told me you'd booked it through an agency.'

'I don't think I actually said that.'

'Yes you did! When I asked you to send me the link, you said it wasn't advertised online.'

'Which is true.'

'That's hardly the point. You lied to me.'

'I'm sorry. It felt awkward.'

'I suppose you used to come here every summer.'

He nodded. 'Christmas too, sometimes. The girls were supposed to come down and help me sort things out, but you know how it's been… They haven't been able to face it. I was hoping you…'

'Oh, right, now I understand,' she said sarcastically. 'We haven't come for a holiday at all, we've come to do a house clearance.'

'No, not exactly.'

'This is ridiculous. I can't do this.' She tugged at the door handle, but the car was safety-locked, the button on his side of the dashboard. 'Let me out. Now.'

'Why?' He looked at her, dismayed. 'Where are you going?'

'Home.'

He put his hand on her arm. 'Don't be silly, Fran. There are no direct trains, it'll take you all night.'

'Then you'll just have to turn around and drive us back.'

'But Noah will be so disappointed. He's been looking forward to it so much.'

'Don't try to guilt-trip me. This is your fault.'

'If you don't like it, we'll leave tomorrow. I promise. Please. We've come so far. We have to see it through.'

She turned to him. 'What do you mean?'

He inhaled deeply. 'There's something I need to tell you, and I can't do it anywhere else.'

'Why are you being so mysterious?'

'Please. Trust me.'

'How can I when you lie to me all the time?'

'I know.' He hung his head. 'But tonight, once Noah's in bed and asleep, I'll tell you the truth. All of it.'

Her heart froze. He was going to confess that he'd been seeing somebody else, or that he'd gambled away all his money, or lost his job… Anything was possible.

'Okay.' She took her hand off the door handle and rested it in her lap. 'But we can't go on like this. You've got to stop trying to manipulate me.'

'Yes, I will. I promise. Everything's going to change. Please, just give me this last chance to put it right.' He looked at her hopefully. 'Deal?'

She sighed wearily. 'Yes… deal.'

He restarted the engine and pulled out into the road. They drove the rest of the way in silence. The landscape became increasingly desolate and unpopulated. After a few more minutes of following the sea wall, they took a right turn up a small private lane, flanked on either side by overgrown hedges. Ned confidently rounded a corner, then the rough track took a sharp upwards incline.

'What is this place?' she murmured.

'It's called Watcher's Rock. Farmers brought their sheep and cattle up here when the land flooded. That was before they built the sea defences, of course.'

At the very top was a tall, exaggeratedly thin house, Victorian and vaguely Gothic in style, rising out of the rock. It was far from the cosy seaside cottage she'd been imagining. The pebble-dashed walls were a sandy grey, the black paintwork was peeling off and the window frames were rotten. The coastguard must have felt very lonely and isolated living up here, with not another house in sight, she thought, deciding that she didn't like it.

She got out of the car and walked to the end of the lane, where the gravel stopped and grass took over, uneven and pitted with rabbit holes. She stepped to the edge, intending to look over, but the land fell away sharply beneath her, and she moved back, her stomach lurching.

Keeping her feet firmly planted, she bent forward, craning her neck. Below was the marsh, green and spongy, thick with ferns and wild flowers. She could just make out a rough winding path leading down, but it looked slippery and dangerous.

She straightened up. There was a stunning view whichever way she looked – flat fields criss-crossed with ditches to her left, rolling hills behind and a large sandstone cliff to her right. But like a spoilt child, it was the sea that demanded her attention. She'd been expecting brown-grey waves churning with sand, but instead she was confronted by a stretch of pale aquamarine, as still and solid as a sheet of glass. She wanted to run down to the beach and throw stones at the water, to see if they would bounce off.

But right now, she had to compose herself, fulfil her side of the bargain. Noah would have woken by now. She knew he'd be very excited to be at the seaside and didn't want to spoil it for him. Yet the thought of stepping into that cottage – *her* cottage – and pretending that everything was absolutely fine was making her feel physically sick.

She walked back down the lane. Ned had removed their luggage from the car and lined it up in the brick-paved courtyard. Noah was already standing by the door, waiting impatiently for his father to let him in.

He waved at Fran happily as she walked up. 'We're here!'

'This wretched key,' muttered Ned, fiddling with the lock. He gave the door a kick and it burst open, bouncing on its hinges. As he bent down to pick up the post, Noah ducked under his arm and charged into the sitting room. Fran followed cautiously behind.

The house smelt damp and musty. There were dead flies on the windowsills and cobwebs hanging in the corners. The furniture looked worn but comfortable, as if it had been there a long time.

'It's pretty basic,' Ned admitted. 'Two bedrooms on the first floor and an attic room with a funny little balcony at the top. We're not sure, but we think it must have been a lookout platform, from when it was a coastguard cottage, that is.'

Don't say 'we', she thought.

Noah seemed already at home. He ran around like a cat spraying its territory, then dived headlong onto the sofa. 'I want to go to the beach!' he shouted.

Ned smiled. 'So do I, but first we have to unpack. That's the rule.'

Noah groaned.

'Why don't you take him for a run around?' Fran said. 'He's been stuck in the car all day – he could do with the exercise. I'll stay here and make up the beds.'

Ned looked at her uncertainly. 'You sure?'

'Of course. Don't worry, I'm not going to burn the place down. It'll still be here when you get back.'

'Don't you want to come with us?'

'Not now. I'd rather stay here and look around by myself, if that's all right. It'll help me adjust.'

'Of course, that makes sense. Whatever makes you feel comfortable.' He smiled again, but weakly. 'I'm cooking tonight, remember?'

'Great.'

'Come on then, buddy. I'll race you.' He kissed her on the cheek as he passed. Then he and Noah ran out together, leaving the front door open. Fran closed it behind them and exhaled. It was time to explore the mausoleum.

She opened the kitchen cupboards and looked at the pots and pans. She pulled out drawers and rummaged through their dusty contents – walking maps, a ball of garden string, an envelope of seeds, a timetable for local buses, various chewed pencils, a couple of joker cards that had escaped the pack. She burrowed into the sideboard and found board games and jigsaw puzzles, a set of champagne flutes with amber stems. She ran her finger along a shelf of wilting paperbacks, their spines cracked white with bending. There were photos of Clare everywhere, but she tried not to catch her eye, afraid she might be glaring at her, mouth twitching in indignation.

There was a door at the end of the room. Fran opened it and found a narrow flight of stairs that hugged the side of the house. She'd promised to unpack and make the beds, but she suddenly felt uneasy about going up. The master bedroom was on the top floor, and she guessed they'd be sleeping in Clare and Ned's old bed tonight.

Why had he really brought her here? she wondered. It wasn't for a holiday, that was certain. She wanted to hear what he had to confess and yet didn't want the burden of knowing. Ned believed he could trust his lover, but he was making a mistake. There'd been a time when Fran would have kept his darkest secrets, when she would have done everything in her power to save him, but those days were a distant memory. They were already broken. The hard shell of their love had been smashed to pieces by the storms they'd been through, and all that was left were a few grains of sand.

CHAPTER THIRTY-ONE

I started searching online for images of the place. Was it a sandy or shingle beach? Was there a lighthouse nearby? A sailing club, perhaps? I tried looking on Google Earth, but all it would give me was an aerial view. The sea, a pale ribbon of sand edged with a dark line of coast road, and on the other side, flat fields criss-crossed with dykes. I zoomed in, but the image blurred, so I had to retreat. Street View wasn't available. There were no streets, I guessed. No houses. No community.

There were a few solid shapes dotted across the landscape, but they looked like barns or sheds. One of those grey squares had to be The Lookout, but viewed from above and at such a distance, it was impossible to identify it.

I sat back, thinking. Edward had never mentioned the place, but then he'd never talked to me about his life with Clare, so that didn't necessarily mean anything sinister. After she died, he could have taken Francesca and Noah to the house for a holiday. If it was the first time Noah had seen the sea, it would have made a lasting impression on him. Hence the strong memories.

A noise broke up my thoughts. I jerked my head up, ears pricked. Listening. Had I imagined it, or had someone just opened the front door? I heard footsteps in the hallway. Now they were heading this way. It must be Edward. Why had he come back? I quickly gathered up the papers and stuffed them back into the filing cabinet, closing the drawer a split second before he entered.

'Lily!' He jumped back in surprise. 'What are you doing in here?'

'I, er...'

'Forgot the bloody tickets, didn't I?' he said, not waiting for my reply. He picked up an envelope from his desk.

'Yes, I was about to call you,' I lied. 'I was upstairs and I suddenly had this weird feeling that you'd gone without them.'

'Oh? Spooky.' His suspicious gaze flew around the room, then landed on me. 'Got to dash. We're going to be late now.' He tucked the envelope into the inside pocket of his blazer and left the room.

'Have a good time!' I called after him.

The front door slammed shut and I finally breathed out. That was close, I thought. Edward hadn't challenged me, but I knew he hadn't bought my excuse either. I would need to have a better story prepared for when he came home after the game. Leaving the office, I went to fix myself something to eat.

It was nearly 11 p.m. when Edward and Noah returned. I was already in bed, watching television. I quickly switched it off when I heard them coming up the stairs.

Edward poked his head around the bedroom door. 'Ah, you're still awake,' he said, mildly surprised. 'I'm going to run Daisy home... Don't like the idea of her catching the Tube at this time of night.'

That was how the affair with Francesca started, I thought. 'Okay,' I replied evenly. 'How was the basketball?'

'It was fantastic. The tricks those guys can do... amazing. Noah was very inspired. Wants to be a professional basketball player now.'

'He's a bit small, isn't he?'

Edward smiled. 'Yeah, but he can dream.' He studied my face. 'How's the migraine?'

'On its way out, I think.'

'Excellent… You'll feel better after a good night's sleep.' He kissed me lightly on the head. 'Daisy's waiting in the car. I'll try not to wake you up when I get in.'

As soon as he left, I got up and went to check on Noah. His bedroom door was closed, so I knocked, and for once he allowed me to come in. He was already in his pyjamas and was lying in bed reading the event programme.

'Hi. I gather you had a good time,' I said.

He nodded. 'It was really cool.'

I sat down on the edge of his bed. 'Dad tells me you're keen to play. Maybe there's a junior basketball team you could join.'

'Hmm… I won't know anyone.'

'Not at first, but you'll soon make friends.'

'Dad wouldn't let me, anyway.'

'He might. I'll talk to him… Anyway, it's late now, time for sleep. You can read the programme in the morning.'

'Okay.' Noah reluctantly closed the brochure and put it under his pillow. Then he lay down on his back and stared at the ceiling, his blue eyes open wide.

'Night-night,' I said, standing up. 'Sleep well.' I waited for him to respond, but he seemed wrapped in thought. I moved towards the door, and was about to leave the room when he spoke.

'Lily?'

'Yes?' I waited again. 'What is it?'

'That lady… the one you were talking to in the park…'

I caught my breath. 'Ye-es? What about her?'

'I think I know her.'

'Really?' I went hot and cold. So he *had* recognised Elaine after all. 'Who is she?'

'I don't know her name, but I've seen her before. Somewhere. Can't remember where.'

I pretended to consider. 'She must live nearby. You've probably seen her in the street or down by the shops.'

'Maybe... I think she knows me too, because when I was playing on the swings and things, she kept staring at me. Every time I looked over to you, she was doing it. Just staring, like she wanted to eat me up. It was a bit creepy.'

'Oh, that must have been my fault. I was telling her about you. Don't worry about that.'

'But now her face keeps coming into my head and it won't go away.'

I didn't know what to say. It was as if a box of memories had been dragged out from the back room of his consciousness, unlabelled and tightly sealed. Now it was sitting there, getting in the way, demanding his attention. He was only young – he didn't know what to do. Should he open it and find out what was inside, or shove it into a dusty corner and try to forget?

'That's strange,' I answered lamely.

'Yes. And last night I even had a dream about her.'

My anxiety went up a notch. 'Did you? I hope it was a good dream. She seemed like a very nice person, you know, she would never harm you.'

'It was a sort of good dream,' he replied. 'We were walking along and she kept making me hold her hand, only I didn't want to. I ran away from her and she chased after me. It was a bit weird.'

'Sounds it.' I bent over and smoothed the duvet cover, although what I really wanted to do was smooth his troubled mind. I was tempted to tell him the truth there and then, but I couldn't. The timing was all wrong. It was late; Edward would be back soon. Noah might get upset. He'd had a fun evening and it would be a shame to spoil it.

'I have weird dreams too sometimes,' I said. 'Everybody does. It's normal.'

'Mine aren't normal,' he muttered.

'What do you mean?'

'I get nightmares.'

'Oh, you poor darling, I'm really sorry to hear that… What sort of nightmares?'

'Scary ones.'

'What happens in them?'

'Can't tell you. If I talk about them now, they'll come back.'

I gave up probing. 'We don't want that. Dream about basketball instead. You can be the hero, scoring the winning goal.'

'They're not goals, they're points,' he corrected, before turning his little face to the wall and closing his eyes. 'Night, Lily.'

'Goodnight, Noah.' I stood up and turned off the light.

I went back to bed and tried to sleep, but it was impossible. I couldn't stop thinking about Clare's house on the coast. I tried to picture it in my mind, but all I could see was Noah's drawing – the beach, the yellow cliff, Mummy in her stripy triangle dress. I wanted to ask Noah if he remembered going to a place called Watcher's Rock, but I didn't dare.

His memories were definitely starting to emerge. I was really encouraged that he'd recognised 'that lady in the park', although I felt bad for not being able to explain who she really was.

What other treasure was stored inside his young brain? I wanted to get inside his head and remove all the dusty boxes. I wanted to tear off the wrapping and open the lids, take the memories out and examine them like a detective. If only I had the training and skills to talk to traumatised children, I thought. Elaine was right, Noah needed to see a specialist. But how could I take him to one without Edward finding out?

Nervous exhaustion eventually took over and I fell into a light, fretful sleep, only to be woken by the sound of the electronic gates opening outside. The security light came on as Edward's car purred onto the driveway. I turned over and picked up my phone. It was nearly 3 a.m. Why was he back so late? Then I remembered that he'd taken Daisy home. That was three hours ago. Geography wasn't my strongest subject, but I knew it didn't take *that* long to drive to Archway and back.

I fumed as I waited for him to come up to bed. Was history repeating itself here? Daisy was young and attractive – I'd already caught him flirting with her. Was I so obsessed with the past that I'd become blind to what was going on in the present?

Edward came into the room and started getting undressed. I flicked on the bedside lamp, blinking at the burst of light.

'What time do you call this?' I said, sounding like somebody's mum.

'Sorry, did I wake you?' He unbuttoned his shirt and threw it at the laundry basket.

I sat up, folding my arms across my chest. 'What's going on, Edward?'

'Nothing.' He took off his trousers, then his socks.

'It took a long time to do nothing.'

'I was yawning, she offered me coffee. We stayed up talking, that's all.'

'Talking. Yeah, right,' I huffed.

He got into bed next to me. 'Give me a break, Lily. I'm tired.'

'I've a right to know what you were doing.'

'And I've a right to know why you were snooping around my office.'

'I already told you, I went to check that you'd picked up the tickets.'

'Bullshit.'

'It's true.'

'Anything you want to know about my business, just ask.'

But I wasn't prepared to let him duck the issue. 'You used to give Francesca lifts home after she babysat. That's how your affair started. It's your modus operandi.'

'My modus operandi? What's that supposed to mean?'

'You were gone for three hours.'

'So what? We got talking. It was interesting stuff, mainly about Noah, if you must know. She's very interested in forest schooling, thinks it might suit him.' I snorted disbelievingly. 'God, I give the girl a lift and you immediately think I'm going to chuck you out and put her in your place.'

'You did it before,' I snapped, unable to stop the words leaving my mouth.

'And what a brilliant idea that turned out to be,' he replied sarcastically. 'Like I really want to do that again.'

'I'm tired,' I said, turning off the light and lying back down, right on the edge of the mattress, as far away from him as I could get. 'I need to sleep.'

'Yeah. Me too,' he grunted.

The room was black and silent. He rolled onto his side, facing away from me. His body was like a furnace, radiating heat throughout the bed. I kicked my feet free of the duvet and tried to settle. But I was annoyed with myself. I shouldn't have reacted so strongly. I should have kept my cool and played my cards close to my chest. What did it matter if he had sex with Daisy? My marriage was over. She could have him, for all I cared.

Edward's voice suddenly pierced the darkness. 'I'm sorry,' he said, his tone completely changed. 'I shouldn't have stayed so long at Daisy's. Nothing happened, I promise, but I can see how it looked. It was stupid of me. Especially with how things are between us.'

I hesitated. 'What do you mean – how things are? They're normal, aren't they?'

'Come on… don't pretend. You've been really off with me lately. Avoiding me. I know you didn't want to come out with us tonight. I'm afraid that you don't love me any more, like you think you made a big mistake.' It was as if he'd just been reading my thoughts.

'Don't be silly,' I muttered.

'Things haven't been the same since you found out about Fran.' He sighed. 'I knew it would happen. That's why I tried to hide it. I was terrified that you'd believe all the lies.'

'Can't talk about it now… Let's sleep.'

'No, please, listen…' His voice choked. 'You don't believe them, do you? Please tell me you don't.'

I couldn't answer.

We lay there quietly for what felt like a long time.

'I didn't kill her,' he said finally. My body shuddered involuntarily. 'I swear on my children's lives, I didn't do it.'

'Please. I don't want to talk about it now.'

He turned over and shuffled up behind me, placing his arms around my waist. I felt his breath on the back of my neck. 'Don't leave me,' he whispered into my hair. 'I love you, more than you can ever know. I can't lose you. Fran took everything from me – my job, my reputation, I nearly ended up with a life sentence. But you saved me.'

'Shh…'

'Don't worry about Daisy, she's Noah's teacher, nothing more. You're my wife, the only one I want. We're together forever, Lily.' He squeezed me tight. 'I promise you. Forever.'

But it didn't feel like a declaration of love; it felt like a threat. I knew in that moment that Edward had seen right through me.

I lay there as tense as a block of wood, waiting for him to fall asleep. Typically, it only took a few minutes for him to drift off. He snored for a short while, then his breathing became deeper and quieter. His hold around me weakened and it was easy to wriggle free without disturbing him. I slid carefully out of bed. Taking my phone, I grabbed yesterday's clothes off the chair and crept out of the room.

The house was still. I quickly dressed in the family bathroom, then tiptoed downstairs. Fortunately, my handbag was in the sitting room. Everything I absolutely needed was in there – cash, bank cards, driving licence. The rest of my belongings I would have to leave behind, for now at least. This was Edward's house, bought with the proceeds of his out-of-court settlement, a monument to his innocence. In the months I'd lived here, I'd made virtually no impression on the surroundings. But I wasn't a ghost. I was very much alive, and I wanted to keep it that way.

Carrying my shoes in one hand and my bag in the other, I soft-footed into the hallway and gently squeezed open the front door. Outside, the air was warm and scented and the sky was fading up from deep blue to lavender. I crossed the driveway and pressed the button on the front gates, glancing up anxiously at the bedroom window as they clunked open. I slipped through the gap, then hurtled down the hill, running and running without looking back, only stopping once I'd turned the corner and was out of sight.

Breathless, I took out my phone and ordered a taxi to take me to Marsha's flat. At this early hour, it was the obvious place to go. My mother lived two hours' drive away, and besides, she was not the right person to turn to in such circumstances. She wouldn't listen to me properly, and would most likely tell me off for walking out on such a wealthy husband.

The nearest car was five minutes away. I confirmed the pick-up point and sat down on a garden wall to wait, hoping and praying that Edward wasn't coming after me. It was the longest five minutes of my life.

CHAPTER THIRTY-TWO

Marsha opened the door in a flimsy dressing gown, her limbs still heavy with sleep. 'Hey, Lily, what are you… It's four o'clock in…' Her eyes flicked across my face. 'What's up?'

'Sorry it's so early. Can I come in?'

'Yes, yes, of course.' She ushered me inside and gave me a hug. 'Are you okay?'

'Not really.'

'It's Edward, isn't it? Oh God, what's he done? Did he hit you, because if he did—'

'No, nothing like that. I just had to get out, couldn't stay there a second longer.'

'Come up, I'll make some tea.' I followed her upstairs, and she sat me down at the kitchen table and put the kettle on. 'How long were you waiting? Sorry, I thought the knocking was in my dream.'

'Sorry, I should have rung. Wasn't thinking straight.'

'Let's stop apologising to each other, eh?' She smiled. 'Breakfast tea? Rooibos? Green with jasmine? Manuka honey? You name it, I've got it.'

'Just normal, please. I need as much caffeine as I can get. I didn't sleep last night.'

Marsha popped two tea bags into a pot. 'Okay. So what's happened? Come on, spill the beans.'

I held up my hand. 'Before that, can I just say sorry for not being in touch for ages. I was angry with you for going behind my back, but most of all I was angry because I knew you were telling me the truth and I didn't want to hear it. I wanted Edward to be innocent and I couldn't tolerate anything that contradicted it.' Tears pricked my eyes. 'But now I realise you were right all along. I've been such a fool.'

'No, you haven't. You've been in an impossible situation. Hey, shh... don't cry,' she soothed, sitting down and taking my hands. 'We're best friends, always have been, always will be. Now put me out of my misery and tell me what's been going on.'

She poured the tea and I told her about the last few weeks, stopping every so often to blow my nose. There was a lot to fill her in on – discovering the mobile phone, asking Alex for help, meeting Elaine, finding the legal documents in the study and finally the confrontation with Edward over Daisy. Marsha's face was a study in shock-horror – mouth gaping, eyebrows almost up to her hairline. She punctuated my story with increasingly colourful curses, all directed at Edward.

'I'm so glad you're out of it now,' she said, once I'd brought her up to date. 'I was really worried about you, didn't know what to do. I kept imagining you in that house with that murderer... I felt helpless.'

'He swears on his children's lives that he didn't kill Francesca.'

She shuddered. 'That's so disgusting.'

'But what if he's telling the truth, Marsha? Nothing was ever proved against him. Somebody else could have killed her.'

'He's a liar – you've proved *that* a thousand times over.'

'Yes, I know, but lying about his past falls way short of actually committing murder. And there have always been good reasons for the lies.'

'There are never good reasons,' she insisted.

I looked into my mug for a few seconds. 'Come on, we all do it from time to time. Little white lies, lies by omission...'

'He's in an entirely different league, girl. Edward married you under false pretences, and he's been emotionally abusing Noah for years. Ask yourself why. If Edward is innocent, why would he try to destroy his son's memories of his mother?'

I shook my head. 'Yes, yes, you're right. That's the conclusion I've come to. It's terrifying, but…'

'Well, I think you should go to the police,' she declared.

'I can't tell them I have a hunch that maybe my husband just might be guilty after all. I need new evidence.'

Marsha steadied her gaze on me. 'Then you'll have to find some.'

'I know… Is it okay if I have some toast or something?' I asked. 'I'm really hungry.'

She nodded, rising immediately and taking a loaf out of the bread bin. I watched her cut two chunky slices and stuff them into the toaster. I'd used that dodgy piece of equipment dozens of times, and remembered how badly it coped with too-thick bread. It comforted me somehow, anchoring me to reality. She refreshed the pot, while I waited for the edges of the bread to burn and the popping-up mechanism to fail.

'Let's work on stuff we actually know,' Marsha said, once she'd extracted the toast with a knife. She found a jar of marmalade at the back of the fridge and put it on the table. 'This house by the sea, for example. Why has he never mentioned it?'

'That's not unusual. He's never spoken about his time with Clare. I always thought it was out of respect for me, but maybe…'

'…he has something to hide,' she finished for me. 'If it's by the sea, it was probably a holiday cottage. For weekends, summer holidays… They probably went there for years.'

I ate my hard, slightly charcoal-tasting toast. 'Yes. The photos in that album were taken when the girls were little.'

'Have Tara and Georgia ever mentioned the place?' I shook my head. 'Don't you think that's suspicious in itself?'

I shrugged. 'Not necessarily – we're hardly best mates.'

'What you really need,' Marsha said, flicking a stray braid behind her shoulder, 'is some proof that Edward took Francesca and Noah there.'

'All I've got is the seaside picture Noah drew.'

'Which could be of anywhere. Even copied out of a book.'

I licked my sticky fingers. 'No, I don't think so. Noah has got a strong memory of his mother associated with the place. Now I'm wondering if it was the last time he saw her.'

'Hey, Lily, you could be on to something here.'

'What I'd really like to do,' I said, adding my plate to the small pile of yesterday's washing-up, 'is to take Noah there and see if he recognises it.'

'You think it might trigger a memory?'

'Yes. If it's the same place.'

She let out a low whistle. 'Isn't that a bit risky?'

'Yes. But I've got no choice. I'd be very careful – I wouldn't push him to remember anything. I just want to see.'

Her expression told me that she was still unconvinced. 'Do you know what happened to the house?'

'No, I didn't get the chance to do any more rummaging. He probably sold it years ago.'

'Let's find out. Do you have the address?'

Marsha wrenched her phone free of its charger. I gave her the postcode and she started searching.

'There's this website. My mum goes on it every time a house in their street is sold. She's the world's nosiest neighbour.' She scrolled down the screen. 'Hmm, interesting.'

'What?' I said eagerly.

'It's not on here. No properties with that postcode have been bought or sold since records began.' She put down her phone. 'Which means it's still in the family.' Her fingers went to work again. 'Maybe it's a holiday let.' But her searches for the property via letting agents and self-catering holiday companies yielded nothing.

'I'm going to have to go there,' I said. 'See the place for myself. But there's no point without Noah.' I screwed my face up in frustration. 'And now I've walked out and left him on his own with that... that monster.'

'Well, I'm glad. I hated the idea of you being there.' She gave me one of her winning smiles. 'I suppose you'd like your old room back.'

'Yeah, but you've got that dancer living there.'

'She moved out last week – I was about to place an ad. But the room's yours if you want it.'

'Oh yes please, Marsha,' I said, hugging her. 'Thank you, thank you.'

It was strange but also comforting to be back in my bedroom at the top of the house. Marsha lent me some clothes and I bought some toiletries and underwear to tide me over. I knew I'd have to go back to Hampstead at some point to collect the rest of my things, but for now I was content to manage with the minimum.

Edward didn't call or text, nor did he try to contact me via Marsha. I was relieved, because I didn't want to talk to him, but I was also surprised, given all the guff I'd had from him that night before I left. For someone who wanted to be with me forever, he seemed to have accepted my departure very readily. Was he too proud to beg, or did he just lack normal human feeling?

I thought about him a lot as I drifted around Marsha's flat, trying to fill the long hours while she was out at work. I pulled our relationship apart then put it back together, like I was doing the same complicated jigsaw puzzle over and over again. I thought about Noah too, and wondered how he was getting on. I felt bad about deserting him, particularly when we had started to bond again, but I hoped, when this whole nightmare was over, that he'd eventually understand. At least he got on well with Daisy. She was a nice woman, even if she *was* screwing my husband.

My husband. How it had once thrilled me to use that term. Now it just filled me with embarrassment. What had I been thinking, marrying him so soon after we'd met, when I knew virtually nothing about him? My biggest worry then had been his first wife and her daughters. I'd thought Tara and Georgia were jealous of me and resented my taking over. Georgia had been okay, but her older sister had given me a hard time. But now I was seeing everything in a new, disturbing light. They'd actively taken part in deceiving Noah into believing that they shared the same mother. And Tara had made a few dark comments to her father about being careful. Did the girls know what had really happened to Francesca? Were they in on the secret too?

After three days, it was Daisy who broke the silence, not Edward. She rang me on her mobile on her way to work.

'I know it's none of my business,' she began, 'but I felt I just had to call you.'

'What about?' I asked cautiously, wondering whether Edward had asked her to contact me.

'Edward said you'd walked out on him because he got back so late the other night.'

'It's a lot more complicated than that,' I replied. 'And you're right about it being none of your business.'

'Okay, yeah, I just…' She paused, and the sound of traffic filled the void. I knew exactly where she was, standing outside the Tube station, which was on an extremely busy road. Her voice became more breathless as she trudged up the hill. 'I promise nothing happened between us,' she continued. 'He gave me a lift home and he was obviously exhausted, so I asked him if he wanted to come in for a quick coffee. We got talking. I must have bored him stiff, because he actually fell asleep on the sofa. Even started snoring. It was embarrassing – I let him snooze for a bit, then I woke him up and told him to go home.'

'Okay, fine, whatever. I couldn't give a toss what happened,' I replied, although her story sounded believable.

'I mean, he's a lovely guy, but not what I usually go for. Bit old for me, if I'm honest.'

'Like I said, I don't care.'

'But *I* do. I've got a boyfriend. Anyway, I'm not that kind of woman. I don't want to be held responsible for—'

'You're not, I already told you. You were just the last straw, that's all.'

'Except nothing happened.'

'Okay, I believe you. Thanks for calling.'

'I like you, Lily,' she carried on determinedly. 'I like Noah, and Edward, I like all of you. I love my job and I hate the thought of causing a problem for the family.' She paused for breath. 'And Noah misses you.'

'I doubt it.'

'No, he does, big time. He keeps asking me where you've gone and when you're coming back. I think he's really rattled by it. Today he asked me if I thought you were safe.'

'Oh God,' I murmured.

'It was such a strange thing to say, it really bothered me. That's why I decided I had to call you and try to clear things up. For his sake.'

Waves of guilt washed over me. It was obvious that Noah was making a connection between his mother's disappearance and my sudden absence. 'Please tell him I'm absolutely fine. I'm taking a break, that's all.'

'Of course. And if there's anything else I can do…'

'Actually, there *is* something,' I said, an idea suddenly popping into my head. 'Could you tell Noah to look behind the ammonite tomorrow morning?'

'The ammonite – what's that?'

'He'll understand. I'm going to send him a little message and some chocolate, so he knows I'm okay.'

'Oh, right. Good idea. Yeah, I can do that, no worries.'

'And probably better if you don't tell Edward – Noah should wait until his dad has started work. It's a secret game, you see, between the two of us.'

'I understand … Look, I'm outside the house now and I'm already late…'

'Thanks, Daisy, and don't forget to tell Noah about—' I added, just before she said goodbye and ended the call.

I immediately went to Marsha's desk and found some plain paper and a pen. I sat down and composed a note.

Hello Noah,

I hope you are well. I am missing you a lot. Would you like to go to the seaside with me for the day? Just the two of us. If the answer is yes, please meet me by the front gate at six o'clock tomorrow morning. It's a secret pirate trip. Don't tell anyone. Maybe we'll find some treasure!

Love, Lily xxx

CHAPTER THIRTY-THREE

Fran woke at dawn, roused by a cacophony worthy of Old Mac-Donald's farm – baaing sheep, mooing cows, screeching gulls, and birds tap-dancing on the roof above her head. Getting out of bed as quietly as she could, she went to the window and pulled back the curtains, drawing in her breath as the view was revealed, even though she'd seen it the day before. They were at the very top of the house, on the highest point of the rock, and the views were stunning. The sea had changed colour from yesterday and was now a deep navy blue, flecked with white. The tide was out, exposing more beach. Seabirds swooped across her vision as if choreographed for her entertainment. A jackdaw landed on the railing of the lookout platform and gave her a dead-eyed stare before taking off again.

Behind her, Ned was sleeping as peacefully as a child, the deep bowl of his conscience emptied at last. He should have poured his guilt into the sea, she thought, but instead he'd filled her up with it. His confession sat uneasily in her stomach, like a bad meal.

She unlocked the door and stepped onto the rickety wooden platform. The salty air whipped across her face, fresh and purifying. She tried to exhale the knowledge from her lungs, but it wouldn't shift. Staring at the sea, she replayed the previous evening.

Noah was in bed – it was late, and they'd drunk a lot of wine. The candle flame was making shadow puppets of them on the wall.

'I did it for you,' Ned said, leaning across the table and stroking her hair. 'I did it for *us*.'

The ghostly light cast a sheen over a framed photo on the mantelpiece – a picture of Clare with her beloved girls, taken long before Fran came on the scene. She sensed Clare's spirit moving restlessly around the room, looking for an object to throw at their heads, but the house remained still and quiet as it absorbed Ned's words into its walls.

'Why are you telling me this?' she asked.

'I don't know exactly.' He ran a finger round the rim of the glass. 'I'm sick of living a secret inner life, I guess. I've told a lot of lies these past few years, I've hurt people I love dearly and made impossible demands of you. But enough is enough. I want a fresh start for the three of us. You, me and Noah.'

She thought of that dear little boy lying upstairs dreaming of sandcastles and rock pools. 'I'm just not sure it's possible, not now… This has changed everything.'

Outside, the night was full of stars and waves were dragging themselves over the shingle. She felt a tug as he tried to reel her in and land her on the beach. He tipped her chin and kissed her so passionately that when he withdrew, she found he'd stolen her breath.

She was still breathless that morning as she leant over the balcony railing, competing and contradictory thoughts churning in her head. Ned was dozing deliciously in the bed he used to share with Clare. He believed he'd sorted it, as he might solve a problem with a neighbour or conclude a tricky business deal, but Fran knew he was wrong.

A short while later, Noah came running down the stairs in his pyjamas and found Fran sitting in the armchair by the window. She was dressed and breakfasted, drinking her second cup of tea.

'Hungry?' she asked, and he nodded. 'One bowl of Cheerios coming up.' She untucked her legs and stood up, moving into the kitchen. Noah jumped onto the sofa and bounced on it like a mini trampoline.

'Careful!' she warned, picking up the cereal packet. 'If you fall and break your arm, you won't be able to go to the beach.' He stopped instantly, landing on his bottom.

'Come and sit at the table, please.' She put his bowl of cereal and a small spoon on the table.

He climbed onto a chair and started shovelling. 'Can we go to the beach again?'

'Of course,' she said.

The staircase resounded with Ned's heavy downwards tread. He opened the door and came into the room, smiling and rubbing his hands together. 'Wow! It's a beautiful day out there!' He winked hello at Fran – breathtakingly casual, she thought – then ruffled Noah's hair as he so often did. 'Still in your pyjamas? You need to get some shorts on, buddy.'

'I want to go swimming.'

'And we will, promise. But we have to wait until the tide comes in.'

'Why?' Fran asked.

He lowered his voice. 'Because it's dangerous. People get caught in the rip tides and they can't get back to land. There are drownings every summer along this stretch of coast.'

'Is it safe for Noah, then?'

'At high tide, yes. Don't worry. I'll be with him.'

'And we're going in the boat,' said Noah, chasing the last few hoops of cereal around his bowl.

Ned pulled a face. 'Hmm… we'll have to see about that. Depends on the weather.'

'But you said!' He jumped down from the table.

'What boat?' Fran asked.

'Daddy's boat! The red one.'

'It's a small dinghy with an outboard motor, that's all,' Ned explained. 'I keep it moored outside the angling club. Actually, I was surprised it was still there, it's been so long. God knows what state it's in.'

'Somehow I don't see you as a fisherman.'

He moved into the kitchen and started to make himself some toast. 'I'm not. I thought it would be fun, but I discovered I get seasick. I need to sell it.' He turned to Noah. 'Get dressed, buddy. Then we'll go and make a sandcastle.'

'And a tunnel, and a bridge.'

'We'll build a whole city if you like,' he laughed. 'But not if you're still in your PJs!'

Noah scooted off. Ned waited until he was out of sight, then turned to Fran, his jolly dad mask slipping to reveal a serious expression. 'Are you okay? Did you manage to sleep?'

'A bit. Woke up very early.'

'That happens here. It's the dawn chorus.'

'No, it was because of last night.'

'Oh…' He put his toast down and looked at her intently. 'How are you feeling? I mean, really.'

She shrugged. 'Don't know. Sort of okay, I think. Shocked. It's a lot to take in.'

'When I woke up and you weren't lying beside me, I thought…'

'No, I'm still here. Just about.'

He smiled. 'I can't tell you how happy that makes me. Come down to the beach with us. It's so beautiful, great for clearing your head. The wide-open horizon…'

'You don't have to convince me.'

'I love you,' he said. 'It's going to be all right. Promise.' She didn't tell him that she loved him too.

Noah bounded down the stairs a couple of minutes later. He was wearing shorts and a T-shirt that he'd managed to put on back to front. He put his jelly shoes on and stood by the kitchen door.

'Daddy! Let's go now!' he declared.

They trooped out of the house. Edward shut the back door and put the key under a flowerpot. 'It's very safe here,' he said.

After collecting some buckets and spades from the coal shed, they strolled down the hill. The sun was shining, the sky was cornflower blue and the temperature was already rising. When they got to the bottom, they made Noah wait to cross the coast road with them, even though there were no cars coming in either direction.

'The lay-bys will already be packed further up the coast,' said Ned. 'But nobody comes this far down. There are no facilities here, thank God.'

Noah remembered the way from yesterday, bounding up the concrete steps, his bucket banging against his legs. Fran and Ned followed close behind, shouting at him to wait, but his attention was gripped by the flat wet sand below. Ned chased after him, but Fran stopped at the top of the sea wall, pausing for a few moments to take in the scene. Close up, everything seemed more alive, although the black weathered groins that held the shingle in place looked like tombstones. She lifted her head and sniffed. The air tasted of seaweed. Gulls and terns circled above her head, their discordant cries underscored by the constant background roar of the sea.

She waded through the bank of deep dry shingle, shaking a foot every so often to release a pebble that had lodged itself between her toes. As soon as she reached softer ground, she took off her sandals, carrying them by their heel straps. It was good to feel the cool wet sand beneath her feet. For a few seconds, she had the childish urge to slap about and make prints, or write her name in large letters, or splash in the icy rivulets trickling in from the sea.

But instead, she stood and watched father and son, who'd chosen their spot several yards ahead and were digging a channel. They seemed to have already forgotten about her.

She walked towards them, raising her voice above the wind. 'Where's this boat, then?' she asked.

Ned straightened up and waved with his spade. 'Over there. You can't see it from here, but there's a low building tucked behind the sea wall. The boats are tied up at the top of the beach.'

'Okay, thanks.' She turned to go back, but he grabbed her arm.

'Only I wouldn't go there if I were you.'

'Why not?'

'It's where the locals hang out.'

She screwed up her face. 'But there aren't any locals. Nobody lives around here.'

'They come from the villages inland. Old guys mostly.' He glanced swiftly at Noah to check that he was fully absorbed in his digging, then dipped his voice. 'They all knew Clare and her family. If they find out I've brought you here…' He pulled an apologetic face.

'What, you think there might be a lynching?'

'Don't be silly. But you might get a frosty reception, a few raised eyebrows at the very least.'

'I see. You're ashamed of me.'

'No, I'm thinking of *you*. I don't want you to feel uncomfortable.'

'Okay,' she sighed, pushing a strand of flapping hair behind her ear. 'I'll go and hide in the cottage, then.'

'That's not what I meant. Stay and help us.' Ned proffered his spade.

'No thanks. I'm going to walk for a bit, maybe have a paddle.'

'Not without swimming shoes.' He looked down at her bare feet. 'Weever fish hide in the sand. They can give you a really nasty sting. Wait till later.'

'Okay, okay,' she replied tetchily before turning round and retracing her steps. She struggled back up the shingle bank, then went down the sea wall steps, crossed the road and walked up the lane. As she rounded the tight corner, she noticed a car parked behind Ned's BMW. Her heart sank. It was Tara's designer Mini convertible, white with a plum-coloured top.

She stopped in her tracks, uncertain whether to carry on or go back to fetch Ned. She was sure Tara's arrival was not part of his plan. Tara would hate Fran being in her mother's house and had probably come to pick a fight.

Gathering her courage, she carried on, entering the cottage by the kitchen door, which had been left wide open. Tara had brought Georgia with her. They were in the sitting room, standing with their backs to her, looking out of the window that faced the sea.

'Hello, girls.' Fran stepped forward cautiously. 'I'm sorry, we weren't expecting you.'

They simultaneously spun around to face her. Tara laughed sarcastically. 'This is *our* house – we don't need permission to come here, least of all from you.'

Fran tried not to react. 'How did you find out we were here?'

'Noah said he was going to the seaside and Daddy was going to take him for a ride in his boat,' Georgia replied.

Tara looked daggers at Fran. 'He's going to sell the house, isn't he?'

'I've no idea.'

'Don't lie to us. If you put Mummy's stuff in the skip, we'll… we'll…'

'For God's sake, we'd never do that.'

Georgia drew herself up importantly. 'Mummy always said The Lookout would be passed on to the next generation, so it could stay in *her* family, not Daddy's.'

'Then she should have left it to you in her will.'

'She didn't make one, you know that,' barked Tara.

'If she'd agreed to divorce your dad, then it would have all been sorted years ago. It's not his fault he inherited.'

'It's *all* his fault. Daddy knows he has no right to be here.'

'Well, legally he *does* have a right, but—'

'And bringing you, too, I mean, that's beyond the limit. It's just… just… all wrong!'

'Tara, let's stay calm.'

'I don't want to stay calm!' Her eyes glittered with anger.

'You won't get away with it,' Georgia said, scowling. 'We're going to see to that. We don't care what we have to do to stop you.'

'It's got nothing to do with me. I couldn't care less what happens to the place. To be honest, it gives me the creeps.'

Tara ignited. 'How dare you say that about our home? You're such a bitch, you're just evil. You've wrecked everything!'

'Don't be so melodramatic. I'm not arguing with you, it's pointless. Go and talk to your dad.'

'Don't worry, we're going to.' They marched past her and stormed out of the house in flames of anger.

In the past, Fran had allowed the girls to upset her, but this time she felt untouched and calm. The dynamic between the three of them had changed. She knew something that neither girl knew, something that Ned would very much not want her to tell them. For the first time since she'd become part of the family, Fran finally had some power.

CHAPTER THIRTY-FOUR

I asked the taxi to wait for me on the corner and walked towards the house. It was 2 a.m. and the street was quiet. I stood on the opposite pavement and looked up at the bedroom window, where I hoped Edward was fast asleep. I knew he'd extended the range of the CCTV cameras, so I would have to be extremely careful approaching the front gates.

Fortunately, the stone ammonite was in the far corner of the garden. I crossed over and crouched down by the railings. It was very dark, but I didn't dare use my torch. I would have to feel my way. I'd put the note I'd written for Noah in a hard-backed brown envelope. Now I took it out of my bag and, holding it tightly between my fingers, pushed my arm through the gap between two railings. My heart was pounding so strongly I feared it might make the whole fence vibrate and set off the alarm. I stretched my arm out in the direction of the stone ammonite, and finally making contact, dropped the envelope behind it. Hopefully Daisy had passed on the message and Noah would be able to find it.

I slowly withdrew my arm, then stood up and ran across the road. At last I could breathe out. The security lights hadn't come on and nobody had been disturbed. The taxi flashed its lights impatiently. It had been a good night's work, I thought, as I hurried back to it. Now I had just over twenty-four hours in which to plan our trip.

*

'This is insane, you can't do it,' said Marsha, when I told her. It was still early morning and she was getting ready to leave for work.

'I'm not kidnapping him,' I said, quietly adding, 'as much as I'd like to.'

'Hmm, but you're taking him away without his father's knowledge or consent.'

'I'm his stepmother, remember?'

She shrugged. 'I'm not sure that gives you any legal rights.'

'Whose side are you on?'

'Yours, of course. What if Edward calls the police?'

'He won't. He hates the police, wouldn't stoop to asking them for help.'

'Okay, but he might come after you himself.'

'He won't know where we've gone. It's only a day trip.'

Marsha gulped down the rest of her tea. 'Maybe you should text Edward to tell him Noah's safe and you'll bring him home by a certain time.'

I thought about it for a few moments. 'Or I could ask Daisy to pretend to take Noah out for the day. That might be easier.'

'No, that's not fair. You've already asked too much of her. She could get the sack and then Noah won't have anyone.'

I heaved a long, heavy sigh. 'I know it's risky, but I *have* to take Noah to that place. It's like I'm being drawn there by an invisible magnet. I owe it to Francesca to find out what really happened.'

'It's not your responsibility.'

'I know, but I feel like it is.'

She grabbed her bag and keys. 'Think about it. We'll talk again tonight.'

'Okay,' I replied, although I already knew she was never going to make me change my mind.

Marsha went off to work and I spent the day on my phone, researching transport timetables and amenities in the local area.

First and foremost, I wanted to give Noah a fun day out. If playing on the beach brought back any memories of being with his mother, then great. If not, then I'd know I'd been barking up the wrong tree and could lay the matter to rest. At least that was how I rationalised it to myself.

The day dragged incredibly slowly. It was warm, and the air in the flat was stifling, particularly in my room, which was nestled under the eaves. I had to get outside. With no garden to sit in, I went to a nearby park and trailed along the paths, dragging my worries behind me. I carried on arguing with Marsha in my head. She was the voice of my conscience, my good angel, always looking after me. But I couldn't see the harm in what I was doing. I wouldn't let Noah get upset; I'd return him safely at the end of the day. If he remembered anything important, I would go straight to the police.

I went to bed early, knowing I'd have to get up at five. Everything was ready. Our train tickets were booked. I'd made up a picnic and packed a bag with towels and sunscreen in case we wanted to swim. All we needed were buckets and spades and we'd be set. I trusted I'd be able to pick some up from a local shop.

As it turned out, I couldn't sleep and didn't need the alarm to wake me. When the cab drew up outside Edward's house, Noah was already standing just inside the gates, stepping nervously from one foot to the other. I got out of the car and crossed the road.

'Hello,' I said quietly. 'Ready for an adventure?' He nodded. 'Push the button then.'

He did so and the gates trundled open. I glanced up anxiously at the bedroom window, but I wasn't going to hang around to find out whether the noise had woken Edward.

'Come on, Noah. Let's go!'

The taxi driver dropped us off by the Tube. I was trying to act like we were doing a normal, fun thing, but Noah wasn't buying it.

As we rattled through the tunnels, he kept his gaze down, twisting his fingers together as if trying to tie them in knots.

'I expect you're hungry,' I said. 'We'll get some croissants and juice at the station.'

'Is it a long way?' he asked.

'No, not at all. We're catching a super-fast train most of the way, then a slow little one for the last bit. Honestly, we'll be there before you know it. And it's good to be early, gives us a longer day. I've brought a picnic. We can build a sandcastle, go for a swim…'

He looked up, alarmed. 'I didn't bring my trunks.'

'That doesn't matter. Just wear your pants, nobody will notice. Anyway, most kids are still at school, so it'll be really quiet down there. We'll probably be the only people on the beach. I can't wait!'

I stopped, aware that I was bombarding him with jollity. There were so many serious things I wanted to say to him, but I knew the timing wasn't right. We were still in London, too close to home. Once we were by the sea, with the clear horizon before us, I hoped the conversation would flow more naturally.

We emerged from the Underground and took the short walk to the mainline station. I stopped at a takeaway café, buying coffee and an almond croissant for me, juice and pain au chocolat for Noah. He helped carry our supplies onto the train, which was already at the platform.

There were ten minutes to go before departure, but it felt like ten hours. I was anxious to get moving. Every time a man entered our carriage, my stomach lurched, thinking it was Edward. There was no way he could have followed us, but I still felt uneasy. What was he doing right now? He could still be asleep. Or he could be running around the house in his boxers, calling out for Noah, panic rising in his throat as he discovered that he wasn't there.

I looked across at my stepson, who was devouring his pain au chocolat like a child who hadn't eaten for a week. Large flakes of pastry fell onto the table. He licked the end of his finger, then picked them up one by one and put them into his mouth.

'Did you tell Daddy you were seeing me today?' I asked, trying to make it sound like no big deal either way.

'No,' he replied. 'I didn't want him to stop us. He never lets me go to the seaside. He hates it.'

'Really?' My heart skipped. 'Why's that, do you think?'

'I don't know.'

'But you've been to the seaside before with him, haven't you?'

'Yes. Only when I was little. He took me out in a boat.'

'Oh, that must have been fun. Did, um… did your mummy go with you?'

'Ye-es,' he said slowly. His blue eyes flashed at me anxiously. 'Is that where we're going today?'

'That's the plan. If I can find the right place. I think it's near a house called The Lookout. Does that name mean anything to you?' He shook his head. 'Do you remember anything about where you stayed? A hotel? A holiday cottage, maybe?' He shrugged his shoulders. 'No worries, maybe you'll recognise it when we get there.' I smiled at him excitedly. 'Who knows what we'll find, eh?'

He suddenly brightened. 'Will Mummy be there? Are we going to meet her?'

'What?' I gasped. 'Oh no, darling, no. I'm sorry, I didn't mean to…' I paused, searching for the right words. 'I wish we *were* going to meet your mummy, but she's… I don't know where she is. Nobody does, I'm afraid.'

His face fell. I was about to talk about the importance of happy memories, but the guard made a passenger announcement and the moment evaporated. Maybe it was just as well, I thought, as the train pulled out of the station.

Noah drank the rest of his orange juice and settled back in his seat. I felt bad for raising his hopes. It wasn't going to be easy, but we were getting there, step by step.

We reached our destination in no time. As we left the station, we were greeted by the cry of seagulls. The air smelt fresh and sharp. There was a taxi rank right outside and we bundled ourselves into the back seat of the first car.

'You're the early birds,' said the driver, starting the engine. 'Where can I take you?'

I read out the postcode and he punched it into his sat nav. 'I don't know exactly where the house is, I'm afraid,' I said.

'No problem, I'll find it,' he assured me. 'There's virtually nothing out that way, so it should be easy to spot.'

I glanced at Noah. 'Everything okay?'

He wasn't listening, looking away from me, nose almost pressed against the side window. As the car drove away, I sensed him devouring his surroundings – winding streets lined with higgledy-piggledy houses, a narrow harbour full of tatty fishing boats. Was it familiar to him? I didn't dare ask.

We soon left the town and found ourselves in open countryside. After a few minutes, the taxi turned left and we passed through some residential housing, which gave way to a caravan site. Then the landscape changed again and we were driving down a long, straight road with a high bank to our left and flat marshland to our right, dotted with grazing sheep. Cars were parked up here and there and a few people were walking along the top of the sea wall, but even that petered out as we drove on, seemingly into the middle of nowhere.

'The sat nav's telling me to go up here,' said the driver some minutes later. He turned off the road and drove up a narrow lane, crossing a small brick bridge over a canal and then turning sharply around a corner. There was a tatty sign nailed to a tree. It read: *The Lookout. Private. Residents only.*

The land started to rise and I realised we were driving up what appeared to be a large rock. I'd spotted it from a distance, sticking out of the marsh like a misplaced chunk of cliff. Noah leant forward expectantly, muscles tensing, eyes darting from side to side.

At the top of the slope was a tall, thin house, standing by itself, with a wraparound view of marsh and sea. Victorian Gothic, I guessed. It looked stern and forbidding, even though the sun was shining and the sky was bright blue.

'It's like something out of *The Addams Family*,' said the driver cheerfully, as he pulled up at what seemed to be the back door. 'You sure about this?'

'We've just come for a look,' I told him. 'We're not staying over.'

'Do you want me to come and pick you up later?'

'That'd be great, but I don't know how long we'll be here for.'

'Give us a call when you're ready.' He handed me a business card.

I paid our fare and Noah and I got out. The car did a cumbersome five-point turn, then rattled back down the slope, disappearing round the corner.

We stood there quietly, staring up at the building. It looked abandoned and semi-derelict, utterly different to the cheerful seaside cottage I'd pictured in my head. The curtains were drawn across the windows, all of which had rotten frames. There were large cracks in the grey masonry where damp had infiltrated. Slates had fallen off the roof and were lying in pieces across the brick-paved courtyard. An outside tap drip-dripped into a stagnant puddle of water.

There were still a few traces left of its holiday-home past. A line of pebbles and shells had been childishly arranged on the downstairs windowsill. A crabbing net was propped up against the wall and a small orange bucket, bleached by the sun and wind, lay at the foot of the steps, a huge wet snail clinging to its side. But mostly the house looked as if it hadn't been lived in for years. Nature had taken over. The gutters were choked with weeds and feathery ferns. Ivy was growing not just above the back door, but right across it. Moss and dandelions had dug themselves in between the cobbles, dead leaves from previous winters were clogging up the gullies, and the windowpanes were dusted with sand.

I turned to Noah. 'Well, what do you think? Have you been here before?'

'Yes. I think so.'

'Is this where you stayed with Mummy and Daddy?'

He nodded his head slowly. 'I'm frightened, Lily,' he said.

CHAPTER THIRTY-FIVE

'What do you mean, Noah?' I asked. 'Why are you frightened?'

He shivered. 'I don't know, I just am. It's coming back to me.'

'What is?'

'I don't know.' He looked up at the house. 'A feeling.'

I crouched down and put my arms around him. 'A bad feeling?'

'Yes… sort of.'

'Look, nobody's going to make you do anything that makes you uncomfortable. If you don't like it here, we can leave right now and go home. Do you want me to call the taxi back?'

He looked down, biting his lip. After a few moments, he lifted his head again and looked right into my eyes. 'No … I want to be brave. I want to go inside.'

'Are you absolutely sure?' He nodded. 'Okay, good. I don't have a key, but maybe we can find a way to get in.'

He sat down on the steps while I walked around the building, trying to lift the sash windows on the ground floor. They were all stuck fast. There was a small door at the side of the building, and a set of patio doors at the back – or was it the front? They were locked, but the wooden frames were so decayed, I reckoned they would cave in with a strong push. Although the house belonged to my husband, I was still breaking and entering, and I was reluctant to do too much damage.

I looked around me, taking it all in. The patio doors led on to a small neglected garden, which was perched on the top of the rock, with stunning views of the sea. Nature had taken back control with a vengeance. Everything was overgrown – the trees spindly and strangled with ivy, the flower beds choking with weeds and wild garlic. The lawn looked like a wild flower meadow, dotted with dandelions and ox-eye daisies. Wisteria was snaking over the walls and trespassing across the windowpanes. It was so beautiful and defiant it took my breath away.

I trampled through the long grass and reached a small wooden fence with a gate to one side. Some crumbling brick steps led to a small patio, perched on the side of the rock face, then continued down to a marshy area below. The steps looked too dangerous to attempt, so I stood at the top, picking out traces of an old garden among the untamed undergrowth: patches of lawn, flowering shrubs and gnarled fruit trees.

At the end of the marsh was a wooden bridge over the canal. Beyond was another wild area, then tall hedges that concealed the coast road. Beyond that, the shingle beach, and then the sea. The water was deep blue, flecked with white-tipped waves breaking near the shore. It held me for a few seconds, its vastness suddenly putting everything into perspective.

What should I do now? I sensed I was on the brink of a crucial discovery and I didn't want to give up, but neither did I want to put pressure on Noah or give him a panic attack. I'd left him by himself; I hoped he was all right. Pulling myself away from the view, I hurried back to check on him.

He was on his feet, fumbling at the door. 'Look what I found, Lily,' he said, holding up a key.

'Hey, well done! Where was it?'

'Under a flowerpot by the rubbish bin,' he said proudly.

'Of course. That's what people do in the country. Why didn't I think of that?' I bounced up the steps. 'Is it the right one?'

'Think so. It goes in, but it won't go round.'

'Let me have a go.' He stood back while I put the key back in the lock and tried with all my strength to make it turn. After a few attempts, there was a click. The door was swollen with rain. I pushed hard and it shuddered open, the bottom edge scraping across the slate-tiled floor.

'You did it,' said Noah, impressed.

'Still sure you want to go in?'

He nodded, tucking in behind me as I stepped straight into the kitchen. It was small and narrow, with old units on both sides and a wooden counter that was stained and covered with knife marks, as if it had been used as a giant chopping board. There was an old-fashioned upright cooker and an ancient fridge in the corner. It had been turned off and the door had been left open.

Noah screwed up his nose. 'Yuck. What's that smell?'

'Not sure. Old cooking? A bit of damp? Nobody has been here for a long time. The place needs airing.' I took the rucksack off my shoulders and rested it on the counter.

There was one small step from the kitchen into the sitting room, a large space with a window at one end and the patio doors at the other. It looked as if it had originally been two smaller rooms. Noah stayed close to me, peeking out from behind my back.

'Recognise it?'

'Yes,' he whispered, as if he didn't want the walls to hear. 'I think so.'

I surveyed the scene. There were two fireplaces. One had a mantelpiece made from a piece of driftwood, and the other housed a log burner with a tall black chimney. The alcoves were lined with shelves stuffed with books and ornaments. In the seating area there was a sagging sofa, two cracked leather armchairs and an old sideboard. A dining suite that had seen a lot of service sat in front of the patio doors. All the furniture was covered in a thick layer of dust, and there were cobwebs in every corner. But it was the family photos that sent a chill down my spine, cluttering up every available surface and space on the walls.

Here were all the images of Clare I'd once longed to see, taken at different ages throughout her short life. Pictures taken on her own, as a child with two people who I presumed were her parents, as a young woman in a group of friends, with Tara and Georgia as babies, young girls and teenagers. Now that she was dead, it looked like some kind of shrine.

Not one image of Edward, though, I noted silently. No romantic poses, no wedding photos, no family portraits. Perhaps I would find them hidden in a drawer somewhere, banished from sight.

Noah had broken free of me and was wandering slowly around the room, trailing his fingers in the dust. He had a faraway expression on his face. I sensed he was thinking about his mother, and I started to conjure her spirit too. What must it have felt like to visit this place? Francesca had been the mistress, the marriage-wrecker and home-breaker, and this had been indisputably Clare's house. I couldn't understand how Edward had had the nerve to bring her and Noah here for a holiday. It seemed so callous, so offensive.

'I remember that,' said Noah, pointing to a large Persian carpet on the floor. He shivered again, then walked over to the corner of the room, where there was a tall pine door. 'And I know what's behind here.'

'What? A cupboard?'

'No.' He pressed the latch and pulled the door towards him, revealing a narrow flight of stairs. 'I sat here,' he said. 'On this bottom step. They thought I was in bed, but I was listening.'

My heart skipped a beat. 'Do you remember what they were saying?'

'Some of it. I don't like this room. Can we go up?'

'Sure,' I replied, desperate to ask him what he'd heard, but knowing it would be wrong to push him. 'Let's explore. Shall I go first?'

We climbed to the first floor, where there was a bathroom and two bedrooms, a larger one overlooking the sea with bunk beds and a smaller one looking over the fields at the back.

'I slept here,' he said, going into the small room. He went over to the window and looked out at the wide, flat marsh. 'I remember the sheep. Look, they're still here.' They were dotted around the landscape in small groups, lambs at their sides. We could hear their intermittent bleating. He turned away and walked back onto the landing.

'What about your sisters?' I asked, following. 'Did they sleep in the other room?'

'Yes, I think so, I don't know.' He stared briefly at the open doorway. 'I don't remember going in there much.'

'And what's up there?' I pointed to a second, even narrower flight of stairs that twisted upwards.'

'I'll show you.'

He led the way this time and we climbed up to a small landing where there was another pine door. The key was in the lock, so we opened it easily and went into the room beyond.

I realised at once that this had been Clare and Edward's room. My eyes flickered over the elegant old furniture, the floral wallpaper, the softly draping curtains, the solid wooden bed covered in a faded patchwork quilt. Everything was covered in dust, but the atmosphere up here was different. It was bright and airy, bursting with life. The large windows at either end brought the outside in. Leafy trees swayed in the wind. The sea was so close you could imagine it rushing in at high tide.

I went over to the balcony door. The bolts at the top and bottom were very stiff, and I struggled to free them. Finally I pushed it open, but a gust of wind immediately banged it shut again. Holding onto the handle this time, I ventured out onto a small platform surrounded by rusty railings, and stood there buffeted by the breeze. The view across the bay was astonishing. I could see the faint grey outline of the power station at Dungeness, and a distant lighthouse.

'Come and look,' I said, beckoning to Noah.

He came to the threshold but wouldn't step outside. 'It's too scary,' he said.

'Can you see the lighthouse? It's got red bands around it, just like in your picture.' He stared at me. 'You know, the one with you and Mummy on the beach.'

'Yes,' he said. 'I forgot you'd seen that.'

I stepped back inside and shut the door behind me. The pretty, bright room seemed as good a place as any for telling him the truth – or at least as much of it as I knew. We climbed onto the bed and arranged the pillows behind our backs. I put my arm around him and drew him in close.

'Noah, I want you to listen very carefully to me,' I said. 'I've got something important to tell you.'

'About Mummy?'

'Yes.' I hugged him tight. 'Remember that lady I was talking to in the park? You were absolutely right when you said you thought you knew her. She's your grandma.' He opened his mouth in surprise. 'Yes, it's true. And she's the one who's been sending you messages and presents.'

His face fell. 'Not Mummy?'

'No, darling, not Mummy. Nobody's seen or heard from your mummy for a very long time.'

I held him as his body started to tremble. 'Why did she leave?'

'We don't know.'

'I thought she was coming to get me.'

'I'm sure she would have, if she'd been able to. She loved you very much, Noah. Your grandma told me that. You were everything in the world to her – she would never have left you.'

'So why did she?'

'We don't know exactly. Your grandma and Mummy's friends and even the police think something bad might have happened to her.'

'You mean she got killed?'

'Mmm… possibly. Or she had an accident, or—'

'They think she's dead.'

'Yes. I'm sorry. But nobody knows for sure. They can't find her, you see.'

He closed his eyes. I could sense his memory waking up after a long sleep.

'It was my fault,' he said solemnly.

'No, it wasn't,' I replied quickly. 'You mustn't ever think that. You were a little boy – it was nothing to do with you.'

'It was my fault,' he repeated. 'I'll tell you.'

CHAPTER THIRTY-SIX

Fran climbed the stairs to the top bedroom and went onto the balcony, suddenly desperate to breathe in some fresh air. She pictured the drama that was being played out on the beach. Georgia and Tara always felt braver together. There would be fireworks, for sure. She was concerned about Noah. He hated people arguing. But she had to keep reminding herself that soon it would be over. She'd made her decision.

She was going to leave Ned, taking Noah with her. If he tried to stop them, she would threaten him with the police. Did he really think she would stay with him, now that she knew what kind of man he was?

She took her clothes out of the wardrobe, laying them out on the bed and folding them into rectangles. She wanted to be ready to escape at short notice, whenever she saw her chance. Today, perhaps; tomorrow at the latest. She would hide her case in a hedge. Then later, when Ned was cooking or resting or taking a shower, she'd take Noah for a walk down the lane.

Her reflection stared back from the mirror. Her jaw was set. She felt stronger and more determined than ever. She put the clothes into the case and shut the lid.

Leaving the cottage, she made her way cautiously down the lane, her damp palm sliding over the handle as she trundled the suitcase noisily over the rough ground. The blind corner was ahead; there was no way she could see past it. If she bumped into Ned and the girls, she would have some explaining to do.

The sun had climbed to its highest point. Beads of sweat popped onto her brow and chest – she couldn't tell whether it was heat or anxiety. On either side, the flat open marsh was singing with insects. Seabirds corralled in the skies above her head. She could feel herself being sucked into the landscape.

She needed to find somewhere to hide the case, and looked around for inspiration. There was an old concrete pillbox in the middle of some wasteland at the end of the lane. It was a relic from the Second World War, now ugly and useless. Its lookout slits had been sealed, and weeds were growing on its flat roof. Lifting the case, she trampled down some undergrowth to form a path. Stinging nettles attacked her legs as she made her way to a narrow-walled entrance at the side of the building.

She edged in sideways and found herself in a dank, eerie room. Her eyes struggled to adjust to the darkness as she kicked the rubbish at her feet. A smell of piss invaded her nostrils. It was disgusting. She guessed walkers sometimes used this place as a toilet.

She hesitated. Would it be safe to leave the suitcase here? Deciding to risk it, she tucked it into the far corner, covering it with a slimy bin liner. She emerged blinking at the sudden light, taking deep breaths through her nose to get rid of the stench.

Now she just had to behave normally. It was lunchtime. Soon Ned and his children would come back from the beach, hungry and thirsty. What could be more natural than for them to find her dutifully making sandwiches? Back at the house, she opened the fridge and took out ham, salad, tomatoes, mayonnaise, the cheesy triangles Noah loved so much. Knowing there were no shops around, Ned had come well prepared with provisions.

Her hands were shaking as she sliced the bread. She'd opened the kitchen window so that she could hear them coming up the lane. After about half an hour, the sound of trudging footsteps drifted towards her. Ned was shouting at Noah to hurry up. She went to the back door and opened it wide.

'Hi,' he said, trying to communicate with his eyes. 'Sorry we were so long. The girls found me – we've been having a chat.'

'Yes, I know. I've made some sandwiches.'

'Oh great. We're all starving.'

Ned made a pot of tea and they ate lunch indoors, out of the sun. Fran found it very uncomfortable to be part of the family group, sitting in a chair where Clare must once have sat, nibbling her sandwich under the hateful gaze of her daughters. Noah seemed oblivious to the tension. He licked the last smears of soft cheese from the wrapper, then asked if he could play in the garden.

'Yes, fine, but keep to the upper lawn, where we can see you,' Ned said.

As soon as he had left the table, an eerie cloud of silence descended. Tara heaved a sigh and leant back in her seat.

'Daddy is giving us the cottage,' she said. 'He's going to make it over to us legally.'

'It's what Clare would have done,' Ned said. 'If she'd made a will, I mean.' He reached out and squeezed Fran's hand. 'I'm sorry, darling. I shouldn't have involved you in all this. It was inappropriate.'

'The thing is, we don't want you here,' said Georgia. 'You need to leave, Fran. Like, as soon as possible.'

'Okay,' Fran replied, looking at Ned for clarification. 'You mean, just me?'

'No, don't be silly.' He let out a small laugh. 'We'll go somewhere else, the three of us. The girls want to stay on. The cottage has been left empty for far too long. Everything needs cleaning and airing.' The various Clares in the photos seemed to nod in agreement.

'Right. So we're leaving now?'

'Preferably,' said Tara.

Ned pulled a face. 'Actually, I've been thinking, we need to stay one more night. There's stuff of mine here, too – books, clothes, a wetsuit. We've got to find somewhere else to stay, and I need to talk to the guys at the angling club about selling the boat.'

'But we agreed—' Georgia began.

'I know, I'm sorry, but there's too much to do.'

Tara rolled her eyes to the ceiling. 'Okay. One more night. Yes, sis?'

'S'pose so.'

'But you're not sleeping in Mummy's bed again. You can sleep downstairs on the sofa.'

'Is that really necessary, Tara?' Ned said. 'What difference will one more night make?'

'Those are our terms,' she replied firmly. 'If you don't like them, you can leave now.'

After lunch, Tara and Georgia went into the garden and lay on the grass, sunbathing and talking in low tones. Fran sensed they were guarding her, fearful that she might rummage around in their mother's possessions or vandalise their home. She cleared the table and washed the dishes. Her head ached and her stomach was unsettled. Instinct was telling her to get out of the hostile atmosphere straight away.

Ned wanted to fulfil his promise to take Noah for a last-chance ride in his boat. He asked Fran to come along, but she refused. As she lay on the sofa, pretending to read one of Clare's books, all she could think about was her escape. She would leave tonight, she decided. Her suitcase was waiting in its hiding place. Her phone was fully charged. She'd found a bus timetable and discovered there was a bus that ran once every two hours to the station. The last one left at quarter past six.

As the sun moved across the sky, long shadows stretched across the upper lawn. Tara and Georgia came inside to make themselves cold drinks.

'What's for dinner?' asked Tara rudely.

Fran removed the cold flannel from her forehead and sat up. 'I don't know. I wasn't aware that it was my job to feed you.'

The kitchen door opened and Noah ran in, followed by Ned. 'Daddy let me have a go,' he said proudly. 'I was good, wasn't I?'

'You were excellent. You should all have come – the sea was really calm.'

Fran shrugged at him, not knowing what to say.

'How about a drink on the terrace? Not too early for a G and T, is it, darling?'

'Not for me, thanks, I've got a headache.'

Ned made some drinks for himself and the girls and they went into the garden. Fran remained in the sitting room. 'Fancy a walk down the lane?' she asked Noah, trying to sound casual.

He screwed up his little nose. 'Why?'

'I need to clear my head. And… I saw a family of ducks earlier. Shall we go and see if we can find them?' She held out her hand. 'Please.'

'Don't want to.'

'Well, I want you to come with me. Go to the loo and put your sandals on. Oh, and bring your jacket.'

'But it's hot.'

'It'll soon get colder. And it's windy by the sea.'

Deciding it would be better not to slip out without saying anything, she went into the back garden. Ned was on the lower patio, sitting on a rusty old garden chair, his girls at either side. They stopped talking when they saw Fran standing at the top of the steps.

'I'm going for a walk,' she said.

He put down his glass. 'Good idea. Blow those cobwebs away.'
She nodded in agreement. 'Want me to come with you?'

'No, it's all right. Noah's going to keep me company.'

'Take him to see the rabbits. There are dozens of them in the meadows at the bottom of the rock.'

'Okay.'

Part of her wanted to say goodbye, just to hear the words out loud and know what they meant even if he didn't, but she was afraid of betraying the relief in her voice. There was yet another uneasy pause. Tara and Georgia exchanged a glance and Ned caught it. 'Don't be too long,' he said. 'I'm going to start cooking soon.'

'I'll be half an hour at the most.'

She collected Noah and they started walking down the lane. The bus was due in eight minutes. She wanted to hurry, but Noah was being recalcitrant. He found a long stick and trailed it slowly behind him over the cobbles.

They reached the end of the lane, by the pillbox. 'Wait here,' she said, looking in vain for the path she'd trodden in the undergrowth that morning. The grass seemed to have completely sprung back. 'I won't be long.'

'Where are you going?'

'To that building. I need to get something.'

'What?'

'A suitcase.'

'Why?'

She took a deep breath. 'We're going away, Noah. Just the two of us.' He looked at her strangely. 'First we're catching a bus and then a train.'

'I don't want to go,' he said.

'I know, but we have to.'

'Why?'

'Because… because…' She stopped. 'I'll explain it to you on the journey. Please, darling, just trust me now. You need to come with me.'

'No. Don't want to. I want to play on the beach.' He turned and started to run back up the lane. 'Daddy! Daddy!' he called.

'Noah! Come back! Noah! Please!'

CHAPTER THIRTY-SEVEN

'Fran!' Ned barked, striding towards her. 'Where the hell do you think you're going?'

'Nowhere,' she replied. 'Just for a stroll by the sea, I told you that.'

'Hmm…' He looked her up and down, observing that she only had a small handbag with her. She thought of her suitcase, lying in wait in the concrete pillbox at the bottom of the lane. There was no chance of retrieving it, but with luck he wouldn't notice it was missing, and it could stay there until she found another chance to escape.

'You can't do this, Fran.'

'What do you mean?' she asked, playing the innocent.

'You can't leave me. Not now. Not ever.'

'Who said anything about leaving?'

'Noah just told me you were taking him on the bus.'

She affected a scoffing laugh. 'He misunderstood. I told him we might *see* a bus, that's all. One's due about now.' She glanced towards the coast road, and on cue, she heard the sound of the last bus of the day trundling past. She suppressed a disappointed sigh. If she had carried on down the lane, she would have caught it just in time and been on her way. But Noah had refused to come and she hadn't been able to leave without him. If only she'd just scooped him into her arms and run, she thought. But now she was trapped.

'Come back to the house, Fran.' It was an order, not a suggestion.

'In a bit. I just want to look at the sea,' she said lamely.

'It'll still be there tomorrow… I want you to come back now. Noah needs a bath before dinner.' He was pretending to be casual, but his tone betrayed him. Even the most ordinary statement sounded like a threat. He took her hand and they walked back up the path. His grip was tight, as if she were a child who might try to wriggle free.

'Mummy!' Noah called out as Ned virtually pushed her through the door. She went into the sitting room. He ran up and flung his arms around her legs. 'You came back. You didn't go on the bus!'

'No, I was just going for a walk, like I told you. Don't worry, it's okay, I'm not going anywhere.'

'Shame,' said Tara. 'We were rather hoping you'd gone to drown yourself.'

'Hey, steady on,' said Ned.

Fran flashed her an angry look. 'Say what you like to me, but watch your tongue when Noah's about.'

'Why should I?'

'Because he's a little boy.'

'A little bastard, you mean.'

'Tara…' said Ned warningly.

'Well, he is! It's all his fault.'

'How dare you say that?' Fran said, cupping her hands over Noah's ears.

'Let's face it. If you hadn't got pregnant, Dad would have dumped you years ago.' Tara turned to her sister, who was busying herself by laying the table. '*Somebody* has to tell the truth around here.'

'Actually, Tara, that's *not* true,' said Ned. 'Noah is just as important to me as you girls are. I love Francesca very much. In fact, I have some special news. Fran and I are engaged.'

The girls stopped in their tracks, their mouths falling open simultaneously.

'You're *what*?' hissed Tara.

'I was waiting for the right moment to tell you.'

'This is so not the right moment, Dad,' said Georgia. She put the bread board on the table.

'Actually, I've decided I don't want to marry your father,' Fran said slowly.

Ned laughed. 'Don't be silly. You already said yes, you have the ring. Of course you want to marry me.'

'That's all you wanted right from the start,' chipped in Tara. 'To get rid of Mum and be the second Mrs Fletcher.'

'Not true, actually.'

'In fact, I'm surprised you didn't make Dad marry you the second after she died.'

'Can we not talk about this?' Georgia put a hand on her sister's arm. 'Not here. It's like Mum's listening. It's making me feel a bit sick.'

Fran turned to Noah. 'Go and play upstairs for a bit, please,' she said quietly. 'I'll be up in a minute.'

'But I want to—' he protested.

'Do as I tell you. Now.'

'Yes, up you go, buddy.' Ned pushed him up the stairs and shut the bottom door. He gave the three of them a pacifying smile. 'Georgia's right, this is not an appropriate place for these discussions. Let's have no more arguing. I've already agreed we're leaving tomorrow. In the meantime, let's try to be civil to each other for one night.'

'Actually, I've changed my mind. I think the three of you should go right this minute,' said Tara. 'This is *our* house, so we can decide who—'

Ned raised his hand to interrupt. 'It's not your house until I've made it over to you legally. For tonight, it's still my property, which makes you *my* guests. So if you don't like it—'

'I am not a guest!' Tara screamed, flying off the handle. 'This is my house! It's her I want out, *her*!' She picked up the bread knife from the dining table and brandished it in Fran's general direction. 'I know it was you! You killed Mum! I know you did.'

'Tara, for God's sake, put the bloody thing down,' commanded Ned.

But Tara wasn't listening. 'I know why, too. It's obvious. It was because she wouldn't give Dad a divorce.'

'You've got it wrong, Tara,' Fran said, trying to keep her voice calm even though her pulse was starting to race.

'Careful, sis,' said Georgia. 'Remember what we said – without proof—'

'I don't need proof. I know she did it. She's guilty, she has to pay.' Tara's eyes were glittering manically. She advanced a few more steps towards Fran, waving the knife around, its jagged blade glinting in the early-evening sunlight.

Fran backed away, stumbling as she bumped into the log burner. A sharp pain shot through her leg, and she yelped.

'I don't know exactly how you did it, but you did,' Tara continued. 'The police were idiots. There's no way her death was an accident.'

'Ned! Do something!' Fran shouted. 'Stop her!'

Tara pushed her to the floor and loomed over her with the knife. 'Go on. Confess. How did you do it? Did you force the bread down her throat? Did you take away her EpiPen? Did you stand there and watch her die, you bitch?'

'Tara, stop this! Leave her alone!' shouted Ned.

'She's not worth it, sis,' Georgia pleaded.

The knife blade hovered over Fran's face. 'If you want to know what happened,' she squeaked. 'Ask your father.'

Ned took a sharp intake of breath. 'Darling…'

She rounded on him. 'Why should I protect you when you won't protect me?' Suddenly she no longer felt afraid. What greater weapon could she have than the truth? She lifted her head and looked Tara squarely in the eye.

'He's the one who killed Clare. He did it because he couldn't wait for the divorce. He wanted the three of you out of the house so he could sell it and keep all the money for himself. He doesn't care about you, he wants to be a new family, just him and me and Noah. Trouble is, I don't want to marry him any more. He's a murderer. He disgusts me.'

'It's all lies!' Ned cried. 'Fran... why are you saying this?'

'Dad? Is this true?' rasped Georgia.

'No. Of course it isn't. If you must know, Fran confessed to *me*. Tara's got it right. She went to see Clare when she was in bed with the flu, pretending she wanted to make peace. She went into the kitchen to make her a hot drink and planted a loaf of sesame bread in the freezer. It was two weeks before Clare defrosted the bread to make herself a sandwich.'

'No, that's exactly what *you* did, Ned.' Fran drilled her eyes into the girls. 'Come on, think about it. Why would Clare have let me visit her? She hated my guts – she wouldn't have let me in the door. Your father told me all this last night. Right here, in this house, *Clare's* house, surrounded by all her photos. He was so proud of himself for committing the perfect crime.'

'She's lying,' said Ned. 'I loved your mother. Fran got pregnant to trap me.'

Tara pointed the knife at Fran's chest. 'You're not going to get away with this!' she screamed.

'Tara, don't...' Georgia lunged forward and tried to grab the knife off her sister. As the girls struggled with each other, Fran got to her feet and tried to help Georgia. Ned just stood there, helpless, not doing a thing. She twisted Tara's wrist around until the knife fell from her grasp, then bent down to pick it up. But Georgia was doing the same, and their heads clashed. Fran fell sideways, her head hitting the edge of the hearth, and Georgia landed on top of her.

Her head reeled with a deep, sickening pain, so intense she couldn't open her eyes. And now there was another pain in her back, dull and heavy, spreading outwards. She tried to move, but her limbs wouldn't work. She tried to speak, but nothing would come. Georgia rolled off her and stood up. High-pitched screams like panicking seagulls filled the room.

'Oh my God.'

'Fuck… fuck, fuck!'

'She's bleeding. Why is she bleeding?'

'You stabbed her.'

'No, I didn't.'

'You did. Look, Georgia! You're still holding the fucking knife.'

'Jesus!' Something clattered to the floor. 'Oh God, look, it's everywhere. We've got to stop the bleeding.'

'I'll get a towel. You call an ambulance!'

'Okay.'

'Listen to me, girls!' A male voice entered the muffled soundscape. It was Ned – Fran's lover, the father of her son, come to save her, she thought. She tried to open her eyes, tried to lift her hand and reach out for him, but she couldn't move. She could feel herself fading away. The pain in her back had sharpened to a point, cutting right through her, letting in the cold.

'Georgia, put that phone down,' he said.

'But Dad, we *have* to. She's going to bleed out.'

'Do as I say. Put the phone down!' There was another scuffle. 'We can't call an ambulance. If she dies, it's murder. Even if she lives, we're in terrible trouble. I won't let my little girl go to prison for that bitch. Not when she killed your mother.'

I didn't kill her... said a weak voice inside Fran's head. *It was you. You told me. You. Edward the Confessor...* But nobody could hear her. The sea was roaring in her ears, the frightened gulls still screeching above her head.

'Then what the fuck *are* we going to do? Let her bleed to death?'

'I don't know. We've got to think. Think.'

'This is insane. Dad, you can't do this.' Tara's voice. 'Get help! Before it's too late.'

Noah... Noah... I want to see my son... said the little voice, gasping for every scrap of breath. *Please, just let me see him... Tell him I love him, that I'll always, always love...*

Her world swirled to black.

CHAPTER THIRTY-EIGHT

'You were right all along, Noah,' I said. 'You *do* remember every-thing, even though it happened when you were little. You have a fantastic memory, you're so clever.' We sat there on the bed with the sun streaming through the window. I pulled him into me and let him cry quietly.

'If only I'd gone with her,' he said, 'she would have escaped.'

'Please, you must believe me, Noah, whatever happened to Mummy after that argument was absolutely not your fault.' I stroked his hair. 'I'm so glad you told me everything. You've had all these horrible memories trapped inside you for so long, all these guilty thoughts going around in your head, but now you've set them free. Do you feel better for it?'

'Yes, I think so… There's a bit more I remember,' he said.

'Okay, go on.'

'After Mummy got hurt, I ran upstairs and hid in my bedroom,' he said, the words flowing freely now. 'I must have fallen asleep, because when I woke up, it was morning, very early. I got up to look for Mummy, but she wasn't there. Nobody was there. The house was empty, they'd left me on my own.'

'So what did you do?'

'I came up here and went onto the balcony. I thought maybe they'd gone to the beach without me, but then I saw the boat. Daddy's boat.'

'The red one, like in the picture you drew?'

He nodded. 'There were three people in the boat. It must have been Daddy with Tara and Georgia. They were sailing back to the beach.'

'Did they see you?'

'No. Don't think so. I came back inside, went back to bed and pretended to be asleep.'

'And you never saw Mummy again?'

'No… Don't think so, anyway. Some of the memories are really clear, but others have gone a bit fuzzy.'

'That's okay. You've remembered all the important stuff. When we get back to London, I'd like to take you to somebody who's specially trained to listen to children talking about their experiences.'

'Hmm… What, like a policeman?'

'Sort of. But not like an interview in a police station like you see on the telly. You've done nothing wrong. Nobody would be accusing you of anything or trying to trip you up. They'd just listen. It would be really good if you could tell them everything you've just told me. I think it could help us find out what happened to Mummy.'

'Okay. Only if Daddy's not there… and you come with me.'

'Of course. Absolutely, that's a promise. But let's not say anything to Daddy about this, eh? He might be cross that we came to the house. Best keep it a secret.'

'Okay.' He unwrapped himself and got off the bed. 'Can we go now? I don't like being here. It makes me feel sad.'

'I'll call the taxi guy. He said he'd come straight away and pick us up.' I took my phone out and dialled the number on the business card the driver had given me. 'Hmm, there's no signal. I'll try somewhere else.'

We went down to the first floor and I walked around, holding the receiver up high and standing by the windows, but I couldn't get even half a bar. The sitting room and kitchen downstairs were no better. I went outside and tried again, but it was no use. The place was too far from a phone mast.

Irritated, I went back indoors and tried the landline, but it had been disconnected.

Noah was starting to look concerned. 'We're stuck!' he said.

'No we're not – it just means we'll have to catch the bus instead. I checked the timetable before we left. Trouble is, they only run every couple of hours. We've missed the morning one, so I'm afraid we'll have to wait until after lunch.'

'I don't want to wait. I want to go now.'

'I know, darling, I'm sorry, but there's nothing else I can do. Perhaps we should just go to the beach. We've still got our picnic to eat. We could build a sandcastle, go for a swim?' I was itching to go down to the beach to see if Edward's boat was still there.

'Can't we walk to the station?' Noah asked, a pleading look in his eye.

'Well, we *could*, I suppose, but it's a very long way.'

'I don't mind.'

'Okay – if you're sure?'

'Yes. Please.' He gave me a grateful hug.

I rubbed his back soothingly, but my mind was in turmoil. I couldn't deliver him to Edward later today pretending that nothing had happened. When we got back to London, our first stop had to be a police station. I was pretty certain that if I mentioned the name Ned Fletcher, I'd be taken seriously. But what would happen to Noah? The information he had was dynamite; he wouldn't be safe. If I wasn't allowed to look after him, he would probably have to go into temporary care. Could I put him through the ordeal of giving evidence against his own father?

My thoughts were interrupted by the sound of a vehicle coming up the lane. 'What's that?' I said, releasing Noah from the embrace.

'The taxi!' he cried happily.

'It can't be… I couldn't get through.' I ran to the window and looked out. A shiny black BMW was drawing up outside.

'Quick!' I said to Noah. 'Run upstairs, fast as you can, back up to the top room!'

'But Lily—'

'It's Daddy! We've got to hide.'

I heard the car door slam. We bounded up both flights of stairs and dashed into the bedroom. I whipped the little key out of the door and locked us in from the inside.

'Keep quiet,' I whispered. 'If he calls out, don't answer. Hopefully he'll give up looking for us and go away.'

'How does he know we're here?' he mouthed.

'No idea.' I gestured to him to hide under the bed. We got down on our stomachs and scrambled into the void, trying not to cough from the dust.

We waited, listening to the floorboards creaking as Edward tramped around the house, calling out our names. Then his feet were on the stairs, climbing to the top floor. We held our breath.

He reached the tiny landing and rattled the door handle. 'Lily? I know you're in there and you've got Noah. Come out. Now.' We stared at each other conspiratorially in the gloom. He tried another tack. 'Noah? It's Daddy here. Are you okay, buddy? Lily has done a very bad thing, bringing you here. I'm worried about you. I want you to come away from her and unlock the door. Please.' I sent eye signals to Noah, begging him not to obey. Bless him, he held my hand and stayed resolutely silent.

Edward started banging on the door with his fist. 'I've had enough. You're making me extremely angry, Lily! If you don't come out, I'm going to bash my way in… I'm warning you. If you don't come out right this second, I'm going to completely lose my temper and I won't be responsible for what happens next.'

'No! Don't hurt her!' shouted Noah. He let go of my hand and crawled out from under the bed.

'Noah, don't!' I hissed, but he was already on his feet and standing by the door. I dragged myself out and stood up too.

'I hate you! Go away! Leave us alone!' Noah shouted.

Edward stopped banging and changed his tone once more. 'Hey, Noah, don't say that to me. I'm your dad, I love you. It's Lily who should leave us alone, buddy. She abducted you and now she's telling lies, trying to turn you against me. She's the bad person, not me. Unlock the door, please, and come out.'

'How did you know we were here?'

'I was in a panic when I found you'd gone. Daisy told me that Lily had left you a note. I found it in your waste basket, torn into little pieces. Good job too, otherwise I wouldn't have been able to rescue you. Open the door, buddy. Please. Do as you are told.'

'Noah is staying here with me,' I said. 'If you don't like it, call the police.'

There was a pause. I knew there was no way he would call the police and invite them to visit the scene of his crimes. We waited. All we could hear was his heavy breathing on the other side of the door. Then he spoke. 'How did you find out about this place?'

'I was snooping in your office. You caught me, remember?'

'Yeah... I knew you were up to something.' He sighed. 'Why did you come here?'

I put my finger over my lips again to tell Noah not to say a word. 'Noah had been talking about this seaside place he remembered visiting when he was little. He really wanted to go back but he knew you wouldn't let him. So I found out where it was and brought him here. I was hoping he'd have a happy memory about his mother.'

There was an electric pause. 'And did he?'

'No. Unfortunately he couldn't remember anything, could you, Noah?' I nudged him.

'No. Nothing,' Noah confirmed.

'So it was a bit of a waste of time. Look, I'm sorry I took him without your permission. It was wrong of me.'

'Yeah, it was,' Edward replied, sounding relieved. Had he bought my lie, or was this another bluff? 'He's my son, Lily, not yours,' he continued. 'I understand him better than you do. I've told you before not to interfere. But let's not fight. Just open the door and we can discuss this like sensible adults… And Noah, don't be scared, you're not in trouble.'

Noah and I looked at each other helplessly. We had no choice. The two of us couldn't stay locked up in the room indefinitely, and I had no way of summoning help.

'Okay?' I whispered, and he nodded. I turned the key and opened the door.

Instantly, Edward lunged forward and shoved me to the ground, winding me badly. I tried to grab his ankle, but he escaped, grabbing Noah by the hand and dragging him onto the landing. Then he took the key and shut the door again, locking it from the outside. Noah started screaming. I think Edward must have picked him up and thrown him over his shoulder, because I only heard one set of footsteps descending the stairs.

Still struggling to catch my breath, I crawled towards the door and tried the handle, even though I already knew there was no point. I sat up with my back against the door, a pain in my stomach, listening for clues as to what was going on below. Was Edward going to drive off with Noah and leave me here? Nobody would know. I could starve to death.

I took my phone out of my back pocket and rushed onto the balcony, holding it this way and that, standing on tiptoe, desperately willing it to connect to the network. Suddenly a large black bird flew towards me, and as I ducked, the phone slipped from my sweaty grasp and fell into the overgrown grass below. I groaned loudly. Not that the bloody thing could get a signal, but now there was no chance. I couldn't even try to call emergency services.

I went back into the bedroom, dizzy with panic. The sound of Noah's hysterical tears drifted up through the floor. What was Edward doing to him? I hoped to God Noah wasn't being forced to reveal what he'd told me. It was my fault. I'd opened up Pandora's box; now the secrets were about to fly out and I wasn't there to protect him. I dreaded to think what Edward might to do to silence his son.

CHAPTER THIRTY-NINE

Everything had gone quiet downstairs. I strained my ears for sounds of life – footsteps, voices, doors shutting, taps running, toilets flushing – but there was nothing. Had Edward taken Noah and returned to London? I hadn't heard the car drive away, but that wasn't surprising – I was on the other side of the house, with no view of the lane.

What was the plan for me? Now that I knew what my husband was capable of, my imagination was running wild. Not only had he killed Clare, but he'd conspired in Francesca's murder by helping to dispose of her body. He and his beloved daughters were in it up to their necks. No wonder they were so damn close, impossible to prise apart. If he allowed the truth to come out now, all three of them would go to prison for a very long time.

I'd bluffed as well as I could, pretending that Noah hadn't remembered anything, but I suspected Edward hadn't believed me. Noah and I were in extreme danger.

But how to escape? The house was in the middle of nowhere. There was no point screaming for help when only the gulls could hear me. I cursed myself for running up to the top floor instead of into the back garden. I was trapped up here.

The only saving grace was the balcony. I opened the glass door and stood out there again. The breeze had whipped up and fine grains of sand were blowing into my face. Leaning over the iron railings, I looked down at the overgrown lawn below. Jumping was out of the question. I craned my neck, searching for a drainpipe to climb down, but there was nothing within reach. What I needed was a rope ladder, or something to lower myself down on. It would have to be long enough, and I'd have to tie it to the balcony railings. They were old and rusty – would they be strong enough to take my weight? I tried to wobble them, and to my relief, they didn't move.

Seized with hope, I immediately went back inside and started ransacking the room, opening the wardrobe and drawers, looking for anything that might serve as a rope. Clare's clothes flew past me as I hurled them onto the floor. I felt her unearthly presence at my side, helping me, urging me on. Soon Francesca's spirit joined us, rising from her watery grave and entering the room on the edge of the breeze. I *would* escape, I *had* to escape, not simply to save myself and Noah, but to get justice for Francesca and Clare.

Of course, there was no rope conveniently curled up in the bottom of a cupboard, but I wasn't giving up. I would make one, I decided. Throwing the duvet off the bed, I took off the bottom sheet and started ripping it into strips. Worrying that they might not be strong enough by themselves, I decided to use the duvet cover too, tearing more strips and plaiting them together.

My fingers shook as I worked at pace, all the time nervously listening for the sound of Edward's footsteps on the stairs. How much longer did I have before he came back to get me? I couldn't believe he would just leave me here to rot. I knew too much. I was too alive.

I completed several long plaits. Now to tie the pieces together to give me enough length to get down to the ground. Firm knots were crucial. I pulled on them with all my strength to make sure they would not give way. My makeshift rope snaked around the bedroom. Would it be long enough? I didn't want to fling it over the balcony to test it out in case Edward was downstairs and saw. I measured it roughly with my hands. It was about twelve metres long.

It was still only mid afternoon by the time I'd finished. My fingers were raw with working the fabric. I'd had nothing to eat or drink for hours and my stomach was sinking with emptiness. There were still no sounds of life downstairs. I went to the door and examined it closely, looking for weaknesses. It was tempting to try to bash it down. But what if Edward *was* below, being very quiet? If he heard me trying to get out, he might come and tie me up, then I'd have no chance of escape.

No, I would stick to plan A. I gazed around. The room was a terrible mess. I rolled up the sheet rope and hid it under the bed, then put all Clare's clothes away. I covered the bare duvet with the patchwork quilt so that Edward wouldn't see that I'd ripped up the sheets. Then I climbed onto the bed and curled up, willing myself to rest, to gather my strength for later.

Edward didn't come to check on me and I couldn't work out why. I tried to imagine what was going on inside his head. Maybe he'd already fled the country. Maybe he'd driven out to get a phone signal so he could talk to Tara and Georgia. Maybe he was trying to decide what to do with me. Making preparations…

And what had he done with Noah? I hoped with all my heart that he hadn't come to any harm. Right at this minute, my husband was a stranger to me, but one thing I knew for certain was that he was a devoted father to all his children and would do anything to protect them. He loved Noah and wouldn't want to hurt him. Even so, the boy had to be careful. I willed him to stay strong, to pretend to forget, to keep his memories secret for a little while longer.

Time dragged on. I stood at the window and watched the tide go out, revealing slimy green rocks and stretches of glistening grey mud. The sun moved across the sky, then disappeared around the side of the house. After a while, an evening chill crept into the room. I went to Clare's wardrobe and found a cardigan to put on.

It felt strangely comforting. My stomach ached with hunger and there was a stale, dry taste in my mouth.

I was feeling increasingly nervous about my plans. I was no athlete, and I didn't have a particularly good head for heights. What if the rope I'd made wasn't strong enough to take my weight? What if the knots came undone? What if I didn't have the courage to climb over the balcony railings? Soon I would find out.

I calculated it must have gone nine o'clock. The light was turning deepest blue. The sea was nothing but a dark smudge, but I could hear the tide rumbling its way back in. It was nearly time to go.

But something was going on downstairs. I ran to the door and listened. It sounded like furniture being moved about. What was Edward doing? All I knew was that eventually he would come and get me. I *had* to make my move now, before it was too late.

I removed the long, plaited rope from under the bed and went onto the balcony. Tying one end as firmly as I could to the side railing, I threw the rope over. I peered down to see if it stretched all the way to the ground, but it was so dark by now that it was impossible to tell. My pulse was racing furiously as I swung my legs over so that I was now standing on the other side of the railings. I stayed there for a few seconds, gripping the top, sweating with fear. But I had no choice. Staying in the bedroom was far more dangerous than attempting to lower myself down.

I peeled my fingers off the rail and grasped the rope with one hand, then the other. The knots didn't move and the plait felt strong. Now it was time to take the leap of faith. I removed one foot, then the other. My body lurched. I hung suspended in the air for a frightening moment, paddling with my feet as I tried to find the wall. Then my shoes hit brick. I'd only ever been abseiling once, years earlier, but in this life-or-death moment the technique suddenly came back to me. Lean back, I told myself. Keep your feet wide apart. Don't rush, take it gradually.

I climbed down, gently bouncing off the wall, step by step by step. I passed the bedroom on the first floor. The room was dark and there was nobody about. I carried on making my way down. A chink of light was coming from around the edge of the curtains on the ground floor, which had been drawn. I went even more slowly and gently, scared they might hear the tap of my feet on the outside wall.

Finally I made it to the bottom, landing in the grass. Never had I felt so relieved to be back on solid ground. I stood up and paused for a moment to catch my breath. The air was sweet, the sky a black coat sequinned with millions of stars. It was very hard to see my way, and I cursed not having my phone to throw a light. I briefly thought about trying to find it, but there was no point. It had probably smashed to pieces anyway.

Feeling my way around the walls of the house, I made it to the side gate. Its hinges creaked as I pulled it open. I paused for a second, ears pricked. Cautiously I peered around the side of the house, staring into the gloom.

Edward was in the lane, his shape backlit from a shaft of light streaming onto the courtyard from the back door. He was carrying what looked like a rolled-up carpet. I held my breath as I watched him stash it in the boot of his car. What was he up to? I couldn't see Noah anywhere. I strained, hoping to catch the sound of his young voice, or to hear Edward talking to him, but there was only silence. Edward shut the boot then went back into the house.

I hesitated for a few moments, trying to decide what to do. I was extremely anxious about Noah and wanted to rescue him, but I knew I'd be no match for Edward in a fight. As reluctant as I was to leave him, I decided to make a dash for it, keeping as close as possible to the hedge in case Edward came back out of the house and drove off down the lane. The ground beneath my feet was rough and uneven, strewn with loose grit and old twigs.

Brambles poked their way through my cardigan and scratched my neck. A dark shape loomed to my right, some kind of concrete building – a good place to hide, perhaps? But no, I needed to get further away from the house.

Why had Edward returned inside? Perhaps he'd gone to check on me. There was no time to waste. I started to hurtle down the lane. It was like running blind; I couldn't see a thing. The ground was slippery. My ankle wrenched as I stumbled over a stone. I let out a small yelp, then covered my mouth.

Within a minute, I was standing on the coast road, the high sea wall straight ahead of me. I could hear the tide dragging itself over the shingle. But which way to go for help? I had no idea what might lie to my right. Another house could be just around the corner, but there could just as easily be nothing at all. The taxi had approached from the left, and I remembered passing through a caravan site. It was about an hour's walk away, probably more in the pitch-black. But what if Edward got in his car and came to search for me?

I couldn't risk it. I would have to go via the beach.

Crossing the road, I climbed the concrete steps. When I reached the top, a blast of wind hit me in the face, almost knocking me backwards. The path along the high wall was narrow and stony, easier to walk on but very exposed. Even though it was dark, I was worried that I might be seen by Edward driving along the road. I had to get down to the strand, at sea level, where I would be well out of sight.

A full moon was shining over the water, casting a shimmering silver cloth over the waves. It was the only light I had to guide me. I surveyed the prospects. Ahead was a deep bank of shingle. Below that, a stretch of flat sand, then swathes of mud and clusters of boulders interspersed with rock pools. In the day and at low tide, the route would have been easy, but the sea was rising and it was very dark.

The pebbles crunched and jostled as I descended the moving staircase of shingle. Tiny sharp stones found their way into my trainers and lodged themselves under my feet. My ankle, already hurting from when I'd twisted it in the lane, started to throb.

Reaching the bottom of the bank, I hobbled over yet more punishing gravel until I found a kinder surface – thick cakey sand sprinkled with tiny water-worn pebbles. My eyes were adjusting now and I could just about see where I was going. There was a zigzag route across the sand, cutting between rock pools and streams, that would take me down to the shoreline. It was flat and open there and I calculated it would be quicker to walk on, even though it was close to the sea. All I had to do was head east and I would eventually reach the caravan site; hopefully I could access it from the beach. It wasn't quite the holiday season yet, but I hoped somebody would be staying there. I imagined a cosy welcoming light and a kind face at the door. I held the images in my mind as I picked my way between pools of water and outcrops of large green-stained stones.

As the sea roared from the sidelines, it felt like it was cheering me on. Every so often, a random wave rushed over my shoes, then retreated. I had no idea that the tide could come in so quickly. The strip of passable sand was narrowing by the minute. My face was sprayed wet, my clothes were getting damp and I was starting to feel cold. I pulled Clare's cardigan across my chest and put my head down, trudging forward, feet slapping in the darkness.

Then I heard Edward's voice trailing on the edge of the wind. He was calling my name, over and over. Turning around, I saw him bounding down the shingle bank, running towards me.

CHAPTER FORTY

'Lily! Come back!' Edward shouted as he picked his way through the rocks. 'You've got it all wrong. Let me explain!'

I'd had enough of listening to his lies. My ankle was really hurting, but I tried to quicken my pace, even though I couldn't properly see where I was putting my feet. The ground beneath me seemed to be softening with every step. I hesitated. Ahead was an expanse of large, slippery boulders, blocking my path. Either I had to walk even nearer to the sea, or I would have to retrace my steps. I didn't want to go back and fall into Edward's arms. If I could just skirt around this outcrop of rocks, I thought, and get to the flatter expanse of beach beyond, then I could run.

'Stop!' he shouted. 'You're going to get cut off!'

I didn't care. Anything – *anything* – would be better than being caught by him. I pressed forward quickly, hobbling over rivulets, splashing through shallow pools that deepened with every incoming wave. My trainers were soon sloshing with icy water. A cold, wet sensation started to creep up the legs of my jeans. Edward was coming after me, getting nearer and nearer. I could hear him cursing as he slid around on the rocks, almost losing his balance.

'This is insane!' he shouted. 'Stop! Come back!'

I got to the other side of a large pool just before it was subsumed by the tide. But instead of reaching solid ground, I landed in a swamp of thick, oozing mud. Suddenly I was in gunge up to my ankles and couldn't move. I tried to release myself, pulling on one leg with all my might. At last it squelched out, dripping with slime, but my trainer stayed behind. I balanced on one foot for a few triumphant seconds before toppling over clown-like and falling face down in the sludge.

For a few seconds, I couldn't breathe. There was mud in my nostrils, eyes and mouth. Lifting my head, I tried to spit it out. I could feel myself being sucked down into the gloop. I tried to get onto my hands and knees, but there was nothing solid to push against. Like a worm, I tried to crawl on my stomach, propelling myself forward inch by slimy inch, but the mud didn't want to let me go.

Edward had reached me. He was standing at my side, his feet sinking into the mud. 'You stupid idiot,' he said, trying to yank me upwards by my top. 'It's dangerous out here in the dark. You'll drown.'

'That's what you'd like, isn't it?' I said, as I slid through his fingers like a fish.

'Don't be stupid. I love you, you're my wife.'

'Is that why you locked me up? Fuck off, Edward – you don't know what love is.'

'I was angry with you for bringing Noah here. I'm sorry, let me help you.' He bent over to try to pick me up, but I pushed him away and he fell backwards into the quicksand. 'Jesus, Lily, you're going to kill us both. The tide's coming in. We have to get out. Now.'

An overexcited wave washed over us, soaking us from head to toe. I coughed out the cold salty water as we sank even further into the slime.

'What were you putting in the car?'

'Just some junk to go to the dump tomorrow. Look, we don't have time for this.' He held out a wet hand. 'Take it. Try to pull yourself up.'

'Where is Noah?'

'Asleep in bed.'

'I don't believe you. What have you done with him?'

'Nothing. Why would I harm my own son?'

'He doesn't remember anything, Edward,' I stressed.

'I know, because there's nothing to remember. For God's sake, Lily, take my hand and get to your feet, then you can help me.'

Another wave engulfed us. Time was running out. I clasped his hand and heaved myself to my feet. Steadying myself in his grip, I managed to pull one foot free and put it on a rock. Then the other leg squelched out. I let go of Edward, almost falling back but managing to steady myself.

'Hey, let me hold onto you!' he cried as I backed away. His face was streaming with water, his hair stuck in thick dark strips to his face.

'Go to hell, Edward,' I said, turning away from him.

He screamed curses at me as I made my way back inland, sploshing through the mud, slipping and sliding on the rocks. I had given up all hope of making it to the caravan site. My ankle was killing me; it would not last the journey. I glanced over my shoulder. How long did I have before the tide caught up with me? It was a matter of minutes rather than hours. Fear spurred me on. The sea was rushing in my ears, the wind slapping me across the cheeks. I was shivering so violently I could hardly control my limbs. The rocks were extremely slimy; it was impossible to stand on them. I had to crawl over each one, scraping my knees and hands, sliding off into freezing pools of water and then climbing out again. All the time the sea was nipping at my heels, threatening to drag me under.

But I made it.

Back on solid, even ground, I slowly got to my feet and bent over to catch my breath. I could hear Edward screaming my name, but couldn't make out his shape in the darkness. I was freezing cold, wet and filthy, and had only one shoe on. My ankle was throbbing with pain, but I was alive. I started to hobble towards what looked like a mountain of shingle.

The sound of distant sirens drifted into my ears. So unexpected that at first I thought it was an animal wailing. I listened hard. The noise was getting louder. The emergency vehicles – police, ambulance, fire engine, I couldn't tell – were definitely heading this way. They had to be; there was nowhere else. Hope and fear struck me simultaneously. Who had called emergency services? What had happened? Had there been an accident, or worse? Was Noah okay? *Please, please let Noah be okay.*

I had to get back to the house. Gritting my teeth, I made my way up the mound of shingle, trying to ignore the pain. I reached the top of the beach and looked around, trying to work out my position. To my surprise, I'd hardly gone any distance. I'd just started to limp towards the steps when two police cars burst out of the darkness, blue lights flashing, sirens blaring. They swooped up the side lane.

I followed them as quickly as I could, my heart thumping as I staggered up the track. Turning the corner, I saw the police cars pulled up behind Edward's BMW. The officers – four of them, in high-vis jackets – were walking around, looking up at the windows, shouting out. One started banging on the door, demanding to be let in. I tried to call to them, but there was no strength in my voice. My bad foot stumbled over a hole in the road and I fell over, crying out with pain, but there was too much commotion going on and nobody heard me.

Then all of a sudden, Noah burst out of the house.

'He's going to kill her!' he shouted to the police. 'He locked her up but she escaped and now he's going to kill her!'

'All right, son, calm down. Did you dial 999?'

'Yes! You've got to help her!'

'Who are you talking about?'

'Lily.'

'And who is Lily?' asked a female voice.

'My stepmum.'

It was the first time he'd ever called me that. His words flooded me with fresh strength as I tried to get to my feet.

'She brought me here,' Noah continued. 'I told her what happened to Mummy, and now Daddy's going to kill her too.'

'Hey, son, slow down.'

'It's okay, Noah,' I shouted feebly. 'I'm all right. I'm here.'

The officers turned as I stumbled out of the darkness. Every inch of me was covered in sticky grey mud, hair matted, features unrecognisable. I looked like a strange, ghostly creature, risen from the oozy depths of the sea.

'Oh my God,' said an officer, approaching me carefully. 'Who are you?'

'I'm Lily,' I said. 'Noah's stepmum. The second wife. The only one who survived.'

EPILOGUE

The sun streams through the sloping window of my attic room. I stuff my toilet bag into the suitcase and zip it up. I'm only going away for a few days, but it's October and the weather is unpredictable. I have T-shirts and thick jumpers, a thin dress, spare jeans and the cardigan I borrowed from Clare's wardrobe that fateful night four months ago. I seem to wear it all the time now. It keeps me connected to her; reminds me of how lucky I am to be alive.

I carry the case downstairs and prop it up against the wall outside the kitchen. It's Friday evening and Marsha is cooking. We take it in turns, although if one of us has to work late, the other steps in and does a double shift. I started a new job last month, teaching at a school for children with complex communication and social difficulties. It's a very peaceful environment, with beautiful grounds and plenty of space for the kids to run around in, or be alone if they prefer. The class sizes are small, and every pupil has their own key worker. I love it. I need to do some specific training before I can take on more responsibility, but I'm looking forward to that. I've found my métier, and for the first time, I have a clear direction in which to travel.

'Packed already?' Marsha says, stirring one of her famous vegetable curries.

I inhale the spices and nod. 'It's an early train tomorrow.' I'm spending half-term with Noah. He's back in Birmingham, where he was born, living with his grandparents, Elaine and Mike.

Marsha glances over her shoulder, grinning. 'It's so exciting. Bet you can't wait to see him.'

'True. I went to the art shop on my way home and bought up half its stock.'

'He'll be thrilled.'

'Hope so.' I cast my eyes downwards. 'I don't know if he still likes drawing. He might be into something else now.' I chew my lip nervously. 'What if he doesn't want to see me?'

'Don't be daft.'

'But he must associate me with some really horrible memories. I don't want to trigger anything… you know…'

Marsha waves her spoon at me dismissively. 'He's a strong kid, he knows how to deal with that shit now. He found your phone and called the police; that was incredibly brave of him. And remember how he clung to you after the arrests? He wouldn't go to anyone else. He thinks the world of you.'

'Yes, that's all true. But it was months ago now. He has a whole new life I have no part in.'

'He'll never forget you, Lily,' Marsha reassures me.

'Hmm… maybe he *should* forget,' I say. 'Maybe I'm being selfish wanting to keep in touch.'

'I'm sure his grandparents would have said if they weren't happy.'

'Yes, I guess…'

I still miss Noah. After Edward died, I wanted him to live with me, but after lengthy discussion with Francesca's family and his social worker, it was decided that he should be looked after by blood relatives. I was very disappointed, but as his stepmother, I had no legal parenting rights. I could have tried to adopt him, but Elaine and Mike would have fought me all the way and I didn't want to cause trouble; they'd suffered enough. Noah is part of Francesca – he will never replace her, but he gives them back a little of what they've lost. And they're good, kind people, besotted with their grandson yet determined not to spoil him.

We all agree that what Noah needs more than anything is to be an ordinary little boy leading an ordinary life. He is finally receiving having specialist therapy on a regular basis, but he goes to school now, to the local primary around the corner from his new home. It was a shock at first, finding himself in a class of thirty kids, but he's doing really well and has made lots of friends. He's even planning to invite some for a sleepover on his birthday.

I pour myself a glass of wine and lean against the kitchen counter. 'What are you going to do without me next week?' I joke.

'Oh, throw a couple of parties, rent your room out.'

'Don't you dare.'

'You know I love having you here, but maybe you should think about going back to the house,' Marsha says. 'It's yours now, after all.'

I shiver involuntarily. 'No thank you. I can't even bear to go back to pick up my boxes from the garage. The place gives me the creeps.' I let out a long sigh. 'I suppose I'll have to confront it once probate goes through and the place is sold.'

'Do you think it'll happen before the trial?'

'Don't know. Doubt it. Anyway, I don't want his money. I'm going to give most of it to a kids' charity.'

'Right, I'm going to leave this to simmer,' says Marsha. 'We'll be eating in about forty-five minutes, okay?'

'Great, thanks.'

'Just need to send a couple of emails.' She takes off her apron and leaves the kitchen.

I put my glass down and set about laying the table. To my annoyance, I find I'm thinking about Edward again. Normal everyday activities requiring minimal concentration are the worst;

they keep sending my mind scurrying into dark corners and it can be hard to get back into the light.

My conscience is clear – up to a point. I might not have been strong enough to pull him out of the mud trap. I told the police that he was stuck and they raised the alarm immediately. But it's remote out there, and by the time the rescue services reached him, he was fully submerged. Sometimes I wonder if he finally accepted his guilt and gave himself up to the sea, but knowing Edward, I suspect he fought death with his very last breath.

Tara and Georgia's trials are scheduled to begin in a few months' time. The media circus has come to town again and the tabloids are full of the case, relishing every gory detail and making half of it up as usual. I try to avoid the newspapers and have come off social media. I dread to think what they're saying about me as the second wife – that I was an ignorant fool, or that I knew all along I'd married a double murderer…

The girls are denying any involvement in Francesca's death. The senior detective in charge of the case says there's a good chance they'll get off scot-free and we must prepare ourselves for an acquittal. The investigation team virtually had to start all over again, refocusing on Watcher's Rock. Tara and Georgia insist that they were never at the house at the same time as Fran, and that their father was totally innocent. The police think Georgia pretended to be Fran when Edward returned to Birmingham after dumping her body at sea, but they can't prove it. Not yet, anyway.

Francesca's DNA was found in the bedroom and kitchen of the house, and specks of her blood were found in the weave of the rug Edward put in the car. After further searches, a suitcase was found in the old concrete pillbox, full of Francesca's clothes. Among them was a pink and green striped summer dress, just like the one in Noah's drawing. Elaine showed the picture to the police and it helped convince the prosecution service that Noah really had remembered what happened to his mother.

But they still haven't found the body. Boats with specially trained cadaver dogs scoured the coast, but without success. They can prosecute without a corpse, but it makes a conviction more difficult. Noah's evidence will be crucial because it ties lots of little things together. Without him, the case will definitely collapse. He's going to have to be very brave, but I know he can do it.

As for Clare's murder, all we have is Noah's account of what he overheard that night. He didn't understand what they were talking about at the time, so never managed to piece it together properly. But we all believe Edward, not Fran, killed her. I suspect even Tara and Georgia believe it, somewhere deep inside their damaged souls. Not that they'd ever admit it. Their father protected them for years and they owe him too much, even in death.

Marsha comes back into the room. 'Right. Just the rice to put on, then we're ready.' She catches the faraway expression on my face. 'You okay, Lily?'

'Yeah… kind of. Just thinking, you know… Same old crap going round and round in my head.'

'Of course. There's a lot to come to terms with.' She gives me a hug. 'You'll get through it – I know you will.'

'How did I make such a colossal mistake?'

'You didn't,' she says, putting a pan of water on to boil. She opens the cupboard and takes out a packet of rice.

'How can you say that? I should never have married him – I didn't know him at all.' She doesn't reply, just pours rice into the pan. 'You knew he was no good, you never liked him from the start.'

'I didn't totally trust him, that's true, but I didn't know why. Instinct.'

'So why wasn't it a mistake marrying him, then?'

Marsha turns and takes my hands. 'Because without you, Noah would still be imprisoned in that house. He had no chance of a normal life until you came along. Edward thought he could suppress his memories until they faded away of their own accord, but they were so traumatic, they were etched on his brain forever. In a strange way, I don't think it matters whether Tara and Georgia are convicted or not. Naturally we want justice for Francesca, but the most important thing is that you saved her son, you gave him a future.'

'Thanks, Marsha,' I say. 'Thanks. I'm desperate for them to go to jail, but you're right.'

'I'm always right, remember?'

I laugh. 'How could I ever forget?'

A LETTER FROM JESS

Thank you so much for reading *The Second Marriage*. If you enjoyed it, and want to keep up to date with all my latest releases, just sign up at the following link. Your email address will never be shared and you can unsubscribe at any time.

www.bookouture.com/jess-ryder

The idea for this book came to me from reading about how memory works. Our memories are not fixed things – they change with time and each retelling. Like old clothes, they need to be taken out of the wardrobe every so often, shaken out and tried on again. With every remembering, the memory is remade. Some elements are forgotten, others are embellished and new details may be created. And so the story changes over time. This is not lying; it's part of the natural cognitive process.

For this book, I also looked into childhood amnesia, which is our general inability to remember events that occurred before the age of around four. Some of us have snatches of memory that have been retained from that time – images, sensations or emotional responses – but most of it is not stored in the brain. Memories can also be manipulated. It seems that if we keep telling a child a story about something that happened to them when they were very little, they can come to believe that they remember the event themselves. Conversely, if we suppress or ignore memories, they can fade and may even disappear. And thus began my fictional story about Noah.

Another source of inspiration for this novel was the coastal location that features in the second half. I moved to East Sussex last year, finally fulfilling my clichéd writer's dream of living on the coast and writing in a room with a view of the sea. The solitary house that I named The Lookout in the novel does not exist, but its extraordinary location will certainly be recognisable to local people. I hope my neighbours will forgive me for the artistic licence I have taken with the geography, purely for dramatic purposes.

I hope you enjoyed reading *The Second Marriage*. If you'd like to write a brief constructive review and post it online in the appropriate places, I'm sure other readers would find it useful.

If this is your first Jess Ryder book, you might want to try my other psychological thrillers – *Lie to Me*, *The Good Sister*, *The Ex-Wife*, *The Dream House*, *The Girl You Gave Away* and *The Night Away*. It's easy to get in touch via my Facebook page, Goodreads or Twitter.

With best wishes and thanks,
Jess Ryder

 jessryderauthor

 @jessryderauthor

 www.jessryder.co.uk

ACKNOWLEDGEMENTS

I would like to thank the following people who have helped me in the writing of this novel:

Brenda Page, for her help with research and proof-reading. Her comments on various drafts are always useful, but this time they were especially valuable.

Rowan Lawton at The Soho Agency, who is a brilliant literary agent – conscientious, supportive and a great listener. Also, Christine Glover, my media agent at Casarotto Ramsay & Associates, who works hard to create new opportunities for my books.

My fantastic editor, Lydia Vassar-Smith, whose notes are always spot on. She shows great patience and understanding, particularly when I keep reworking the plot and sending her almost entirely new drafts to read.

Everyone on the Bookouture team. They work incredibly hard for their authors and I really appreciate their efforts.

My sons and daughter, their partners and my three grandchildren. Their love and support have kept me going throughout this difficult time, even though it was mostly via Zoom!

And finally, as ever, my husband, David. We have been through a period of great change together recently, and I can honestly say I couldn't have done it without him.

Made in the USA
Middletown, DE
16 January 2022